THE LOVE OF A RAKE

THE BROTHERS OF THE ARISTOCRACY

LINDA RAE SANDE

Twisted Teacup
PUBLISHING

The Love of a Rake

ISBN: 978-0-9964433-1-9

V1.3

Cover photographs © Novelstock, Inc. and iStockPhoto.com

Cover art by Twisted Teacup Publishing

All rights reserved - used with permission.

Library of Congress Control Number: 2015918333

Linda Rae Sande, Cody, WY

PRINTED IN THE UNITED STATES OF AMERICA

ALSO BY LINDA RAE SANDE

CHAPTER 1
A RACE TO THE FINISH LINE

*M**ay 20, 1817, Epsom Downs, Surrey*

"He's holding his own," Alistair Comber commented, his eyes darting between the pocket watch he held and the opera glasses he was using to better see the jet black horse as it powered its way along the U-shaped race course.

Although the track at Epsom Downs started with a bit of a climb, the finish featured a slight downhill grade. An early morning rainfall had settled the dust, but clods of soil flew up from the horse's hooves as they took flight with each gallop. "It's a good thing the Derby isn't a two-mile race any longer, though," he added with a frown as he noted how the Thoroughbred's overall pace seemed to slow down after the first turn.

"Agreed," Randall Roderick, Marquess of Reading, replied as he watched his newest racehorse, Zeus, round the last turn and head for the finish line. "He doesn't have the stamina for two miles. But this one-and-a-half-mile track may just be his forté—if he can do it in under three minutes. If he can't ... well, I suppose I would rather he race than pay the forfeit fee."

Alistair gave him a nod. "Two-hundred guineas is a rather rich fine for pulling out," he agreed. "Have you had any luck finding a suitable cold-blood mare for him? He would probably make an excellent stud."

Shaking his head, Randall worried that Alistair was suggesting he simply put Zeus out to stud rather than continue his training as a racehorse. The man was an expert when it came to horses, whether they raced or were used for farming or puling equipage or for simply riding. "I have not," he replied as he watched Zeus finish the run.

"Looks like two-minutes, fifty-five seconds, my lord," Alistair said with a nod. "I think you may have yourself a racehorse."

Randall breathed a sigh of relief. He pulled a cheroot from his waistcoat pocket and offered it to Alistair.

The second son of an earl shook his head. "Thank you, but no." At the raised eyebrow the marquess gave him, he added, "I brought my wife along on this trip to Surrey, and I shouldn't want to smell like a men's club when I'm escorting her to dinner this evening." He nodded toward the young woman who sat in a curricle positioned so she could watch the practice runs. She gave a tentative wave when she noticed his gaze. "Julia wanted the chance to get away from London for a bit."

The marquess dared a glance toward Julia Harrington Comber. The daughter of Stanley Harrington, Earl of Mayfield, Julia might have been expected to make a match with a duke or marquess' son, but she had opted to accept the marriage proposal of her father's then-groom and now the head of his stables and horse breeding program—and a frequent consultant to Tattersall's. It was Alistair's connection to the horse trader's business that had Randall seeking his advice when it came to his racehorse.

Randall felt a stab of jealousy that a man of Alistair's age— six-and-twenty, if he had heard correctly—had figured out it was time he take a wife and start a family. "And how do you like being leg-shackled?" Randall asked when he returned his attention to Alistair.

The groom gave him a nervous grin. "I like it far more than I thought I would," he answered with a nod. "But then, I'm one of the lucky ones. I ended up with a spirited filly," Alistair said, one eyebrow arching up.

Randall dared another glance in the direction of Mrs. Comber just as she blew her husband a kiss. Despite his reputation—Randall was known in London as the Rake of Reading—he found himself rather shocked by the young woman's gesture. Shocked, and just a bit, well, *jealous* of the earl's son. "I see what you mean," he said with an arched eyebrow of his own.

Noting how the jockey who had ridden Zeus was heading his way with the horse in tow, he held out his right hand. "Thank you for your help. I'll see to your fee when I'm back in London."

Alistair shook the man's hand and gave him a bow. "Good luck, my lord." Stepping back, he made his way to his curricle as Randall turned his attention to the jockey.

"Any trouble?" he asked. The man shook his head and pulled Zeus so the horse stood even with him.

"He's fast, my lord, and I'd be willing to wager a year's earnings on him winning the Derby."

Randall took a deep breath and let it out slowly. "Well, there won't be any of that, son," he said, knowing anything could happen between now and the race two days hence. Zeus could end up poisoned, or drugged with cocaine, or come up lame from an injury in the stables. The marquess was determined nothing egregious would happen, though. His stable-hands were more than they seemed. Should anyone try to get near the black Thoroughbred, at least one of them would see to it Zeus was protected. "Run him easy tomorrow, and take care you're not pissed day after tomorrow."

The jockey bowed. "Of course, my lord."

Randall gave Zeus a quick pat and took his leave of the racetrack, his mind on cold-blood English mares.

It was well past time he found himself a spirited filly—and not just the mare he needed for the next generation of Reading racehorses.

He needed a wife.

And at five-and-thirty, he needed an heir before *he* crossed the finish line.

CHAPTER 2
A BIRTHDAY PRESENT ARRIVES IN THE FORM OF A PUZZLE

Very, very early in the morning of September 15, 1817 Lord Charles Henry Goodwin, Earl of Wakefield, glanced in the cheval mirror. Not a particularly vain man, he still wished to leave his next visitor with a somewhat positive first impression. If he did, perhaps she would return to his bed another night and ply her trade again. As it was, he had few ladies of the evening who made the trip up the two flights of stairs and to his bedchamber more than once—despite the fact that his bedchamber was located in the fashionable Curzon Street terrace he called home when he was in London.

He wondered if there was something about his body they did not care for (doubtful, but possible, he considered), or if perhaps he was a bit too quick with his tumbles and left the ladybirds less than satisfied.

It could not be their compensation, for he was quite generous with his sovereigns. *No,* he thought as he gazed at the candlelight image of himself in the looking glass. It was probably the Rule. For no matter what time his appointment arrived, they were to be out of his bed at two o'clock in the morning and out of his house no later than two-oh-five.

A man had to have his sleep, after all.

So, if he returned from White's or a ball at one-thirty on one of those two nights a week, a trollop would no doubt be waiting in a chair just past the vestibule, sometimes incensed that she had been left waiting for hours and then had to undress quickly, be available for whatever debauchery he thought of as fun for the evening, and then be out the front door before she'd had enough time to properly redress herself. Such were the vagaries of being a prostitute sent to the home of Lord Wakefield by her madame.

The brocaded dressing gown he wore, closed in front with a loosely knotted belt, covered most of his firm, muscled body. The opening at the top revealed a dusting of dark hair on the bronzed skin of his chest. The deep brown color of the fabric nearly matched the closely cropped hair on his head, a lock of which always seemed to hang above one eyebrow.

His face, too broad to be considered oval, sported high cheekbones, a nose that had at one time been broken and not quite put back into place, and a broad mouth. Wakefield prided himself on the condition of his teeth, all of which were still intact and kept as white as possible with the frequent use of tooth powder and a brush. That way, when he smiled, he could dazzle his peers in Parliament or impress the ladies at the theatre or a ball. He was in the process of testing their whiteness with a grimace aimed at the mirror when his valet stepped close.

"My lord," Chester spoke quietly. "Your appointment is here. Miss Eleanor Merriweather."

Wakefield tore his attention from the mirror and gave his valet a glance. "Thank you, Chester. You may retire for the night," he said with a nod, wondering at the name his valet had offered. Usually Chester only gave him first names. Or nicknames. He rather doubted any of the ladies of the evening used their Christian names.

When the valet stood his ground, apparently trying to decide whether he should say something else, Wakefield regarded him with furrowed brows. "What is it?"

Chester angled his head in the direction of the girl who stood near the door to his bedchamber. Wakefield followed suit, giving the chit a quick look. Although her head was bent down, and despite the pelisse she wore, he could see she was petite, pale, and brunette, his favorite set of features in a lightskirt. "She seems ..." Chester paused, not wanting to anger his employer. "Not like the others," he whispered, his eyes as downcast as the girl's.

Wakefield was about to crack that it was about time Lucy Gibbons sent him a truly naughty wench, but another glance at the girl told him that she probably wasn't very naughty. She looked as if she could be a rather proper girl except for the messy bun atop her head and the wrinkled gown she wore.

Rolling his eyes, Wakefield nodded. "Thank you for the insight, Chester." He motioned with his hand. "Does she know the Rule?" he remembered to ask when his valet was just about to leave the bedchamber.

"Yes, my lord," Chester replied before giving the young girl what could only be described as a look of sympathy.

Lord Wakefield regarded his visitor, a slight alcoholic haze clouding his sight just a bit. At the sound of the door closing, the young woman looked up, making brief eye contact with the earl before averting her gaze. *She is young*, he thought, wondering why his image of her seemed somewhat blurred. He hadn't had *that* much to drink.

A puzzle, she was, but wasn't everyone when he first met them? A ten-piece puzzle with uneven edges and some pieces not always interlocked with the others. He imagined dumping them out of their wooden box onto a card table, turning some over so their images were right side up and quickly arranging them so they were evenly spaced out.

He moved closer. "What should I call you, Miss Merriweather?" his question coming out a bit louder than he meant it to.

The girl nearly jumped off the floor at the sound of his voice, but then she executed a perfect curtsy, her reticule bobbing from one hand. "Eleanor, my lord."

Wakefield bowed, impressed by the young woman's poise. "How old are you?" he asked, guessing seventeen but thinking she was probably already past her majority. Young women's ages were always so tricky.

"Eighteen, my lord," she replied quietly, a slight quaver to her voice.

A puzzle piece clicked into place.

Her eyes finally looked up and locked on his. *Brown eyes*, he realized, or perhaps hazel given the dark brown hair that curled around her face and was otherwise knotted on the top of her head in that loose, messy bun.

Not so very young, he considered, *but why is she blurry? I am not that foxed that I can't see straight.* As he moved closer, he realized her entire body was ... *vibrating*. Shivering, he realized. The fire was still ablaze and the room was a bit warmer than he liked for these late summer nights, so why ...?

"Are you cold?" he asked then, moving slowly to stand before her. She was pretty, he decided. Very pretty. Her skin was like porcelain, with no blemishes, and her cheeks were rosy. At first he thought she might have used cosmetics to redden her lips and color her cheeks, but upon closer inspection, he realized she wore none. *She's truly blushing.*

Not a typical lightskirt.

A puzzle piece hung for a moment, not quite fitting.

"I am very warm, thank you, my lord," she replied, again with the quaver in her voice.

A different puzzle piece clicked into place.

She's frightened, he realized. *Good God, what have the harlots been saying about me at Lucy's place?* he found himself wondering. "Well, you needn't be frightened of *me*," he said defensively. "I promise, I will not hurt you," he added before glancing at the clock. It was already after one. "You should be getting undressed, though. We don't have a lot of time," he said then. "You can hang your garments over there," he pointed in the direction of a richly upholstered chair located near the fireplace. As he was about to untie his dressing gown, he noticed she had removed her pelisse but hadn't made an effort to remove her dress. "Well?" he asked impatiently, noticing her pelisse was of recent construction, the fabric showing little in the way of wear and tear. Even her gown seemed new, although whatever she had been doing in it that day seemed to have wrinkled it. For a moment, he thought she might have come straight from another tumble, one in which she hadn't had to remove her gown. For some reason, the thought excited him. Most of the women sent from Lucy's shed their garments before they climbed onto his bed, but one or two wore their chemise and corset.

Although he was tempted to tup her over the edge of his bed, he decided he wanted her undressed.

Completely.

Naked and in the middle of the bed.

The young woman's large brown eyes looked up at him again. They were bright, as if she were on the verge of tears. He had seen those eyes before, he remembered. On a doe he had discovered in the back gardens of the Wakefield estate in Hampshire. She had been eating the rosebuds. And those eyes had looked at him in sudden fear as he drew his bow and let loose the arrow that killed her.

That deer had been dinner for several nights.

And that look haunted him now as he regarded Eleanor Merriweather.

"I cannot undo the buttons by myself," she replied, turning slowly until her back faced him.

The earl blinked. *Well, this is a first,* Wakefield thought as he reached out to the row of jet buttons that held her gown closed. "You'll have to remember to wear a gown that doesn't have buttons the next time you're here. I've no lady's maid in this household," he scolded lightly, quickly finishing the task of unbuttoning her gown as if he did it every night. Then he reached down to grab a handful of muslin to pull the gown, and while he was at it, her petticoat, over her head.

A puzzle piece was still hanging out there, he remembered, wondering what it was about this chit that had him behaving, well, a bit more civilly than he might normally. He ignored her gasp as the gown and petticoat were freed from her body. He tossed it rather unceremoniously toward the chair and then moved to undo the ties of her corset. Within a few seconds, he had that garment as well as her chemise removed.

Eleanor's arms instinctively wrapped around the front of her body, covering her bared breasts. Wearing only black slippers, stockings and garters, she held herself very still.

From Wakefield's perspective, she was the most erotic sight he had ever laid eyes upon. And he was merely looking at her backside —a long neck and longer back, slim waist, perfect bottom and shapely legs. He sighed in appreciation, and Eleanor dared to look at him from over her shoulder. "I'll remember, my lord," she murmured, her eyes turning down again.

Another puzzle piece clicked into place.

"Call me Henry," he replied, surprising himself as he reached out to place a hand on her shoulder. He found he felt a bit of relief when she didn't flinch at his touch. With a gentle shove, he turned her body slowly until she faced him. He reached out to lift one hand from a breast and raised it to his lips.

Eleanor's eyes followed the motion, and she watched while he kissed the back of her fingers. His eyes took in the front of her. She gave him her other hand when he raised an eyebrow. He held both hands in his much larger hands while he continued to gaze at her. "You're very pretty," he murmured, suddenly feeling very sober.

And very aroused.

Her pale breasts were pert and round, tipped with nipples that were especially dark and already tightened into hard buds. And her mound of brown curlies, so small between the creamy white thighs, caught his eye. He licked his lips in anticipation.

The puzzle was nearly complete.

"Thank you. Hen ... Henry," she stammered. "I am to tell you, 'happy birthday' ... I am ..." She paused a moment to take a breath and to swallow hard. "I am your birthday gift."

The words were nearly strangled coming out, but Wakefield heard them clearly enough. "Indeed?" he replied in delight, a smile making his face appear friendly. He hadn't thought much about his twenty-seventh birthday. *Next week sometime*, he remembered absently.

So if Lucy had sent Eleanor for his birthday, he thought he should figure out why the chit had been chosen as his gift.

Another puzzle piece!

What special talent did she possess that he might find enjoyable or more pleasurable than the regular whores Mrs. Gibbons sent to him twice a week? He felt Eleanor relax a bit and realized he had probably been scowling at her all night. "Well, since I have unwrapped my present, I shall have to decide what to do with you," he said lightly, placing her hand on his arm and leading her to the bed. *Perhaps she is an accomplished kisser*, he thought happily. One didn't usually kiss whores, but with those red, full lips, she seemed imminently kissable.

Or perhaps she would straddle him and ride him like a racehorse, bending low over him so that he might capture her dark nipples with his teeth and tongue. "Climb up," he said happily, removing his dressing gown in a flourish and tossing it toward the chair by the fire.

The young woman let out a squeak and stepped back, trying hard as she did so to avert her gaze from his sudden nakedness.

Wakefield grinned. "No need to be shy," he said, leaning over to grasp Eleanor by the sides of her waist and lifting her onto the bed. Her hands had instinctively reached for his shoulders, her warms fingers pressing into his flesh so that the ends of her fingernails left little half moon brands in his skin. The thought of the way she clung to him for that moment had his cock hardening even more than the sight of her breasts.

He felt her body shiver and realized she was trembling.

Her entire body was quaking. *Such anticipation*, he thought, arranging the puzzle piece so it fit into the picture he was slowly creating of her. He lowered his mouth to one of her breasts, breathed in the soft scent of her skin. She wore no perfume but smelled faintly of lemon soap. *She bathed for me,* he thought in wonderment, his body responding more quickly than usual to the feel of her body against his.

Another puzzle piece clicked into place.

Laving his tongue across the ruched bud, he felt delight when her entire back arched up and an audible gasp escaped her lips. He drew his tongue across to the other breast, repeating his quick seduction of that nipple while a thumb and forefinger pinched her other nipple. The double hitch in her breath told him she was feeling something from his ministrations.

I usually don't do this to a whore, he considered. He was usually the one being pleasured, the one being stroked and suckled. This night was different, though. This woman was soft and silken and responsive, clean and fresh, her innocent act from a few moments ago a powerful aphrodisiac that made him want to pleasure her until she fractured. He wanted to take her right then, though. Bury himself deep inside her and allow his release. The mere thought of spilling his seed inside her nearly had him climaxing right then.

Hold on, he thought. He wanted this harlot back in his bed. The puzzle of her was nearly complete, but what was the hurry in completing it in one night? This was no time to turn selfish and take his pleasure before he had seen to hers.

From the corner of one eye, he watched as her fingers clutched the bed's counterpane. It was if she had to anchor herself to the bed or risk floating above it from the shear pleasure of his touch, he thought with some amusement. If he continued to pleasure her, he was sure she would return to his bed, perhaps even *beg* to be sent back to him. Yes, this was one puzzle he would gladly welcome to his bed again and again.

He slid one knee over hers, forcing her legs to spread apart just a bit as he slid the fingers of one hand down her sides and across her belly, barely touching her skin as he did so. She continued to gasp, continued to hold onto handfuls of the counterpane as her body arched up, her dark nipples erect atop the beautiful mounds of her breasts. *Nipples of Venus,* he thought, wondering briefly where he had sampled the chocolate confection. But these were so much better, he considered, offered to him on a plate of silken skin that tasted slightly of salt and smelled of pure womanhood.

Another puzzle piece clicked into place.

Lifting his body over hers, he watched as her brown eyes widened, watched as her mouth shaped into an 'o', and smiled when she nearly screamed as his thumb caressed the swollen folds between her thighs. *God, she's beautiful*, he thought, lowering his head to her belly. He slid the palms of his hands beneath her, lifting her bottom until her thighs fell apart. Once she was opened to him, he reached out with his tongue and laved it across her womanhood. Once, twice, and then, after a pause, his lips suckled the swollen mass.

When the sound of her sudden cry and subsequent mewling reached his ears, he allowed a smile. *Success!*

Straightening his body so he stood on his knees, he rested his hands on her bent legs as he regarded his nearly completed puzzle. Her entire body was flushed in a becoming pink glow. Her hair, which had been barely held up with a few pins, was now splayed across the dark counterpane in a golden brown halo. *She looks like an angel*, he thought happily, deciding it was his efforts that had brought about the glow.

He gave her a nod, and then glanced down when he saw the object of her shocked gaze. He shrugged. "I'm sure you've seen many like mine," he teased, indicating his hardened cock as it bobbed from its nest of dark curls.

A last puzzle piece was almost ready to be put into place.

"Or perhaps not," he commented with amusement as he regarded his member. "I am told it is larger than most," he announced proudly, just as he lowered the object of her attention into her wet, warm sheath, thrusting himself a bit harder than he intended when he felt a hint of resistance. Before he could register the shock and subsequent wince he noticed on her face, or hear the sudden hiss of air she sucked in through her teeth, he let out a growl at the tightness that surrounded his manhood. He let out another growl when he felt her body arch against his, and still another when her knees raised up and pressed against his hips, allowing him deeper inside her warm cocoon. He hadn't even had a chance to begin the rhythmic motions of intercourse when his body betrayed him, the contractions of a climax so intense he nearly passed out from the sudden pleasure.

"I am quite sure I would not know," Eleanor said quietly, her lips nearly touching his ear as she spoke the words. Her short breaths seemed to caress his hair, ruffling a few of the strands near his ear so they tickled.

The earl stirred and lifted his head from where it had fallen above her shoulder. "What did you say?" he asked. He had expected her to at least agree or counter his claim with a playful guffaw as any other harlot would have done.

And then he considered what had just happened.

"I've never done this before," she whispered, her head shaking back and forth against the counterpane.

Click!

CHAPTER 3
A RAKE PAYS WITNESS TO A VISIT

A bit after midnight of September 15

Randall Roderick watched from his bedchamber window as what appeared to be a hackney pulled up in front of the townhouse across the street and to the west of his own. His butler, Giles, had informed him that an earl occupied that particular property. "He is in residence almost year 'round, my lord," the butler had said in a manner suggesting he was the aristocrat and not the marquess he served. "Young, unmarried, and he has the reputation of a libertine."

This last comment had Randall arching an eyebrow. He was quite sure Giles knew the name of said earl and was probably holding it back in the hopes he could impress his master with it when asked as to the identity of the earl.

Randall didn't ask.

He would meet the man soon enough—if not on one of his morning walks, then in the chambers at Parliament.

And so what if the man was a libertine? Randall had just spent the evening at White's in the company of just such a gentleman, although to be fair to the Earl of Wakefield, he was better known as a rake rather than a libertine. And Randall was quite sure his butler was aware of his own reputation as the Rake of Reading.

He had earned the moniker at an early age, delighting in seducing young widows and bedding lonely matrons whose husbands were busy at men's clubs and brothels. Handsome and possessing an ease with conversation and an education commensurate with his position as a marquess, Randall was soon a father four times over. He never married the mothers of his bastard sons, although he would have been unable to do so in the case of two of them, considering they were already married. He kept in touch with the boys he was allowed to, though, and saw to the placement of the two born to unmarried women in homes of well-to-do cits.

He also saw to their education. The oldest was already seventeen, the age at which Randall had impregnated his daughter-of-a-viscount mother. She was long gone from London, married to a baron who claimed to love her despite her having been ruined. The two were now raising a brood somewhere in Northumberland.

Randolph Roderick—Randall had made sure the boy had his surname—was now at Oxford. Randall could only hope his son had taken his advice regarding the use of French letters whilst at university. "There is nothing more frightening to a man of your age than to discover you're about to become a father," he warned Randolph. "Nor more expensive. Illegal or not, use them," he had commanded. He rather wished his own father had suggested he employ condoms. Had he done so, he was quite sure he wouldn't have fathered three more sons in the next seven years.

Four sons and not a single heir. Well, it was past time he do something about his status as an unmarried aristocrat. He needed a wife and a legitimate son.

The marquess returned this attention to the hackney across the street. The driver had stepped down and opened the door, appearing a bit impatient as he waited for his passenger to take her leave.

The figure that emerged was definitely a woman, although the gas lights lining Curzon Street proved too dim to illuminate her. Having seen the same situation occur just a few days ago at exactly midnight, and a few days before that at midnight, the marquess realized his neighbor must have arranged a regular liaison with a courtesan or two. Having still been awake a few nights ago, he had been aware of a hackney returning to the townhouse at two o'clock in the morning, its passenger the very woman who had been left there two hours earlier.

Randall couldn't help the bit of envy he felt at knowing a neighbor didn't have to seek female companionship but rather had it delivered to him. The earl was probably just like Randall had been ten or fifteen years ago. Young, handsome, too confident—and randy.

Hell, I'm still handsome and confident, Randall thought, noting his reflection in the window glass. If he held his head up just a bit, his second chin wasn't the least bit evident.

The sound of horse hooves had him returning his attention to the earl's visitor. The hackney pulled away, leaving its passenger regarding the townhouse for a moment before she finally made the short walk to the stairs.

When the young woman reached the top step of the townhouse, she paused and glanced around. Randall was quite sure she was barely out of the schoolroom, if she had ever been in one. Young, dark of hair and wide-eyed, she paused before she lifted a gloved fist to rap on the door.

He wondered at her hesitance. The other ladybird he had seen approach the townhouse had done so with confident steps and her head held high, as if she were proud of her status as one of London's ladies of the evening being sent on a house call.

Perhaps this one had never been dispatched to a lord's home before, plying her trade at the brothel from which she had been dispatched. Or perhaps she was new to the trade entirely.

The thought had Randall reeling. *What if the chit was a virgin?*

He frowned as he watched the door open and the young woman step into the brightly-lit vestibule. And then the door closed behind her and the night swallowed up the bit of light that had been there.

Randall sighed and turned away from the window. He had come to his room intending to dress for a return visit to White's, but the thought of spending the early morning hours in the company of other men held little appeal. Even the thought of a glass of port or brandy while reading that day's *The Times* didn't convince him it was worth his time or effort to dress for the short trip.

Sighing, he turned to regard the bed, his gaze finally turning back to the window and the townhouse in which the supposed prostitute had disappeared. None of the windows held shadows of the people within; in fact, no lights were visible in any of the windows.

Deciding the earl's bedchamber—or whatever room he used when bedding a woman—must be on the back half of the townhouse, Randall pulled shut the heavy velvet drapes and climbed into bed.

For the few moments before sleep took him, he considered his rather odd mood and how he might overcome it. He knew why he felt this way, at least. And he couldn't exactly blame it entirely on the long letter he had received just before he left for White's earlier that evening. But its message had left him feeling a bit lost. A bit lonely.

And very alone.

This kind of melancholy required a morning walk, he decided. An early morning walk in the park.

After all, one never knew what—or who—they would find in Hyde Park in the early morning hours.

CHAPTER 4
DECISIONS, DECISIONS

One-thirty in the morning of September 15

Charles Henry Goodwin did something he normally didn't do in the company of a female. He cursed. Then he cursed again as he lifted his head from where it had fallen above her shoulder. He stared at Eleanor Merriweather. "You're a *virgin?*" he whispered hoarsely, his voice seeming to roar given how close it was to his bed companion's ear. His breathing was still heavy, his chest heaving against the front of her soft body.

Eleanor, terror evident in her eyes, reluctantly nodded. "Well, I was," she replied, her lower lip trembling. Which didn't help Wakefield's situation one iota—part of him wanted desperately to capture that lower lip with his own and kiss the girl senseless. "Mrs. Gibbons said ... she said it was your birthday and that you should have a special present."

Wakefield's eyes blinked twice and then rounded in shock. "That *bitch!*" he cursed, making sure he wasn't looking at Eleanor when he said it. He tried to calm himself, not wanting to frighten the poor girl in whom his cock was still firmly planted. His erection had thankfully subsided somewhat, but what good did that do when the deed had already been done? He had experienced one of the most satisfying and pleasurable couplings of his entire life, only to discover too late that he had taken a girl's virtue. And it wasn't as if he had any experience with a virgin to know what to expect—or not—when it came to a tumble.

Whatever was he to do now? This ten-piece puzzle had suddenly doubled, nay, *quadrupled* in size.

"Why ... why didn't you *tell* me?" he whispered, his anger abating somewhat, his attention focused on the top of her shoulder. He couldn't bear to look at her just then. He certainly wouldn't have bedded the young woman if he had known she was a *virgin*. He might engage in sexual romps that would shock even the most jaded trollops and some of his peers, but he would never knowingly deflower a maiden!

The sensation of her hand against the side of his face made him slowly turn his head to regard Eleanor. Even in the dim light, her face seemed to glow, her complexion flushed from their coupling. She was gazing at him in a way that made him feel far too naked—as if she could see through him. "Would you have believed me?" she whispered, her lower lip still trembling. While her fingers rested along his jaw, her thumb had moved to the edge of his mouth, threatening to cover his lips if he didn't tell the truth. Tears had already collected in the corners of her eyes, a testament to her realization that she was most thoroughly and completely ruined.

Wakefield closed his eyes as he lowered his head back down to her shoulder. All the signs of her innocence had been there—her clothes, her hair, her eyes—even his valet had known she wasn't like the other whores Mrs. Gibbons sent his way.

Had she told him she wasn't a prostitute, would he have believed her? "Probably not," he admitted finally, thinking he should have removed himself from her just as soon as he realized what he had done. But her other hand had moved so it rested on his back, her knees were still held firmly against the side of his thighs, and she was staring at him in a way that suggested he had better stay right where he was. Not that he had any strength to move. His entire body felt spent, his head felt as if it weighed several stones, and sleep was threatening to overcome all his senses. "I apologize, my lady," he whispered, dozing off.

Eleanor Merriweather felt the weight of Lord Wakefield's body settle onto hers as he slowly fell asleep, the sensation at once comforting and a bit disconcerting and, well, a bit frightening, too. She had never in her life been this close to a member of the opposite sex. Never had she lain with a man, nor even been so much as kissed by one. Thank the gods the bed's ropes were especially tight, otherwise she might have suffocated in the soft mattress.

She slowly lowered her legs, her stockinged feet barely grazing the sides of his legs as she did so.

Fighting off the sense of panic she felt—not for the first time that day given everything that had happened—she dared a glance toward the fireplace. It took a moment to read the time on the elaborate mantel clock. *One-forty-five.* She still had fifteen minutes before she had to be out the bed and dressed and out of his bedchamber. The earl would certainly roll off of her before then. He had to. Then she would be able to climb off the high bed and get dressed. How she would manage to get her gown rebuttoned, she had no idea, but she had a pelisse that would cover her back if she could not. At least her stockings were still on; she had no idea where her slippers had landed.

At this last thought, she chastised herself. Here she was, concerned about finding her slippers when she had just lost her virtue to Charles Goodwin, Earl of Wakefield!

Of all the men in the *ton*, why, oh why did it have to be him? Why did it have to be one of the most well-known rakes in the *ton?* And the brother of the one man she had secretly wished to do this very deed with during one more than one sleepless night?

Be careful what you wish for ...

Eleanor closed her eyes and tried to envision Arthur Goodwin's face, tried to remember his lean, muscled body. Instead, the vision of the Earl of Wakefield appeared as he was when he was lit by the fire. She had never imagined that thighs could be so large on a man whose waist was so trim and not the least bit fleshy, and whose chest was so broad she wondered how he passed through doorways. And his upper arms—she was sure she wouldn't have been able to span their circumference with both her hands spread out two times over. His phallus, quite large when he had removed his robe, wasn't at all like those on the Elgin marble statues at the British Museum. She found it rather repulsive at first, but then a shiver that wasn't fear had gripped her body and sent a rather pleasurable feeling coursing through the core of her body. A faint version of it passed through her body even as she relived the past few minutes, a sense of foreboding filling her when she felt his manhood still inside her.

She had known exactly where that organ was supposed to go in a woman. Had just learned that very afternoon and been rather appalled at the thought of it. Had this happened only the day before, she would be sobbing uncontrollably, screaming in fear and using her fists to fight off the earl.

But after the events of this afternoon, she found herself feeling rather defeated. Feeling like such a fool, since she had been the one to make the mistake so many innocents made when they decided to venture to London without benefit of a chaperone. Without benefit of a protector.

She had trusted a sign in a window shop.

Earlier that evening, she had spent nearly an hour locked in a cabinet with a peephole, peering onto a bed in one of the rooms at Lucy Gibbons' brothel. Within minutes of Mrs. Gibbons' departure from the room, one of the prostitutes entered with a rather rotund gentleman on her arm. Eleanor kept one hand over her mouth as she was forced to watch (and listen) as Lord Edward Sinclair repeatedly shoved his cock into the redheaded whore. He did so from several different angles, all the while grunting and moaning as if he were about to die. And when he was finally finished—she had thought the man would never tire—and the room was vacated, Mrs. Gibbons had come for her.

The overweight madame instructed her on how she was to behave with Lord Wakefield. "If I get no complaints from him, I'll see to it you get my better paying clients," she said with a grin, as if that was some kind of favor Eleanor should appreciate. "And if he likes ya, I'll send you his way again next week."

This was not how it was supposed to be, Eleanor thought as she reviewed the events of the past two days in her mind. She had seen the posting at the mercantile's shop in Epping. *Wanted: Young ladies to help display the newest fashions from Paris to London's finest gentlemen! One evening show every week! Dozens of new gowns!* The advertisement promised that some gowns could even be kept by the model. The gentlemen were apparently shopping for their wives or mistresses, she supposed.

Eleanor wrote down the Covent Gardens address along with the list of days the offer was valid, and then, when no one was looking, simply removed the advertisement from inside the window and tucked it into her reticule.

Once home, she plotted how she would tell her mother of her plan to visit her father in London to arrange her come-out, never mentioning to her that she planned to meet the Lucy Gibbons mentioned in the posting.

But she never had a chance to share her plan with her mother. Opportunity had presented itself early that morning, and she had embraced it.

She closed her eyes and wished it was all just a bad dream.

Oh, how I wish I had never seen the advertisement!

CHAPTER 5
A COUNTRY CHIT

*F*our days ago

Eleanor Merriweather took a deep breath before stepping over the threshold of the breakfast parlor. As she expected, her mother, Laura Merriweather, Countess of Middleton, sat opposite her uncle at a table just a bit too large for their morning meal. There were just the three of them on any given morning, and except for the fact that sunshine actually streamed into the room from the east window instead of the gray gloom that had been omnipresent for the past three weeks, this morning's breakfast might have been the same as all the others.

That is, if Eleanor hadn't decided that very morning to insist her father's promise to her be kept as an excuse to get to London. She had another reason for wanting to go; an advertisement she had seen posted in the mercantile window the day before was folded up and tucked into her reticule.

"Good morning, Mother," she said brightly, leaning over to give her mother's upturned cheek a quick kiss. "Uncle," she added before taking the chair a footman held for her.

Henry Tuttlebaum, Viscount Whittingham and older brother to Laura Tuttlebaum Merriweather, gave a quick glance over the top of that morning's *The Times* to acknowledge his niece's greeting.

"Morning," he managed before returning his attention to the newspaper.

At least three footmen scurried about, filling the serving trays on the sideboard and the coffee cups in front of the countess and viscount. A plate of toast, coddled eggs and a rasher of bacon appeared in front of Eleanor, the steam hovering above it a testament to how quickly a footman had managed to get it from the kitchen. "Thank you," Eleanor spoke quietly, knowing her mother might admonish her for thanking servants. "It's their job to serve you, so there's no need to thank them," she had said on more than one occasion. But Eleanor had been in enough households to know that the best service was provided by servants who were well treated by their masters. Saying 'thank you' seemed the least she could do in her mother's household.

"And what have you planned for the day?" Laura asked, turning from her own breakfast to acknowledge her daughter. One dark eyebrow arched up at the sight of the amount of food on Eleanor's plate. "A very long walk, I would hope," she added with a nod toward the breakfast.

Eleanor fought the urge to cringe. Couldn't her mother see she was wearing her newest riding habit, the fit of which was quite snug and meant to display her trim figure to it best advantage? "A ride, in fact," she responded, taking up a fork in defiance of her mother's implication. "Mr. Greaves has agreed to accompany me," she added before her mother could ask, remembering how enthusiastic the head groom's response had been when she wondered if he might act as her chaperone on that day's ride.

At first, she had thought he was being facetious with his reply, but his smile seemed genuine, especially when he made a comment about how beautiful the day would be for a ride. If the rays of sunshine still illuminating the breakfast parlor were any indication, the day would be glorious, indeed.

"Well, don't be too long. We should pay an early afternoon call on Lady Winstead. The gossip has it she just learned of her husband's new mistress, and I should like very much to see how she is faring."

Eleanor resisted the urge to scold her mother, knowing full well Laura Merriweather felt no fondness for Lady Winstead. She merely wished to call on the poor viscountess at a time when the woman was no doubt most embarrassed.

Or most relieved, perhaps.

Penelope Winstead had never voiced much in the way of fondness for her husband.

"I was thinking I might take a trip to Mayfair," Eleanor replied, continuing to eat her breakfast as if mentioning a trip to London was something she did every day.

"Mayfair?" Henry repeated, folding his paper and setting it aside as if he was interested in the women's conversation.

Eleanor swallowed. "Yes. To visit my father. It's been some time since I saw him," she managed to get out before reaching for her coffee. "He promised he would help me arrange my come-out." Although she was sure she sounded confident in her announcement, her stomach threatened to cast up her accounts. "Of course, I would have to meet with a modiste to have an appropriate gown made for my presentation to the queen," she added, mostly to hide her nervousness.

"You'll do no such thing!" her mother replied, the look of shock on her oval face quite at odds with her otherwise elegant appearance.

As the daughter of a marquess, Laura had spent her entire childhood in Mayfair amongst the *ton*, her own come-out a rather lavish affair in the form of a ball given in her honor by her parents. She had met her future husband that night, dancing with him just the one time but obviously impressing him enough that he would eventually ask for her hand in marriage.

Exacting George Merriweather's proposal of marriage during her first Season was considered quite a coupe. The older earl was handsome, rich, politically important in the House of Lords, and not the least bit interested in living the life Laura had imagined for them. Of course, she didn't discover this last bit until she was expecting their first son and was forced to spend her confinement at the Merriweather country estate. Before she could resume London's busy social life the following Season, she was with child once again, this time presenting her husband with a spare heir during the hunting season.

A year later, Eleanor was born.

Having missed three Seasons in a row, and three years of London theatre, fashion and soirées, Laura Merriweather realized life as a young matron in the *ton* would be difficult to resume. She loathed the London gossips, afraid of what they might say about her extended absence and well aware of the damage that could be done should their suppositions be believed. A night at the theater meant many expected more entertainment to be had from the audience than from whatever was taking place on the stage. The crush of carriages and horses made a shopping excursion in New Bond Street a chore. She despised the way the omnipresent soot turned falling snow to black slush.

Despite a childhood spent living in the city, or maybe because of it, life in London no longer appealed to the countess.

Instead of rejoining her husband in Mayfair the following Season, Laura remained in his Surrey estate home, opting for a smaller social circle and the slower pace of country life.

Eleanor gave her mother her best look of surprise. "Why ever not? You had your come-out when you were seventeen," she countered, suppressing the urge to allow her sudden anger to show. As it was, she was sure her cheeks had turned a splotchy red.

"I *lived* there," her mother replied, one shoulder lifted as if a come-out was expected of a London-based chit. "I would hope to spare you the ordeal of a London Season and see you settled with some young gentleman from around here," she added before taking a sip from her coffee cup.

"*Spare* me?" Eleanor repeated, stunned at her mother's words. "But, I don't wish to be *spared!*"

Henry straightened in his chair, the sound of his throat clearing a warning shot across the table. Eleanor forced herself to sit back in her chair, sure he would admonish her for arguing with his sister.

"She makes a good point, Laura," Henry stated, much to Eleanor's surprise. "Every young woman wants to spend at least one Season attending balls and such. And it would do you some good to spend some time in the city. When was the last time you bought a new gown?"

Laura regarded her brother with a look of surprise—and perhaps a bit of annoyance. "Are you implying my gowns are unfashionable?" she countered, her attention no longer on her daughter. "I just had this one made last month. Mrs. Stader assures me the design is straight out of the latest *La Belle Assemblie*."

The viscount let out a sigh. "That wasn't my point, sister," he replied carefully. "I just think you may need to spend some time with your husband. Show the *ton* you two are still ..." He paused, one eyebrow lifting suggestively.

"Still ... *what?*" Laura asked, her face pale.

Eleanor held her breath for a moment, realizing her uncle's meaning right away. She had read the same gossip he had in last week's *The Tattler*. Although she didn't believe her father would ever consort with a courtesan, someone thought they had seen the earl in the company of one at the Drury Lane Theatre. She was quite sure the rag had been wrong; her father had assured her on several occasions that he held her mother in high regard and would never do anything to embarrass his countess.

When Eleanor wrote to him about the incident, he sent word the very next day assuring her he hadn't attended the theatre in years, nor did he spend time with courtesans. *Besides, I love your mother*, he had explained in his even script, nary an ink droplet staining the parchment. *There is no other woman for me.*

"That you're still married," Henry finally said, a bit too harshly.

Before Laura could respond to her brother's comment, Eleanor placed a hand on her mother's shoulder. "Father loves you. He wrote to tell me that it was not him at the theatre, and that he does not employ a mistress."

Laura's eyes widened. "He wrote to *you* of mistresses?" she whispered, glancing about to be sure no servants were within earshot.

Sighing, Eleanor nodded. "Only because I wrote to him about them first," she said, *sotto voce*. "He is devoted to you, Mother. Perhaps you should pay him a visit, though. A dinner together at the Clarendon Hotel will put to rest any doubts about your marriage."

Tears welled up in Laura's eyes, her expression still one of shock. "So the wags have been speaking of him again?" she whispered, her attention entirely on her daughter. She knew Eleanor read everything about the *ton* she could get her hands on in Epping. If there were gossip regarding her husband, Eleanor would know.

Henry, too, perhaps. Damn him.

"Mistaken identity," Eleanor replied as she shook her head. "You've nothing to worry about when it comes to Father."

Settling back into her chair, Laura used the corner of her linen napkin to dab away a tear that had escaped the corner of one eye. "I should forbid you to read those awful gossip sheets," she said, suppressing a sob.

"Probably," Eleanor agreed, a mischievous grin lighting her face until she remembered the odd comment made in the latest issue of *The Tattler*. She wasn't sure it had anything to do with a certain man for whom she had felt a growing affection since the last dinner party she had attended in London. But she was at a loss as to figure out anyone else who fit the initials used in the article.

A certain knight, AG, had better take himself a wife, or he'll be forever known as a molly. We shouldn't want him arrested. Guilt by association is still guilt.

Try as she might, the only knight she could think of with those initials was Arthur Goodwin. Handsome, debonair and ever so refined that night she had sat across from him at Worthington House, Sir Arthur was hardly one she could imagine in the company of a man, at least in *that way*. Especially given some of things she had imagined him doing to her many a night in her bed. Especially on cold nights. Well, any night really, but cold nights were quickly made tolerable when she imagined her body pressed against his, imagined her head tucked into the small of his shoulder and her legs tangled with his. Even now, the thought of Arthur Goodwin made her feel warm all over. Almost uncomfortably so. Hot, really. Her cheeks seemed almost on fire.

It was a good thing she was about to go for a ride.

Realizing she had stayed too long at the breakfast table— the head groom would be waiting with her Norfolk Trotter at the stables —Eleanor excused herself. "I'm off for my ride. And, if it's all right with you, I'd really rather not pay a call on Lady Winstead this afternoon. If this weather holds, I would prefer to take a walk to town. See what's come on the latest mail coach."

She didn't add that she intended to *be* on that coach when it departed for London at noon.

CHAPTER 6
ANOTHER DAY, ANOTHER RAKE

*E*arlier *in the evening of that fateful night, well before the clock struck midnight*

"Do you ever feel guilty? Given our past behavior, I mean," Randall Roderick, Marquess of Reading, asked as he reached for his brandy balloon. One of the footmen at White's had just set it down on the table next to his chair. He waited for Charles Goodwin, Earl of Wakefield, to do the same before holding up his glass in a salute.

The earl matched the marquess' move and sniffed his brandy before taking a sip. "To what behavior do you refer?" he asked, allowing the footman to light his cheroot. For a moment, he wondered if the marquess had him confused with his brother, Sir Arthur. The damn gossip rags were at it again, suggesting the man had been seen in the company of other men, and not for the purpose of gambling or whoring.

Randall gave Charles a quelling glance. "Our rakish behavior, of course. I never thought it would ... *interfere* with my life as much as it seems to have done this past week," he explained.

Charles regarded the marquess for a moment, his gaze intercepted by a swirl of smoke from his cheroot. Once the smoke had cleared, he allowed a shrug. "I've done nothing for which to feel *guilty*," he replied. "Unlike you, I pay for my tumbles, and I haven't had the comforts of a widow in ... well over a year," he added, his voice lowering so only the marquess could hear him. "And then it was only because she trapped me in Lord Weatherstone's library and *insisted* on it during his annual ball."

His eyebrow's dancing, Randall gave a snort. "What? Did she put a gun to your head?" he teased.

The earl frowned. "Not the head you're thinking about," he replied with a wince. "And I rather like both of them, so I did as I was told. I left quite sure she was satisfied, although we did have to be quick given the queue waiting outside to use the room."

The Marquess of Reading shook his head, wondering if *he* had been in the line to which the earl referred. Goodness! Lord Weatherstone's balls were always the best attended and probably because they always promised a willing woman or two with whom a tryst could be arranged in the gardens.

Or the library.

Except for this last ball, Randall remembered. "I was kissed by a virgin at Weatherstone's last ball," he murmured, his gaze taking on a faraway look. "Something that's never happened before and probably never will again."

Charles straightened in his chair, intrigued by Randall's claim. "Because you plowed her in the garden? By the fountain?" Charles countered, his amusement disappearing when he caught sight of Randall's somber face. The man looked positively sorrowful. Another moment, and Charles was sure the marquess' bright eyes would shed a tear or two. "Good God, man! What did you *do* to her?" he asked, struggling to keep his voice low despite his alarm.

The question seemed to bring the marquess back to the present. "Nothing. I did *nothing*," he replied. "Well, except speak of marriage. I proposed. I even made a promise to her that I would keep a vow of fidelity should she accept my offer."

Charles stared at Randall for a full ten seconds before his eyebrows drew together into a deep frown. "Where is the Rake of Reading and what have you done with him?" he asked in a menacing voice.

The marquess frowned. "It's not funny, I tell you," Randall said with a shake of his head. "I am five-and-thirty. My hair is graying. A second chin appears at the worst possible moments. My ears are growing hair, and I am deathly afraid of growing one of those paunches that seem to make men look as if they're breeding and about to give birth." He took a breath and let it out, sounding ever so frustrated. "And a young lady—the same age as my oldest bastard son—kissed me on the corner of my mouth—right next to Weatherstone's fountain—and told me she would consider my suit."

Blinking as if he couldn't believe what he was hearing, Charles shook his head. "Was she a ... a gold digger?" he asked carefully, thinking the marquess had realized the proposal was a mistake. Or perhaps the marquess wasn't worth as much as everyone thought he was. He did spend a good deal of coin on jewelry for all the women he kept happy between the bed linens. And then there was his love of race meetings. Rumor had it that his horses cost him a small fortune.

Perhaps he needed to marry for a dowry.

"Hardly," Randall replied. "Her dowry was probably worth twenty, maybe even fifty thousand—"

"Good God, man!" Charles said again, thinking *he* might be compelled to promise fidelity in exchange for such a large dowry.

Or perhaps not.

He liked variety in his bed. It was part of the excitement of putting together a new puzzle every time he hosted a harlot at his townhouse, something he would be doing later that night. "When is the wedding?" he asked then, thinking the marquess was merely feeling sorry for himself because he had promised to keep his wedding vows. The thought had Charles allowing a sudden shiver, for the idea of fidelity was inconceivable despite the promise of a large dowry.

Randall Roderick took a long sip from his brandy. "Yesterday. I received a note from the lady saying she had accepted another's suit, and, in fact, has already married the young man. A commoner, no less," he said with sadness.

In fact, he hadn't yet read the entire letter but planned to do so in the morning whilst on his usual walk in Hyde Park.

The Earl of Wakefield shook his head, stunned by the news and wondering just who the marquess referred to in his story. Realizing Randall would probably drain his brandy in a single gulp, he said, "Look on the bright side, man. You don't have to keep your promise. You can still be a rake."

Sighing, Randall leaned forward in his chair and rested his elbows on his knees. "I don't *want* to be a rake anymore," he said quietly. "I *want* to be married. It's time I take a wife. Time I sire a legitimate heir," he added in a whisper. "And deuce take it, but I have no idea where to start."

Reeling from the older man's confession, Charles merely shook his head back and forth. Randall Roderick was a role model for rakes everywhere. Past middle age, the gentleman was so well known as a rake, widows and matrons eagerly sought his company. Unlike a libertine, Randall took pride in making sure his partners were all willing. And able. Nothing could be done for the women who were said to be cold fish in bed, after all.

"I have to admit to a bit of disappointment at hearing your news, Reading," Charles said finally. "But I suppose when I am your age, I will have come to the same conclusion." *But not before then.* He couldn't imagine the idea of marriage. Not now, and certainly not in the next ten years.

Randall lifted his eyes to meet his younger counterpart's. "Do not wait that long, Wakefield," he warned. "Find a wife while you still have a single chin and all of the hair on your head. Learn to pleasure her and do it over and over again so she won't be tempted to invite another to her bed. Bestow her with jewels she will wear only for you. And for God's sake, get yourself home before one o'clock in the morning."

Stung by the man's words, Charles winced. "Now you sound like Grandby," he accused, trying to lighten the mood.

Randall nodded. "That's because *he* figured it out first," he spat out. "Notice how he left at exactly seven o'clock this evening so he could be home in time for dinner at Worthington House. He has a loving wife at home who's about give him a child. And he's got at least ... seven, eight years on me. I am not about to wait any longer."

With that, the Marquess of Reading gave the earl a nod, stood up, and took his leave of White's.

Damnation! Charles thought as he watched the man retrieve his hat from a footman. *Was the Rake of Reading truly turning over a new leaf?* Randall Roderick had never spoken of marriage, of fidelity or home, and certainly not of children.

Noting the time on his own chronometer, he realized he had some time before he needed to take his leave of the men's club. A harlot was scheduled to arrive at midnight, and given his rule about her being out of his house by two o'clock in the morning, Charles wanted to be sure to get home by one.

Tossing a coin in the direction of the footman, he finally took his leave of White's at half-past midnight.

CHAPTER 7
NOW THAT THE DAMAGE
IS DONE

Back to the fateful morning of September 15
When the mantel clock displayed the time to be ten minutes of two o'clock, Eleanor allowed a sigh. She was tired, travel weary, and rather traumatized by the events of the day. Although she was tempted to simply fall asleep—Wakefield's Rule be damned—she realized she really should take her leave of the earl's house while it was still dark. Perhaps she could leave by way of the back door in an effort to escape notice by the hackney driver who was no doubt watching for her out front. Although she didn't know her way around London, she thought she might be able to hide in a mews until morning. Then she could hire a hackney to take her to her father's townhouse. A small purse with a few coins was shoved into the pocket of her gown, a measure meant to allow her some money should she need to purchase a cup of tea when the mail coach made its frequent stops. Now it would be her way to pay a hackney driver.

Escaping Lucy Gibbons was paramount, she decided, even if it meant abandoning her valise. The madame had taken possession of it prior to sending her to Wakefield's house, explaining to Eleanor that she could have it back when she returned later that night.

Eleanor thought briefly about asking her father to retrieve the traveling case, but then she would have to explain how it got there.

And if someone saw the Earl of Middleton enter the brothel, word would no doubt get to *The Tattler*. The gossip rag would suggest her father was employing one of the Gibbons' girls! The mere thought of her father doing what she had seen Lord Sinclair doing just a few hours ago had her cringing worse than she had when Lord Wakefield had impaled her with his rather prominent prick.

Perhaps she would be better off claiming the valise had been stolen whilst on the mail coach. The idea of her jewelry and her favorite gowns in the possession of the brothel owner rankled, but she could not abide the thought of returning for it.

Still trapped beneath the earl's prone body, she wondered how she could extricate herself from the bed without waking him. She moved one leg in an attempt to slide it under his legs. When he stirred, she stopped and held her breath. A moment later, she tried again, stopping when he rolled to one side, his head coming to rest on the pillow next to her head and the front of his body pressed against the side of hers. One of his beefy arms remained wrapped around her midriff, however, while his hand ended up cupping the side of her bare breast. Attempting to slide off the bed from beneath his arm proved impossible; the earl's arm was like a steel band! As for his hand, well, Eleanor might have thought its place-ment rather scandalous except there were too many other far more scandalous activities she had witnessed or participated in over the course of the day to be particularly scandalized by a mere hand on her breast.

She sighed. "Could you please let go?" she whispered, hoping the earl would simply lift his arm and allow her to leave his bed.

His reaction was exactly the opposite, though, his arm pulling her body hard against his.

Eleanor let out a yelp when she realized her bottom was cush-ioning his manhood. At least, she was pretty sure that's what was tucked up against her. Not having spent much time studying his male anatomy when she'd had the chance—she was thoroughly scan-dalized at that point in the night—she could only imagine it was his weapon seeking a sheath in which to bury itself for the night.

"Where do you think you're going?" he asked, his voice such a surprise to Eleanor, she nearly let out a squeak.

"It's nearly two o'clock, my lord. According to your rule, I need to—"

"You're not going anywhere, my lady, except to sleep."

Eleanor dared a glance over her shoulder, rather surprised to find the earl's eyes closed. "But, I'm supposed to take the hackney back. Mrs. Gibbons has my things," she pleaded. She thought about telling him of her plan to hide until daylight, but she rather doubted he would allow her to leave his house given his curt words of only a moment ago. But if she were to attempt to leave once it was light, she took the risk of being seen by a neighbor.

"I'll have Chester see to your things in the morning. But you're *not* going back there," he murmured, his fading voice evidence that slumber was about to take him once again. "Besides, you're my birthday gift, and I have no intention of giving you back."

A moment later, Eleanor could tell from his even breathing that the earl was sound asleep.

No intention of giving you back?

Goodness! What did he intend to do with her? Make her his private concubine?

The thought should have had her feeling scandalized, she supposed, but a flutter just beneath her skin had her thinking it might not be so bad.

Offer her carte-blanche?

Eleanor thought of her earlier conversation with her mother and uncle—had that just been earlier that morning?— and wondered what it might be like to become a mistress. To have a townhouse, servants, beautiful clothes, jewelry ... but for how long?

She might have pondered his comment a bit longer, might have allowed the tears that once again threatened to have her sobbing, but instead, she simply sighed and allowed exhaustion to take her away.

When he was sure Eleanor was sleeping, Wakefield gave a sigh of frustration.

What have I done?

Acted like the worst rake on the planet. Taken a virgin to his bed. Kept her there against her will, although he rather doubted she really wanted to leave his bed to return to the brothel. *I am the lesser of two evils*, he thought with a sigh.

Remembering his earlier conversation with the Marquess of Reading, he was about to make a vow never to bed a woman again but thought he would never be able to keep it. He rather enjoyed a good tumble. Twice a week. More if he was so inclined and could arrange a willing partner.

At least he hadn't simply tumbled Eleanor. At least he'd had enough sense to employ a bit of foreplay before he had unceremoniously plunged himself into her. He was about to relive the memory of the exquisite pleasure he had felt when he chided himself.

There were no two ways about it. He would have to own up to his mistake. He would have to admit it to the affected parties. He would have to do the honorable thing.

He would have to marry Eleanor Merriweather.

The thought must not have surprised him as much as it should have, for he was sound asleep within moments.

CHAPTER 8
A REFORMED RAKE
PONDERS HOW TO PURSUE
A WIFE

Eight o'clock in the morning of September 15

Ignoring the early morning fog, Randall Roderick donned a coat and hat and left his Curzon Street townhouse on foot. Although he could have taken a shortcut through the Marquess of Devonville's yard and been in Hyde Park in a matter of moments, he instead opted to stay on the tarmac as he made his way.

He patted the side of his coat where he had stuffed the letter he had received from Lady Lily the day before. Not particularly surprised the young lady would forgo his offer of marriage—he was quite sure he hadn't completely convinced her of his intention to give up his life as a rake—he was surprised she had written of far more than her refusal of his suit.

Having been about to leave for White's when the letter was delivered the night before, Randall read the first paragraph and quickly tossed it aside. A bit hurt, he thought only to drown his sorrows at the men's club and pay a call on a widow he had comforted the week before. However, after his time lecturing poor Charles Goodwin, Earl of Wakefield, on the virtues of finding and honoring a wife, he could hardly spend the night tumbling a widow, no matter how willing she was.

Once he was home from White's and had finished his observation of the delivery of the harlot to the terrace across the street, he had gone to bed—alone—and slept rather hard. Awake too early but unable to settle his mind to return to slumbering, Randall surprised his valet by getting up before seven and announcing he was going to the park. He had a letter he wished to finish reading and some planning to do.

Along the way, he was surprised when he came upon the Earl of Norwick and his countess pushing a perambulator in which two small babes were wrapped in flannel blankets. "Good morning, Lady Norwick," he said with a tip of his hat and a quick bow. "Norwick," he added with a nod to Daniel Fitzwilliam. "And who do we have here?" he asked as he dared a glance into the wide baby carriage.

"These are the Ladies Diana and Dahlia," Clarinda said proudly. "Three weeks old and rather early risers."

Since both babies seemed sound asleep, the marquess figured they must have been awake at some point earlier that morning. "Goodness! Look at all of that hair," he muttered, resisting the temptation to reach down and smooth the shocks of dark fuzz into place.

Clarinda grinned. "They were born with it," she said proudly.

"I do hope they didn't wake you, Lord Reading," Daniel said from where he stood, watching the marquess closely. He thought perhaps the man had just left a widow's home and was making his way back to his terrace.

Randall shook his head. "Not at all. I went to bed before one and found myself wide awake at seven. Figured a walk in the park would do me good."

At that moment, a footman wearing the colors of Worthington House hurried up to them. Breathless, he said, "Pardon me, my lady, my lords," with a hastily performed bow. "Lady Torrington has requested Lady Norwick's presence at her earliest convenience." Before anyone could give him an answer, he gave another bow and hurried back the way he came.

Clarinda dared a quick glance in Daniel's direction before

turning her attention to the marquess. "Forgive me, but it seems Grandby's baby is about to make its debut."

Randall's eyes widened. "*Now?* Well, that seems rather inconvenient," he replied with a frown.

Suppressing a grin, Clarinda said, "Babies rarely come at the most convenient time, actually. Please do excuse me. I must be going," she said, taking a step back and giving the marquess a curtsy.

Daniel gave an apologetic nod. "As must I," he said, motioning to the perambulator. "Do have a good walk, Reading."

And with that, the Norwicks were hurrying off toward Worthington House.

Randall watched the couple take their leave, rather touched that an earl would accompany his wife on a walk with the children—with babies that were not even his own but rather his nieces.

Despite his own father never having done such a thing, Randall thought perhaps he would go on walks with his wife and children. He imagined strolling around Cavendish Square, pushing a perambulator, a woman's arm on his as they made their way.

He rather liked the image.

Sighing, he continued his daydream as he made his way into Hyde Park.

By eight-thirty, the fog had lifted and a hint of morning sun lit the park in a golden glow. Randall paused to regard a series of rose bushes, their blooms still brilliant despite the early fall temperatures. Lowering himself to sniff a particularly red rose, he closed his eyes and was reminded of Lady Lily.

Well, this won't do, he thought as he glanced about and headed for the nearest park bench. Until he read the rest of her missive, he wouldn't be able to leave thoughts of her where they belonged.

He removed the note from his pocket and carefully unfolded the corners. Holding it out until his eyes could focus on the feminine script, he took a deep breath and began to read.

> *Dear Marquess of Reading,*
> *I am writing to give you my answer regarding your marriage*

proposal. As you may recall, you asked me to marry you whilst we attended Lord Weatherstone's ball in June. If in the event you do remember, let me inform you I was honored a marquess would consider an illegitimate maid for his wife ...

What?! *Did she think I had forgotten her?* Randall thought, at first offended by the young lady's words before forcing himself to remain calm. In her defense, she knew he was a rake. Perhaps she believed he proposed to every woman he managed to get into the gardens behind Lord Weatherstone's mansion as a means to have his way with them.

Little did she know she was the first to ever have him considering marriage. The first woman to whom he had promised fidelity should she consider his suit. The first woman to ever kiss him first, even if it was just on the corner of his mouth.

He reached up to touch the spot with a gloved hand, remembering the feel of her soft lips as they had made contact, the scent of her more enticing than all the floral scents in the garden surrounding them.

He shook his head, determined to erase the image from his mind. Taking a breath, he resumed reading the missive.

Although I am led to believe no fewer than four aristocrats wanted my hand in marriage, yours was the only formal proposal I received. My heart, however, already belonged to a young man I met many years ago in Vauxhall Gardens.

I married him yesterday.

Well, the chit certainly didn't waste any time! But the fact that she had penned a letter to the marquess after only a day of marriage said she must have held him in some regard.

Frowning, Randall continued to read.

During your proposal, I truly believe I heard more in the words you did not speak than in those you did. Perhaps I am being presumptu-

ous, but I do believe you are a lonely man who has come to the conclu-sion his life can only be complete with the addition of a wife and a necessary heir. As a marquess, I also believe you think you must pursue a wife from those women who are daughters of others like you.

From my recent lessons in history (my brother, Lord Trenton, insisted I be educated), and should your marquessate be at war with another, or should your coffers be in need of funding, I would agree you should consider a marriage for political or economic gain ...

Faith! The young woman was writing of strategic marriages!

Randall lifted his head and glanced around to ensure he was still relatively alone in the area of the park in which he sat. He held out the note and resumed reading.

... However, I do not believe you require such a union. Given the circumstances, you have a distinct advantage over your peers, my lord, for you can do what most of them cannot.

You can marry for love.

Stunned at the words, Randall straightened on the bench. Aris-tocrats didn't marry for love. That's what their mistresses were for!

Although, to be fair, he did know of some who were quite fond of their wives—perhaps even in love with them. Anyone who had been at a soirée at Carlington House had to know the Marquess of Morganfield and his marchioness were in love. They seemed to spend an inordinate amount of time in the company of the nearest potted palm, believing they were hiding their affection for one another from their guests as they engaged in a good deal of kissing and other fondling pursuits. Just a few minutes ago, he had been in the company of the Fitzwilliams. Why, the newly minted earl and his wife seemed rather fond of one another. But then, Clarinda had been in love with the older twin, he remembered, and Daniel *was* the spitting image of his brother. He wondered if she sometimes forgot her husband had died. She certainly hadn't spent much time in mourning before marrying his brother, but given how the two behaved when he came upon them that morning, he had to believe they were in love.

Intrigued by the thought of marrying for love, Randall relaxed back onto the bench. He searched and found where he had left off reading.

> *You can marry for love.*
>
> *Having spent over two months in the company of my brother, Trenton, and his countess, Sarah, I can tell you their marriage is one such. And as such, they are a happy couple, engaging in spirited conversation and shared responsibility and public displays of affection I find most embarrassing.*
>
> *I can imagine you in such a union, my lord. Your marchioness at your side, sneaking kisses whilst at the theatre and singing your praises in the parlors of Mayfair, a public face for your favorite charity and your one (and only, dare I say it?) lover.*
>
> *I do believe she would make you a very happy man.*
>
> *So in your pursuit of a wife, I would remind you there are hundreds of young women—commoners, yes, or those on the fringes of the ton, but many educated and not looking to marry for money—who would strive to make a happy marriage with you. I implore you to consider one of them to be your wife.*
>
> *Yours most sincerely, Lady Lily Overby.*
>
> *Post Scriptum: Had I not given my heart to another, please know I would have accepted your most generous offer.*

Randall glanced about again, stunned by the young lady's words. She spoke of marriage as if she had been married her entire life, and yet she made her point so plain.

Marry for love.

How hard could that be? He sighed.

Nearly impossible, he reasoned. For to marry for love meant he had to be in *love* with someone, and he couldn't think of a single woman he knew for whom he might somehow develop a tendré. Someone with whom he could fall in love.

Which meant he probably hadn't yet met the woman, he reasoned.

Which meant another Season of balls and soirées and musicales and evenings at Almack's.

Damn!

Groaning, Randall carefully arranged the pages and refolded the note, his gaze directed at the lawn beneath his feet. Although he was tempted to feel sorry for himself—Lily had seen through his façade of confident rake and guessed at his loneliness—he also felt a bit emboldened by her words.

You can marry for love.

He didn't have to pursue a daughter of the aristocracy to be in his wife. He could court whomever he wished.

Taking a deep breath, he stood up from the bench and was about to take his leave of the park when he realized he was no longer alone. A startled young woman regarded him from the crushed granite path, her maid several steps behind her.

Randall stared at the young woman for a full five seconds before he realized he was staring. "Good morning, my lady," he finally managed to say as he gave her a deep bow. The sunlight illuminated one side of her face, making her porcelain skin even more luminous than it probably was in the midday. Her hair, although mostly hidden by a rather stylish hat festooned with large flowers and a bright red bow, was definitely blonde, and her eyes were a shade of blue. Or green, perhaps. *The color of the ocean*, Randall thought briefly.

He would have spent more time deciding on their color except that the young woman blinked and dared a glance back at her companion. It was then he realized she was probably a bit older than he first surmised. *Thirty, perhaps?*

The maid was definitely younger than her mistress, but probably not by much, he figured, and she was much more comely. She was staring at him as if she recognized him. He was quite sure he had never seen her before. But then, who noticed servants?

A sense of panic settled over him as he wondered if the maid knew of him from one of his trysts with a widow. Or a matron who had invited him to her bed because she was lonely. Or one of his younger conquests who pretended not to want his attentions but were just as enthusiastic as his older lovers once they were undressed and beneath him on a bed.

But the woman before him wasn't a woman with whom he had ever shared a bed. He was quite sure he would remember her. Positive, in fact.

When the young lady returned her attention to him, she gave a curtsy. "Good morning to you, sir," she replied, a hint of uncertainty in her voice. "Have ... Have we met?" she asked, as if she might or might not recognize him.

Randall shook his head. "I'm quite sure I would remember you ..." *and your maid*, he almost said, "...if I had, my lady." He hesitated before introducing himself. "Randall Roderick, at your service, my lady," he finally managed, stepping forward to take her hand.

He brushed his lips over her ill-fitting white linen glove, noting how her hand seemed to quiver in his hold. Was she frightened of him? Or cold, perhaps? Although the morning had started out rather chilly, the sun was now clear of the clouds and the air was warming nicely.

The woman seemed to deflate a bit at hearing his name, but she quickly recovered. "Miss Constance Fitzwilliam," she said before daring another glance back at her maid. "So good to make your acquaintance," she added as she pulled her hand from Randall's gentle grasp.

"And yours," he countered, rather surprised at hearing her name. Goodness! How unusual to come across so many Fitzwilliams in one morning! He was about to ask if they might be related when he realized he needed to offer his arm. "May I ... escort you somewhere?" he asked. "I seemed to have interrupted your morning walk. I do apologize," he added, hoping she would accept his invitation. He needed a bit more exercise and an opportunity to practice what he realized might be one way to court a lady—walk with her whilst engaging in conversation.

Another backward glance at the maid, who merely gave her a curt nod and a look of impatience, was followed by the young woman's own nod in his direction. "Yes, thank you," she replied.

Randall gave the maid a nod of thanks and offered his arm to the young woman. "Where would you like to go this morning, Miss Fitzwilliam?" he asked then, turning so he was headed in the same direction she seemed to be heading when he spotted her.

"I ... I'm not sure," she replied, turning once again to the maid. "Simmons?" she said in a hoarse whisper.

The marquess was aware of the maid's audible sigh of what sounded like frustration. "Back to the carriage, my lady," the servant replied, as if she were growing impatient with the chit.

"Of course, thank you, Simmons," the young woman said before turning around. She was about to repeat what the maid said when Randall angled his head in her direction.

"I heard," he said with a grin. "Perhaps if we walk this way, the path will lead us back to where your carriage is parked," he suggested, not wanting to turn around just then. With the sun at their back, he could better see the woman who barely touched her hand to his arm. "I will not bite, my lady," he said *sotto voce*. "Unless you wish me to do so, and then ..." He stopped himself and nearly cursed. *Good God!* What was he saying? It wasn't as if she was a typical widow looking for a bit of companionship and a tumble!

He cleared his throat as he placed his other hand over the one on his arm. "Tell me, Miss Fitzwilliam. Why the ... uncertainty?" he asked outright. The chit was so nervous, he thought she might faint.

"Oh, Simmons, this isn't working," she said, pulling her arm from his.

Frowning, Randall turned his attention from Miss Fitzsimmons to the maid. "What, pray tell, is going on?" he asked the servant directly.

Giving her mistress a quelling glance, the maid stepped forward and, keeping her voice low, said, "Miss Fitzwilliam recently inherited some funds and has been elevated in Society as a result. She ... She is *practicing* everything she needs to learn."

Randall blinked. The scenario sounded ever so familiar. Lady Lily had been a maid when she was suddenly elevated in Society when her brother, the Earl of Trenton, had claimed her as his sister. "Elevated?" he repeated quietly as he dared a look at Miss Fitzwilliam.

The maid sighed. "She recently reached her majority, my lord," she replied, her brief explanation expected to answer his question.

Well, it did to some extent. For a woman to reach her majority meant she wasn't married, wasn't betrothed to be married, and had probably inherited some funds kept in escrow for just such an occasion. "Congratulations, Miss Fitzwilliam," he said with a nod, still wondering if she were any relation to the Fitzwilliams he had come upon earlier that morning. Although Norwick's father had died years ago and his twin brother had perished in a traffic accident earlier that year, Randall wasn't sure about the earl's uncle. A simple comment would help determine if he had guessed her familial relationship correctly. "I suppose I should offer my condolences."

The young lady's eyes widened. "How ... How do you know about ... Did you know my ... father?"

Of all the times to have guessed right, Randall rather wished it wasn't this time. But at least he had the young woman conversing. "Norwick's uncle?" he ventured.

At her slight nod and sideways glance toward the maid, he took a deep breath. "I knew him in passing. We both had horses on the racing circuit." He nearly stopped talking when he heard the maid's soft gasp behind him, but decided to continue. "As I recall, his Thoroughbred won most of the races a few years ago. Did Edward die ... recently?" Randall asked, hoping she wouldn't begin crying at being reminded of her father's death.

She shook her head. "It's been three years ago now. Now I am ..." She paused before daring a glance back at the woman who followed them. "I feel a bit lost whilst attempting to learn what it is to be out in Society. And I'm making a cake of it," she added in a whisper.

Even though he agreed with her self-assessment, the marquess shook his head. She certainly looked as if she were lost. Why else would she continue to look to her maid for guidance? Especially when the maid was definitely younger than she was? For when he dared another glance back at the maid, he was quite sure there was at least five years difference in their ages—perhaps even ten. "Hardly, my lady," he said as he lifted her hand back to his arm. "At least you were not a maid suddenly elevated to the position of an earl's daughter," he offered when he noticed her look of surprise, noting how her eyes widened even more at the comment.

She apparently didn't need to think about the scenario for even a moment. "You're referring to ... to Lady Lily, aren't you?" she guessed, a nervous smile forming on her lips.

Randall gave some thought as to what it might be like to kiss those lips, but he didn't find the thought as enchanting as he should have. Now a quick glance back at the maid, and he found he rather liked the idea of kissing *her*.

What the hell?

Had he developed a desire for lady's maids given what had happened with Lady Lily? He dared another glance back at Miss Fitzwilliam's chaperone and wondered at the woman's apprehension. When might he kiss the maid?

"I am," he finally replied with a nod in response to her question about Lady Lily. "She is married now."

This news seemed to surprise the Norwick cousin. "But, when did this happen?" she asked in disbelief.

Randall gave it some thought. "The day before yesterday, I believe," he replied. "She married a commoner. A clerk." When he noted her continued look of surprise, he added, "It was for the best. She married for love, you see."

"Oh," the woman who had introduced herself as Constance breathed, and once again Randall was left wondering if he should kiss the woman, just to discover if he could get away with it, and if he did, if she might consider him for matrimony.

If Constance Fitzwilliam had reached her majority, then she was probably five-and-twenty, Randall figured. Much older than most debutantes, but certainly not a spinster—at least, not yet. "How is it you have managed to avoid marriage?" he asked then, not realizing how personal the question sounded until he heard the maid's gasp behind him.

The young woman stared straight ahead, wondering how best to answer. "I was betrothed once," she finally admitted. "But I despised my father's choice for me, and I—"

"My lady, we should be getting back to the carriage," the maid interrupted.

Randall bristled at hearing the maid's comment, just as Miss Fitzwilliam was about to impart a crucial bit of information. Had Simmons done so on purpose? "We should be coming up on the carriageway momentarily, my lady," he said with a pat on the white-gloved hand that rested on his arm. "I suppose you have already met your new cousins?" he ventured, wondering if the lady had paid a call on the Earl and Countess of Norwick and their new twin daughters.

"Cousins?" Miss Fitzwilliam repeated, appearing a bit confused. "Oh! You mean the twins," she said. "No. Not yet, as I've just recently come to London. But I shall do so in the next ... week or so," she added at Randall's look of surprise.

"Does Norwick even know you're in town?" Although his only interaction with the new earl had occurred only the hour before, he would know more about the man when Parliament resumed in November—or perhaps at a Society event even before then.

Miss Fitzwilliam seemed to deflate before his eyes. "He does not," she replied.

At this tidbit of information, Randall allowed an audible sigh. "Do not delay in making your presence in London known to Norwick, my lady. You require protection," he warned. *From men like me*, he almost added. Instead, he said, "And he can provide it."

When they cleared a stand of hedgerows, the carriageway appeared straight ahead. A barouche, a single Yorkshire Trotter, and a driver and stood ready and waiting for the young lady and her maid.

"I shall call on the earl this week," Miss Fitzwilliam promised as she regarded the marquess, apparently surprised that their walk had taken them in a large circle around the hedgerows. She stepped up into the barouche with the help of the driver. Once she was seated, the young woman gave Randall a nod.

"It was very good to make your acquaintance, my lady," Randall said with a bow. "I shall look forward to a dance with you at the first ball." When he realized the maid hadn't yet stepped up into the carriage, he dared a glance to his right and found her nose-to-nose with the horse. Apparently she admired the Trotter, for he witnessed her whispering so only the horse could hear her words. The horse knickered and tossed its head as the maid stepped away.

Rather touched by her action, Randall held out his hand in her direction. After a slight hesitation, she took it, her gloved hand sending a jolt of *something* through the marquess' arm. He tightened his hold on her fingers in response as she easily stepped up into the conveyance. Her look of sudden surprise and quick glance in his direction had Randall thinking she might have felt the same *something* he had. He thought of holding on for a moment more, but realized he had to let go. And just as quickly as the *something* took hold of him, it left him. The moment was lost as quickly as it had occurred.

Apparently surprised by his comment about dancing with her at the first ball, Miss Fitzwilliam afforded him a nod. "As do I with you," she said as her maid took her seat in the back of the equipage.

Randall tipped his hat when the driver returned to his seat and set the horse in motion.

Puzzled by their conversation, especially by the maid's reticence, Randall wondered about Constance Fitzwilliam. And he wondered more about her maid. Wondered because, damn it to hell, he was quite sure he wanted to get to know far more about *her*. Everything about her. Maybe even ask for her hand in marriage.

What *was* it about *maids?* Prior to meeting Lady Lily, he hadn't given a maid a second glance. Now he found himself curious enough to make a damn fool of himself.

Then he remembered Lady Lily's missive.

You can marry for love.

Perhaps he could.

CHAPTER 9
ANTICIPATION OF A BIRTH

early nine o'clock in the morning of September 15
While he waited for his wife to join him in the breakfast parlor, Milton Grandby, Earl of Torrington, read that day's edition of *The Times*. He was rather pleased to see the notice of the marriage of Lady Lily Wellingham to Mr. William Overby, the union effectively ending any speculation as to which the young lady would choose to marry during the Little Season. Although he had to admit to a bit of surprise at learning she had married a clerk—four aristocrats had been rumored to want either her hand in marriage or her dowry—Grandby thought her choice of a commoner a better fit. Although she had been the darling at balls during the two Seasons she had attended *ton* events, Grandby wondered how the ladies of the *ton* would have received her if she had married an aristocrat. Some of the women could be quite cruel with their words and their gossip, and given her illegitimacy, he thought she might suffer the cut direct among her fellow young matrons.

If Lady Lily hadn't made a decision as to a spouse, Grandby was quite prepared to arrange a suitable one on her behalf. Given how his life would be changing any day now, though, he was rather relieved the matter was out of his hands.

He glanced at his chronometer, surprised that his countess,

Adele Slater Worthington Grandby, hadn't yet appeared for breakfast. About to summon a footman to check on her, he was rather startled when one suddenly appeared, breathless, in the doorway.

"My lord. The countess says to beg your forgiveness, but she won't be joining you for breakfast this morning," the young man managed to get out before having to inhale to catch his breath.

Grandby blinked. "Oh. Did she say why?" he asked, hoping she wasn't feeling any worse than she had the night before. She had complained of backaches and swollen ankles, conditions he found he could help alleviate with a bit of sexual intercourse and by rubbing her feet. Despite her repeated admonishment of his advances—"I'm as big as a house, Milton. Honestly, how can you stand to be in the same *room* with me?"—Grandby found he rather liked his wife in her current condition, all soft and round and ready for his arousal no matter the time of day or night. He had to admit to feeling a bit exhausted, however; he had never engaged in this much intercourse, even when he was an unmarried earl bedding a different widow every Season.

The footman colored up and stammered a bit before he said, "She's going to have a baby, my lord!"

Grandby set aside his newspaper and nodded. "I'm well aware of Lady Torrington's condition," he replied with a grin. *Have been since March*, he nearly added.

Swallowing, the footman nodded. "Today, my lord."

Having taken a drink of his coffee, Grandby nearly choked as he comprehended the words. "*Now?*" he countered, rising quickly from the table. "Send for the midwife—"

"The butler is seeing to it," the footman interrupted.

"Then see to it word gets to Lady Norwick," Grandby ordered, knowing Adele would want Clarinda Fitzwilliam at her bedside. The Countess of Norwick was Adele's best friend and confidante, and she had just delivered twins a few weeks ago.

"Another footman has already been dispatched to Norwick House, my lord," the tall man countered.

Grandby frowned. "What? Am I the *last* to know?" he asked in alarm.

The footman, deciding he really shouldn't attempt to answer the question, simply bowed and took his leave of the breakfast parlor.

The earl wasn't far behind, making his way to the stairs just as Clarinda Fitzwilliam appeared in the vestibule of Worthington House. She cradled a blanket-wrapped baby in one arm.

"Clare!" Grandby called out, changing his direction of travel in order to make his way to greet her.

"Grandby. So good to see you," the new mother said as she held out the baby. "Here. Take her so I can get out of my pelisse, won't you?"

Blinking, Grandby was suddenly in possession of a three-week-old girl. Although he was the godfather to twenty-one—no, make that twenty-two—women of various ages, Milton Grandby hadn't held a baby in his arms in over twenty years. He had *seen* this one before, as well as her twin sister, but both were in their perambulator and snoozing on their morning walk with their mother and uncle.

The baby, although awake, didn't seem the least bit bothered at being handed off to a man who was probably old enough to be her grandfather. "Which one is she?" Grandby asked as he adjusted his arm so her head was better supported. *This isn't so hard*, he thought, rather pleased with himself that the newborn wasn't howling at the sudden change in view. Perhaps his own baby, apparently on the way at any moment, would feel the same.

He could only hope.

"That is Lady Diana Dorothea," Daniel Fitzwilliam said as he stood in the vestibule helping his wife remove her pelisse with one hand while he held another bundle in his other arm. Having helped deliver one of the twins—the midwife had assisted with the first and then left the bedchamber while Clarinda gave birth to the second— Daniel was a far more involved stepfather than most aristocratic fathers were. "And this is Lady Dahlia Davida," he said as he held out his bundle. "We're quite sure we haven't used up all the names beginning with a 'D'," he added with an arched eyebrow, apparently daring the fellow earl to make some pithy comment.

"Of course not," Grandby replied, although, if pressed, he was quite sure he wouldn't have been able to come up with any other names for girls beginning with a 'D'. It was rather fortunate that none of the names he had in mind for his about-to-be-born child began with the letter 'D'. If it were a boy as Adele kept claiming it would be, he would probably name him George after his father and his father before him. But if it were a girl as he'd been hoping for since he discovered his wife was expecting last March, he would name her Angelica.

Rather surprised both girls were wide awake, Grandby was about to ask how the new parents were faring when a servant appeared at the top of the stairs. "Oh, milady, 'tis so good to see you. She's been asking for you. And the midwife still hasn't arrived."

Clarinda gave Grandby an arched brow, gathered up her skirts, and made her way up the stairs. "I trust you can entertain Diana for a while," she called out, knowing her husband would help if need be.

Having been at Worthington House many times in the past, Clarinda knew her way around and headed straight for the mistress suite. She hurried in without knocking, a bit startled to find Adele leaning up against pile of pillows.

"Thank the gods!" the Countess of Torrington said as her lady's maid wiped her brow. "I was about to send for Milton to help, but I have a feeling he would faint," she managed as her face screwed into a grimace.

"I don't know how much help *I'll* be," Clarinda said just as Adele let out a rather unladylike howl. Alarmed, Clarinda moved to lift Adele's chemise. "How long has it been since your water broke?" she asked, her brows furrowing.

Adele dared a glance at the mantel clock. "A few hours now," she said, her voice weak. "I am too old for this, Clare," she added before her face took on an expression of pain.

"Nonsense. You're younger than Queen Charlotte was when she

had her last. Do you feel like … pushing?" she asked, remembering what she had been through with the quick birth of her twins.

"Anything to get this boy out," Adele countered.

Another servant appeared, this one apparently more familiar with childbirth than Adele's maid. She carried several linens and a bowl of water, setting them aside before seeing to Adele.

"You look as if you know what to do," Adele commented.

"Aye," the woman nodded. "Twins?" she questioned as she settled herself.

"Yes," Clarinda replied. "Three weeks ago," she added when the servant turned to regard her.

"Oh, congratulations, milady," the maid said with a smile. "But I was asking Lady Torrington."

Clarinda stared at the servant for several seconds before returning her attention to Adele. "Why didn't you tell me?" she asked in surprise. The two countesses were the best of friends, went on frequent walks in the park together, and took turns hosting other Mayfair matrons for morning or afternoon tea. Although Adele had said nothing about having twins, it would certainly explain why the countess had grown so large in the last few months.

Adele blinked. And blinked again as she shook her head in alarm. "No one said I was having *twins*," she replied just before another contraction had her crying out.

Wide-eyed, Clarinda looked to the servant. "You get the first. I'll get the second."

Within a half-hour, the Grandby twins made their debut.

CHAPTER 10
THE MORNING AFTER

Half-past nine o'clock in the morning, September 15

Warmth and comfort and the scents of sandalwood and brandy were pleasant aids to sleep, but at some point, their hypnotic effect wore off, and Eleanor slowly awakened. Light showed from around the edges of the heavy velvet drapes covering the windows.

Unfamiliar drapes.

And the soft mattress beneath her was far more comfortable than usual. *Goose feathers*, she thought with a wan smile. The heavy arm around her middle was also unexpected, as was the soft snoring she heard above and behind her. When she was aware of the soreness at the apex of her thighs, she bolted up. She would have left the bed entirely but for the arm that kept her anchored to the bed.

"Let go of me!" she nearly shouted, pulling the bed linens so as to cover her nakedness.

Charles lifted himself onto an elbow and reluctantly released his arm from around Eleanor. "Shh," he hissed, his annoyance quickly dissipating as he took in the sight of his bedmate's sleep tousled hair and bare shoulders. Despite the wide eyes staring at him—either she was very afraid or very angry—Charles found himself rather happy. And aroused. Although he usually awoke with a slight headache and a cotton mouth, he found he felt rather refreshed this morning. "Good morning, beautiful," he murmured, moving toward her with the intent of kissing her.

Eleanor scootched farther from him, taking the bed linens with her as she attempted to take her leave of the bed entirely. The movement had the bed linens sliding off of the earl, which left him almost completely uncovered. "Oh!" she cried out at the sight of his bare chest and the instrument of his manhood bobbing from a nest of dark curlies. She covered her eyes with one hand as she attempted to toss back part of the covers in his direction, which left her mostly exposed. "Oh!" she cried out again as she nearly fell off the bed.

Capturing her around her midriff before she could tumble off the bed, Charles had to stifle a chuckle. "I've got you," he said as he pulled her into the middle of the bed. He hoped she would cease her struggles—she was making a mess of the bed—but she didn't.

Charles sighed and rolled Eleanor, who was still squirming in an attempt to free herself from his hold, so her body was atop his as he collapsed back onto the mattress. "Now that's better," he murmured, one of his arms holding her bottom immobile while a hand moved to pull her head down until his lips could reach hers. He kissed her then, effectively silencing her protest.

His joy at the feel of her lips against his was short-lived, however, for Eleanor gave up her fight and slumped atop him. He ended the kiss as quickly as he had begun it, his hand lifting her head away from his so he could see her face.

Even in the dim light from around the drapes, he could see tears brightening her eyes. "What is it? Have I ... did I hurt you?" he asked in an urgent whisper. He had never had a woman cry whilst in his bed. Titter and laugh, yes. Scold him on occasion, of course, because he behaved like a rake. But then, that was his reputation. One lady of the evening had even bitten him, although she could be excused since he had asked for it. Something about having learned about vampires and such ... but never had a woman *cried* in his bed.

Flipping her over so her back was on the bed linens covering the mattress, Charles held himself over the top of her body as he studied her face. She seemed familiar, and not just because he had seen her the night before, all prim and wide-eyed innocence. He had met her somewhere else, some place in the past, but he couldn't quite remember where or when.

Noting she didn't look at him—her attention was directed to her left—he followed her gaze to the twisted pile of mussed bed linens and a telltale bloodstain therein. The events of the night before came crashing back.

I've never done this before.

Christ! Charles lowered his face so it rested between her breasts.

"You ruined me," Eleanor whispered, one of her hands coming to rest on the back of his head as a sob escaped.

Charles felt her body shake beneath him, felt her heart beat race against his cheek. "I did," he acknowledged, barely moving his head as he attempted to nod. He inhaled slowly, reveling in the scent of her skin, the feel of her soft breasts, the rise and fall of her chest with each labored breath. Finally lifting his head, he regarded her for a moment. His brows furrowed. "I am sorry, my lady, but in my defense, you could have said something. You should have pushed me away. You didn't exactly warn me."

"I was frightened out of my mind!" Eleanor countered, her sudden ire evident in her response.

The earl frowned. "There was no need to be *frightened* of me," he countered, sounding a bit offended. "I'm a very agreeable man ..." At her roll of eyes and pointed look, he realized she meant something else. "Oh. That," he murmured. "Yes, I suppose to the ... *uninitiated*, my prick can be a bit ... intimidating," he reasoned, cocking an eyebrow with his response.

"Intimidating?" Eleanor repeated, her mouth rounding into a rather large 'O'. "It *hurt!*" she cried out.

"And I do apologize for that, my lady, but ... I am led to believe it hurts just the one time, so ... so now you've got the painful part all out of the way," he replied with a rather proud nod. "So the next time won't be so bad. Won't be bad at all," he amended, his face screwing up as he realized she was angry. Angrier than she had been.

Eleanor blinked. She blinked again as she slowly shook her head. "Led to *believe?* Do you expect me to believe I'm the first ... *virgin* you've ever ... *pricked?*"

It was Charles' turn to blink. "As a matter of fact, yes, you *are* my first," he claimed, not having to give it a second thought. He was quite sure he had never before taken a virgin to his bed.

Or hers.

"And the term is really *plowed*, but I wouldn't expect a virgin to know such a thing."

Eleanor's eyes widened again.

Would the horrors never cease?

"You consider me a .... a wheat field?" she asked in a hoarse whisper, wondering how the term 'plowed' ever came to represent what he had done to her the night before.

The earl repositioned himself atop her, wanting to be sure she wouldn't notice the topic of their discussion trying to plow its way back into her. And 'plow' was definitely the wrong term, he considered. 'Seeding' was the more appropriate term, although he knew it would never catch on as a popular word to describe what he wanted to be doing to her just then.

He wondered if she would notice his seed drill attempting to make its way back into her.

She noticed.

"What ...? Are you ...?" Her eyes widened again and she attempted to squirm out from beneath him. With his legs betwixt hers and his rather wide arms anchored into the mattress on either side of her torso, she finally gave up. Tears threatened once again until she found him staring at her, his brows furrowed and his eyes filled with remorse.

"I am sorry about what happened," he whispered. "Truly. And I meant no offense with the term 'plowed'. It's ..." He shook his head. "Crass and wholly inappropriate to describe what I must admit was a rather ... *special* ... tumble."

Even before Eleanor could put voice to her new reason for being angry—didn't the rake realize he was making her case for her?—

Charles knew he had bungled his apology. "First and foremost, I am not attempting to ..." He was about to say, "plow" and then, "tumble" before he left out a sigh. "As much as I truly want the pleasure of your body again, I am ... abstaining," he managed to say. "For now."

Eleanor stilled herself at his words, until his final two, and then she resumed her struggle to get out from under him. "You *rake!* Get off of me!" she said in a hoarse whisper. She thought about screaming and then worried that the only other person in the house might be his majordomo. The tall, gangly man would be of no assistance.

Charles sighed and finally lifted himself to his hands and knees, but before Eleanor could wriggle out from beneath him, he pinned her with a strategically placed hand over one of her breasts. "You came here the same way all of Lucy's harlots do," he said quietly. "How was I to know ..?"

"All?" Eleanor repeated in horror. "How many ... how many have you ..?" She was about to say "plowed" but thought better of it.

His head dropping so his lips could reach the breast he wasn't holding, Charles kissed it, secretly satisfied at Eleanor's sudden jerk and inhalation of breath. "I ... I don't know. I certainly don't keep track. I'm a rake, you see." At her body's jerk beneath him—not one caused by his fondling or his kisses but because she seemed determined to leave his bed—he added, "It's not as if I carve a notch in my bedpost for every woman I bed." He raised his head and pinned her with his gaze. "Although, I am thinking I should for you. I do not believe I have ever had such a satisfying evening with a woman."

Eleanor stared up at the earl, a bit stunned by his words.

For a moment, she didn't know whether to be incensed or proud.

"Please, let me make this right," he whispered. When Eleanor simply stared at him, her expression not giving away her immediate thoughts, he lowered his lips to hers and captured them in a light kiss.

Never having been kissed, Eleanor held her breath as the earl's lips slid over hers, as they seemed to suckle and lock onto hers until she was forced to breathe. Her chest rising a bit in the process, she was aware of how the palm of his hand pressed against her breast, of the skitters of pleasure that seemed to emanate from the tips of his fingers. When his lips left hers to trail down her cheek to her jaw line, she inhaled sharply. His hand moved to her other breast, his fingertips barely skimming her sensitive skin and sending darts of pleasure in every direction. By the time his kisses reached her throat and the top edge of her collarbone, Eleanor became aware of a slight throbbing at the apex of her thighs, at the very place where she felt a bit sore and yet still yearned for that magic touch he had provided the night before.

Perhaps she had put voice to her thoughts, for Charles' hand continued its journey of slight caresses, making its way down the front of her body, around one of her hipbones to slide along the top of her thigh, to delve between her legs and caress the tender flesh before finally—*finally*—pressing against the sensitive spot that seemed to throb as fast as her heart raced. At the very same moment, his lips captured one of her nipples, gently suckling it as his hand rubbed her, slow at first and then harder and faster as her breaths quickened until she seemed to fracture beneath him. Her cry of ecstasy was silenced by his hungry kiss. Her arched back forced her breasts against the front of his chest as he buried himself in her, his groan breaking the kiss as he gasped for air.

The sudden sensation of fullness had Eleanor clenching on the intruder, gasping as she struggled to hang onto him. Her fingers dug into his sides, the pads sensing the play of hard muscle beneath his skin. The thought of "how dare he do this to me again?" warred with the thought of just how wonderful the feel of his hand in her most private place had been, of how the rolling waves of pleasure were still coursing through her body. At any moment, she was sure she would feel as spent as she suddenly felt alive.

Although his thrusts seemed uncomfortable at first, she soon realized she could counter his forward thrusts with her own. His whispered "Yes" had her secretly pleased, his mouth covering her breast had her momentarily stunned, and when he stopped and moaned, she stilled her movements. Tendrils of pleasure passed through her lower body just as a wash of warmth filled her from within. One of his arms moved beneath her, lifting her so the entire front of her body was pressed against his.

"Zeus," Charles murmured, his face buried into the space above her shoulder. "I have found my Aphrodite," he whispered as he slowly allowed his body to settle atop hers. After kissing her temple, he drifted off to sleep.

Eleanor stared at the ornate ceiling above, at once wondering just how she could have allowed him to do to her what he had done the night before and then wondering how she could have prevented him from doing so.

Why hadn't she fought him off? Put more voice to her objection? A skitter of pleasure darted beneath her skin, and she realized she had her answer.

Nothing else had felt as wonderful as the pleasure she had just experienced. And it was all because of Lord Wakefield's expert ministrations, his confident manner, his rather impressive manhood.

Oh, but why couldn't he be Arthur?

Did Sir Arthur Goodwin know how to pleasure a woman like Lord Wakefield did? Would he find her ... what had Wakefield said? *I've found my Aphrodite.* She allowed a wan smile at the memory of how he had said it, as if he truly believed his words.

He had probably already forgotten them, she was sure.

Sighing, she turned her attention to the muscled shoulder just below her chin. A shiver passed through her body at the memory of how those muscles had moved beneath his skin as he held his body over hers, of how taut they appeared at that moment just before ecstasy gripped him, before the rush of warmth filled her lower body. Her wan smile grew into a grin at the thought of the pleasure she had felt, his touch so sure and so perfectly placed. *How did he know what to do?* she wondered for a moment, the thought quickly replaced with the obvious reason.

He was a rake.

He bedded women several times a week—perhaps more than one a day! Of course, he would know how to pleasure a woman. How to keep her coming back to his bed for more. How to keep her in his bed, just as she realized he had succeeded with her, for she had no desire to leave his bed.

Sighing again, Eleanor relaxed into the mattress and allowed sleep to take her once more.

CHAPTER 11
AN EARL ADMITS A MISTAKE

bit later in the morning of September 15

"I have to think you're hoping for a boy," Daniel said as he settled into one of the leather chairs in Grandby's study, his niece alert and making bubbles as he held her in one arm.

"I am hoping for a girl, I'll have you know. But at this point, I don't really care what it is as long as Adele ..." He allowed the sentence to trail off, worry evident on his brow. "I don't know what I'll do if I lose her," he finally managed to get out, his attention turning to the baby he still held in his arms. "Geez, she's a heavy little—"

"Watch your language," Daniel interrupted, thinking Grandby was about to say 'bugger'.

"Chit," Grandby finished without missing a beat.

"She'll be fine," Daniel said, aware one of his best friends was going through what he had gone through only a few weeks ago. At least he hadn't had a chance to be worried for very long. Clarinda's labor had gone so fast, there was barely time to send for the midwife.

"We'll never have intercourse again," the older earl announced.

Daniel blinked. "Yes, you will," he said with a nod. "And, please, my nieces do have ears," he added with a frown.

"Have *you?*" Grandby asked.

A bit confused by the question, Daniel had to think a moment. "Well, not yet, but we will. In a … a few weeks," he ventured. "The Norwick earldom needs an heir, and my wife is willing to have as many babies as it takes. She's quite adamant when it comes to doing her duty," Daniel said as he raised Dahlia to his shoulder. He wasn't about to get another child on Clarinda anytime in the next year, but the Earl of Torrington didn't need to know that he had a supply of French letters on order. Thank the gods he had a discreet importer seeing to it. Wellingham Imports might be better known for the unusual products they imported from countries all over the world, but sometimes their most prized products were made in England.

Thanks to sheep.

"Fuck duty," Grandby cursed.

"Grandby! Language!" Daniel nearly shouted, which had Dahlia fussing at his shoulder. He bounced her a bit, which seemed to settle the girl. Diana wasn't as easily assuaged when Grandby tried to bounce her, though, her face screwing into an expression of unhappiness. She let out a cry.

"I apologize," Grandby said to the baby he held. "Please, don't cry," he added.

Diana blinked and stared at the man whose face filled her vision. She grinned, which had the man looking ever so startled.

"You'll do fine," Daniel murmured, rather amazed at how Grandby was doing with Diana. "In fact, Clare wondered if you would agree to be the godfather for these two," he said in a quiet voice.

The earl stared at him a moment. "Are you sure? I can't say as I did right by her when it came to you," he replied after a pause. Although Clarinda had been his first goddaughter, he had helped her father see to it that she married David Fitzwilliam, older twin brother of Daniel, even though he was pretty sure she had been courted by Daniel. Given David and Daniel were identical twins, and Clarinda was barely allowed in the company of Daniel for more than a few minutes at a time, she had accepted his suit and married David thinking he was Daniel.

When David died in a horrible traffic accident earlier in the year, Daniel had stepped in as earl—he was the rightful heir since neither of Clarinda's babies turned out to be boys— and taken Clarinda as his wife despite her mourning period having just begun. "No one will notice," Grandby had assured Clarinda, knowing she was due to give birth in the late summer. "The *ton* has a short memory, and the two men look so much alike, most won't even realize David has perished," he said.

Daniel's head jerked up at Grandby's question and comment. "Whatever do you mean, 'you didn't do right by her'?" he asked in surprise.

Grandby gave a shrug, which had Diana studying him with a furrowed blonde brow. He watched the baby's face as he said, "I knew David was a rake. Knew he owned that brothel and gaming hell. But I also knew he needed to marry. He needed an heir—"

"Which turned out to be *me*," Daniel interrupted, his manner rather serious. Had Grandby undermined his attempt to marry Clarinda Anne Brotherton, the daughter of an earl? They had been in love back then—still were, in fact—which made her marriage to David cause a rift that would take years and their recent private wedding to mend.

"True," Grandby agreed. "But I knew that Clare's father wanted her settled with a titled man."

Daniel stared at the Earl of Torrington for a long time, anger passing through him as he considered the hell he had gone through when he learned Clarinda had married David instead of him. Instead of the man who had courted her with pink roses and walks in Kensington Gardens and soft words and softer kisses. "Then it's a good thing I still ended up with her," Daniel said with a hint of menace.

Milton Grandby regarded Daniel for a moment. "It is indeed," he agreed. "I made a mistake with my first goddaughter, but I promise you, I did not and will not make the same mistake with any of my other goddaughters," he vowed.

"And what of your own daughter?" Clarinda asked as she stood in the threshold of the study, a blanket-wrapped baby held in her arms.

"Why, I plan to send her to a nunnery ..."

Grandby was on his feet, staring at Clarinda, the bundle in his own arms cooing in delight at the sound of her mother's voice.

"A girl?" Grandby whispered, his face splitting into a huge grin. "Let me trade with you," he said as he hurried to collect his daughter from Clarinda while she took Diana from him.

"Yes," Clarinda hedged before she motioned for the midwife to join her. "And what of your heir?" she asked as she nodded to the bundle the midwife carried.

Daniel, who had stood up upon his wife's entrance into the room, noted how pale the other earl appeared and was ready to retrieve the baby from him should the older man faint.

But Grandby's face continued to betray his joy. "A boy?" he whispered, readjusting his daughter so he could take the baby boy into his other arm. "Jesus, Joseph and Mother Mary," he murmured. He looked up to find Clarinda weeping. "Well, there will be none of that," he said with a shake of his head. "Christ. I should take a trip to Ludgate Hill right now and buy every bauble in every jewelry store for my beloved wife, but before I go, I should like to see her. Is she ... is she well?" he asked in a whisper.

Clarinda nodded. "She's tired, of course. Sleeping now, in fact, but I'm sure she wouldn't mind being awakened by you and your children," she added with a grin.

Grandby nodded and took his leave of the study. "Help yourself to the brandy. And the champagne and whatever else you want," he said as he made his way up the stairs with his prize possessions. "Hell, take everything!"

Daniel frowned as he stood in the threshold of the study.

"*Language!*" he called out.

But the Earl of Torrington and his twins had already disappeared into the mistress suite.

Daniel turned his attention to Clarinda, his brow furrowed so a fold of skin appeared between them. "How is it he is able to carry both babes in his arms like that?" he asked. "It took me a *week* to be able to do that."

Clarinda reached up and kissed him on the cheek. "He's had far more practice than you, my love. He has over twenty goddaughters, you know."

Daniel wasn't about to counter her comment, but he was quite sure Grandby had never held a baby in his arms before that day. At least not recently if he had ever.

"Well, I certainly have no intention of helping myself to a brandy given the early morning hour," he commented, moving back into the study. "Champagne?" he suggested.

Clarinda sighed as she settled into the leather sofa, Diana propped up so her head rested against her shoulder. "Despite the fact that it's still ..." She dared a glance at the clock on the mantel. "Goodness, it's not even ten o'clock!" she said in surprise.

Prior to the arrival of her twins, she would normally still be abed. She thought of how her friend's life was about to change. At least Adele would have a wet nurse—or two— to see to her babes. "I do believe a bit of celebration is in order. Grandby finally has his heir and the daughter he's always wanted. Champagne sounds divine," she finally murmured.

Daniel gave her a knowing smile before lowering the babe he held onto the settee next to her mother. "I'll see what I can find," he offered, wondering if the butler was back in residence. Although the household had been rather quiet when they first arrived—no servants had greeted them at the door, nor had there been any footmen about—Daniel could hear voices outside the study.

He disappeared for a moment and returned, holding a white parchment in one hand and a bottle of champagne in the other.

"What is that?" Clarinda asked as Daniel moved to the sideboard.

He shook his head, attempting to read the note while he worked to free the cork from the bottle. "One of our footmen just brought it over. Apparently, it was delivered just after we left this morning." The popping cork had both babies jerking with the sudden sound, their matching expressions of wonderment sending Clarinda into giggles. "It's not bad news, I hope," she said, sobering at the sudden thought.

Daniel's familiar frown reappeared. "Well, it's curious more than anything," he said as he carried a crystal-stemmed glass to his wife. "It's from the Norwick solicitor in Sussex."

Clarinda took the glass and sipped the bubbly fluid. She hadn't had champagne since the last ball she had attended at the end of the Season. "I've missed this," she murmured, her attention still on her husband. She was about to ask him about the solicitor when she saw his face go pale. "Daniel? What is it?"

The earl folded the missive and closed his eyes a moment. "*Who* is more the thing. Constance Fitzwilliam. My late uncle's only daughter. Seems she paid a visit to our solicitor expecting to be given her inheritance."

Taking another sip of champagne, Clarinda wondered at Daniel's tone of voice. "You make it sound as if she isn't entitled to it."

Daniel shrugged. "Well, if she's reached her majority and hasn't married, then she is," he said, his attention back on the missive. "Dammit."

Clare's eyes widened. "*Language!*" she said in a hoarse whisper.

Pulled from his reverie, Daniel straightened and allowed a guilty expression. "Forgive me. I ... I had no idea Connie was already five-and-twenty. Truth be told, I hadn't given her much thought in a long time."

Curious as to why news of his cousin seemed to have upset Daniel, Clarinda allowed him another minute before she asked, "Is there an inheritance for her claim?" she asked carefully.

Daniel took a deep breath and nodded. "Oh, I'm sure Uncle Edward saw to it before he died. I just ... I realize from this note that the solicitor is unaware of it, is all," he stammered. "I'll be sure to send him a letter with the details." He nodded as he made the comment, his attention still on the folded note he held.

"Is she not very ... agreeable?" Clarinda asked before finishing off her champagne, closing her eyes a moment so she could enjoy the sensation of the bubbles as they bounced about on her tongue.

"Agreeable?" Daniel repeated.

Clarinda nodded. "In order for her to claim her inheritance, she couldn't be married. Which I suppose means the money would have been her dowry. But is she really unbiddable?"

Daniel seemed to struggle for words. "I don't know. It's been ... *years* since I last saw Connie," he replied, obviously bothered by the conversation.

Frowning at Daniel's odd behavior, Clarinda straightened on the settee. "Why do you suppose she has never married?"

The simple question had Daniel shaking his head. "Last I knew, she was still living at Fair Downs near Boxgrove. Other than a monastery, there's really not much there, and I rather doubt any Benedictine monks are looking to marry," he said lightly. He sobered again, though. "I'll see to it she's suitably ... settled," he stammered.

"Daniel!" Clare's hoarse whisper had the earl's attention back on her.

"What?"

"You're hiding something," she accused. "I don't believe I have ever seen you so ... *discombobulated*," she added. The babe on her shoulder gave a slight cry before settling down again.

Daniel reached down to pick up Dahlia. "It's nothing. I just ... I just lost track of time. I invested her funds along with most of David's way back when. I'll see to making sure she gets it," he promised before joining her on the settee, Dahlia propped against one of his shoulders. "When we're back at the house," he added with a nod.

Clarinda nodded and allowed a wan smile, thinking it would be some time before she would be able to walk.

The champagne had gone straight to her knees.

CHAPTER 12
A MARQUESS RECONSIDERS
A LADY

ine-thirty in the morning of September 15

Randall watched the barouche pull away, wondering about the skittish woman he had escorted to the equipage. Throughout their entire stroll, a walk that lasted no longer than fifteen minutes, the marquess had hoped to put the woman at ease. He couldn't help but think she was more frightened of him now than when she had first come upon him whilst he sat on the bench. *Perhaps I was scowling*, he thought, wondering if his appearance was to blame or if Miss Fitzwilliam was simply uncomfortable in the company of a man.

About to turn around to make his way back to his townhouse, he was rather startled to see not Miss Fitzwilliam, but rather the maid turn around to regard him from where she sat in the back of the open carriage. Despite her earlier manner— she seemed most displeased when she and her mistress had come upon him in the park —the expression on her face now suggested she might have changed her opinion of him.

Randall acknowledged her gaze with a tip of his top hat, rather pleased she didn't turn around quickly, as if she were embarrassed at having been discovered glancing back in his direction. Instead, she continued to watch him until the barouche passed beneath a tree and around a bend in the road, lost to his sight as it made its way back to South Carriage Drive.

Now that was rather odd, Randall thought as he continued to puzzle over Miss Fitzwilliam. Well, if she were one of Norwick's relatives, it would be easy enough to discover more about her. He would simply pay a call on Norwick House and ask to speak with the earl.

The thought of the Earl of Norwick reminded him that the older twin, David, had died earlier that year—a traffic accident in Oxford Street, if he remembered right—which meant the younger twin was now in charge. He puzzled over the man's name, thinking it was fortuitous for the man to have inherited since David hadn't sired an heir before his death.

What was the younger twin's name?

Dweezle? Dunbarton? Dwayne? Daniel?

Daniel!

Yes, that was it. Randall wondered how he could have forgotten, for to be fair to Daniel Fitzwilliam, the younger twin was the real reason the Norwick earldom was rather flush despite its base in Sussex. David might have seen to it the earldom's coffers were full with monies from his gaming hells and the lucrative brothel he owned prior to inheriting the Norwick earldom, but it was his younger brother who managed the earldom once David had the title.

The marquess frowned. *Discover more about Miss Fitzwilliam?* What was he thinking? The young lady was ... well, she certainly wasn't marchioness material, he thought, realizing he had been considering her as a possible wife.

Faith! Thoughts of matrimony were certainly at the forefront of his brain these days.

Sighing, he turned and made his way back toward Park Lane, his thoughts not on Miss Fitzwilliam but rather on her comely maid and the expression on her face as she watched him from the carriage. *Now there's a chit I would welcome in my bed*, he thought with a grin, his rakish thoughts certainly more comfortable than those centered on matrimony.

He imagined her arriving at his back door, like any other servant, and then making her way up the back stairs and to his bedchamber. Grinning, he thought of how she would let herself into the room and undress slowly, carefully placing her pelisse and gown over the back of a chair before slowly removing her silk stockings and petticoats. She would require help with removing her corset, of course, which meant he would have to be there to pull the bow and loosen the ties. To pull it up and over her head. To remove her translucent chemise and allow it to fall to the floor in a silken puddle. Then he would pull the pins from her simple bun and slide his fingers through the mass of dark, curly hair. Lift her to the bed. Watch her as his simple kisses and soft strokes readied her for when he spread her shapely legs and entered her slowly.

His mouth would cover one of her breasts as her torso would rise in response to his first thrust. Would move to the other breast and feast on it during his second thrust. His third thrust would have her legs wrapping around his thighs, her fingers clutching his sides. His fourth would leave him nearly breathless but remembering he needed to see to her pleasure before taking his own. Sliding his hand down the side of her breast, his thumb brushing the tender flesh, he would continue his exploration by lightly sliding the pads of his fingers over her midriff, down to her belly and finally to her dark curlies. Then he would gently press against her wet, throbbing womanhood at the very place their bodies met. He would watch in wonder as her body succumbed to his erotic touch, thrill at her soft cries and murmured pleas, and allow his own moan of pleasure as the ecstasy took him under, leaving him breathless and broken and feeling ever so blessed.

Randall Roderick, Earl of Reading, stopped short on the path toward Park Lane. *Good God!* He had never bedded a maid before, and yet, just then, he had imagined a rather satisfying scenario with Miss Fitzwilliam's maid!

What is happening to me? At that moment, he found he wanted to know far more about the maid than he did about Constance Fitzwilliam.

Remembering he was trying to reform his rakish ways, he quickly sobered and took his leave of Hyde Park.

CHAPTER 13
AN IDENTITY REVEALED

ine-thirty in the morning of September 15

Charles awoke slowly, his nose buried in hair that smelled of lemon. He allowed a smile at the woman who lay beneath him. *Eleanor ...* He closed his eyes in an attempt to remember the rest of her name. She had mentioned it when introducing herself the night before.

Merriweather.

Yes, that was it. Eleanor Merriweather.

He carefully rolled off her body, rather glad she was sleeping so soundly. Had she been awake, he would have been tempted to take her again. Zeus, she was beautiful! A bit on the young side, but older than most of the debutantes mothers took great pains to keep away from him at *ton* balls and soirées, she seemed at once naive and innocent and then quite suddenly more jaded and mature. How could that be?

Did she live in London?

No. She mentioned having come to town on the mail coach. That meant she was probably from the country, but her manner of speech suggested otherwise. A pile of puzzle pieces were stacked up in his brain.

Well, he would have a lifetime to put them into place. He would be marrying the chit at the first opportunity.

Daring a glance at the clock over the fireplace, he decided he had best get up. His brother, Arthur, had said he would stop by later this morning. Although the knight hadn't given a reason in his message that arrived the day before, Charles hoped the man was coming to announce his betrothal.

Arthur was younger than Charles, but the knight's days as a bachelor needed to come to an end—Arthur was rumored to be a molly, and if he didn't marry soon, Charles was afraid he would be arrested. The word circulating at White's was that Arthur had been in the company of a man known to host parties of like-minded men in his public house. Charles winced when he realized the news had probably appeared in one of the scandal sheets.

The Tattler, no doubt.

He glanced again at the jumble of bed linens, verifying his guilt in having taken Eleanor's maidenhead. Well, he would see to making everything right. He had promised her that. He would acquire a special license to marry her that very day, if he was allowed to do so. Perhaps the two of them could be married before this evening, and she could spend the night in his bed again! His arousal made itself evident.

First things first, he chided himself. He left the bed, pulling up the velvet counterpane to cover Eleanor. Retrieving his robe from the floor, he was about to use the bell pull to summon Chester when he remembered Eleanor was naked beneath the coverlet. He couldn't exactly have his majordomo come to his bedchamber while she was still abed! Charles instead made his way to the bedchamber door.

Charles had barely pulled the door open when he realized Chester stood just beyond the threshold, a tray bearing a cup of chocolate and slices of toast held in his bony hands.

Chocolate? He dared a glance at Eleanor and realized what the butler intended.

"Rather considerate of you," he whispered as he took the tray and set it on the table next to the bed. He took his leave of the room and motioned for Chester to join him in the next room. "Especially since she is to be my wife," he added as he made his way to the dressing room and bathing chamber that connected two bedchambers. A tub of steaming water sat in the center of the room, and he gingerly stepped into it.

The majordomo's eyes widened considerably. "Very good, my lord," he replied, obviously stunned by his master's words. "May I remind my lord that Sir Arthur is due here later this morning?" he added, as if the news of Lord Wakefield's impending nuptials was secondary.

"I remembered," Charles said as he took a seat in the tub, hissing as he lowered himself into the hot water. "Otherwise I wouldn't have bothered to get up before Miss Merriweather," he added as he settled his back against one end of the copper tub.

Chester immediately moved to seat himself behind the tub so he could shave the earl. "Should I contact an agency about procuring a lady's maid for Miss Merriweather?" he asked in his baritone voice.

Charles arched an eyebrow and nodded, thinking his majordomo seemed rather pleased with the idea of his taking a wife. "That is an excellent idea. With any luck, we'll be married later today," he claimed, rather satisfied with his plan. "Tomorrow at the latest." He gave a passing thought to just how odd it was that he was planning a wedding when only last night whilst at White's, he had assured Lord Reading he had no intention of taking a wife for ten years or more!

My, how just a few hours can change a man!

Chester paused before slathering shaving soap over Charles' face. "A trip to Doctor's Commons is planned for after your brother's visit then?" the majordomo replied, his voice rather neutral despite the news his master had dropped on him.

"Indeed. But before my brother arrives, I believe I need to make a trip to Mrs. Gibbons' establishment. It seems she holds my intended's valise as collateral for her return," he explained with a roll of his eyes. "I was going to send you after it, but since Miss Merriweather was a birthday gift to me—and I have no intention of returning her —I have decided to inform Lucy in person." At his butler's sudden pause in shaving him, he added, "Lucy needs to learn she cannot lure innocents to her brothel and expect them to become harlots."

Chester pondered this tidbit of information as he continued to shave Charles, not offering a response. The two sat in silence for several moments as Chester continued to shave Charles' face. "You're rather quiet. Do I sense disapproval?" Charles asked when Chester finally pulled the straight edge away from his neck.

The majordomo regarded the earl for a moment. "Is the young lady aware of your plans to marry her?" he finally asked, wiping the shaving soap from the razor with a linen.

Charles blinked. "I made it clear I would ... make it right," he replied with a nod. In a lower voice, he said, "You could have been a bit more ... *emphatic* with your objection last night. I could have arranged to have her sent ..." He paused, realizing he didn't know where he could have sent her. *To whom did she belong? Who was supposed to provide protection for her?*

Chester pulled a bath linen from a nearby shelf and held it for Charles. "It wasn't my place to interfere with your plans, my lord," he replied as Charles stood up and allowed the water to sluice off his body before yanking the linen from Chester's hands.

"What do you know of her?" Charles asked, thinking the major-domo knew more than he was admitting.

Chester sighed. "It's possible Miss Merriweather is Lord Middleton's daughter," he suggested in a whisper. "She is of the same age and should have had her come-out last Season."

Charles stared at his butler for a long moment before shaking his head. *Middleton's daughter?* Was it possible the girl who slept in his bed was another earl's daughter? Lord Middleton's daughter?

Well, this certainly changed things.

Or did it?

He had ruined the chit. It didn't matter if she was a princess or a pauper or an earl's daughter. He promised her he would make it right.

He would marry the chit.

He found he *wanted* to marry the chit, if for no other reason than to have her in his bed every night.

His earlier thoughts of variety came back to haunt him at that moment. Randall Roderick's comments from the night before had him remembering his own beliefs about fidelity. Could he be true to just one woman? Would he be satisfied if he bedded the same woman twice a week, every week, for the rest of his life?

To hell with twice a week! Perhaps he could bed her every night!

The thought of Eleanor's body beneath him had his own reacting rather strangely. Desire mingled with anticipation and lust had him aroused once again. Despite having bedded her twice in the past eight hours, he found he wanted her again. And again.

This was new! He had never before wanted the same woman again.

He decided he could forgo any of the best Lucy Gibbons could offer from her brothel if he knew Eleanor Merriweather would be sharing his bed. His days of being a rake would be over, of course, but was that such a bad thing? According to the Marquess of Reading, it was about time he became respectable. About time he was regarded as something other than a ne'er do well in Parliament. He would be married before the next session began, in fact. By then, he would have appeared at several balls with his new wife, perhaps attended a soirée or two and the opera with Eleanor on his arm.

My countess, he thought with a sense of growing satisfaction.

The Countess of Wakefield.

Charles sighed and allowed a slight grin as he dressed for the day.

CHAPTER 14
A WOMAN CONTEMPLATES
A MAN

en o'clock in the morning of September 15
  "I apologize, my lady. I've made a cake of it, and I am so sorry."

Constance Fitzwilliam shook her head, rather pleased she could do so without having to worry about a ridiculous hat escaping from its pins. The simple bonnet she had borrowed from her maid, Simmons, was comfortable and managed to display her dark brown curls to great effect. "You did fine, Esther," she said as she patted the back of her housekeeper's gloved hand. "Meeting Mr. Roderick was good practice for you," she added with an encouraging grin. "We'll probably never see the man again, so it won't matter what first impressions he was left contemplating."

Dressed as her own lady's maid and rather pleased with the anonymity the mode of dress provided, Constance found herself enjoying the morning outing immensely. Only a few riders were up and about in the park this early.

Coming upon the handsome gentleman—he had been reading what appeared to be a rather long letter—had been almost unexpected. Almost, because Constance was fairly certain she had seen the man take his leave of a townhouse very near to the one in which she had taken up residence in Curzon Street. He, too, had been heading in the direction of the park.

His destination was entirely unknown to her at the time, of course, but seeing him on the park bench, his brows furrowed and his posture suggesting he had just read some rather sad news hadn't surprised her in the least.

It was too bad her housekeeper had panicked, though. And worse, that she had continually sought Constance's counsel throughout their brief walk with Mr. Roderick.

The poor woman had only reluctantly agreed to this morning's outing, believing Constance's claim that no one would even be in the park at such an early hour. But it gave her housekeeper the opportunity to practice her curtsy and engage in the art of conversation with a gentleman.

Too bad she did it using my name, Constance thought with a sigh, cringing when she remembered how many times Esther had turned to her for guidance whilst they strolled with the man.

He seemed rather at home escorting them through the park, as if he knew that the path on which they walked would eventually lead them back to their rented barouche. He was certainly at ease with Esther Simmons on his arm, his attention entirely on her except when she needed help. And he seemed ever so patient with Esther, as if he dealt with uncertain chits every day.

Perhaps he did. Perhaps he was a shopkeeper who had to deal with young ladies who couldn't make a decision if their very life depended on it. Or perhaps he had a business and employed some women who required a good deal of handholding.

One thing she knew for certain—if the man had met her father because they both had horses on the racing circuit, then he must either be an inveterate gambler or be employed in a trade where he could afford to be away for weeks at a time. Given the cost of racing— trainers, stable hands, and feed as well as the time required—traveling to the race meetings in Doncaster, Newmarket and Epsom Downs— meant that Randall Roderick had to be a man of some means.

And he probably liked horses, too.

Constance dared a glance at Esther, glad to see she had settled into the squabs and was enjoying the early morning ride. They would have to do this more often now that they were in London. Both of them.

Time was running out.

Annoyed by the sudden thought about why they had come to London, Constance turned her attention back to Esther. The young woman was more than adept at housekeeping. One day, she might even secure a position as the head of housekeeping for a large manor house or an estate home, but she wouldn't until she was more at ease among those who might employ her. And if she couldn't secure another position soon, Constance worried the woman would end up in the poor house.

Her thoughts scattered, Constance wondered at how often Mr. Roderick visited the park. She wondered if he ever rode a horse or simply preferred to walk whilst there. It was rather unlikely they would ever again see the gentleman, even though she was quite sure he had been the one she had seen leaving the nearby townhouse earlier that day. But even if she came upon him in another part of London, she doubted that he would remember having met *her*.

No one paid attention to the servants, after all. Or those dressed as the hired help.

Remembering his first name was Randall, Constance thought to ask about him when she was next in the company of Londoners. Based on the superfine of his top coat, his embroidered waistcoat, and the top hat he wore—Constance was sure the hat was from 'Fitzsimmons and Smith' in Oxford Street—he was no doubt a well-to-do cit. She now wondered if he might be a member of the aristocracy, but he hadn't identified himself with a title during his introduction. Certainly he would have if he were a titled man!

Wouldn't he?

Not having been in London more than a fortnight, Constance was still finding her way around the city. Mr. Roderick's suggestion that she make her presence known to Daniel Fitzwilliam was a sound one, she had to admit. Her cousin might be of help. She had no idea if the Earl of Norwick knew she had reached her majority, or if he had learned of her missing inheritance from the solicitor in Chichester, but she needed the money to secure her future.

Thinking she had an inheritance on which she could live for the rest of her life, Constance had thought to remain a spinster. Why put herself at the mercy of a husband who would essentially own her and all her assets when she could enjoy the freedom the life of an unmarried woman provided?

Avoiding courtships was easy enough once she was past three-and-twenty. Now that she was five-and-twenty, she rarely had to fend off a marriage-minded man. At the moment, however, she realized that's exactly what she needed to find. The funds she had brought with her from Chichester would last a month at most. After that, she would have to dismiss Esther and seek housing arrangements elsewhere, especially if the current Earl of Norwick discovered she had taken up residence in the abode he used prior to his marriage to Clarinda Fitzwilliam.

Finding the key to the back door had been easy. Maintaining a low profile on such a high profile location as Curzon Street, directly off of Park Lane and the residences of most of England's aristocrats, was proving difficult. Everyone seemed interested in their comings and goings.

Her mind wandered once again to Randall Roderick. *How old is he?* She remembered the hint of gray at his temples and the tiny lines around his eyes. He appeared well groomed. Well-fed, but certainly not fat. Confident.

And entirely too handsome.

A frisson passed through Constance as the barouche made its way out of the park and turned left. She was sure the man had seen her watching him, but try as she might, she couldn't look away from his gaze. He had stared at her as if he knew her secret, knew she wasn't who she appeared to be as she accompanied her housekeeper in the park.

Had he guessed she was more than a lady's maid? Surmised she was really a relative of the *ton* and in dire need of funds? Of a husband?

Of course not. He thought she was the maid!

She bristled at the thought of having to marry because someone had drained the bank account that held her inheritance. There were only a few men who would have had access to the account. Her late father, of course. Her brother, perhaps. Someone at the bank. It was unlikely a bank employee had done such a thing, but it was still possible. Until she had an opportunity to speak with the London-based solicitor her own family's solicitor had recommended, she really didn't think she should bother her cousin with the issue. He was an earl, after all, and probably far too busy with matters of the Norwick earldom, a new wife, and twins to concern himself with her missing inheritance.

Besides, there was that issue she'd had with him all those years ago. *Never find yourself in a situation requiring complete and utter secrecy,* she now knew.

If only she had known when she made her debut at Norwick Park in Sussex. Her entire body shook on remembering that rather unfortunate evening. He had been so patient. So understanding. So generous while he introduced her to his friends and associates. While he arranged dances on her behalf, seeing to it her dance card was full even before the first minuet had begun. And then she had made the mistake that could never be forgiven. Could never be forgotten.

Never find yourself alone in a dark stable at night.

Even thinking of it now had her cheeks reddening with embarrassment, her body shaking with the memory of how frightened she had been, of how angry the Earl of Norwick had been.

Constance lifted her eyes to find Esther staring at her. "What is it?" she asked, straightening against the squabs.

"The earl will help you, I'm quite sure," the housekeeper said as she leaned toward Constance, her voice kept low lest the driver overhear her remark.

Constance silently cursed, displeased by the fact that Esther knew far more about her situation than any servant should know.

But the woman was as much her housekeeper as her companion these days, and lately, she had become her confidante, as well.

"Of course, he will," Constance agreed. "I am just hoping he won't need to," she added as the barouche pulled in front of the small Norwick townhouse in Curzon Street. *Praying he won't need to*, she thought as she stepped down from the barouche and made her way toward the front door. For she rather doubted Daniel Fitzwilliam would welcome her into his home.

Not after what had happened all those years ago.

CHAPTER 15
A BROTHER PAYS A VISIT

Eleven o'clock in the morning of September 15

Sir Arthur Goodwin used the lion-head knocker to announce his presence at Lord Wakefield's residence. Although he was merely a year younger than the earl, Sir Arthur had made a name for himself in London, and not for the kind of activities his older brother was known.

Arthur was a philanthropist, a researcher, and a sometimes-professor at a local college. He was not popular with the ladies, mainly because he avoided any interaction with them. Oh, he spoke with them in shops and occasionally danced with one during a ball, but he avoided bedding them, which meant he was able to avoid the kind of reputation Lord Wakefield seemed to be suffering at the moment. Or enjoying, if one considered the lifestyle Charles seemed to be living these days.

Unfortunately, Arthur's reputation was of an entirely different sort. He could claim it was guilt by association. He could argue he was never in the company of a man who hosted other men at his public house. He could even state that he had never been in that particular public house. But anything he said at this point would be denying the truth.

He preferred the company of men. The company of men who preferred other men.

Now that *The Tattler* had all but pegged him as such—who else in London Society was a knight with the initials AG?— Arthur was desperate to take a wife. He needed to take a wife or risk arrest.

He had just asked a viscount's daughter for her hand in marriage. Unlike most young ladies of the *ton*, the shy bluestocking had given him an immediate answer. "Yes, I will," she had said, removing her gold wire-rimmed spectacles from the end of her nose as she gave him her answer.

Arthur could hardly wait to tell his brother of his impending nuptials. With any luck, Charles would share the news at White's tonight and put some of the rumors to rest.

Chester opened the door and bowed to the knight. "Sir Arthur," he murmured in his low voice as he stepped aside. "Lord Wakefield will be in his study shortly," he intoned, his voice suggesting the earl was on his way there to solve all the world's problems from behind his large mahogany desk.

"Is he sick?" Arthur asked as he stepped into the vestibule and handed the majordomo his top hat.

The question caught Chester off-guard. "Not that I know of," the majordomo replied. Although if he had given the question a bit more thought, he might have responded in the affirmative with the word, 'lovesick,' but the man had just returned from Lucy Gibbon's establishment, a valise in one hand and a rather disgusted look on his face. The majordomo no longer knew if his master was as inclined to want to marry as he had been earlier that morning.

Arthur afforded the butler an arched eyebrow. "I can find my way," he said as he handed over his coat.

The knight rarely paid a call on his brother. The two had so little in common, there didn't seem to be a reason to spend time in one another's company. But it had been several weeks since he had seen Charles, and he had his good news to share, so he had sent a missive the day before. *Are you alive? If so, I'll pay a call on you in the late morning. Arthur.*

Arthur figured the note would at least get his brother's attention, and even if he only ended up gaining a few minutes of his time and a cheroot out of the visit, it would be worth the trip.

Charles returned to his bedchamber, sighing as he considered his less-than-satisfying meeting with Lucy Gibbons. Could the madame be any more disagreeable?

"How dare you lure young ladies to your establishment and then press them into service!" he had accused once she finally descended the carpeted stairs into the front parlor of her brothel. He had obviously awakened her, his demanding demeanor scaring a prostitute into hurrying up the stairs to fetch her from her slumber.

The madame frowned at her visitor. "Lured?" she repeated. "Why, every girl who comes to my door does so of her own volition," she claimed, pulling her loose satin dressing gown tighter around her middle. The action only emphasized that she wore nothing more than a corset beneath.

The earl angled his head and glared at Lucy Gibbons. "Do you even know *whom* you sent to my house last night?" he asked in a hoarse whisper. Although no one else was in the parlor, he didn't wish to be overheard by any of the patrons or harlots who were in residence.

Lucy rolled her eyes. "Did she claim she was a princess? Or the daughter of an earl?" she countered, one hand going to her hip.

Charles narrowed his eyes. Actually, Eleanor hadn't claimed an association to anybody. It was Chester who had suggested she was Middleton's daughter. "And if she *is* the daughter of an earl? Should I send *him* your way?" he asked in a hoarse whisper.

Her confidence faltering, Lucy took a deep breath. "She didn't entertain anyone here," she replied. "So if you bedded her, then her loss of virtue is on you," she accused with a nod of her head. "And I expect you to pay for her, too. She was my newest lightskirt."

Shaking his head, Charles stepped forward. The madame held her ground while he wagged a finger in warning. "Now, you see here. You'll give me her valise—with all the contents intact—and I won't have a Bow Street Runner arrest you for kidnapping."

Lucy gasped. "You do that, my lord, and I'll never again send you another harlot."

Well, that was certainly a threat worth throwing back in her face. He had absolutely no intention of allowing another prostitute into his home, nor did he think he would ever again employ one anywhere else, for that matter.

"Done," he said, his chin thrust out. The valise landed in a heap at his feet. "As for compensation, I hardly think I need to pay for a *gift* when I was told she was my birthday present."

The look on Lucy's face had been so satisfying, Charles dared not say another word but merely picked up the valise and took his leave of the brothel.

Thinking of Eleanor had him wondering where she might be. His bed was empty. Moving to the bathing chamber's door, he found it ajar and peeked in to find his future countess in the copper bathtub, a mound of bubbles hiding her body from view. The sight of her with her dark hair loosely piled atop her head had his breath catching. "Good morning, my lady," he murmured as he made his way into the tile-floored room.

"What do you think you're doing?" Eleanor replied, a look of shock appearing on her face. "Get out!"

Charles paused before taking a step back. "I merely wish to bestow you with a kiss, my beautiful," he said in his softest voice.

Eleanor gave him a quelling glance. "Now?" she whispered hoarsely, afraid the majordomo might be somewhere nearby.

"Well, anytime really," Charles replied as he resumed his approach toward the tub.

Straightening in the tub so that her breasts were atop the bubbles, Eleanor lifted the bar of soap in one hand and held it as if she intended to throw it at him.

"Oh, an invitation to join you, I see," he teased, his arresting smile having its desired effect on her. She paused, as if she were confused by his response to her threat.

"Don't you dare," she replied, her hand—and most of her torso —disappearing beneath the bubble-topped water.

Charles grinned. "Or you'll ... what?" he responded, his next step taking him close enough so that he could bend down and kiss her on the forehead.

Before he had a chance to straighten up, a wave of sudsy water splashed onto the front of his breeches. "That!" Eleanor replied with a satisfied 'huff'. "Now get out!"

Soaked from the placket of his breeches down, Charles managed to refrain from putting voice to a curse and instead merely took a step back. The sudden look of hurt on his face was unmistakable, however. "I ... I apologize. I didn't mean to anger you, my lady," he managed to say before he quickly left the room and shut the door behind him.

This isn't going well, he thought before realizing he would have to change his breeches. Given the circumstances, he supposed it would take some time for Eleanor to accept her new role, time to learn how a countess behaved. Perhaps countesses didn't particularly like being visited during their morning bath, though. Which had him wondering, since a particular baroness not only wanted him to visit her in her bathing chamber, she expected him to join her in the tub!

Charles glanced back toward the closed door and realized he would have to acquire a larger tub in order to share a bath with Eleanor. *That will have to wait for another day*, though, he reasoned as he changed his breeches.

He reviewed what he would need to accomplish on this day, his excitement at the idea of marrying Eleanor growing with each passing moment. Acquire a special license, buy a ring, arrange for a modiste, and secure someone to marry them. *How hard could that be?*

By the time he made it down the stairs, he was smiling broadly. When he burst into his study to find his brother already ensconced in one of the upholstered chairs holding a brandy balloon in one hand and a cheroot in the other, he was downright giddy. "I have news, brother," he announced happily.

Arthur regarded Charles as if his older brother might be a candidate for Bedlam. "Indeed?" he replied dryly. "And to think, I thought my news would be the only news of the day."

Charles took an adjacent chair and cringed at the thought of a brandy before breakfast. It wasn't like his brother to imbibe during the daylight hours. Then he wondered if Arthur had even gone to bed. Perhaps he was just ending his evening, despite the clock showing it was nearly eleven in the morning. "I do hope I am about to hear I'm to gain a sister in the form of a viscount's daughter," he said in a voice filled with warning. "While you are about to gain a sister in the form of ..." He paused then, not actually positive Eleanor Merriweather was Lord Middleton's offspring. "A probable earl's daughter," he finished rather proudly.

Arthur blinked. And then he blinked again as he shook his head. How did Charles already know his good news? Arthur hadn't shared it with anyone, nor had he been to White's in the past week.

And then the rest of the statement hit him.

"Who did you get a child on?" Arthur asked in disgust.

It was Charles' turn to blink. "No one," he replied, rather proud of the fact that he regularly employed French letters, although he had not done so the night before.

Or this morning.

He frowned when he realized his brother was staring in disbelief at him. "At least, not yet," he amended, the thought of having possibly impregnating Eleanor not as scary as it should have been.

Perhaps he *would* have a brandy.

He was about to reach for the bottle when he stilled himself. "But I should think I will do so immediately. I plan to marry before tonight."

Arthur stared at the earl for a long time. Who was this man and what had he done with his brother? "Do I need to contact someone about having you admitted to Bedlam?" Arthur asked, his brandy all but forgotten and his cheroot burning so the ash was about to drop onto the Axminster carpet below their feet.

Charles frowned at the obvious cut direct. "I am perfectly sane, I'll have you know," he responded, his chin angling up. At least he didn't have to be concerned about a double chin appearing like it sometimes did on Lord Reading.

"Who's the *probable* earl's daughter? I take it you haven't actually proposed yet?" Arthur added with an arched eyebrow.

The question had Charles frowning again. Well, he hadn't exactly *asked* Eleanor for her hand in marriage, but he had made it perfectly clear he was going to make it right. Certainly she understood his meaning.

Charles was about to respond when a light knock sounded at the door. Thinking Chester was delivering the coffee service, he called out, "Come."

The door slowly opened to reveal Eleanor staring at him— or was she staring at Arthur? Charles was on his feet in an instant, surprised to see the girl looking nearly as prim and proper as she had the night before. Only her hair seemed out of place, still pinned up as it was in the messy bun he had seen her sporting in the tub—a rather charming look for her, he decided. Otherwise, she was completely dressed in the gown he had helped remove the night before.

He was about to wonder whether or not she had managed to put on her corset when he realized he couldn't think of such things just then. His arousal was about to become rather evident behind the placket of his doeskin breeches.

"Miss Merriweather!" he said as he moved to join her at the door. He performed a bow as he took her hand and kissed the back of it. When he straightened, he couldn't help but notice her attention was on his brother. Attention that made her appear as if she might faint. He leaned over and kissed her on the temple, which had the young woman glaring at him.

"Lord Wakefield!" she admonished him, her widened eyes displaying her dissatisfaction with him.

Charles continued to hold her hand and turned toward his brother. "Eleanor Merriweather, I would like you to meet my brother, Sir Arthur Goodwin," he said as he used his other hand to wave toward his brother.

The knight made his way to stand in front of Eleanor.

"We've met," the two said in unison.

"My lady," Arthur managed to get out before he took her other hand and brushed his lips over the back of it. He straightened and angled his head. "What's ... going on?" he asked, his attention never leaving the young woman.

Her pulse pounding in her ears, Eleanor afforded the knight a curtsy, sure her face was splotched in bright red. Although she had only been formally introduced to Arthur Goodwin the one time, she had admired him from afar ever since his return from France. Wounded by a bullet, he had been granted his knighthood for his bravery during one of the last conflicts against Napoleon. And then she had been seated directly across from him during a dinner at the Earl of Torrington's residence. "It's very good to see you again, Sir Arthur," she said with a nod, rather glad her gown hid her knees, which had suddenly become rather rubbery.

"And you, my lady," the knight answered with a hint of uncertainty. He turned his attention back to Charles. "I sent you a note about my good news, but I have to admit I am rather ... *surprised* at yours."

Faith! What the hell was the woman doing here in his brother's townhouse? Had his brother ruined her? The thought was barely formed in his mind when he realized the explanation had to be something of the sort.

Charles nodded, tempted to say something like, "So am I." Instead, he said, "I couldn't have my younger brother beat me to the altar." He glanced nervously in Eleanor's direction as he made the claim. "Sweeting, I must speak with my brother for a few more minutes. Perhaps you can start breakfast in the parlor without me?" he suggested, hoping she wouldn't protest having to leave what he was sure would be an uncomfortable exchange with his brother.

Eleanor was about to protest—she had silently wished to be in Arthur's presence for at least a year now—but Charles' fierce expression had her realizing she needed to take her leave of the men. "Of course," she replied with a nod, her attention flitting to Sir Arthur before she took her leave of the study with a quick curtsy and yet another moon-eyed glance in the knight's direction.

Charles watched as Eleanor departed, wondering at how she gazed at his brother. *What the ...?* He was about to put voice to a question about the circumstances of how Arthur and Eleanor had previously met when his brother took the chair in front of the desk and said, "What the hell is going on here? And why is the Earl of Middleton's *daughter* in your *house?*" This last came out harsher than intended, leaving a frown on the knight's face.

Charles took a deep breath. Well, that confirmed it, he supposed. Eleanor Merriweather was indeed the Earl of Middleton's daughter. But what could he say to explain the young woman's presence in his house? Arthur would eventually figure it out if Charles didn't tell him something close to the truth. "Would you believe me if I told you she was sent by Lucy Gibbons and arrived on my doorstep at midnight last night?"

Arthur blinked. "No," he answered with a shake of his head.

So much for the truth.

"Well, she did. And I ruined her." Charles didn't allow his brother to interrupt as he continued, "Quite by accident, I assure you, but nevertheless, I have done so."

Blinking, Arthur shook his head. "As I recall, sexual intercourse with a woman isn't exactly something that can be an *accident*," he said in measured words. "But the fact that you recognize what you did was wrong at least prevents me from suggesting you check yourself into Bedlam."

It was Charles' turn to blink. For years, he had thought his brother a molly, a man more interested in other men than the fairer sex, although he didn't have any compelling proof or reason to believe such a theory—being in the company of a known molly certainly wasn't enough of a reason.

Now that he had confirmed Arthur was engaged to be married, albeit to a bluestocking, Charles wondered if perhaps his brother wasn't a homosexual but merely late to the party. "She was kidnapped by Lucy and sent here last night as my birthday present," Charles stated, allowing a hint of anger to color his voice.

Arthur stared at Charles for several seconds, as if the words were spoken in a foreign language and he was attempting to decipher their meaning. "Good God!" he finally replied. "What is she? Seventeen? I don't think she's even had her come-out," he said. "Have you spoken with Lord Middleton?"

Charles stared at his brother, rather surprised he would know more about Eleanor than he did. Enough more that he felt a hint of jealousy. "Of course not. I rather imagine I'll be drawn and quartered should I tell him what actually happened."

His brother shook his head again. "Why would he find you at fault for what that despicable madame has done? Although, in her defense, I should think you should have recognized Lady Eleanor, but something tells me you were too inebriated to do so." He spread out his hands, his head continuing to shake as he did so. "Am I right?"

Sighing, Charles gave a slight nod, realizing his brother wasn't going to provide any solutions—nor solace. "Except, I don't know why you would think I should have recognized Eleanor. I don't recall ever having met her," he answered in his own defense.

Arthur gave him a quelling glance. He couldn't help but notice his brother's use of the girl's given name, and the hint of intimacy when he had kissed her at the door. "We attended a dinner party at Worthington House. Right after Grandby married Lady Worthington. Although, to be fair, you were seated rather far from Lady Eleanor whilst I was seated directly across from her." An image from that night filled his mind's eye. He had caught the doe-eyed young woman staring at him more than once that evening, her porcelain complexion taking on a rather telling blush both times he had caught her.

She couldn't have been more than fifteen at the time, which had him wondering why she would even be seated at a table of lords and ladies. The last thing he had wanted that night was a young lady to develop a crush on him. Not when he had finally accepted that he would never be attracted to a woman. Deciding to marry Lady Priscilla Sinclair was merely a way to deflect rumors of his homosexuality. Given the prevailing laws, he couldn't afford to have his secret revealed any more than last week's *The Tattler* had already intimated it.

"How old is she really? All of sixteen?" he asked rhetorically.

"Seventeen, actually," Charles countered. "She came to London for her come-out. Seems she expected her father to help her with arranging her introduction to the queen and whatever else it is chits do their first Season."

Arthur shook his head. "Rather early for her to make her way to London, seeing as how Parliament won't convene until November," he chided.

Charles frowned. "I suppose," he replied, not really sure of her other motives for coming to London. What did he know of Seasons and such? The Goodwin boys didn't have a sister, although if they did, Charles would have summoned her to help before speaking with his *brother* on the topic. He knew what he had to do; he just wanted to be sure he went about it the right way.

"Anyway, I will marry her, of course—"

"Of course," Arthur agreed.

"But I wonder how I should proceed with the announcement of the impending nuptials."

Arthur blinked. "I should think a letter to her father informing him of your intentions should precede a trip to the bishop's office for a special license. She's too young, of course, so you'll have to have his permission to marry her. Unless you wish to take a trip to Scotland."

Charles stared at his brother for a moment. The thought of simply taking Eleanor to Gretna Green seemed the easiest approach to marrying the chit. They would have days and days together in his coach, time they could spend bouncing about ...

He had to stop thinking of Eleanor. If his brother noticed the growing bulge in his nether region ...

"Really, brother, is sexual intercourse *all* you can think about?" Arthur asked rhetorically.

Charles gave up and shrugged. "I cannot help myself. I ... I feel *affection* for her ladyship." The admission was rather freeing just then, for the idea of facing Lord Middleton wasn't exactly something he wished to do, even though the man was also a fellow earl. And at some point, the earl would discover his daughter had traveled to London and didn't make it to his townhouse. Perhaps the man already had Bow Street Runners searching for her. The ten days it would take to get to Scotland and back would no doubt have her parents in knots with worry. No, better he send a note to her father post-haste. And probably by way of a footman rather than a postman.

"*Lust* is probably a more appropriate term for what you feel. Have you even *proposed?*" Arthur asked, one eyebrow arching up in amusement. From Eleanor's earlier behavior, he could swear the chit recoiled at Charles' kiss, and not just because he had paid witness to it.

"Not exactly," Charles answered carefully. "I suppose I can give the lady that courtesy," he added sadly. "I will, in fact, after I have everything sorted."

Arthur allowed a sigh. For probably the first time in his life, he felt sorry for his brother. "Do you have a ring?"

Charles dared a glance at his signet ring. Although it was gold and featured a rather large onyx gem, it certainly wasn't suitable to the occasion. "No," he replied with a shake of his head. "I'll have to pay a call on a goldsmith," he added, deciding he didn't wish to raid his mother's extensive jewelry collection to search for an appropriate bauble.

Sighing, Arthur angled his head to one side. "A trip to Ludgate Hill is in your immediate future. I suppose I should go with you to help you pick out something appropriate. God knows, you won't know a wedding ring from a cock ring."

Frowning, Charles regarded his brother. "I'll have you know, I have never worn a ..." Before he could finish, there was a knock on the study door. He gave a 'humph' and called out, "Come!"

Chester appeared with a tray on which was perched a bottle of whiskey and two glasses. "Lady Eleanor requested I deliver this," the majordomo stated when he noticed the look of surprise on his master's face.

"Rather sporting of her, don't you think, brother?" Arthur asked with an arched eyebrow. "Unless she poisoned it," he murmured under his breath as he took the glass of whiskey the majordomo offered and lifted it in his brother's direction. "Congratulations on your impending marriage, Charles." And then he downed the entire contents of his glass in one gulp.

Charles stared at his brother for a long time, finally taking a sip from his own glass. "Same to you, of course," he replied, realizing after a moment that he meant the comment. He would soon have a sister in the form of Lady Priscilla.

Although the viscount's daughter preferred to spend her days with her nose in a book, she wouldn't be a demanding chit. Nor would she drain his brother's accounts with frequent trips to modistes or gaming hells. Now, his brother's money would be spent at The Temple of Muses. Or Hatchett's, perhaps.

His thoughts turned to his own future wife. Eleanor could have spent the morning crying. She could have spent the morning in denial, lamenting the loss of her maidenhood.

Her innocence.

She could have been angry, yelling at him with a series of cruel words and crueler actions. But the woman had seemed rather calm. Rather collected. As if she accepted her fate, which surely she realized included a marriage to him.

Charles couldn't help but wonder at her reaction to his brother, however. *Is she attracted to Arthur? Had they met just the one time? And what had they talked about?* A pang of jealousy had him imagining one of his fists impacting Arthur's impressive jaw line. Blinking at the image, Charles gave his head a slight shake, and he tossed back the rest of the whiskey in his glass.

Charles saw his brother out to the vestibule and watched while Arthur climbed up onto his sporty yellow phaeton and took his leave of Mayfair.

When Charles turned around, he found Eleanor staring daggers at him.

CHAPTER 16
A MARQUESS WONDERS ABOUT A WOMAN

eanwhile, back in the park

Remembering he was trying to reform his rakish ways, Randall quickly sobered and took his leave of Hyde Park, his thoughts scattered as he made his way along the path he had followed earlier that morning to get to the bench on which he had read the letter from Lady Lily.

He blinked back a tear, stunned at how the former maid's letter had affected him. *I am happy for her*, he thought stubbornly. *I am.* In reality, he felt a good deal of jealousy toward the young man who had captured her heart—and her hand in marriage. *I am old enough to be her father*, he reminded himself. *Jesus!* She was the same age as his oldest bastard son!

His thoughts drifted back to the maid he had just met. A rather comely woman. Confident and proud, her speech suggesting she was an aristocrat rather than a servant or the paid companion she probably was.

A moment of daydreaming had him imagining her in a red satin ball gown, her brown curls piled atop her head in an arrangement he would take great delight in watching fall down in a cascade around her shoulders when he pulled the pins from her hair. A cascade of curls he would see on his pillows as he bedded her.

Christ! If he wasn't careful, he wouldn't make it the rest of the way home given how uncomfortably tight his buckskin breeches had become in the last few minutes! It was time he think of something else. Something less ... arousing.

Randall considered his mansion in Cavendish Square, rather glad he had put it on the market to let. Although he usually lived there while he had to be in London for Parliament, he had instead taken a townhouse in Curzon Street upon relocating from Reading the month before. "Just until Christmastime," he told the broker who had asked about his plans for his future. "By then, I should be married." The Cavendish Square mansion would then be a more appropriate place to live. A perfect house his marchioness could oversee. A perfect home in which to raise a family.

Now, it was entirely too large for just him. Well, just him and the army of servants it required for its upkeep.

His Reading manor house, located on the southwest edge of the largest city in Berkshire, was an entirely different situation. The Portland stone edifice had been designed and built by Randall's great-grandfather, the second Marquess of Reading, as a wedding gift for his beloved wife. The records found squirreled away in a priest hole off the study suggested the marquess had chosen his wife, Faith, when the two were but children. Faith, the daughter of a duke, was apparently intended for someone else, but his great-grandfather had whisked her off to Scotland for a quick marriage and made sure she was with child before the two returned to Reading.

Randall wondered if perhaps he should pursue a similar approach when he found a woman he wanted to marry. He quickly dismissed the idea, though, realizing it sounded rather archaic. Tempting, but entirely inappropriate. His fellow aristocrats would think him a barbarian!

He was nearly to his townhouse in Curzon Street when he once again caught sight of the barouche carrying the two women from the park. Instead of entering the street from Park Lane, as Randall had done, the driver had gone several streets beyond and turned onto Curzon Street so that the barouche was now coming towards him, no doubt so it could drop off the ladies on the other side of the street.

Feeling the sudden need to hide, Randall was about to step behind a tree trunk when he realized the conveyance had pulled over several houses up the street. Pausing in mid-step, he watched as the driver jumped down and hurried to open the door for the two women. From his vantage point, he couldn't see them once they existed the barouche—until they were climbing the steps to a town-house on the opposite side of the street from his own.

They're practically neighbors, he thought with some surprise. He was even more surprised when, not the maid, but the one who had introduced herself as Constance Fitzwilliam, hurried ahead to open the door, holding it until the maid had passed over the threshold. Then she followed and was lost to his sight as the door closed.

Well, that was rather odd, he thought as he made his way to his own front doors, one of the burgundy painted panels opening even before he had reached the top step.

"My lord," Giles said as he stepped aside and took the marquess' hat. "Is something amiss?" he asked, taking a look out the door before closing it.

Randall unbuttoned his topcoat and regarded the servant for a moment. "Giles, were you made aware of any new ladies ... uh, *people* in the neighborhood? Across the street and down several houses?" he asked as he removed his topcoat and handed it over to the butler.

Giles angled his head to one side. "There are a number of new neighbors, my lord," he replied, rather surprised the marquess would ask him.

He knew the rumors about Randall Roderick, Marquess of Reading. *The Rake of Reading*, some called him. Apparently rather popular with widows, lonely matrons and younger unattached misses looking for a randy man's attentions, the marquess would seem to be the first one to know about any new female neighbors. At his master's startled look, he shrugged. "Lord Trenton has returned to town and brought with him his new countess. A young lady from

Sussex arrived about two weeks ago and has taken up residence in the townhouse the Earl of Norwick used to occupy on occasion ..."

Randall was about to stop his butler, but decided to allow him to continue, thinking he might have some tidbit of information about Constance Fitzwilliam to share.

"... Lady Fletcher has just returned from her trip to Bath ..."

Rolling his eyes, Randall nearly huffed. The baroness was nearly old enough to be his mother. She was Lord Bostwick's aunt, for goodness sake!

"And a young couple, a Mr. and Lady Overby, have moved into the townhouse on the corner opposite. I do believe Lady Overby is Lord Trenton's—"

"Sister, yes, yes, she is," Randall interrupted, wincing as he remembered that the letter he had received from her was still tucked in his waistcoat pocket. "And a fine young woman, too. There's to be no disparaging words of her made by anyone in this household. Is that understood?"

One of his eyebrows rising in alarm, the butler nodded his head. "I'll see to it, my lord," he said, nodding again.

Randall immediately regretted his comment. For some reason, he found it necessary to protect the young woman, despite the fact that she had married and had a husband to see to her reputation. The servants would assume she had been one of his conquests should they be ordered not to exchange gossip about her.

Or perhaps they would think Randall and Lily were having an *affaire!*

"I ..," he paused, not sure how to make his butler understand there hadn't been, nor would there ever be, any relationship with the newlywed half-sister of Gabriel Wellingham, Earl of Trenton. "Had she been a few years older, I might have made her my marchioness," he finally managed to get out, deciding it better that he not admit that he had proposed to Lady Lily during Lord Weatherstone's last ball.

Understanding his master's words, Giles lowered his eyes. "I'll see to it, my lord," he said again. "Would my lord wish to send a floral arrangement to the Overbys, perhaps?"

The marquess considered the idea for only a second. "No, but I should think one would be appropriate for Miss Fitzwilliam," he countered.

The butler's eyes glanced to the right for a moment. "Miss Fitzwilliam?" he repeated, obviously unfamiliar with anyone with that name.

"Yes. Constance Fitzwilliam. The young lady who just moved into Norwick's old bachelor quarters," he clarified.

Giles's eyes widened. "Of course, my lord. I'll see to it right away." He gave a bow and hurried from the vestibule, leaving the marquess to heave a sigh of frustration. If it hadn't been so early in the day, he might have made his way to his study for a drink. If it had been the afternoon, he would have made his way to White's for a game of hazard and a glance at the betting books. But it was neither.

The problem with being in town well before Parliament was due to convene meant a month or two of boredom. This was the time he usually spent at someone's house party in Kent or at a friend's hunting lodge or in a villa on the coast. For some reason, none of his friends had arranged such pursuits this year, although given how cold the weather had been this time the year before, he couldn't blame them for thinking the snows would come early again.

Randall made his way upstairs and to the end of the hallway where a large window overlooked the street to the east. He glanced in the direction of the Norwick townhouse, angling his head as he gave some more thought as to what had occurred in the park earlier that morning. And then just a few moments ago when the two women had made their way into the house that had his attention.

He had just about decided to pay a call on the Earl of Norwick and ask about Constance Fitzwilliam when he noticed the front door of the Norwick townhouse open. A woman dressed in yellow emerged, a yellow parasol held aloft as she made her way down the stairs and then off toward the east. No one joined her on her walk, a situation he found rather odd given there was at least one maid in the household.

Not quite sure what compelled him, Randall was suddenly back down the stairs, calling for Giles. "My coat, please," he said as he reached for the topcoat the butler hadn't yet delivered to his bedchamber. "I'm going out."

Before the butler could reply, Randall made his way through the vestibule and to the front door, buttoning his coat as he did so. "Let Cook know I won't be home for luncheon."

The butler nodded. "Very good, my lord," Giles replied, the words said in the direction of the empty vestibule.

Lord Reading had already taken his leave of the townhouse.

CHAPTER 17
RUINATION IS A REALITY

Eleven-thirty in the morning

"What did you tell him?" Eleanor asked from where she stood at the edge of the vestibule.

Charles frowned but allowed a shrug. "That I ruined you," he answered simply. "That you would be his sister-in-law."

Eleanor's eyes widened at the same time a combination of anger and remorse seemed to wash over her face. "How *dare* you?" she whispered, keeping her voice down in case any servants were nearby. "We could have ..." She stopped, taking a deep breath when she realized her vision was graying at the edges. "No one needed to know, my lord," she whispered, tears collecting in the corners of her eyes. "No one but us."

Charles furrowed his brows as he approached her. He reached an arm around her shoulders, pulling her into a hug. He felt her stiffen and attempt to resist the move that brought the front of her body against his. Why didn't she succumb to his hold as she had earlier that morning? Was she merely playing coy?

Or did she intend to offend him?

"I promised you I would make this right, and I will, my lady," he said as he planted a kiss on the top of her head. "Now, I must take my leave of you as there is much to do today."

Eleanor pulled away from his hold. "Like what?" she asked in alarm. "Other than to take me to Mrs. Gibbons' to retrieve my valise and then to my father's townhouse," she added in a hoarse whisper.

Charles wondered why she whispered. "Oh, I've already paid a visit to Mrs. Gibbons' brothel. Your valise is upstairs. In our bedchamber," he added, rather satisfied with how the words sounded.

Our bedchamber.

She could have her own, of course. There was a mistress suite on the other side of the bathing chamber, but the thought of her sleeping in it wasn't something he could abide just then.

Unless he was sleeping in there with her.

That thought had a slight smile replacing his look of consternation at her apparent anger. "You need to stay here, my love, as I have the nosiest neighbor in all of the *ton* directly across the street and the second nosiest neighbor to the east. Should either one of them see you leave this house, by the front or by the back door, you will indeed be ruined beyond redemption," he claimed, rather glad Lady Pettigrew and Lady Fletcher lived so close—the first time since occupying the Curzon Street townhouse that he felt that way.

Eleanor's eyes widened, the tears threatening to spill over the edges of her lids. "Are you holding me *prisoner* then?" she asked, rather annoyed at the frisson that shot through her body just then. *Traitor*, she thought.

And just what did the earl mean by his mention of 'our bedchamber'? Didn't he realize there was a mistress suite on the other side of the bathing chamber?

Probably not.

He seemed addle-brained. But none-the-less, she had no intention of stepping into his bedchamber ever again!

"Of course not!" Charles replied with a shake of his head. "I am merely seeing to your ... *reputation*." He realized just then that having admitted to telling his brother of their encounter was counter to his claim. But how else would he have explained her presence when she showed up at his study door? "Arthur will tell no one, I assure you."

The sense of sorrow settled over Eleanor again. She realized Sir Arthur would never consider her to be his wife now. Certainly not now that he knew his brother had ruined her. "I don't suppose it matters any longer," she whispered, no longer fighting back the tears. Before the first teardrop fell, though, Charles had his handkerchief out and was offering it to her.

"I know I said I was sorry," he murmured as he reached down to kiss her on the forehead. "And I am. For you. But now I am finding I cannot regret last night." Before Eleanor could process his words, he let go of her, gave her a bow, and took his leave of the house by way of the front door.

Charles didn't make it down the front steps before he realized he needed to say more to Eleanor. From her behavior and curt words, it was quite apparent that she didn't realize he intended to marry her.

Turning around, he climbed the stairs and took a deep breath before reopening the front door. "I beg your pardon, my lady, but ..." He would have continued his comment but for the need to duck as the vase from the vestibule's table suddenly sailed overhead and crashed into the transom above the front door. Shards of Egyptian glass rained down behind him, littering the marble floor and making tinkling sounds as they came to rest around his feet.

"If you think for one minute that I will stay here and be your *prisoner*," Eleanor said with a vehemence Charles found rather frightening, "then you have much to learn about women!

"I hate you!"

Charles stared at Eleanor, noting her sudden look of stunned surprise, as if she hadn't expected the vase to miss him and break into a thousand pieces. His own look of surprise must have appeared more like anger to her, for she straightened and gasped, her body tensing. Then she turned and ran for the stairs, her skirts bunched up into her hands so she could keep from tripping on them as she made her way up the stairs.

"Lady Eleanor!" he called out, finally able to move from where he stood in the vestibule. *This isn't going well*, he thought as he realized he needed to go after her. He dared a glance back at the broken vase, secretly glad to see it was beyond repair. He had never much cared for the thing, even if his mother had managed to bring it with her all the way from Greece.

Taking the stairs two at a time, he reached the top step just as he heard the door to his bedchamber—*our bedchamber*, he remembered thinking—slam shut. "My lady, please," he called out. He made it to the door, rather surprised to find the handle wasn't locked. Stepping in and prepared to duck in the event he needed to avoid any flying *objets d'art*, he was stunned to find the room unoccupied. The connecting door to the bathing chamber was open, however, but the door to the mistress suite beyond was not. Making his way to the door, he tested the handle and found it locked. Heaving a sigh, he raised a fist and knocked three times.

"Who is it?"

Charles frowned. *Was she joking?* But he heard the sound of a sob beyond. "The Earl of Wakefield," he responded in his firmest voice. "I wish to pay a call on Lady Eleanor," he added, wondering if someone else was in the room with her. "The future Countess of ..."

The *snick* of the lock being undone silenced him. However, the door didn't open. Waiting a moment, Charles finally tested the handle to find that it turned. He opened the door a few inches. Thinking she might slam the door shut on his fingers should he attempt to use his hand to open the door, he instead placed the toe of one of his Hessians into the opening at the bottom and gave it a slight kick.

When he didn't immediately find her beyond the door's opening, and nothing airborne came flying in his direction, Charles dared a glance around the edge, shocked to see she was making her way out of an open window! "My lady!" he cried out, stunned she would attempt to leave by way of the second-story window. "What ..?" He reached around her shoulders and clasped his hands around whatever he could grab onto, pulling her back through the opening while she kicked and struggled.

"Let go of me!" she insisted, her voice filled with as much sorrow as anger.

"I'll do no such thing," Charles countered, his frustration finally apparent. "You'll break your neck," he added as he managed to get her free of the window frame, one arm wrapped below her breasts while another was behind her thighs, which left her in danger of falling face down onto the floor should he loose his grip on her. "Or mine, if you don't stop struggling!" he claimed. "*Dammit*, woman!"

The tone of his voice, or perhaps his curse, must have been enough warning for Eleanor, for she finally went limp in his arms. Slowly, Charles lowered her legs to the floor but kept both his arms around her shoulders in the event she decided to flee the house by way of the door. His anger abating somewhat, he used a hand to lift her head so that she would have to look at him. Despite the tears that limned her lids, her eyes blazed with anger. "Please, don't do that again," he whispered, his lips pressing against her forehead.

"Or what?" she whispered hoarsely, her voice full of venom.

"My lady, you must—"

"*Must?*" she interrupted, her eyes turning to slits.

The response brought him up short. He stared at her, wondering of what she thought he might be capable. Did she think he would hurt her? Force her to do something she didn't wish to do?

"Marry me," Charles said in a voice so quiet his words were barely heard. "Become my wife. My countess."

Eleanor's eyes widened at his words and then blinked at the way he had said them. As if he truly *wanted* her as his wife. The thought was momentary, though. "You're a *rake*, Lord Wakefield," she accused.

"I am," he agreed with a nod. "*Was*," he added. At her arched eyebrows, he shook his head. "I promise, I will ... I will honor my marriage vows. I will ... forsake all others," he claimed, hoping the wince he felt wasn't visible.

He tried to remember the words said in the last wedding he had witnessed. Witnessed while feeling ever so sorry for the man who had said those very words. Although, to that man's credit, he had believed every-thing he said when he repeated the vows. And apparently the man was enjoying a rather happy marriage to a woman who felt affection for him.

Truth be told, Charles wasn't sure if he could trust himself to keep the marriage vows. He had never thought about marriage beyond knowing he would at some point have to be married in order to sire a legitimate heir. *Duty, and all that*, he thought with some derision. "I have already told Mrs. Gibbons not to send anymore harlots to the house. Just give me a chance," he whispered, lifting one of Eleanor's hands to his lips, bestowing a gentle kiss on her bare knuckles.

"When did you do that?" Eleanor asked as she angled her head back to regard him, wondering at the pleasant tingle she felt in her fingers when his lips kissed them.

"This morning. When I went to retrieve your valise. I ... Lucy said some things might be missing, but if that is the case, then I will take you shopping tomorrow so that you might ..."

But Eleanor was already pulling herself from his hold and glancing about the bedchamber in search of the traveling case. "Chester may have put it in here," he murmured, hoping beyond hope that the few items still in the valise were everything she had brought with her to London. Any missing clothing items he knew could be replaced—he would take her shopping on the morrow—but if she had brought mementos with her—priceless items—they were probably now in the hands of the harlots at Lucy Gibbons' brothel.

He followed Eleanor to the other side of the bed, pausing when saw her lift the valise onto the counterpane. She opened it, and he saw how her anticipation was palpable. He watched as she rifled through the few items of clothing. His heart clenched as she let out a stifled cry and flung the valise to the floor.

Daring to join her on the bed, Charles pulled her into his arms and held her for several moments as she cried. Her sobs shook her entire body, sobs that had him tightening his hold on her. "Tell me what is missing. I shall replace whatever it is," he said, burying his face in her hair.

Eleanor shook her head against his arm. "My gowns. My silk stockings. Dance slippers. My *jewelry*," she sobbed.

Charles felt relief at hearing the list. At least nothing irreplaceable had been taken. "Then I suppose a shopping trip in New Bond Street and in Ludgate Hill is called for," he whispered. "Will you join me tomorrow?" he asked gently. "I think I should like to escort you, my lady."

Eleanor heard the earl's words and forced herself to stop sobbing. "I think I would rather die, my lord," she managed to get out.

Charles stilled himself, rather hurt by her curt words. "Nevertheless, I think you could do with a bit of air, my lady," he countered with a sigh.

Needing to be away from Eleanor, away from his townhouse and away from what he had done, Charles said, "You will have to excuse me, my lady, as I have an appointment."

Just as quickly as he had taken her into his arms, Charles removed himself from Eleanor and left her slumped over on the bed. "I'll check on you when I return," he added, not trying to hide the hurt in his voice.

Unsure of what else to say and looking ever so confused, he speared his fingers through his dark hair, gave a slight bow, and took his leave of the room.

Bereft at the loss of Charles' strong arms to hold her up, Eleanor slumped onto the bed and wept.

CHAPTER 18
A VISITOR TO A SOLICITOR

One o'clock in the afternoon of September 15
Constance double-checked the address on the note her solicitor in Sussex had provided on her last visit. The Fitzwilliams had employed the short, balding man for as long as she could remember. If she couldn't trust him, she didn't know whom she could. As for the solicitor he recommended she see whilst in London, he angled his head and peered at her over his gold-rimmed spectacles. "He's well-regarded and well-connected," Bernard J. Asherman stated when he had handed her the sheet with the details. "You may require an appointment. Be sure to mention my name if that's the case."

Constance gave the man her thanks and took her leave of him and of Sussex that very day. The trip to London, a whirlwind of a coach ride in the company of Mrs. Olivia Cunningham and her housekeeper, Esther Simmons, had been accomplished in the course of a long afternoon and evening. Although she had originally turned down the offer of a ride with the future viscountess, she found herself changing her mind when she realized she could use the time in the coach to learn everything she needed to about London.

Having spent her entire life near Horton, Olivia Waterford Cunningham had been somewhat of an outcast upon her arrival in the world's largest city. But after two years in a Grosvenor Square townhouse with her husband, Michael, she had settled into a life of a typical aristocrat's wife—paying calls on other young matrons, hosting them in her parlor, shopping in New Bond Street and Oxford Street, and overseeing the Cunningham household. By the end of the year, she would also be a mother, a tidbit of information she had put voice to when they were discussing the birth of the Norwick twins and the impending birth of the Countess of Torrington's baby.

Constance couldn't imagine marrying, let alone giving birth to a baby! She was already five-and-twenty! When she mentioned this to Olivia, the younger woman merely shook her head. "The Countess of Torrington is in her late thirties," she countered. "And although she was married and widowed before she became a countess, Adele claims she adores her husband and looks forward to motherhood."

Well, the Countess of Torrington was married to Milton Grandby, apparently one of the most agreeable men in all of London, so of course his wife would adore him, Constance thought with a sigh.

She glanced up at the shingle that hung above the door marked No. 30, Oxford Street. *Lady E's Finding Work for the Wounded*, she read to herself. That would be Viscountess Bostwick's charity, she thought with a smile, rather happy to have met the viscount before he inherited.

George Bennett-Jones was almost a hero to those who lived on his lands in Sussex or who worked in his coal mines. The man was considered fair and agreeable, even during the horrible summer of 1816 when there was no summer and so many crops failed.

Then there was his willingness to allow her to borrow one of his horses, Bounder, the same one she had "borrowed" when she was a year from her come-out.

The year she had decided it was time her mare produce a colt.

Any other aristocrat would have denied her simple request out of concern for their horseflesh, or expected a large payment for leasing the beast, or charged her an exorbitant stud fee, but the viscount seemed rather honored she would request his assistance. "No one else seems to want anything to do with him," he commented, despite knowing the resulting Thoroughbred from the first time she had "borrowed" the horse had done rather well on the racing circuit.

She couldn't help it if her father had gambled away all the winnings.

Despite not having participated in the largesse the stallion's first progeny generated, George Bennett-Jones seemed rather happy to learn the product of two Arabians behaved himself whenever Constance was leading him. The stallion had never been properly trained, but she seemed to have a calming effect on the headstrong horse.

Or perhaps Bounder knew what he was expected to do and simply went willingly. He and Amasia got on quite well the first time they were introduced to one another, after all.

Constance made a mental note to pay a call on Viscount Bostwick so she might meet his wife and give him her thanks in person.

The solicitor was next door to the charity, she remembered being told by Mr. Asherman. She moved to the next door and paused before going in. The hair on the back of her neck seemed to rise, and she turned around just as a well-dressed gentleman disappeared into the charity offices. No other people were about just then, so she took a deep breath and let herself into the solicitor's office.

Andrew S. Barton, Esquire, looked up from the stack of papers covering the middle of his desk and then attempted to get to his feet. "Pardon me," he said, bowing awkwardly after another moment. A glance at the end of his desk showed a pair of crutches leaning against the mahogany top.

Constance curtsied. "No need, sir. I am sure I have caught you at an inopportune time. I wondered if I might make an appointment ..?"

"Please, have a seat," Barton said as he indicated the padded chair in front of his desk. He held out his right hand, as if he expected her to grasp it. Constance did so, giving it a firm shake.

"I am Constance Fitzwilliam. I was referred to you by—"

"Asherman," he interrupted. "Yes. I've been expecting you. For a week, at least," he added as he held out his hand again.

Constance blinked, realizing Bernard Asherman, Esquire, had sent word she would be paying Mr. Barton a visit. She regarded his outstretched hand for another moment and realized he expected her to provide Asherman's note. Pulling open her reticule, she extracted the document and handed it over to the middle-aged man. *How much does he already know?* She watched him read the carefully scripted parchment. After a moment, he lifted his head.

"Have you an aversion to marriage, my lady?" he asked, his brows furrowing.

Surprised by the question, Constance shook her head and then allowed a shrug. Until her coach ride with Mrs. Cunningham, she might have answered in the affirmative. Now, she wasn't quite sure how she felt about the matter. "I am five-and-twenty, Mr. Barton. I have never been courted, nor do I expect to be anytime in the future. Therefore, it is imperative my inheritance be restored so that I might see to my own welfare," she said in what sounded like a well-rehearsed speech.

Barton regarded her for a moment and then gave a sigh and a nod. "In the meantime, how are you meeting your expenses?" he asked, one of his bushy eyebrows cocking up with the query.

Constance sighed as well, realizing the solicitor did not have time for pleasantries, nor for beating around the bush. "I have a bit of money," she replied, deciding she didn't need to be specific.

"How much?" Barton asked.

Her eyes widening in surprise, Constance shook her head. "How is it any of your concern?" she countered as she shifted in her chair.

The solicitor took a deep breath and sighed again. "Although I believe I will be able to help you ... in time ... I may not be able to resolve the situation for a few months. Perhaps a year—"

"A *year?*" Constance interrupted, panic setting in. She wouldn't last a year on the monies she had managed to squirrel away. She didn't think she would make it another *month* given the cost of goods in London. She struggled to fight back tears that threatened the corners of her eyes. "I've only enough for a month. Maybe two if I ..."

Mr. Barton settled back in his worn leather chair and sighed. "Certainly Lord Norwick could see to your expenses—"

"*No*," Constance said with a shake of her head. When she saw the solicitor's look of surprise, she added, "We are ... estranged," she said in a whisper. "I rather doubt he would be willing to pay for anything for me given our ... given my father's past with the man," she struggled to explain, not wanting to tell the solicitor about the reasons for her estrangement. She was quite sure the man would laugh at her.

The oddest things happened at balls.

"I don't see as you have much choice, my lady," he said. "Unless you can find a husband or have Lord Norwick cover your expenses, you will ... you will be *destitute*."

The word echoed in Constance's ears.

Destitute.

How was she supposed to find someone to help her in a month's time? How was she supposed to find a husband? Especially when she didn't particularly want to get married?

The solicitor crossed his arms over his ample chest and leaned forward. "Perhaps you could pay a call on the countess and present your case to her? Lady Norwick is a rather agreeable woman," he suggested. "I've heard she's just given birth to twins."

Constance considered the idea, realizing she might have to prevail upon her cousin's wife for help. She was about to thank the solicitor for his time when he angled his head to one side. "Or you could seek employment."

Her eyes widening again, Constance considered the idea. "Doing what?" she asked, nervous as to what the man might suggest.

"Servant, governess, mistress," he said quickly.

Feeling as if she had been punched in the stomach, Constance stared at the solicitor for several seconds before she finally blinked. And blinked again at just how direct the man could be. "I will seek an audience with Lady Norwick," she whispered. "Thank you for your time," she added as she slowly stood up.

"I'll have my resources work on finding your inheritance right away, Miss Fitzwilliam," Barton said as he carefully got to his feet, hanging onto the edge of the desk since he needed it for support. "But if the money was stolen, it may be lost for good," he warned.

Feeling sick, Constance nodded. "I understand." She gave a curtsy and took her leave of the solicitor's office, completely unaware of the gentleman who watched her as she dried her tears and made her way down Oxford Street toward Mayfair.

CHAPTER 19
A MARQUESS BECOMES CHARITABLE

*M*eanwhile, next door...

Realizing the woman he was following would probably recognize him as she entered the solicitor's office, Randall Roderick stepped into the offices of 'Lady E's Finding Work for the Wounded' and stopped short. A beehive of activity beyond the small lobby area was visible, and several men who looked as if they hadn't eaten or slept in days were lined up on a bench along one wall.

"May I help you?"

The marquess turned to find Lady Lily ... he blinked, unable to remember her new last name.

Overby.

"Good morning, Lady Overby," he said as he removed his hat.

"Lord Reading! 'Tis so good to see you," Lily replied as she offered her hand. The marquess took it and brushed his lips over her knuckles, giving a bow as he did so.

"And you, my lady. Although, I wouldn't have expected to find you *here*," he added, his brows furrowing as he jerked his head toward the men who sat on the bench. "Seeing as how you were just recently wed."

The young lady gave him a brilliant smile with her curtsy. "I was, although I won't be going on a wedding trip for a few weeks. Mr.

Overby's presence is required at Wellingham Imports until the owners return from their holiday, so it makes sense for me to continue my work here," she said as she led him into the main office of the charity. Several older gentlemen were seated at desks, quills in hand as they performed their duties.

"But, my lady," Randall started to say and then stopped when one of the men stood up from his desk and glared at him. "You seem to be the only ... *female* ... here. Is it ...?"

"Lord Reading, I'd like you to meet my husband's uncle, Mr. Augustus Overby," Lily interrupted, understanding the marquess' concern for her. Given the appearance of the men in the lobby, any gentleman would be concerned for the welfare of a lady in their presence. "He's my protector, and Lady Bostwick's when the viscountess is in the office," she explained as she angled her head toward the clerk.

The two men nodded to one another. "My pleasure," the two said in unison. When the marquess turned his attention back to Lily, he found her gazing at him, her eyes having taken in the sight of him from head to toe.

"You received my letter," she said, not making it a question. He had greeted her using her married name.

"I did," Randall replied. "And I ... thank you for informing me of your decision," he struggled to get out, rather annoyed that his face was taking on the reddish cast of embarrassment. He had never in his life felt embarrassment in the company of a woman, and could not now understand his reaction to Lady Lily's presence except that he had felt affection for her.

Enough so that he had proposed marriage.

"Thank you for having offered, my lord, but I do believe there is a better choice for your marchioness out there," she said in a voice meant only for his ears.

Possibly, Randall thought as he gave a nod. *And she might be right next door in Barton's office.* "Let's hope so," he finally replied. "In the meantime, I came ... well, I hope to visit with the solicitor next door once his current appointment is finished. Until then, I thought I would do what you suggested regarding charity," he explained, his brief glance in Mr. Overby's direction confirming the man was still staring at him and would pounce should the marquess attempt to do anything untoward with respect to Lily.

Lily smiled again and the marquess felt a twinge of regret at knowing he wouldn't see that smile everyday as he had hoped when he proposed to her at Lord Weatherstone's ball. "Have you come to make a donation?" she asked then, anticipation apparent in her tone of voice.

The marquess allowed a grin. "I am. I ... I have a bank draft here," he said as he pulled the paper from his waistcoat pocket. Relieved he had stuffed the cheque into his coat earlier that morning, he thought of what he had originally intended to purchase with it.

Jewelry.

A bauble he would probably only see once on its intended recipient. Although Rachel hadn't expected such a gift—he had only spent a few days with her at her Chiswick estate—the second youngest daughter of Mary Margaret Merriweather and George Grandby was rather discreet and rather thankful for his time and attention. Despite her age—she had to be in her late-forties—the woman lived the life of a spinster, quite happy in her independence and wealth.

Rachel made it quite clear she had no designs on him for marriage or even a continuing liaison. "Darling, you have more than satisfied an old woman," she had said when he took his leave of her bedchamber. "But now it's past time you find a wife."

Seeing Lady Lily and remembering the words in her letter to him, he decided right then and there he would never again buy jewelry for a woman unless she was either betrothed to him or his sister.

"May I ask how my donation might be used?" he asked as he surveyed the office again. Every desk was neat, with small stacks of what appeared to be applications on either side of where the men were busy transcribing information. In one corner, a tailor was measuring a man, apparently for a suit of clothes, and in another, a man spoke in low tones to an older man whose face displayed the ropy scars of burned flesh.

Lily lowered her voice and leaned in closer to the marquess. "Only yesterday, I learned of positions for several of those who are waiting for employment, but the business owner requires a substantial ... deposit."

Randall's eyes widened, wondering at the meaning of her comment. "Do you mean a *bribe?*" he asked with some alarm.

Lily stepped back and angled her head. "I'm not to use that word," she countered quickly. "It's a guarantee of sorts, insurance that the men will report to work and remain in his employment for some length of time."

Frowning, Randall angled his head to match hers. "And at the end of that time? Does the money get returned to you?"

The young woman blushed and lowered her head. "I do not know. Lady Bostwick makes those arrangements with the employers," she whispered.

Not particularly pleased his donation might go to some cit who probably didn't need it, Randall was about to beg forgiveness and take his leave, but Lily motioned toward the tailor. "However, I believe your monies would go to pay for the suits required for the men who are waiting to be fitted." She indicated the line of bedraggled looking men who sat in the lobby.

Randall dared a glance back at the men and gave Lily a nod. He handed the cheque to her. "Would one-hundred pounds cover it, do you suppose?" he asked as he angled his head.

Lily allowed a slow smile to show. "More than enough, my lord," she said with a nod. "I'll be just a moment. I need to write you a receipt." She moved off to one of the desks, handing the cheque to Augustus Overby.

Randall dared a glance back toward the lobby, wanting to be sure he didn't miss seeing the young woman he had followed to the solicitor's office. Before Lily rejoined him, he was rather surprised when he spotted the woman through the glass in the door. She stood for a moment in front of the charity's office, staring at her reflection in the glass as she used a gloved hand to wipe the sides of her eyes.

Alarmed, the marquess was about to hurry to her when he realized he needed to say a farewell to Lily.

"My lady," he said as he took her hand. "I really must take my leave. Congratulations on your marriage. Your Mr. Overby is a very lucky man," he added as he lifted the hand to his lips and kissed the back of it.

Blushing, Lily gave the marquess a curtsy and thanked him for his generosity. "Do come again," she said as he made his way out the door.

By the time Randall was able to leave Lady E's office, the young woman he had been following was no longer in front of the building, nor did he see her on the cobbles. Looking left and right, he finally spotted her walking rather fast as she made her way back toward Mayfair.

Damn it! he thought as he moved next door to the office of Andrew S. Barton, Esquire.

So much for offering the lady an escort.

CHAPTER 20

A MAID MAKES A MAIDEN'S DAY

*O*ne-fifteen in the afternoon of September 15

Eleanor regarded the embroidered handkerchief she still clutched in her hand, its edges damp from where Lord Wakefield had touched it to her face when she was crying earlier. The initials CHG were carefully stitched with a swish of curlicues at the ends of each letter. She briefly wondered what the 'H' stood for, but found she really didn't care. She imagined instead what 'C' might look like if it were an 'A'. *Arthur Goodwin,* she thought with a wan smile. Well, she probably wouldn't find out what that particular initial would look like given he wouldn't be marrying her.

Spying her bedraggled appearance in the corner cheval mirror, she nearly let out an audible gasp. *Goodness!* It was a wonder anyone would want to marry her when she looked so disheveled. About to get up from the bed, she paused when she heard footsteps outside the door.

Despite expecting the knock, she still jumped when it finally happened. Taking a deep breath and ready to resume her battle with the earl, she opened the door with a flourish and let out a squeak. Instead of finding the Earl of Wakefield beyond the threshold, a young woman of about her age stood in front of the majordomo.

"How do?" Eleanor managed to say as she regarded her visitors.

Chester gave Eleanor a nod. "Lady Eleanor Merriweather. May I present your lady's maid, Miss Alice Foster?" he intoned, his baritone voice causing a bit of vibration in the floorboards beneath the carpet. "Lord Wakefield requested that I hire her from an agency."

"My lady," the girl said as she performed an awkward curtsy.

"Oh," Eleanor replied in surprise, giving the girl a nod. *When had the earl had time to order a maid be sent?*

"I will work to have her quarters ready upstairs by dinner," the majordomo said before giving a bow and retreating.

Eleanor blinked. *A lady's maid? Of my very own?* Well, of course, she reasoned. It wasn't as if there was another woman in the household needing a maid. She had to share a maid with her mother back home. "Do come in. As you can see, my hair is in need of a repair," she said as she lifted one hand to the back of her head and grimaced.

"Yes, my lady. I can pin it up for you right away," Alice said as she moved into the room and quickly removed her pelisse and bonnet. When Eleanor didn't make a move toward the dressing table, the younger woman pulled out the chair. "It will be easier if you sit here, my lady," she hinted.

Blinking, Eleanor gave a start. "Of course," she agreed, hurrying to take a seat before the dressing table. A quick look into the mirror had her wincing. "Oh, I look a sight," she breathed as the maid took out the pins that held up her messy bun. Staring at her own reflection and then at the reflection of the room's furnishings and wall coverings behind her, Eleanor found herself rather surprised at just how beautifully the bedchamber was decorated.

When Alice had all the pins out of her hair, Eleanor dared a glance at her surroundings. She realized the earl had to have purchased the terrace already furnished; it was rather doubtful the man would have had a hand in choosing such rich fabrics in the deep scarlet and pale pinks that covered the chairs and bed, or the French furnishings with their elegantly-turned legs and drawer fronts. The room looked as if it had been made for the palace at Versailles!

"We'll have you fixed up right quick, my lady," Alice assured her, helping herself to an ivory comb from a set on the dressing table top, a set that appeared rather expensive. "Do you have more pins than this, my lady?" the maid asked as she waved to the small pile she had removed from Eleanor's hair.

Not about to admit she probably did but they were either scattered in the earl's bed or on the floor of his bedchamber, Eleanor gave a shrug. "I'm sure they're here somewhere," she replied, realizing they would be very apparent given the few accoutrements in the uncluttered room. She studied the matching hairbrush, admiring the decorative enamel finish on the back and down the handle. Two perfume bottles were the only other embellishments on the dressing table, the Egyptian glass appearing almost pearlescent in the light from the window. Studying the swirls in the delicate glass reminded Eleanor that she had packed her only bottle of perfume. The thought reminded her that she had tossed her valise when she discovered it was missing some of what she had brought with her to London.

She glanced about, finally spotting the bag near the door to the bathing chamber. "There should be some hair combs in my bag," she said as she pointed toward the valise. "And a gown for dinner," she remembered, wishing she had brought more clothes. But she had figured her father would help with her come-out, and help with seeing to it she had an appointment with a modiste and a cobbler, and hire a chaperone to accompany her on trips about London.

Alice opened the valise and pulled out several items of clothing, only one of which seemed appropriate for dinner with an earl. Unable to locate any hair combs, Alice finally turned over the valise so that its contents dumped out onto the counterpane.

Eleanor turned around, feigning shock at discovering some of her clothing was missing. Was all the jewelry was missing, too? Although she had looked through the bag earlier, she had done so in such haste and with tear-filled eyes, she hadn't actually seen any of its contents.

She remembered the look on Lord Wakefield's face when she had tossed the bag. Strained—sad almost—as if he truly felt sorry for her. And then he had promised they would go shopping to replace any missing items.

Of course, he would make such a promise, she realized. She had been crying. He was desperate to make her stop. He probably would have promised her the royal jewels, if necessary.

Unable to breathe, Eleanor struggled to maintain her composure. At Alice's quick glance in her direction, she said, "I was ... I was robbed. On my way here." Which, for all intents and purposes, was a fairly true assessment of her situation. *Robbed of my innocence, the only man I've ever felt affection for, and now my clothes.* She allowed an audible sigh. Although she was tempted to resume crying, she realized she had been a watering pot for too long. It was time she accept her lot and move on.

The maid's eyes widened. "Goodness! No wonder you look as if you've been ..." She paused, apparently about to say 'tumbled'.

Or 'plowed'.

"Been what?" Eleanor replied, her eyes wide.

"As if you've been *robbed*," the maid quickly responded, picking up the hair combs from the counterpane. "We'll have you ready for the modiste in no time," she added as she moved to work on Eleanor's hair.

"Modiste?" Eleanor repeated.

The maid nodded to Eleanor's reflection in the mirror. "Aye. His lordship had Mr. Chester arrange for her to pay a visit this afternoon at two o'clock. She's to bring some finished gowns as well as fabrics and pattern books for your approval. For your riding habit and walking gowns and ball gowns and such," Alice added as she began the task of pinning up Eleanor's brunette hair.

Staring at her reflection, Eleanor had to remind herself to close her mouth. *The earl had ordered a modiste be sent?* Well, the man was certainly not as much of a barbarian as she had first thought, she realized with some surprise.

"Your wedding must have been quite the affair," the maid said as she continued dressing Eleanor's hair.

Eleanor blinked. *Wedding?* The maid must have thought she was already married to the earl! She was about to set the young woman straight when she realized she couldn't. How would she explain her presence in Lord Wakefield's home without admitting what had happened the night before?

"Hardly," Eleanor said with a slight shake of her head, the move made nearly impossible with Alice holding onto a lock of hair as she stabbed another pin into the mound already piled atop her head. At the maid's look of confusion, she added, "We were married by special license. A small affair." At least, that's what she imagined it would be if she was truly forced to marry the man, which was looking more and more likely as this awful day continued.

"It sounds rather romantic," Alice commented with a sigh. "Were you betrothed to him since childhood?"

Eleanor considered how to respond. Before last night, she had only met the man once! "Not at all. We merely met ... quite by accident, and the next thing I knew, I was to be married to the man."

The maid allowed another sigh. "So, it *is* romantic. Are you a daughter of the aristocracy?"

Noting how the maid seemed to hold her breath in anticipation of her answer, Eleanor gave a shrug. "My father is ..." She was about to say his name and realized it might give away her situation. "An earl, of course," she merely responded. "My mother prefers living in the country, so I haven't spent much time here in town," she added, hoping the maid wouldn't ask where she lived.

She asked.

"Just outside of Epping," Eleanor replied after a pause. "Are you familiar with it?" she asked carefully.

The maid gave a sad shake of her head. "I've only ever lived here in London, my lady," she answered, lifting the last lock of hair and pinning it into place.

"What a vast improvement!" Eleanor commented turning her head left and right as she admired her maid's work.

"Oh, I'm not finished, my lady," Alice replied. At Eleanor's quizzical expression, she added, "I still have to pin the curls into place."

Eleanor settled back onto the small chair and watched as her maid worked her magic, wrapping the ends of her hair into pin curls and anchoring them into place with the rest of the hairpins. "I'm hoping the modiste has a ribbon we might use to finish it, my lady," Alice said as she aimed a critical eye at Eleanor's coiffure.

The earl's daughter dared a glance in the mirror, stunned at the transformation. She looked positively elegant. Elegant and at least a few years older. "You've worked wonders, Alice," she murmured just as her stomach grumbled.

"Would you like me to bring up your luncheon, my lady? Or will you be eating in the parlor?"

Eleanor hesitated with her response. She didn't even know where the parlor was located, but she supposed it was about time she familiarized herself with the townhouse. "The parlor, of course," she said with a nod. "Since I am ever so much more presentable than I was," she added, giving her maid a nod. "Thanks to you."

"My pleasure, my lady."

Frowning, Eleanor wondered why a maid with her hair dressing skills wouldn't already be employed. "For whom did you work before Lord Wakefield?" she asked as she stood up from the dressing table.

Alice's face fell. "My employer was Lady Pettigrew," she said sadly.

Eleanor's eyes widened. Hadn't Wakefield mentioned that Lady Pettigrew was a neighbor? "Next door?" At the maid's nod of agreement, she added, "Why did you leave her employ?"

The maid seemed to deflate before her eyes. "Her ladyship's hair, or rather what was left of it, burned off when I tried to use the curling iron on it. She regularly wears wigs, you see, and with most of her hair gone, she had no need of my services."

She didn't add that the woman had fired her.

Eleanor gave the maid's response some consideration. "Well,

since I don't have a curling iron, burning my hair off won't be a possibility, now will it?" she responded.

With that, she took her leave of the bedchamber and made her way downstairs, wondering if there wasn't just a bit more to the story of Lady Pettigrew's hair.

CHAPTER 21
A MARQUESS MEETS A SOLICITOR

One-thirty in the afternoon of September 15

The solicitor glanced up from the document he had apparently just put into place on his blotter and sighed upon seeing yet another person coming through his office door.

"Good day," the gentleman said as he removed his top hat and nodded toward the solicitor.

"I haven't yet decided if it is."

Randall Randolph, Marquess of Reading, regarded the solicitor for a moment. "If I were to exchange some coin for information about the young woman who just left your office, would that help to make it a good day?" he asked, cringing at how his question sounded like a bribe. He now had a better understanding of how Lady Bostwick had to conduct business on behalf of her charity.

Andrew Barton frowned but leaned back in his chair. "Depends on who is offering the coin, I suppose," he answered, his face showing his suspicion as his eyes took in the cut and quality of the topcoat his visitor wore.

"Randall Roderick, Marquess of Reading," Randall said with a nod. Although the solicitor didn't offer it, he took the seat opposite the man's desk.

Barton leaned forward, his hands resting on the front of his desk.

"I apologize for not recognizing you, my lord," he said in a quiet voice. "I expected you to be ... older," he stuttered.

At that moment, Randall noticed the two crutches leaning against the side of the desk and realized the man probably wouldn't have been able to stand upon his entrance. "I expected you to say 'younger', so I guess we're even," Randall said with a grin.

Barton leaned back in his leather chair. "She is a cousin to the Earl of Norwick," he said without preamble. "And having just come into her majority, she has discovered her inheritance is ... missing."

Randall blinked. "Missing?" he repeated. But that wasn't what had him blinking in disbelief. He could have sworn the woman he followed wasn't the relative of Norwick but rather the maid who had accompanied her on her walk in Hyde Park. Although he was quite sure they were both brunettes—their bonnets had covered most of their hair, but their eyebrows were visible—he now wondered if he had mixed up their identities.

Or had he?

The solicitor sighed and pulled open a desk drawer. He pulled out a bottle of Macallan scotch and two tumblers, setting them with a *thud* on the mahogany desktop. "I usually don't imbibe until after luncheon, but I'm finding my day rather trying already," Barton stated as he opened the bottle and poured three fingers' worth into the glasses. He held one out to the startled marquess.

"Thank you," Randall said as he took the glass, rather shocked the man would have such good liquor in his office, let alone offer him such a generous portion.

The solicitor lifted his glass and held it out. "To chits who don't know any better," he said.

Randall blinked and held up his glass. "To chits," he said before taking a sip of the smoky liquid.

Barton did the same, savoring the scotch before he allowed it to drip down his throat. "I was about to pen a note to a Runner I use for cases such as these," he said as he indicated the parchment in front of him. "He's rather good at investigating, especially when bank accounts go missing or an embezzler is involved. But I have a feeling that's not the case in this instance."

Frowning, the marquess regarded the solicitor for a moment. "Well, if the money hasn't gone missing, then why hasn't Miss Fitzwilliam been able to find it?" he asked before taking another sip of the fiery liquid. Although he rarely drank before his afternoon visit to White's, Randall could understand why the solicitor did so.

Fortification.

Barton shook his head. "It's possible there's no money involved," he answered.

The marquess frowned. "If not money, then ... what?"

The solicitor took a deep breath. "I received a letter from a solicitor who worked for the young woman's father, Edward Fitzwilliam. Seems he was an inveterate gambler, and a rather poor one at that, which is why I suspect there wasn't any money left for Miss Fitzwilliam's inheritance. There was, however, a stable of horses."

"Horses?" Randall repeated. His eyes widened. "Yes, I remember now. Fitz had a racehorse. A three-year-old that did rather well a few years back," he recalled. "In the Derby at Epsom Downs."

The solicitor nodded. "It did indeed, but Mr. Fitzwilliam's winnings just gave him more grist for the gambling mill. According to Mr. Asherman—the family's solicitor in Sussex—Mr. Fitzwilliam died a widower leaving only enough for his daughter to keep the estate and pay a few servants until she reached her majority."

The marquess nodded but his brows were elevated on his forehead. "Will she lose the house?" he asked in alarm.

Barton gave a look of surprise. "She cannot. It's entailed to the Norwick earldom."

Randall felt a bit of relief at hearing that bit of news. At least the woman would have a home in which to live, even if she didn't have any funds. "And what of the horses?"

Andrew Barton blinked as he regarded the marquess for a moment. "Yes, indeed," he whispered, his attention moving to a document that had been folded at some time. "What of the horses?" he murmured as he perused the document. "There's nothing mentioned here about the stables. But I should think there's got to be a horse or two of some value. Probably the racehorse and a foal or two from it," he reasoned as he returned his attention to Randall. "Unless Mr. Fitzwilliam sold them. But whether or not there was money involved, stolen or not, it still means the young lady will be left destitute when her funds run out in a month or so."

Randall's eyebrows arched. "Destitute?" he repeated. "She's a ..." He stopped, trying to remember how she was related to the Earl of Norwick.

"Cousin," Barton said with a sigh. "Apparently estranged and not particularly motivated to seek Lord Norwick's help, it seems. I encouraged her to pay a call on the countess instead," he explained. "Lady Norwick has just given birth to twins and may be more amenable to a request for help."

Randall gave a nod. "Good advice," he said. *And she'll be more sympathetic to a unmarried woman's plight*, he considered.

As am I.

"Can you ... can you be sure the woman who was just here was indeed Constance Fitzwilliam?" he asked then, wondering if the solicitor had sought some proof of identification.

Andrew Barton inhaled slowly. "She had documents in her possession, and there is certainly a family resemblance, but not having met the woman before, I cannot confirm that was she, indeed, Miss Constance Fitzwilliam. Should I suspect otherwise?" he asked, cautious with his query.

The marquess shook his head. "No," he said. "I am just ... suspicious is all," he added before draining his drink. "How much was the woman's inheritance supposed to be?"

Barton allowed a sigh and drained his own tumbler. "Fifty-thousand pounds," he replied with an arched eyebrow.

Randall's eyebrows joined the solicitor's in elevation. "Good God!" he said as he placed his tumbler on the desk. "It's a wonder no man has insisted she marry him," he said.

The solicitor gave a shrug. "Although I recommended she marry in order to avoid the poor house, I got the distinct impression Miss

Fitzwilliam did not relish the idea of marriage," he explained in response.

Randall allowed a nod. "Perhaps she can be ... *compelled* should an offer be made," he suggested, wondering how he might accomplish such a feat. Although most women could be compelled with a bauble from Rundell, Bridge & Rundell, he rather doubted Constance Fitzwilliam could be.

Barton frowned. "Just because she is owed her inheritance does not mean she will be able to collect it," he said with a hint of warning.

Furrowing his brows, Randall said, "So?"

The solicitor sighed rather audibly. "You cannot count on her inheritance as a form of dowry," he clarified with impatience.

"I am not looking for a *dowry*," Randall countered, his annoyance at the comment sounding in his voice. "I am, however, looking for a suitable *wife*."

This bit of news seemed to surprise the solicitor. "Then perhaps you should see to courting Miss Fitzwilliam," he suggested, his manner most serious.

"I plan to," Randall responded before he realized what he was admitting. *Although I would like to know if it's the maid or the Norwick cousin I should be pursuing.* He did not put voice to his thought but rather pulled out a guinea and placed it on the solicitor's desk. "Thank you for your time."

Randall was about to take his leave when he paused and regarded the solicitor for a moment. "Could you send word if you learn anything more about her inheritance?" he asked, pulling out his calling card and offering it to Barton.

The solicitor gave a nod. "I will send you word at the same time as I send word to Miss Fitzwilliam," he promised. "But something tells me you'll know before I do."

Giving the man a nod, the Marquess of Reading took his leave of the solicitor's office, intending to find the object of his interest and offer her a ride home.

CHAPTER 22
A MEETING WITH A GODFATHER

Turning back the clock to one in the afternoon ...

Upon leaving his townhouse, Charles thought at first to pay a visit to White's, but then considered the man he sought would probably not be at the men's club until later in the day. The other man he thought might be of some help would probably be at his manor home, a man who prided himself on the number of goddaughters he had amassed over the course of nearly thirty years.

Never having given a thought to those goddaughters, Charles now wondered if the current crop of unmarried daughters of the *ton* shared Milton Grandby, Earl of Torrington, as their godfather.

Well, that was rather unlikely, he considered. But for the ones that were his earliest goddaughters, Grandby had made sure they were all either married to appropriate men or would be when they were old enough, even if those men weren't always the most logical choices. And the chits were from the best families, with nary a poor word written about them in the gossip rags.

The thought of Grandby had him wondering if Eleanor was one of his goddaughters. Charles considered returning to the townhouse to ask Eleanor but thought better of it. Grandby always made an appearance at White's at seven o'clock every night. Perhaps he would simply go to the club later and confront the man. But Charles decided he couldn't wait that long for the earl to appear.

He would instead pay a visit to Worthington House and find out from the Earl of Torrington right then, giving a passing thought to the fact that it had been at Worthington House when he was first in the presence of his future wife.

How ironic.

Charles tossed a shilling to the young boy who still held the reins of his bay—he had been doing so since Charles returned from Lucy Gibbon's brothel earlier that morning—and climbed up onto his phaeton. He took his leave of Curzon Street and turned onto Park Lane.

Although he had heard some women of the *ton* were especially cruel with their gossip, he couldn't help but hope Eleanor would be spared. She would be under his protection, after all. Being the wife of an earl had to count for something.

He blinked, realizing that his reputation as a rake made her the perfect fodder for gossip and for gossip rags like *The Tattler*.

What am I doing? Of course, everyone would assume he had ruined her and was forced to marry her. Better they think that than know the truth of what had happened to her.

Or was it?

Although he meant to visit with Grandby to learn if he was Eleanor's godfather, Charles had a much longer list of concerns by the time he appeared at the front door of Worthington House.

The butler answered, blinking when it was apparent he didn't immediately recognize Charles. "Lord Wakefield to see Grandby," he stated, his hands clasped behind his back.

Stepping aside to open the door, the butler bowed. "My lord, the earl is ..." Fitzroy paused, as if he wasn't sure he should say what he had been told to say when greeting a visitor on this auspicious day.

"Indisposed?" Charles offered as a possible response.

The butler shook his head. "In the nursery. He says if a visitor isn't opposed to spending time in the company of a newborn baby and the odors associated with such, then they are welcome to join him."

Charles blinked. And then blinked again before he remembered Lady Torrington had gone into confinement a few weeks ago. "Oh! The earl's a father now, isn't he?" Charles asked rhetorically. "Well, did his countess give birth to a boy or a girl?" he asked, deciding to take a chance and join the earl in the nursery. He had never actually been in the company of a baby, but from what he knew of them, they were small and didn't speak.

"Yes, my lord," the butler replied with a nod.

Charles removed his top hat and gave it to the servant. He was about to blink again at the butler's odd response but thought carefully about what the man had said. "An heir?" he guessed.

"Yes, my lord."

Well, that certainly had to be good news. But the butler's expectant look made him realize there was more information to be had. "And a ..?"

The butler's eyes flitted about before he finally blinked. "A ... a *female.*"

Charles' eyes widened. "Twins?" he said with some excitement. "*Faith!* Why, the Countess of Norwick just had twins a few weeks ago," he murmured as he made his way to the stairs. Which was really a rather efficient way of going about procreation, he thought then. He imagined Eleanor round with child—with twins—and his heart clenched just as he reached the stairway. He paused a moment, thinking of her large brown eyes, of her brunette hair splayed out on his pillow, of how she had felt with her soft body pressed against the front of his as he slept. Of how he had slowly awakened that morning feeling better than he had in months. Years, perhaps. It had taken every bit of self-control not to help himself to her body that morning and then ... then he had. The thought he could do so on occasion should she agree to marry him had him bounding up the stairs.

Before he realized it, Charles was at the top and working his way down the wide hallway toward the quiet conversation he overheard.

He poked his head around one open doorway, rather surprised to see the Earl and Countess of Torrington each seated in wooden rocking chairs and each holding a blanketed bundle in their arms.

"Pardon me, my lady, Grandby," he said by way of announcing himself. Fitzroy had probably planned to do so, but the poor man was probably still only halfway up the stairs. He bowed in the direction of Adele Grandby, who gave him a brilliant smile.

"Why, Lord Wakefield, do come in," she said as she readjusted the baby she held so she could hold out her hand in his direction. He leaned over and brushed his lips over her knuckles.

"I hear you have an heir and a daughter," the earl stated as he released Adele's hand.

The countess beamed as she held out the baby in her arms so he could better see the newborn. "Indeed," she said proudly.

"She's beautiful," Charles commented, deciding not to put voice to his real opinion of the scrunched up face below a shock of dark hair. Goodness! How could something so newly born look as if it were ninety years old?

"*He* is," Adele corrected him gently. "My daughter, Angelica, is the one his lordship won't allow anyone else to hold. Unless she's hungry or wet, and then he's happy to hand her over," she said with a wink in her husband's direction.

"And if you think I'm going to allow a rake to hold my daughter, think again, Wakefield," Milton Grandby warned from where he gently rocked the baby he held. "She may end up in a nunnery on the occasion of her sixteenth birthday due to the likes of you." He made the claim with a wink aimed in his wife's direction.

The rake was about to claim his days of being a rake were over, but he thought it better to discuss that with the other earl in private. "As I don't know the first thing about holding babies, I will not ask for that honor, my lord," Charles said from where he stood admiring the nursery.

He could imagine Eleanor in just such a room, a blanket-wrapped babe held in her arms as she hummed a lullaby.

His baby.

Charles blinked and quickly shook his head, wondering how he had managed to conjure such an image.

"What brings you to our nursery, if not the desire to hold a babe?" Grandby asked, slowly getting to his feet and moving the babe he held so it rested against his shoulder.

Daring a glance at Lady Torrington, the younger earl allowed a shrug. "I am in need of some advice," he replied.

Grandby seemed surprised by the response. "Let us retire to the study then," he suggested as he moved toward the door.

"Aren't you forgetting something?" Adele asked with a raised eyebrow.

The older earl paused and regarded his wife for a moment. "Oh!" he managed as he hurried back into the room and planted a kiss on her cheek. "I won't be gone long," he said as he moved to the door again.

"Milton!" Adele admonished him, both of her brows arched up. "I'll not have you smoking whilst you hold your daughter," she said.

Grandby regarded his wife for a moment. "I promise I won't smoke," he replied.

When Charles realized the countess had turned her attention on him, he shook his head. "I won't either," he said quickly, realizing Lady Torrington was quite serious.

The two earls took their leave of the nursery and headed down the stairs. "Something tells me you wanted a daughter and she wanted a son," Charles ventured as they reached the bottom step.

Grandby allowed a grin. "My wife is all about duty, and I ... I always thought my cousin, Gregory, would inherit the earldom," he replied. "He'll be relieved to learn my beloved delivered a boy. Although he would make an excellent earl, Gregory didn't really want the responsibility," Grandby explained as they made their way into the study. "So my son, George, will have to do so."

Charles was rather surprised Grandby didn't hand off the baby to the nearest servant when they took their seats in the overstuffed chairs near the fireplace. The earl continued to hold the sleeping baby girl against his shoulder, occasionally bestowing her with a kiss on her hairy head. "You seem to have ... experience with babies," Charles commented, accepting the glass of brandy a footman offered him.

Grandby took his brandy balloon and set it aside. "I do. I have the honor of being a godfather to two-and-twenty goddaughters and six godsons," he said with some pride. "I hope to add two more when I talk my oldest goddaughter into allowing me to be the godfather to her twins," he added.

Charles realized the earl referred to the twins the Countess of Norwick had delivered just a few weeks ago, but the news that the older earl was her godfather was a bit of a surprise. He figured the man could only have been in his late teens when he took on the responsibility. Wondering again if Grandby was also Eleanor's godfather, he cleared his throat and put voice to his query. "And Lord Middleton's daughter, Lady Eleanor. Are you her godfather as well?" he asked carefully.

Grandby frowned as he considered the question. "And if I am?" he countered, a suspicious expression developing on his face.

"I wish to marry her," Charles responded, deciding not to take the sip of his brandy he was about to just then.

Had Grandby taken a sip of his, the brandy would have been spewed out onto the hearth near their feet. "What?" he said in reply, leaning forward so he had to catch Lady Angelica from falling from his shoulder. The baby squirmed but was soon sound asleep as he moved her into a crook of one arm.

The younger earl sighed. "I wish to marry Lady Eleanor. I admit I ... I ruined her. By accident. But I find myself rather enamored with the young lady and have decided I would like to make her my wife," he explained, ignoring Grandby's expression of surprise coupled with horror and a good deal of disbelief. Realizing he had to provide more details in order so he wouldn't seem the absolute worst of rakes, Charles proceeded to explain what had happened. "Mrs. Gibbons was rather angry at my insistence that I would not be sending Lady Eleanor back to her brothel," he finished.

Grandby held out a hand. "*Language*, man. There's a young lady in our presence," he added in admonishment.

"Oh. I'm so sorry. House of ill repute?" he ventured.

"Well, it's too late *now*," Grandby countered. But his sigh of frustration was followed by a shake of his head. "How long had the young lady been there before she was sent to your house?" he asked in a whisper. *Good God!* What had Eleanor Merriweather done to end up at Lucy Gibbons' brothel? He knew she wasn't the first to suffer the indignity of being kidnapped by the wily madame, and she wouldn't be the last despite his warnings to the contrary. It was most unfortunate she enjoyed such a rich and varied clientele. And that she could abide an occasional retribution from a powerful lord.

The Earl of Wakefield shrugged. "Just yesterday is all. But ... she was placed in a cupboard and forced to watch Lord Sinclair spend time with his favorite lady of the evening in the middle of the afternoon." The older earl's wince was quite evident to the younger earl. "So, you see the predicament. I wish to do right by the lady and marry her," he explained, finally draining his brandy.

Grandby rubbed his forehead with his free hand. "Have you spoken with her father yet?" he asked in a low voice.

Charles eyes widened. "I haven't. I thought to come to you first," he said.

Grandby gave him a quelling glance. "A godfather is not a replacement for a father until the man has died," he said. "Although I sometimes wonder if some of them haven't lost their minds," he murmured. He took a deep breath. "Talk to him. I'm sure he'll be quite relieved to have his daughter betrothed before the Little Season even starts. He has no clue what he would be in for should he have had to help with her come-out," he added. "And her mother hasn't been back to London in so long, it's doubtful she would be of any help, either." His brows furrowed. "Perhaps this is a bit of a blessing," he murmured. When he looked up to find the younger earl staring at him in surprise, he said, "For her, of course. You ... I'm not so sure about."

Charles shook his head. "It's time I reform my ways, my lord.

Time I take a wife and ... and father a child," he struggled to get out, his attention going to the bundle Grandby still held in the crook of his arm before he frowned.

"Well, you needn't make it sound so God awful," Grandby countered. "It's not, you know. It's rather ... wonderful knowing you have a household complete with babes. And all the odors that tend to go with them," he added, sniffing experimentally and then deciding whatever foul odor he had just sniffed wasn't due to his newborn daughter.

The younger earl's eyebrows arched to the middle of his forehead. "*Language*, my lord," he said with a nod to the baby.

Grandby looked suitably admonished. "Then go forth and get married, Wakefield. Let me know if you need any help with Middleton," he added with a sigh.

Charles nodded to the earl and stood up. Leaning over the baby, he carefully lifted the baby's hand with a single finger. He noticed the miniature fingernails, the tiny wrinkles outlining each knuckle, the way her fingers clenched on his as he lifted it to his lips. "It was very good meeting you, my lady," he whispered.

Before Grandby could scold him, Charles made his way out of the study and out of Worthington House.

CHAPTER 23
A MOTHER DISCOVERS THAT SOMEONE IS MISSING

Four o'clock in the afternoon of September 14, 1817
Laura Merriweather entered her parlor at exactly four o'clock, anxious to tell her daughter of what she had discovered that afternoon during her call on Lady Winstead. Although Penelope didn't seem the least bit disturbed by reports of her husband's recent hiring of a mistress—"Goodness, I should think I would need to be rather worried if he hadn't," she had replied with an elegantly arched eyebrow—the news that someone had paid witness to Eleanor climbing into the mail coach in Epping did. "I do hope she is off to visit a friend and not in pursuit of a husband," Penelope had said, all sweetness and light.

Laura had angled her head. "I'm sure the reports are unfounded. I'm not expecting her to her leave until the Little Season actually starts. In a month or so."

But as the half-hour call neared its end, and the two other local ladies in attendance were taking their leave of Lady Winstead's parlor, Laura had begun to wonder if her daughter had, indeed, run away to London. She would know in a few moments. If Eleanor didn't come for tea in her own parlor, then she was no doubt on her way to London.

With none of the servants apparently missing—Laura had asked the butler when she returned—Laura realized Eleanor probably left without the benefit of a chaperone. At least the trip to London would be quick. In fact, she was probably already in London, probably already at her father's townhouse, arranging for modistes and who knew what else in order to prepare for her come-out, Laura reasoned.

She hurried to the escritoire, pulling a sheet of parchment from the top drawer and the quill from the ink pot. Her quick note, penned to Lord Middleton, asked that he send assurances that Eleanor had arrived in London and was staying at his townhouse. She thought of dispatching a footman, but she didn't know if the servant could be trusted to make the thirty-mile trip before sundown and be back sometime the following evening. Perhaps a courier could be hired in Epping.

Shaking her head, she decided she would have her brother decide what was best to do when he returned from his business. After all, how much trouble could Eleanor get into on her way to her father's townhouse? she reasoned.

Laura wondered briefly at whose ball Eleanor would first appear. Wondered at what she might wear. How many dances she would dance. How late she would stay.

Not too late, Laura figured. For she knew her husband wasn't fond of *ton* events, apparently opting instead for quiet evenings in the card room at White's. But she also knew that the sooner Eleanor was betrothed, the happier her husband would be. She knew he wanted his daughter married off, even if it meant divesting himself of the money he had set aside for her dowry. Although he claimed to love her dearly, he also claimed he couldn't live in the same household with a teenage daughter.

Until Eleanor Merriweather was married off and out of his country estate, George Merriweather would remain in London.

CHAPTER 24
A VISIT WITH A COUNTESS

Two-thirty in the afternoon

Lady Clarinda Norwick screwed up her face and watched as the baby she held responded with a grin. "You are a little flirt, aren't you," she whispered as she used a forefinger to rub the girl's belly. "Just like me," she added, stunned at the sudden feeling of sadness that settled over her just then. She looked up and around, wondering if the ghost of her first husband, David Fitzwilliam, might be watching them.

Chiding herself on thinking he might be in the nursery, Clarinda returned her attention to her first daughter. Having just finished nursing, her eyelids drooped in a familiar manner. "Going to fall asleep on me again, are you?" Clarinda whispered. She leaned down and placed a kiss on Diana's forehead, rather satisfied she had been able to put the babe to sleep so easily. The nurse never seemed to manage the feat with the older twin girl. The younger one, far more peaceful and easily put to sleep, was already napping in the nearby bassinet.

"I admit to feeling rather jealous of the attention you shower on your daughters," Daniel Fitzwilliam said from where he leaned against the nursery door's frame. "But then I remind myself that someday you will do the same for my sons, and I find I cannot find fault."

Clarinda regarded her husband with a grin. "I should be the one who is jealous at how much attention you pay to the girls," she countered. The man had become quite adept at holding both babes in his arms whilst he sat in his study and took turns making faces at them. She was quite sure he had held them for nearly an hour the day before, and only gave them up to the nurse because their nappies needed changing.

"But you cannot, as I shower you with attention every night once they are abed," he said as he moved into the nursery and kissed her forehead. Clarinda leaned her head back and angled it to kiss him on the lips. The thought of just what he had done the night before had her entire body shivering in response. The kiss merely reminded her of his gentle caresses and the pleasures he had incited. Another week, and she would once again welcome him into her body. The thought had her insides tumbling about in a most pleasant series of sensations.

"Attention I spend the entire day looking forward to," she murmured happily.

Daniel kissed her again. When he pulled away, he reached down and took the baby from her arms. "As do I. However, right now you have a visitor in the parlor," he said, "So it's my turn to put her to bed," he added as he moved to place the babe in the bassinet she shared with her twin sister.

Clarinda frowned. "Who is it?" she asked as she rocked herself out of the chair and up to her feet. She shook out her skirts, relieved when she didn't feel any wet spots in the sprigged muslin.

"I've absolutely no idea. I intercepted Porter on the stairs and said I would let you know. It is about time for tea, though," Daniel said as he offered her his arm and led her down the grand staircase to the main floor. "Do be sure to have an extra cake or two," he encouraged as he paused before they reached the parlor doors.

Clarinda was about to protest but gave her husband a brilliant smile. "I like how you spoil me," she said, angling her head to one side.

Her first husband had never suggested such a thing, but then, David Fitzwilliam had never known of her craving for cakes or for pink roses. Daniel knew because Daniel had courted her first, courted her and asked for her hand in marriage, and then watched in horror as his older twin brother had stepped in and taken Clarinda as his countess.

Having only been courted by Daniel for a few weeks, and then only for a few stolen moments at a time, Clarinda had had no idea how to tell the twins apart. No idea until she discovered her father said she would be marrying the earl—a rake with a reputation. "I made arrangements long ago," he told her. Then she had only agreed to the match when David assured her he would divest himself of his brothel and gaming hell and give up his mistress. Clarinda had seen to it he made good on his promises when she hired a Bow Street Runner to provide periodic updates on her husband's whereabouts and activities.

True to his word, the Earl of Norwick had been faithful to his young wife for the four years of their marriage. Only four years, for David had been thrown from his horse in Oxford Street and broken his neck when he hit his head on a shipping crate filled with Lord Everly's tropical fish.

That had been six months ago.

"Enjoy the cakes," Daniel whispered before he bestowed another kiss on Clarinda's forehead.

"I will," she replied, giving her skirts another shake before making her way into the parlor. "See you at dinner," she whispered. She turned her attention to her visitor and noted the woman's pale complexion and look of fright.

And her uncanny resemblance to her husband.

"Good afternoon," she ventured, moving farther into the parlor. She waved to one of the settees that faced the low tea table. "Will you join me for some tea and cakes?" she asked brightly, hoping to put the poor thing at ease. Given her guest's appearance, she thought it better to ply her with food and drink rather than attempt to coax an introduction out of her just then.

Clarinda didn't recognize the young woman as someone she had met before, but thought she must be in her mid-twenties. A surreptitious glance at her bare hands—she had removed her gloves and clutched them tightly in her left hand—told Clarinda the young woman was unmarried.

"Yes, of course. It's rather kind of you to offer, my lady," Constance said as she positioned herself in front of a settee. She curtsied. "I am Constance Fitzwilliam," she added with a nod. "I am honored to make your acquaintance."

Clarinda's eyes widened and then she blinked. "Clarinda Fitzwilliam. You must be a relative of Norwick's," she added, relieved at knowing why the woman resembled Daniel.

Constance nodded, her nervousness still evident. "I am his cousin, my lady," she replied with another curtsy.

Her own eyes widening at the revelation, Clarinda studied the young woman who stood before her. She was taller than most aristocratic women, although not so tall she would attract unwanted attention. Her dark hair was the same color as Daniel's, and the set of her eyes and cheekbones were similar enough to the earl's that they might have been siblings.

"Why didn't you introduce yourself to Daniel? To *Norwick*, I mean?" Clarinda asked, waving a hand to indicate the young woman should take a seat.

Constance gave her hostess a slight shake of her head. "I didn't wish to bother the earl. I know he is a busy man," she added.

Clarinda frowned. "He would be pleased to know you're here. In fact, let me ..." She reached over to grab the porcelain bell on the side table, but hesitated when she saw the young woman shake her head. Constance looked positively frightened. "What is it, Miss Fitzwilliam?" Clarinda asked, one of her brows furrowing so a fold of skin appeared between them.

"Please, do not," Constance answered with another shake of her head. "I do not believe the earl would be ... happy to know I am here," she said carefully.

Alarmed, Clarinda rang the bell anyway. When a footman appeared only a second later, she said, "Bring the tea tray, please. And be sure there are cakes," she added, giving Constance a wink.

The footman bowed and took his leave of the parlor. When the two women were once again alone, Clarinda regarded her guest with an arched eyebrow. "Do tell me what this is about, won't you?"

Constance allowed a nod. "Of course, my lady," she agreed with a sigh. After a long pause, she explained how she had met with the Norwick solicitor in Sussex. "Imagine my shock when I learned my inheritance was missing," Constance said. "Mr. Asherman, the solicitor in Sussex, knew I would have to come to London. He was the one who recommended I meet with Mr. Barton," she explained, "Which I did just before I arrived here. His news was not good, I fear, and he was the one who recommended I pay a call on my cousin."

Clarinda angled her head, rather concerned for the young woman who sat across from her. She was about to speak when a maid appeared with the tea tray.

"I'll serve," she said as the maid lowered a tray to the low table in front of Clarinda. She smiled when she noted the number of cakes that were artfully arranged on the porcelain salver along with a selection of lemon biscuits and berry scones. "How do you take your tea, Miss Fitzwilliam?" she asked.

The younger woman noted how the countess addressed her. "Connie, please. A bit of milk and two lumps of sugar," she replied, secretly glad for the opportunity to take tea the way she was accustomed to doing so in Sussex. Since moving to London, she had chosen to eschew the milk and use only one lump of sugar as a cost-saving measure. "I implore you not to bother my cousin with my problems, though," she added as Clarinda handed her the steaming cup of tea.

"Nonsense," the countess responded. "The Norwick earldom is responsible for your situation, and it shall make good on your inheritance," she added as she helped herself to a cake. "Would you like a biscuit or a scone?" she asked as she held out the decorated porcelain plate on which the sweets were arranged.

"Thank you," Constance said as she helped herself to a biscuit. "Truth be told, I have reason to believe my inheritance may have been ..." She paused, not sure if she should tell Lady Norwick of the solicitor's assertion that the monies were missing because they were stolen. "Taken," she finally said.

In the middle of eating one of the cakes, Clarinda stared at the Norwick cousin. She swallowed and quickly took a sip of her tea, glad she hadn't had a mouthful of tea when Constance made the comment, for she was sure the tea would have ended up sprayed all over the tea tray.

"Taken?" she repeated. "As in ... *stolen?*" she whispered, not wanting any nearby servants to overhear their conversation.

"Yes," Constance nodded before taking another sip of tea. She nearly sighed aloud at the pleasant taste. *So much better than what we've been drinking!* she thought as she reveled in the high-quality steaming liquid. "It's possible the money has merely been ... moved, or borrowed, perhaps. But, if so, the solicitor in Sussex is unaware of when or what it might have been used for." She didn't add that she suspected her father might have gambled it away, despite his assertion that she would be set for life.

Clarinda frowned, her eyebrows drawn together so that the fold of skin appeared between her brows. An alarm bell was going off in her head, one that wouldn't subside until she had a satisfactory answer for the cousin. "Given Daniel ... *Norwick*," she corrected herself, "Has been personally seeing to the earldom's finances, I cannot imagine the inheritance would have been ... *borrowed* or otherwise used for some other purpose. I'll take up the matter with him when I have dinner with him later this evening. Or before, should I have occasion to see him," she promised with a nod. "Now, do tell me where you're staying whilst in Mayfair," she said as a means of changing the subject.

Constance held her breath a moment, realizing she didn't have an answer unless she told the truth.

"If I tell you, will you promise not to tell Norwick?" she asked in a whisper.

The alarm bell sounded even louder in Clarinda's head. "Of course," she finally said, realizing the young woman wouldn't share her secret until Clarinda promised to keep the information from Daniel. *What exactly had happened to cause Constance to fear Daniel?*

"I am staying at the Norwick terrace in Curzon Street," Constance whispered. "With my maid, whom I am afraid I shall have to dismiss by month's end, as I won't be able to afford her salary when my funds run out."

Clarinda felt a bit of relief coupled with concern. At least the Norwick cousin wasn't staying in an expensive hotel or paying exorbitant rent for a Mayfair townhouse. "You're welcome to stay there as long as you need to," Clarinda insisted as she helped herself to another cake. "It's been quite forgotten since Norwick last used it." That had been back when David housed one of his mistresses there, back before Clarinda had agreed to marry him. *Forgotten* was not exactly the truth, though, as another courtesan had lived there until recently. Lord Pettigrew's mistress, Angelika, had left the viscount's employ and was apparently happily married to a baronet, the man rather proud of an Italian wife who looked as if she could be the sister of Adeline Carlington, Marquess of Morganfield.

At the look of surprise on Constance's face, Clarinda realized the young woman feared she would be evicted from the residence. "Tell me, Miss Fitzwilliam. Are you ... betrothed or expecting an offer of marriage anytime soon?" Clarinda asked, finishing off the cake.

Constance sighed. "I am not, nor do I expect an offer of marriage, my lady," she replied.

"Clare, please," the countess insisted. "I don't understand. Are there no worthy gentlemen in Sussex desiring your hand in marriage?" she asked outright.

Wincing, Constance shook her head. "I haven't had interest

from the males in Boxgrove for several years now, which isn't surprising since most of the men are Benedictine monks," she said with a wan smile. "If I may speak plainly, I find I prefer I find I prefer life as a spinster," she explained.

"I see," Clarinda replied with a nod. Having heard similar claims whilst in Lady Torrington's parlor from several older unmarried women, she wondered at the appeal of living with only a companion and attending events without the benefit of a chaperone. "I understand," she finally said with a nod. "Then, is it your intention to return to Boxgrove once you've secured you inheritance?" she asked carefully. She imagined life in the small village would be rather lonely for an unattached woman.

Constance nodded. "Yes. A stablehand is looking after the horses, and the butler and housekeeper are under the earl's employ," she explained, "So if the earl allows it, I can continue to look after the estate."

"Horses?" Clarinda repeated, leaning forward.

"Yes. They're my pride and joy, my lady," Constance said with the first real smile Clarinda had seen her display. "The estate has excellent pasture land, so they do not cost much to keep."

"You ride, then?" Clarinda asked.

"Oh, yes," Constance replied happily. She didn't add that she preferred to ride astride, and not just because she had outgrown her child-sized side-saddle. "I find a good ride is invigorating, and all eight horses love to run as much as I let them."

Clarinda blinked as she remembered something her first husband had said long ago. "Is one of them a racehorse?" she asked then.

Constance sobered. "Mr. Tuttlebaum was at one time," she answered carefully. "He won all his races. But my father gambled away all his winnings." She stopped speaking and gave a sigh of frustration. "I apologize. You didn't need to hear that," she whispered before taking a breath and letting it out again.

The countess angled her head to one side. "Mr. Tuttlebaum must be quite a valuable stud," she remarked, wondering who was seeing to those arrangements. *The stablehand?* She rather doubted it.

"Oh, he's only sired a couple of horses, my lady, and both of his colts are in the stables."

Before Clarinda could react to this bit of news, a footman appeared at the threshold. "I beg your pardon, my lady, but Lady Pettigrew is in the vestibule."

Constance was up in an instant. "I should be going." she announced, as if she had been waiting for an excuse to take her leave of Norwick House. "Thank you for agreeing to see me. And for the tea, my lady," she said as she gave a quick curtsy and hurried out of the parlor.

The countess stared after the retreating back of Constance Fitzwilliam, not just stunned by her sudden departure but stunned by her news. For she found herself wondering if Constance Fitzwilliam's inheritance wasn't money at all but rather what resided in the stables at the Norwick estate in Boxgrove. Before she could give it more thought, though, Lady Pettigrew appeared on the parlor threshold, and Clarinda was forced to play hostess again.

CHAPTER 25
CONFESSION IS GOOD FOR THE SOUL

hree o'clock in the afternoon

"You're quite sure you saw the lady in yellow go into that house?" Randall asked of the street urchin who was quick to take his sixpence, his forefinger directed at the Park Lane residence better known as Norwick House. Despite the young woman's head start when leaving the solicitor's office, Randall had simply retraced their steps, occasionally catching sight of her bright yellow ensemble as he hurried along. When he made it to Park Lane, however, she had disappeared.

"Aye, guv'nor," the boy nodded.

"How long ago?"

The filthy boy seemed to think on it awhile before giving a one-shoulder shrug. "I dunno. Not long, though."

Randall gave the boy a nod and another sixpence. Truth be told, he was quite surprised to find an urchin in this part of Mayfair. Boys of his ilk seemed more prevalent in the Seven Dials. Or in Whitechapel. "Fair enough," he said, wondering how we was going to approach Miss Fitzwilliam when she took her leave of Norwick House.

Just as he was about to walk in that direction, a town coach pulled into the half-circle drive. He recognized the seal on the coach

as that of Lord Pettigrew, so he wasn't surprised to see Lady Pettigrew step down from the coach when a footman opened the door.
He watched as the older woman ascended the front steps and
decided to bide his time. Once she was announced, he rather imagined Miss Fitzwilliam—or her maid—would take her leave.

He wasn't disappointed.

The lady in yellow appeared at the dark green double doors only
moments after Lady Pettigrew had disappeared into the house, her
yellow parasol popping open in response to the sudden wash of
sunlight on her face.

Randall gulped and swallowed.

He was quite sure she was the woman who had been the maid
that morning in the park. And she was positively beautiful. Lovelier
now that she was properly dressed and wore a stylish hat instead of
the serviceable bonnet she had been wearing that morning.

He made his way up the half-circle drive so he would meet her
when she made it to the bottom of the stairs.

"Oh!" Constance managed to get out when she was forced to
stop or walk into the marquess.

"Miss Fitzwilliam, I presume?" Randall said as he bowed and
reached for her gloved hand. He brushed his lips over the back of it,
aware of how she stiffened.

"Mr. Roderick, isn't it?" she responded, giving him a curtsy.

"Indeed," he replied, rather happy she remembered his name.
"May I escort you?"

Constance dared a quick glance to her right and then to her left.
"I ... I suppose," she said, her cheeks flushed with a pink cast.

Randall offered her his arm. "To your home?" he asked. "Or
would you like to walk in the park?"

Her look of guilt was quickly replaced with one of contrition. "I
feel as if I have been walking all day," she replied.

The marquess was about to agree but thought it better he not
admit to having followed her through half of Mayfair that day.

"Home, then," he said with a nod.

Constance sighed. "Yes, I suppose," she agreed.

"Or, if we walk just a bit further, we could be at Gunter's Tea Shop. We could enjoy an ice whilst you explain why it is you and your maid exchanged identities earlier today."

Angling her head to one side as they made their way toward Curzon Street, Constance sighed. The thought of an ice was enough of an incentive to walk the additional two streets or so, but she wondered about propriety. She hardly knew the man on whose arm hers rested as they walked. She could hardly accept the offer of an ice, and she dared not spend the bit of coin she had left to get her through the month in London.

Randall regarded the woman on his arm for a time before he realized she was uncomfortable strolling with him. "I mean you no harm," he said. "And, in fact, I only mean to learn more about you since you so thoroughly intrigued me with your subterfuge earlier today."

"Subterfuge?" she countered, her eyes widening with his words. "I assure you, there was nothing done to offend or ... *mislead* you," she added hastily.

"Your maid introduced herself as you," he stated.

Sighing, Constance angled her head to the other side. "An unfortunate mistake on her part—"

"That you did not correct," Randall interrupted.

"Because I did not wish to embarrass her," she said quickly. "She is uncomfortable in social situations and could not think of a suitable name on such short notice."

"She could not use her own?" Randall countered, rather liking how the young woman defended her servant.

Constance gave a shrug. "I have already admonished her on the matter." She paused a moment. "Look, I know now that I should have insisted my maid not adopt my identity whilst she went about the park, but I assure you, it will not happen again."

Randall regarded Constance for a moment, rather glad she wasn't the maid she had appeared to be that morning. He had already wondered about why he found himself attracted to maids.

"Your loyalty to your servant is to be commended," he said then, leading them east on Curzon Street toward Berkeley Square.

Surprised by his comment, the young lady looked confused. "Thank you, I think," she managed. "I just ... I wanted her to learn how to get about in London should she ... should I be unable to continue to employ her." She pursed her lips, frustrated to hear the words spoken aloud. They were a testament to her failure in securing her inheritance, and despite the positive meeting with Lady Norwick, she couldn't help but believe her cousin would deny her request for funds. "I fear she won't gain employment in a suitable house, and I hate to think of her on the streets of London without a place to live, or without a protector—"

"Nonsense," Randall interrupted. "If it comes to that, she can work at my house in Cavendish Square," he said shortly. "I believe there will be an opening for a maid as early as next month, in fact," he added, thinking if he took a wife, there would be a need for a lady's maid.

Whirling to face him, Constance's move forced the two to stop in their tracks. "You would do that?" she whispered, her words out before she considered she hardly knew the man with whom she walked. If he had a house in Cavendish Square, though, it meant he was probably a physician or owned a lucrative business. And everyone knew the houses in Cavendish Square were some of the very best in that part of London.

Randall regarded the young woman for several seconds, rather liking how she gazed at him, her blue eyes full of question and query and gratitude. "For you, I would. Yes," he said with a nod.

The words were out before he could censor them. Before he realized how they could be interpreted. How they could be misconstrued.

Although relief had settled Constance somewhat, the marquess' last words had her on her guard once again. "In exchange for *what*, my lord?" she asked, a blaze of anger appearing in her eyes.

Randall angled his head, curious as to what she implied with her question. He finally shook his head. "Nothing. That is, nothing but a simple 'thank you'. What ... what did you think I meant?" he demanded to know, pretending to be offended by her comment.

A bright blush colored her face just then, a blush the marquess found rather fetching. "The worst, of course," she whispered.

Then Randall really did feel offended, but he put himself in her place. She had no idea he knew all about her, no idea he had followed her about town as she looked for her missing inheritance. "As I said before, you have nothing to fear from me," he repeated. "However, I am in a position to help, should you require it. I have the good fortune of having a good fortune, which gives me the means to help where I can," he explained. "Were you, perhaps, paying a visit to an office in Oxford Street earlier today?" he ventured carefully. "I was sure I saw a woman in yellow whilst I paid a visit to Lady E's 'Finding Work for the Wounded'," he added when he saw her look of surprise.

Constance finally nodded. "I was visiting with a solicitor. He was recommended to me. I was hoping he might be able to help me with something."

Randall feigned ignorance of the situation, hoping she would provide her side of the tale. "And will he?" he prompted.

Sighing, Constance gave a shrug. "I rather doubt it. I'm beginning to wonder if ... well, it is of no matter now," she hedged, wishing she hadn't allowed the gentleman's question.

Sure she was about to shed some tears, Randall considered reaching for his handkerchief when he realized her words were more of disappointment than sadness, which meant she expected to hear what she had been told. "You ... you don't seemed surprised by what you've discovered," he replied, his brows furrowing. He was quite sure she was going to say something about her inheritance, but she didn't.

"I am not," she agreed, shaking her head. "My father was a gambler. Whatever monies he made, either from the Norwick estate in Sussex or from his one racehorse, he gambled away."

One racehorse? The solicitor had implied there was a stable of horses. Surely there would be more than one suitable for the racing circuit. But perhaps they were too old. Most races required a horse be three years old.

Or perhaps they were too young. A horse had to be six to compete in the Ascot.

"Was the horse a winner?" Randall asked, wondering if he might have seen the nag in action at the Royal Ascot or at Epsom Downs.

"Mr. Tuttlebaum won every race he ran. He started when he was three and then won the Ascot when he was six," Constance claimed.

Randall inhaled sharply, now quite sure he had seen the horse in action. "How old is he now?" he asked, thinking the horse wouldn't be too old to use as a stud. He made a mental note to speak with Alistair Comber, the head groom at Lord Mayfield's stables. The young man had been quite helpful the prior racing season, even if Randall's horse had come in second.

"He's nearly nine," Constance replied. "Still runs as fast as he can. His brother is almost six. There's a course set up on the grounds near Boxgrove where I live," she explained. "I like to ride him and Mr. Wiggins there. It's very invigorating."

Randall watched as Constance's face lit up with her description of the horse, witnessed how she seemed to come alive when remembering riding him.

Invigorating, indeed, he thought, imagining the woman on horseback, her dark hair loose from its pins and flowing behind her as the horse raced around the track. In an effort to tamp down the sudden arousal he felt at her excitement, he turned his thoughts back to the horse. He was about to ask how much the stud fees were when he realized the young woman probably didn't know about matters of money. He hoped a man of business was seeing to it, though. The income might be a way for her to remain independent.

He was about to ask who her man of business might be when he realized he didn't *want* her to be independent. At least, not so independent that she would eschew his presence in her life. The thought brought him up a bit short when he remembered his thoughts of her earlier that morning. He had spent a good part of the day either in pursuit of her or in her company. He knew more about her than he knew about any other woman of the *ton*.

And he found he wanted to know even more.

They were in sight of the tea shop when he was about to ask who her man of business might be. The solicitor mentioned there was a family solicitor in Sussex—wouldn't that man know if there were income to be made off of a retired racehorse?

"Have you been to Gunter's before?" he asked as he held the door open for her. A row of open carriages lined the road in front of the confectioner, their occupants engaged in conversation while they drank lemonade or enjoyed dishes of sorbet under the shade of the plane maple trees lining the square.

Constance shook her head as her eyes widened. Her attention wasn't on the tea shop but rather on a town coach that was pulling away from the curb. "Poor thing," she murmured, her face taking on a look of worry.

"What is it?" Randall asked, following her line of sight. He watched the conveyance she seemed to be studying but didn't recognize its occupants.

"The right lead. He's lame. His back leg. See how he favors it?" she replied, nodding in the direction of the departing town coach.

Randall turned his attention to the horses that pulled the town coach and realized after watching them for a moment that the horse she described was, indeed, lame, although he wasn't obviously so. "You've quite an eye, Miss Fitzwilliam. I rather doubt the driver even realizes it," he responded, half-tempted to go after the coach and inform the driver. But the busy Berkeley Square traffic swallowed up the town coach, and he was forced to turn his attention back to the woman on his arm. "I'm sure he'll realize it and see to its care once he's back in the mews, my lady," he said quietly.

Constance glanced up at him, apparently wanting to believe him. "Of course," she replied with a nod. She glanced up at the shingle above the tea shop. "I have not been here before, Mr. Roderick," she murmured, gripping his arm tighter as they entered the crowded shop. "But I have certainly heard of it."

Randall felt a hint of satisfaction at feeling her hold on him increase. He thought by now she probably trusted him enough to share more about herself. She already seemed to trust him with her concerns for horseflesh. What was her favorite color? What was her favorite past-time, if not riding a horse?

"What is your favorite flavor?" Randall asked, giving a nod to a fellow lord when the man acknowledged him from where he sat in the back of the shop.

Constance appeared stunned. "There's more than one?" she countered. When Randall pointed to the menu board, her eyes widened even more. "I have absolutely no idea!" she replied, her eyes taking in the list and then darting about the small tables surrounded by fashionably dressed patrons as if she might find a flavor she liked that way.

"Do you trust me?" he asked, his manner most serious.

The young woman stilled herself, a shiver of excitement passing through her body and forcing her breath to catch. "I suppose," she finally allowed.

Momentarily appeased, Randall led her to a table that had just been vacated. He pulled out a chair for her and took the one directly across from her. A waiter appeared, his pencil poised over a small tablet of paper. "Good afternoon. What may I get for you?" he asked.

"Two lemonades, and for ices, we'd like a strawberry and a bergamot pear," he stated, watching Constance's reaction as the waiter gave a short bow and hurried off. Randall wasn't disappointed to see her look of anticipation turn to one of pure joy.

"I love strawberries," she said in a hoarse whisper. "Unless you ordered it for yourself," she said, her eyes widening.

Randall felt a bit of relief at hearing her claim. "I did not," he replied with a grin. Had she said strawberries made her break out in hives, he would have given her the bergamot pear, his favorite flavor. "What else do you love?" he asked, realizing just then he had never before asked the question of a woman. *How odd!* After spending so many evenings in the company of women, how was it he was only now asking it of his companion?

Having glanced about the shop, Constance returned her attention to Randall. "Horses. Roses. Bubbles in my bath. Champagne. The color purple." Her eyes widened as a carefree giddiness seemed to possess her.

Randall swallowed, stunned at her simple responses. He had expected she might mention Paris or Rome or the Kew Gardens, or gemstones like sapphires or diamonds. "Easy to please then, are you?" he responded, allowing a smile at her infectious behavior.

Her happiness seemed to abate some. "I ... I suppose," she replied uncertainly, her eyes once again darting about the room, her manner betraying her nervousness.

Damnation!

Randall realized his mistake too late. "What else do you like?" he asked, hoping to restore her unguarded manner. But before she could answer, the waiter appeared with their order.

"Thank you," he said as he gave the man a coin. "Keep the change," he added when he saw the waiter reach into his apron pockets.

"Much obliged, my lord," the waiter said before scurrying away.

Randall lifted his lemonade and held it up. "I hope you enjoy it, my lady," he said before he drank nearly half the glass.

Constance tore her eyes from Randall's cravat, her attention having been on his throat as he swallowed the lemonade. On his Adam's apple as it bobbed up and down. She couldn't remember having noticed it on another man, probably because it was always hidden by a cravat. Or a second chin.

She blinked as she turned her attention to the pink confection in the porcelain dish. "I most assuredly will," she said, lifting a spoon the waiter had delivered with their order. "I will pay you back, of course," she said as she regarded the sorbet for a moment before bringing the spoon to her lips.

"You will do no such thing, my lady," Randall replied, tucking into his own dish of sorbet. "I appreciate your company. Indeed, I hope that I might be allowed to spend more time in your company," he added carefully, watching to see her reaction.

In the middle of her first taste of the sorbet, Constance's eyes widened. She swallowed and regarded Randall for a moment. "For what purpose?" she asked, suspicious of the man's motives.

Randall realized he might have said too much. "The Little Season doesn't start for several weeks, and I find myself rather ... lonely. I merely wish for the company of someone to walk with me in the park or ... have an ice with me here," he explained. "There is nothing else implied, I assure you," he added, realizing she might be left with the wrong impression.

She was left with the wrong impression.

Constance left her spoon in her dish and moved to stand up.

"My lady, please," Randall said quickly, one ungloved hand waving to indicate she should retake her seat. "Your hasty exit will be noticed," he warned with an arched eyebrow. "Please, do not leave me looking as if I have offended when no offense was intended."

Glancing about to see if anyone had noticed her sudden move, Constance pretended to readjust the skirts of her gown as she slowly lowered herself back into her chair. "I am not offended, Mr. Roderick," she said, her eyes going to the rather large signet ring he wore. The dark purple stone embedded in a gold band reminded her of what she had admitted only moments before. *Goodness!* She had dropped her guard and given him a list of everything she loved! He probably thought her a mindless chit. "I am merely being—"

"Cautious," he finished for her. "Yes, I understand," Randall agreed. "As you should be. London is not a town in which a young woman should be walking about without the benefit of a companion or chaperone. I merely wish to act in that capacity."

Constance relaxed in her chair and regarded her dish of sorbet. The man seemed sincere. And the well-dressed man a few tables away seemed to have recognized him when he gave them a wave upon their entrance to the tea shop. "Very well," she finally said. She took another bite and allowed the cold confection to slide down her throat. Realizing her comments had stilled their conversation, she wondered what she might say to restore the ease they had enjoyed only moments ago.

Remembering how she had offered information about herself, she thought to coax some out of her companion. "Tell me, Mr. Roderick. What do *you* love?" she asked boldly.

Randall allowed a grin, understanding her need to clear the air and let him know she accepted his explanation. "Well, now," he replied with a nod, realizing he couldn't say things like "a well-turned ankle" or "bedding a woman", not that he particularly *loved* bedding a woman. At least, not like he used to. Not when he knew there would be nothing beyond the bedding. No waking up in each other's arms. No breakfast together in the parlor. No dinner together. No sitting by the fire until it was time to share a bed.

Randall shook himself from his reverie, hoping he hadn't paused too long before providing an answer. "I can admit to loving a good scotch. Reading a book." He paused, his face screwed up in disgust. "Not those dealing with farming, however. I am speaking of fiction here," he clarified. After another pause, he added, "My horse." He said this last as he dared a glance in her direction, secretly glad to see her look of approval. "And, at some point in my life, sooner rather than later, I would hope to love the woman I marry. And my children, of course."

Constance was forced to tear her gaze away from the handsome man who sat across from her. Did he have any idea of how his words affected her just then? She would never marry, so there would never be a husband to love. Never a man with whom to share her bed. A man to wake up next to every morning. A man to read the paper while they enjoyed the morning meal in the breakfast parlor. A man with whom to eat dinner. To sit with by the fire once he had enjoyed his brandy and a cheroot in his study.

She would never have the children he spoke of so sweetly, but she found herself imagining them. She imagined what they might look like given their handsome father. Imagined him lifting them into his arms, hoisting them into the air. Imagined hearing their high-pitched voices as they giggled and begged him to do it again.

Her chest felt as if a great weight had settled on it. Sure tears would form any moment, she tried to concentrate on her strawberry ice, tried to remember how delicious the cold treat tasted. When she could not, she reached for the lemonade and took a long drink, trying hard not to allow her gaze to rest on Randall Roderick.

Did he have any idea of just how handsome he was? How debonair he appeared with his hair cut and combed into place so precisely? Did he know his eyes were the perfect color of *everything?* That the fine lines on either side of them gave him the air of someone who had lived a good life and enjoyed it? And then there was that jaw line, so bold, with just a hint of stubble that hadn't been there this morning when they first met. His mouth ... well, she had to swallow when she considered what it might be like to kiss those lips.

Or be kissed by them.

A delightful shiver made its way to her core, forcing her breath to catch and reminding her she was on the verge of tears.

Constance set down her glass and placed her hands in her lap. She managed to take a deep breath without sobbing and regarded her escort for a moment. "You really should warn a woman before you say such things," she admonished him.

Randall angled his head to one side, wondering what had her scolding him. He had spoken of a wife and children. He had spoken hoping she might see herself in the role of his wife, for he was quite sure he wanted her in his life, and he knew he wasn't looking for a mistress.

"I apologize, my lady," he said quietly. "I really do love my horse," he teased. "He's a cross between a ..."

Constance giggled, one hand moving to cover her mouth as the sound burbled forth.

"You dare laugh at my love of a horse?" he asked rhetorically, a smile replacing the dour expression he had displayed only moments before.

"Mr. Roderick!" she replied in a hoarse whisper. "That is not what I meant, and you know it," she said as she leaned toward him.

Given the small size of the table, Randall thought he could kiss her without having to leave his seat. "Ah, so you were moved by my words of love for a wife and children I do not yet have?"

Constance sobered and leaned back. "I was," she admitted with a nod. "It is refreshing to know there are romantic men in London."

Randall sighed. "There are, indeed. Like them, I can imagine seeing to it my wife has bubbles in her bath as well her champagne glass, and a stable full of horses. And I would arrange for her salon to be redone so she is surrounded by roses and the color purple."

Gasping at his words, Constance stared at him for a long moment before she blinked and shook her head. "Your wife will be a very lucky woman, indeed," she murmured, feeling jealousy at the idea of someone other than herself enjoying his generosity.

As much as she wanted what he suggested with his words, she knew it could never be for her.

Taking a breath, Constance glanced down at the table and realized he had finished both his lemonade and his sorbet. "Now, perhaps you can tell me all about your horse while we make our way back," she suggested brightly, the quiet moment gone.

Randall gave her a nod. "As you wish, my lady," he said.

As they took their leave of Gunter's, the waiter hurried to open the door for them. "Thank you, guv'nor," he said as he gave them a nod.

Randall placed his top hat on his head and gave it a thump on its lid to be sure it was secure. Holding his arm out for Constance, he was relieved she took it without him having to invite her to do so.

"Why did he call you 'governor'?" Constance asked, noting how the man matched his steps to her own, despite his longer legs.

Randall gave a shrug. "Can't say as I know," he replied quickly, not wanting to tell her he was a titled man just then. "Now, my horse is a cross between a Cleveland Bay and a descendant of an Arabian that was bred to other bays," he said, picking up where he had left off in the tea shop.

"A half Thoroughbred, then?" Constance queried.

Randall allowed a chuckle. "Half of that and half of that

again, I suppose," he replied. "Apollo is large, but he's fast, and he has the stamina for a hunt or a good ride around my entire property."

Constance frowned. *Goodness! He must own all of Cavendish Square and half of London if his horse has the stamina he claims it does.* "Do you ride him in Cavendish Square then?" she asked.

The marquess laughed out loud. "No. He's not even in London, my lady," he said with a grin. "I wouldn't subject him to such torture as having to live in London. He's on my property in Reading. Not too far west of here," he added, in case she wasn't familiar with the geography.

A bit surprised the man would have a townhouse in Curzon Street, a house in Cavendish Square, *and* property in Reading, Constance was about to ask him what else he might own when she realized he was watching her. "What is it?" she asked as she angled her head so she could see him better.

"You're not the least bit impressed, are you, my lady?" he asked with a smirk.

Her eyes widening with his claim, Constance shook her head. "I am if you wish me to be," she countered. "From the moment you introduced yourself this morning, I figured you had to be well-to-do." When Randall displayed an arched eyebrow, she added, "From your manner of speech, and your clothes, and your boots. And your ... address, I suppose."

Randall blinked. "You know where I live then?" he asked in surprise before remembering he had mentioned the house in Cavendish Square. *Of course, that was the address she was referring to,* he thought.

A blush colored Constance's face. "I wasn't sure until I saw you leave early this morning. You were headed toward the park."

Randall nodded, realizing he wasn't the only one who noticed what his neighbors were doing. *Goodness!* He had been watching her come and go without any thought to her doing the same of him! "Truth be told, I saw you earlier today, as well," he admitted. "When you and your maid returned from the park."

Constance nodded. "I thought you did. I do hope you've forgiven me for my maid's behavior earlier."

"Of course," he answered, giving her gloved hand a pat with his own. He would have to be requesting the same of her once she learned his true identity.

If it ever came to that.

Realizing they would be coming upon her townhouse— or Norwick's, rather—within the next street, he turned the subject back to one of her comments. "Now you must tell me about the horses you love," he insisted. Even without looking at her, he could tell the topic had her filled with joy.

"There are eight of them."

"Eight?" he repeated in surprise. *All racehorses?* he nearly asked.

"Yes, and they all have the sweetest of temperaments and the most attractive coats."

"Indeed?" he interjected. "What breeds are they?"

Constance sighed. "The mare, Amasia, is a Cleveland Bay—"

"Good choice," Randall said with a nod.

"And her colt, Mr. Tuttlebaum, is a Thoroughbred, as is his younger brother, Mr. Wiggins. Then there are five others, four of whom are draft horses we use for haying, and finally, one who is Yorkshire Trotter. The Yorky is the one I like to ride," she added as she returned her attention to Randall. Her smile faltered when she saw his expression. "What is it, Mr. Roderick?" she asked in a whisper.

Randall had to prevent himself from pulling her into his arms and simply kissing her senseless. Did the chit know how she lit up when she spoke of her horses? How she turned into a completely different person when she described life in her native Sussex? "Nothing, my lady," he said. "But I must commend you for your love of horseflesh. I have never met a woman who was so enamored with horses. It's a pleasure to know one such as you exists."

The pleasant sensation of flutterbies passed through her belly, forcing her to inhale sharply and hope the man didn't notice. "Thank you, Mr. Roderick," she finally replied.

"But what of the sires?" he asked, remembering her comment about the mare and two colts. The one had been a racehorse. *What of the younger Thoroughbred?*

"Bounder?" she replied.

Randall frowned and stutter-stepped. "Are you accusing me of being a bounder, Miss Fitzwilliam?" he asked, trying to decide if he she felt offended or happy she was comfortable enough with him to tease him.

Her wide eyes told him she wasn't teasing.

"Of course not!" she replied. "Unless you are?" she added, one eye nearly winking.

Chuckling, Randall shook his head. He had been called far worse than "bounder" in his younger years. "Tell me about this ... bounder, then," he encouraged.

Constance gave a slight shrug. "Bounder is Viscount Bostwick's Arabian. He sired both of Amasia's colts," she said in an off-hand manner.

Randall nearly stopped in his tracks. *Zeus!* Was it possible the younger Thoroughbred could be a racer? "Do you plan to race Mr. ... Mr. Wiggins, was it?" he asked, hoping he remembered the name correctly.

"Yes, but I rather doubt it," she replied with a shrug of one shoulder. "The racing, I mean," she clarified, wishing she could see his reaction more clearly. But Randall was facing forward and she couldn't make out his expression.

"A bit of a shame. Seems he might be worth a try on the track," he commented, wishing they weren't already at her townhouse. He wanted to know more about Mr. Wiggins. "Will I see you again in the park? Tomorrow morning?" Randall asked just as they arrived at her townhouse.

Her eyes widening, Constance wondered if he thought to arrange a liaison. Perhaps he *was* a bounder. "I don't yet know my plans for tomorrow," she managed to say before digging her key out of her reticule.

Randall felt a stab of disappointment. "I'll be happy to escort you whilst you're in the park, should our paths cross again," he said. "I should like to speak with you more about your horses. And thank you for going to Gunter's with me. I hope we can do it again very soon." He lifted her hand and kissed the back of it before tipping is hat. "Good day."

Constance gave him a curtsy. "Thank you, Mr. Roderick." Without a look back, she quickly ascended the few stairs to the front door and disappeared inside.

CHAPTER 26
A MEETING WITH A FATHER

Four o'clock in the afternoon

"Has Lord Middleton arrived yet?" Lord Wakefield asked of the footman who held open the front door to White's. The men's club seemed busier this afternoon, no doubt because many of its members had returned to London for the start of the fall sessions of Parliament. However, few balls or soirées had been scheduled; most invitations would go out next week for the Little Season events.

"I believe Lord Middleton is in the card room, my lord," the footman answered as he took the earl's hat. Despite the slight chill in the air, Charles had elected to leave his townhouse without a coat. He tossed the man a shilling and made his way through the club, nodding at acquaintances and passing by others with his eyes on the card room door.

Once inside, he glanced around until he spied Eleanor's father at one of the whist tables. Although he was tempted to simply walk straight to the Earl of Middleton, he instead wandered about, looking as if he were searching for a game to join. When he finally stood next to the earl's table, he held his hands at his back and waited until Middleton gave him a glance. "Wakefield," the fellow earl acknowledged with a nod.

"Middleton," Charles replied. "When you're finished here, I

would appreciate a word, please," he said and then took his leave of the card room.

The Earl of Middleton watched the Charles Goodwin take his leave of the room, wondering why the younger man would want a word with him. His curiosity piqued, he gave his fellow card players an apology and made his way out to the main room of the men's club.

He found the Earl of Wakefield settled into an upholstered wing chair, a glass of whiskey held in one hand as he stared at the fire. "Curiosity has me stepping away from a rather lucrative game of whist," Middleton said as he took a seat in an adjacent chair.

"I didn't wish to interrupt," Charles replied as he straightened, rather surprised at the other earl's sudden appearance.

Middleton frowned. "Good God, Wakefield. You look as if you haven't slept in days. Whatever is wrong?"

Charles blinked. He thought he had actually slept better than normal the night before, Middleton's daughter tucked against his front for most of the night. "Have you heard from your daughter recently?" he asked, not sure how else to broach the subject of Eleanor.

Middleton shook his head. "Well, I had a note from her saying she wanted some help with her come-out, but I haven't yet replied," he hedged. "Why, pray tell, do you ask?"

Charles let out the breath he had been holding. At least the Bow Street Runners hadn't been dispatched. "I would like to request your permission to marry her," he said, surprised at how easily the words came out.

The Earl of Middleton regarded Charles with an arched eyebrow. He had a passing thought to laugh at the younger earl, but the man's countenance didn't appear as if he were in the mood for humor. "How do you even know my daughter?" he finally asked.

Charles felt relief at not being denied outright. "She was in attendance with you at a dinner at Worthington House. Shortly after Grandby married the Worthington widow," he answered, hoping the earl wouldn't require more of a reason.

He did.

"How is it you want to marry Eleanor after only one dinner? One dinner that took place over ... two years ago," he amended, his suspicion evident in his furrowed brows.

Charles let out the breath he had been holding. "She's rather ... beautiful, my lord, and I am in need of a wife. 'Tis time I did my duty and took a wife."

Lord Middleton stared at Charles for a moment, his mouth opening and closing like one of the goldfish in Lord Everly's giant fish tank. "Why my Eleanor?" the earl finally asked.

Charles was about to reply with, "Why not?" but thought better of it. "Truth be told, I ... I feel affection for her," he said, which wasn't entirely untrue, for he found himself rather enamored with the chit. He had to be, given his reaction to her sobs when she had opened her valise to find some of her belongings missing. He had truly felt sorry for her, a feeling he didn't think he was capable of unless there was some affection involved.

Narrowing his eyes, Middleton stared at Charles. "Did you ruin her ... somehow?" he asked in a whisper.

Sure he had been discovered, Charles nodded. "Yes. Yes, I did. And I would apologize, but I find I cannot as I truly wish her to be my wife."

The Earl of Middleton stared at him for a moment before bursting into laughter. When Charles merely frowned at him, no doubt thinking he was a candidate for Bedlam, Middleton sobered. "Your confession was so believable, I could not—"

"Yesterday, your daughter took the mail coach to London and was kidnapped by Lucy Gibbons," Charles whispered, realizing the earl wasn't going to take him seriously unless he told him the whole sordid story. "She was sent to my house last night. As a birthday gift. I didn't recognize her at first. However, the fact that she's been in my home—and is still there, in fact—means she is hopelessly ruined. I wish to make it right by making her my wife. Will you please give your permission so that I might obtain a special license and marry her in a day or two?"

Middleton stared at Charles for a long time, his look of amusement slowly changing to one of anger. "Is this some kind of sick joke?" he asked.

Charles shook his head. "I assure you, it is not."

The two earls stared at one another, eyes blazing. "What have you done to my Eleanor?" the older one demanded to know.

Closing his eyes in an effort to rein in his sudden anger at the other earl's reaction, Charles sighed. "I stripped her bare and made mad, passionate love to her. I kissed her. I held her in my arms as she slept. I made love to her again this morning. *Good God, man!* What do I have to say to get you to agree to a marriage?" he asked with a good deal of exasperation.

Middleton bounced his head from side to side. "Well, when you put it like that, I suppose my answer is ... of course. Whatever I can do to help," he said with a shrug.

Charles blinked. And blinked again. "Just like that?" he replied, stunned at the other earl's rather cavalier attitude.

Shrugging, Middleton nodded. "Truth be told, I had no intention of helping with her come-out. I have no idea what to do or whom to speak with about what's involved. Her mother won't come to London. With Eleanor married, I won't have to find her a sponsor, or worry about her staying out too late at balls, or find a modiste to make her one of those ridiculous gowns she would have to wear to be presented to the queen."

The Earl of Wakefield frowned. "Ridiculous gowns?" he repeated, not sure what the other earl was talking about.

"Oh, you know. Those gowns that have the wide ... hips and the stomacher." He motioned with his hands to indicate a form fitting gown that then stuck straight out at the sides. "So wide a woman cannot pass through a simple doorway without turning sideways," he added. "I hear they're rather expensive, and since they're years out of fashion, they cannot be worn for anything else except perhaps a masquerade ball. Why should I pay for such an extravagance when she cannot wear it to a regular ball?" he asked rhetorically.

Charles didn't have an answer for such a query, but if Eleanor brought it up, at least he would have a logical rejoinder. "Would you like to be present for the wedding?" Charles asked, *sotto voce.*

The Earl of Middleton gave the question some thought. "How much is it going to cost me?" he countered.

Charles sighed. "I'll marry her by special license. I'll see to it it doesn't cost you a pence," he replied, not hiding his disgust with the other earl until he remembered a dowry might be involved. "Other than her dowry, I suppose."

Middleton frowned and sighed. "Ten-thousand pounds," he said. "But I should think it's forfeit given the circumstances."

Tempted to forego the dowry, Charles decided he would not. "Take it up with Lucy Gibbons," he replied, thinking he would like to be present when the Earl of Middleton presented his case for reimbursement to the madame.

"I will," Middleton replied, rather indignant.

"Good. It's settled then. I'll secure a license on the morrow," Charles said as he stood up. He would have liked to do it that day, but he realized it was probably too late to pay a call at the bishop's office in Doctors Commons. "Is there a message you would like me to pass along to your daughter?"

The Earl of Middleton shook his head, but decided his wife must be sick with worry. "I'll dispatch a courier to Epping right away. Laura is probably worried to death if Eleanor has been gone since yesterday." Then he remembered his wife might not be so amenable to her daughter marrying a known rake. "Tell Elly to write to her mother. She'll need to apologize. And beg forgiveness. But tell her to remind my countess that she will be spared having to come to London for a wedding."

Charles frowned, wondering at the odd comment.

"Spared?" he repeated. "I would have thought she would welcome a trip to the city." *At least for her daughter's wedding*, he thought, wondering if he was being selfish for wanting to secure a license and marry as soon as possible.

The Earl of Middleton regarded Charles for a long moment. "Once your future countess has been subjected to the barbed tongues of the shrews that make up the so-called fairer sex of the *ton*, then she, too, will want to flee London and never return," he warned with a nod. He took a deep breath, as if trying to decide if he should say anything more. Apparently he decided to hold his tongue and instead said, "I have a game to return to." With those words and a nod, the earl took his leave of Charles and made his way back to the card room.

Charles watched as Middleton disappeared through the door to the card room, and he wondered at the man's parting words.

Barbed tongues? Shrews? Faith! *Just what kind of women made up the current crop of young matrons?*

CHAPTER 27
A KNIGHT RETURNS

Four-thirty in the afternoon

Arthur Goodwin was nearly to Marylebone Street when he realized he could not simply accept what his brother was about to do—marry a chit because he had ruined her.

It wasn't fair to the chit!

Eleanor Merriweather was the daughter of an earl. *Poor girl*. She didn't deserve to be saddled with his rake of a brother. Didn't deserve the gossip that would surely follow her no matter where she went in London. Every young matron and most of the old ones would find her the perfect fodder for their parlor talk. Other than her father, she had no family in town to see to it she had protection. And he rather doubted his brother was capable of controlling the harsh words that would be said of her. It was bad enough he was well known as a rake, and he certainly didn't seem the least bit bothered by what they said of him.

Arthur frowned as he halted his horse near his brother's terrace. A town coach was parked directly in front, and two footmen were pulling a trunk from the back and hauling it up the front stairs while a woman he didn't recognize spoke to them with a French accent. *Spoke* was probably too nice a word; she was actually yelling as she motioned for them to hurry with their burden. When she spotted him, though, she changed her words to the footmen, thanking them for their kind assistance.

As Arthur gingerly made his way up the stairs, he found Chester just inside the front door. "Lady Eleanor's maid?" he asked under his breath.

"The modiste, Sir Arthur. Lord Wakefield asked that I have her pay a call on Lady Eleanor," the majordomo countered. "I believe that is the last of the trunks she's having taken up to milady's bedchamber."

The knight blinked. "What the hell, Chester?" he said *sotto voce.* "What's going on?"

The majordomo straightened to his full height. "Lord Wakefield is to marry Lady Eleanor, sir. Miss Clos du Bois is here to see that the future countess has a proper wardrobe and bride clothes."

Arthur realized he probably should have taken his leave of the terrace right then and there, but he would never forgive himself if he didn't check on Lady Eleanor, at least see to her well-being.

What if she was miserable about her impending nuptials? What if she despised his brother and was only doing this because she saw no other option? Indeed, what were a ruined chit's options if she turned down his brother's offer of marriage? It wasn't as if she could return to her life as an innocent earl's daughter about to make her come-out.

When he reached the top of the stairs, he passed the two footmen who had brought up the trunk as they headed down the stairs. Aware of voices coming from near the end of the hall, he followed the sound until he was suddenly the witness to a whirlwind of feminine activity.

Lengths of fabrics, ready-made gowns, ribbons and what-not surrounded Lady Eleanor as she stood on a small box. At least three —no, make that four—other women were in the room. One was hemming the gown in which Eleanor was standing, another was measuring her arm, another was arranging fabrics on a display for Eleanor's perusal and yet another was standing off to the side with a bemused expression on her face.

That would be the lady's maid, Arthur thought as he realized she was having nothing to do with the modiste or the seamstresses intent on creating what had to be a bridal gown. He almost cleared his throat to announce himself, but Eleanor's attention went from the fabrics she was studying to him, her eyes widening to what could only be described as dismay.

"Sir Arthur," she breathed.

Having absolutely no experience with women who fainted, Arthur was caught completely off-guard when Eleanor's head fell back and she seemed to float downward. He was aware of a trio of gasps as the seamstresses and her maid realized what was happening, but despite his quick step or two forward, he barely had a hand on her when Eleanor fell from the box. He managed to prevent her from hitting the carpeted floor too hard, though, when his other arm reached under her neck and shoulders.

The shrieks of the other women were stifled as they all backed away from Eleanor's prone body, Arthur's arm still under her shoulders and holding them above the Aubusson carpet. "Do any of you have a vinaigrette?" he asked, his manner most calm, as if women fainted upon seeing him on a daily basis.

Miss Clos du Bois stood in the doorway, apparently finished overseeing the unloading of her trunks of clothes. Despite her surprise at her client's sudden tumble from the box, the modiste moved first and fished a vinaigrette from a nearby reticule. "Please don't spill it, sir," she cautioned him as he moved to open it.

Frowning, Arthur handed it back to her. "Perhaps you should do the honors, my lady," he said.

A second later, the offending odor of vinegar wafted through the room, and Eleanor's eyes fluttered and then opened. Despite Arthur's hold beneath her shoulders, or perhaps because of it, Eleanor merely stared at him. Her expression brightened as she did so, a smile finally lighting her face. "Sir Arthur," she breathed.

The knight gave a quick glance about the room. "I do believe I will need a moment with her ladyship when you are quite finished here," he said, his eyes sweeping the room. He lifted Eleanor to her feet and made sure she was steady before he gave a bow. "I'll be in my brother's study," he said before he took his leave of the bedchamber.

He cursed as he made his way back down the marble stairs. He recognized the look in Eleanor's eyes as she gazed up at him. The doe-eyed look of a chit who thought she was in love. He had seen that same look the night of the dinner party when she had been seated across from him. The blush that colored her face only one of the telltale signs that Eleanor Merriweather had a crush on him. They spoke little for he rather doubted she was capable of conversation. Every time he brought up a suitable topic, she was barely able to form a coherent sentence. When she could, he thought her an interesting woman, but he knew even then he would not look to a debutante to share his bed. Nor a widow or even a harlot. Even back then, he had known he wouldn't be satisfied sharing his life with a woman.

He was too handsome, Arthur knew. His lover had told him so nearly every night they spent together. His betrothed had told him as well when they brokered the deal that would make her his wife. But he couldn't help how he appeared to others. He could change their opinion of him so they wouldn't be so enamored of him, though, which is what he realized he needed to do with his future sister-in-law. It would do no good to have her giving him that doe-eyed look every time he had dinner at his brother's house. He dared not give Charles a reason to despise him more than he already did.

He settled himself into one of the overstuffed chairs after helping himself to a snifter of brandy, tempted to also light a cheroot. His brother would know he had been there, though, and he dare not give his brother reason to wonder why he might have paid another call at the terrace.

Not quite a half-hour later, Lady Eleanor knocked lightly on the study door before she entered. Arthur stood up and gave her a bow before pointing to an adjacent chair.

"How do, Sir Arthur," she said lightly. "I apologize for keeping you waiting. The modiste was rather ... demanding," she said as she lowered herself into the proffered chair. "I hope this day finds you well."

Arthur nodded, rather surprised at Eleanor's words. At least she could string them together better than she had that night of the dinner party at Worthington House. "Very, in fact," Arthur said as he took his seat. "I thought I might take a moment to welcome you to the family, seeing as how you'll be my sister very soon."

Eleanor's face displayed a smile that visibly faltered. "Thank you," she answered with a nod. "Am I to understand I'll be gaining a sister as well?" she ventured, her hands clasped together in her lap in an effort to keep her fingers from pleating the fabric of her skirt.

"You have heard about my impending marriage to Lady Priscilla then?" he half-questioned. "She is a lovely girl."

Angling her head to one side, Eleanor allowed a sigh. "A blue-stocking, is she not?" she said, trying hard not to sound too terribly catty with the comment. She knew it was an opinion shared by many in the parlors of Mayfair.

"She is," Arthur agreed with a happy nod.

Eleanor couldn't help but notice how Arthur's response had his face to lighting up. "You don't find that ... appalling?"

Taking a deep breath and letting it out slowly, Arthur shook his head. "I do not. In fact, I find Lady Priscilla's knowledge of the world to be quite refreshing in a member of your sex," he said care-fully. "She is educated. Open-minded. Perhaps a bit too ... *uninhib-ited*," he added, one of his eyebrows arching up with his words despite the slight smile he allowed.

Her eyes widening at the simple description of Lady Priscilla, Eleanor shook her head slightly. "In what way do you mean?" she asked carefully.

Arthur settled back into his chair, his mannerisms rather effemi-nate. "Why, despite knowing I have taken a lover, she is quite deter-mined we be married. It was her suggestion we do so, you see," he said, one of his fingers settling against his temple as his elbow rested on the arm of the chair.

Eleanor blinked. "Lover?" she repeated. "A ... a mistress?" But that couldn't be. She was quite sure she would have read about it if *The Tattler* knew anything about the knight arranging for the services of a mistress. The gossip rag seemed to know about every arrangement made in that regard.

Shaking his head slowly, Arthur made a slight humming noise before he finally said, "Not exactly, although Robert does share my bed. We plan to live together, you see, but in order to do so, it was necessary to arrange for one of us to be married. When Lady Priscilla came to me with her ... *proposal*, we both readily agreed to it."

Swallowing hard, Eleanor nodded. "How fortunate for you," she offered. "May I ask what she proposed?" she asked, trying as she might to imagine a man as handsome as Sir Arthur sharing a bed with a man and finding it impossible. Worse, she couldn't abide the thought of Lady Priscilla with him, either.

It didn't matter what she thought, though, she realized. The rumors were apparently true.

Sir Arthur is a molly!

"An arrangement," Arthur said quietly. "We provide her pleasure in bed every so often—she wishes for a child, you see—and she allows us our nights, together" he explained, realizing he was scandalizing the poor girl who sat across from him. "Anyway, I didn't mean to shock you, but I thought you should know," he said lightly. "Seeing as how you'll be my sister and will be expected to keep our secret. Now, tell me about your wedding plans."

Eleanor impassive expression brightened. "Charles is seeing to a special license," she answered. "I expect we'll be married tomorrow. And you?"

Arthur felt relief when he realized Eleanor wouldn't be fainting upon seeing him again. "I expect I'll be married within a fortnight," he said with a nod. "Charles has agreed to stand with me."

Nodding, Eleanor leaned forward. "I would like to be present, as well, should you need another witness," she offered, her heart beating far too fast.

Obviously surprised by her offer, Arthur gave her a nod. "I would like that very much," he said.

She dared a glance at the clock above the fireplace. "Oh, dear. I expect Charles for dinner this evening, and I haven't even dressed for it yet. You will excuse me, brother?"

Arthur got to his feet and gave her a bow. "Of course, El. Do have a good evening," he said, wondering what she thought of him using a nickname for her.

"You as well," Eleanor said as she curtsied. She took her leave of the study, apparently fine with him referring to her as 'El'.

Arthur listened to the tapping of her slippered feet as Eleanor hurried up the steps to the mistress suite. He downed the rest of the brandy in his glass and stared into the dying embers in the fireplace, hoping beyond hope that he hadn't jeopardized the arrangement he had made with Lady Priscilla and Robert, or traumatized his poor future sister-in-law with the news that he was what *The Tattler* claimed him to be.

At least she would no longer look at him with the doe-eyed expression of a chit in love. Perhaps she would turn that gaze onto his brother.

He would be a lucky man if she did, the rake.

CHAPTER 28
A MARQUESS PAYS A LATE CALL

even o'clock in the evening
"How old is Mr. Wiggins?"

Constance Fitzwilliam straightened from where she had been tending to a series of rather messy flower beds. Since she was living in the Norwick townhouse without having to pay rent, she figured the least she could do was attempt to restore the garden to its former splendor, a task that hadn't been done in at least a few years. Her pruning shears were suddenly in front of her, as if she intended to use them as a weapon.

Randall Roderick took a step back from where he had come through the back gate. Determined to see Constance again, he had decided to try the back door, thinking a servant would answer since no one had come to the front door. "You've nothing to fear from me, my lady," he said. "I tried knocking, but there was no answer. I grew … concerned."

Letting out the breath she had been holding and lowering the pruning shears to her side, Constance gave her visitor a slight curtsy. "Mr. Roderick," she managed. She dared a glance down at what she wore, rather embarrassed he would see her in what had to be her oldest, most out-of-fashion gown. The apron she wore over it covered the worst of it, she supposed, but still. This wasn't how she imagined meeting Mr. Roderick again, especially so soon after their afternoon walk.

Randall approached her then, taking her gloved hand in his and raising it to his lips.

"Oh, please don't. It's rather filthy," she said as she pulled her hand from his.

Releasing her hand, Randall gave her a raised eyebrow. "The glove perhaps, but not you, my lady," he said. He glanced around, now aware of what she had been doing in the garden given the cuttings that had been gathered into heaps along the garden paths. "Has your gardener quit you, my lady?" he asked then, his brows furrowing with concern. Goodness! Had she managed to do all this in just the few hours since he had left her at her door?

Constance had to suppress a grin. "I rather doubt there ever was a gardener, Mr. Roderick," she replied with an arched eyebrow.

"Randall," he replied. "I insist. We're neighbors, Miss Fitzwilliam. I hardly think we should be so formal."

"Randall," the young woman repeated with a nod. "I thought I would try to put it to rights." She waved to the area she had been working to restore. Despite the growing season nearing its end, there were still late summer flowers scattered throughout the garden, and a series of rose bushes displayed blooms in a number of colors.

"You're doing a fine job of it," Randall remarked. "Imagine the results if I were allowed to send my gardener from my Cavendish Square household. Why, you could instruct him on exactly what you want done, and it could be accomplished in a day. Maybe two," he added.

Constance inhaled sharply. Finding her in the garden by having come in through the alley entrance was one thing, but to offer his personal gardener was quite another. "That won't be necessary. Mr. Rod ... Randall," she corrected herself. She remembered what he had said about knocking on her front door and wondered as to his reason for paying a visit. "What is it that brought you back to the Norwick townhouse today?" she asked, her curiosity piqued.

Randall wished the woman wasn't so skittish. He was reminded of a newborn filly, curious but nervous in the presence of its owner. "I was wondering about your Mr. Wiggins," he answered. "You mentioned him earlier. Does he share the same lineage as your Mr. Tuttlebaum?" he asked, his hands going to his back so that he could clasp them together. He was afraid he would be tempted to touch her if he didn't keep them away from her.

Constance angled her head, wondering why he would be so interested in her colt. "And if he does?" she countered, deciding not to admit that the two horses were essentially brothers.

Randall took a breath. "Do you plan to race him?" he blurted. "Is he three years old?"

Eyeing the man for a moment, Constance finally gave him a nod. "He will be in time for next season's races," she admitted. "Why ... why do you ask?"

Randall gave a nod. "Do you have someone lined up to see to it he's delivered to the race meetings? To Doncaster? To Newmarket? Epsom Downs? Is he in the book at the Jockey Club?"

The young woman swallowed, a bit surprised by his query. "And if I do not? Are you offering your resources to see to it that he is? And, if so, how much will this cost me?" she asked, her head angling up in a manner suggesting she was rather incensed by his questions.

Randal lowered his own head, realizing immediately that he had offended with his offer. "I apologize. I meant no offense, my lady. I just thought ... I only meant to offer my help. I can afford to do so without recompense, of course," he added, hoping she wouldn't think he was trying to take advantage. Realizing he needed to give her a reason, Randall allowed a shrug. "You see, I used to place one of my Thoroughbreds in the race meetings every year. But try as I might ... try as *they* might ... none were ever completely successful. Since your Mr. Tuttlebaum won all of his races, I have to believe Mr. Wiggins could do so, as well, provided he has a good trainer and a jockey."

Constance clutched the front of her apron in one hand, rather surprised at hearing Randall describe what she had thought could be a way to stretch the funds for Fair Downs for a few years or more.

But to have a horse entered in the various race meetings throughout the racing season meant employing a trainer, hiring a jockey, and paying for the travel necessary to get a horse from one track to the next. And there were no guarantees Mr. Wiggins would perform as well as Mr. Tuttlebaum. She might incur all the expenses of racing the Thoroughbred but never receive any prize monies to offset the costs.

"I cannot afford a trainer for Mr. Wiggins," she said. "But I do thank you for your interest," she said as she stepped back and gave her visitor a curtsy. "Good day, Randall."

"I have a trainer," Randall blurted. "He is paid the same no matter the horse. Would you at least think about allowing me to see to it Mr. Wiggins is allowed to race next season?"

Constance regarded Randall for a moment and shook her head. "Why?"

Randall took a deep breath and held it a moment. *Why, indeed?* In the two hours since he had left her at her front door, he had plotted how he might ingratiate himself into her life. How he might provide some service she would find useful. Some reason that he might spend more time in her company.

Perhaps the rest of his life.

"I have the means to help, my lady, and I've no Thoroughbred of an age eligible to race next season. I would like to offer those means to you so that you might have the income you seek."

Her eyes widening at his statement, Constance blinked. "In return for what, Mr. Roderick?" she asked again. "I cannot believe you would offer such expensive services and not expect some kind of recompense," she argued.

Randall winced at her use of his formal name. He couldn't blame her for being suspicious. She had only just met him that morning! "All right then. Ten percent of his winnings," he stated. "You get the rest, of course."

Constance blinked, realizing she probably should have accepted his offer of providing the services gratis. But what guarantee did she have he would actually do what he claimed? Perhaps he was only after her horse. Perhaps to use Mr. Wiggins as a stud. Or as a training partner, made to deliberately lose so that another horse could learn how to win races.

Randall realized the woman was considering all the reasons she shouldn't agree to allow him to race the horse. After all, what assurances did she have that he wouldn't just disappear with Mr. Wiggins, never to be seen or heard from again?

"I would insist you accompany me to all the race meetings, of course. And pay an occasional call at my home in Reading so that you might follow your colt's progress whilst he's in training," he said, as if he expected her to bring up the most logical reasons for turning down his offer.

Constance's eyes widened. "I hardly think that would be proper, Mr. Roderick," she replied, wondering how he thought she could afford the travel, let alone the paid companion that would be required for the trip.

The marquess sighed. "I would, of course, see to a companion for you, my lady. As well as arrange travel on your behalf. I've a rather new coach-and-four available. Very comfortable, if I do say so. Tilbury certainly seemed to think so when he sent the bill." He didn't add that the cost of the coach was more than he had paid for Zeus' sire.

Constance regarded her visitor with a wary eye, still wondering why he was being so generous with his offer. Ten percent hardly seemed enough of an incentive to offer such expensive services. Was the man really so enamored of the racing circuit that he would go to such extremes merely to have a competitive horse to race?

"It seems to me there must be some other racehorse available to you, Mr. Roderick," she said with a sigh.

Randall shook his head. "But none of them would be championed by you, my lady," he responded, his manner becoming rather sullen.

Stunned by his comment, Constance could feel a blush coloring her throat and face. "I hardly know what to say," she said. The offer was generous. The idea of traveling in a comfortable coach to visit a well-funded horse training facility wasn't exactly a trip she had ever thought possible—indeed, had never dreamed of when she imagined Mr. Wiggins on the racing circuit.

Doncaster, Newmarket, Epsom Downs. Her father had been to all of them and more, several times, in fact. But she had never accompanied him. *Next year, Poppet,* he would say. *When you're older and out of the schoolroom.* But that next year had been the year he died. The year she was forced to fend for herself and those who worked at Fair Downs. The year she discovered her mother had been squirreling away money in hidey-holes throughout the house. It had been that money that allowed her to keep the household running, to pay the bills and buy food and pay the salaries of the few servants left on the estate.

"Then say nothing right now," Randall stated with a nod. "Think on it, and give me your answer when you've had a chance to mull it over."

Constance angled her head to one side. "You don't seem like a very patient man, Mr. Roderick." Curious as to how he might respond, she was rather surprised by his response.

"I am not," he agreed. "However, if you had given me an enthusiastic 'yes', I might have thought you a bit fast," he chided.

The pink blush reappeared on her cheeks. "I am not, I assure you," she murmured.

Randall allowed a grin. "I'll have the gardener sent over first thing tomorrow morning. Either tell him what you'd like to have done here, or let him know you trust his judgment. Either way, you shall at least have a decent garden, my lady."

He glanced around, as if he had just then noticed the late hour. The summer sun would be setting in a couple of hours, and worse, someone in a neighboring townhouse might pay witness to his presence in the garden. Constance didn't have a chaperone in sight. "Good evening, my lady," he said, giving her a bow and placing his beaver back onto his head.

Constance curtsied and watched as her late afternoon visitor took his leave by the back gate and headed down the alley, all the while wondering if she was the reason for his unusual visit or if it was because of Mr. Wiggins. Perhaps she would never know for sure, but she couldn't help but hope it was the former more than the latter.

Randall hurried down the alley, counting off the townhouses as he went to be sure his gardener would tend to the correct one in the morning. He rather hoped the man could do what he claimed. Truth be told, he really didn't know the extent of the man's skills with regard to landscaping. He hadn't taken up residence in his Cavendish Square mansion in over a year, opting to remain in Reading for the summer last year and in the townhouse this summer. Otherwise, he was at his estate in Reading. He merely trusted the butler there to oversee the staff, house, and grounds.

In his missive to the man later that night, he included not only the instructions for the gardener to see to Miss Fitzwilliam's townhouse, but also to the creation of a salon decorated entirely in purple. *Hire the decorator who can do it the quickest,* he wrote. *I am considering matrimony.* He briefly thought of suggesting the color scheme also be applied to the mistress suite, but thought that might be a bit much. If Constance wanted a purple bedchamber, she could request it once she was his wife.

Satisfied with his missive, he rang for Giles and asked that a footman be dispatched immediately. "Time is of the essence," he explained when Giles' eyebrows lifted to new heights on his forehead.

When the man had taken leave of his study, Randall allowed a chuckle. He loved it when he was able to discombobulate the staid servant.

CHAPTER 29
AN EARL AND COUNTESS IN THE LIBRARY

Seven-thirty in the evening

Clarinda met her husband in the library at exactly half past seven o'clock, intent on having a glass of claret before the dinner bell sounded. The butler had seen to the wine and a plate of walnuts just before the Earl of Norwick arrived. As he stood on the library's threshold, daring a peek into the room in search of his wife, Clarinda smiled.

"I was beginning to think you weren't coming," she accused in a soft voice, reaching for Daniel's hand to pull him farther into the room. She gave the door a shove so it closed behind the rather startled earl.

"I wouldn't miss dinner with you for the world, and you know it," Daniel replied, leaning over to give her a kiss on the corner of her mouth.

She returned the act of endearment and hooked her arm into his. "Is all well in the Norwick earldom?" she asked as they made their way to the settee in front of the fire.

Daniel gave a shrug as he took her glass from her so she could be seated. "As well as can be expected. Maybe better. Early reports say we will have a decent harvest this year."

Clarinda allowed a wan smile as she leaned over the earl and lifted a glass of scotch from the side table. She offered it to him, making sure he was aware of what her low-cut dinner gown exposed. "That is good news, considering what happened last year," she said in a quiet voice.

The summer of 1816 had been horrible for nearly everyone in England. With so much rain, cool temperatures, and very little in the way of a growing season, many tenant farmers had nearly starved. Only those who owned coal mines seemed to have made any money, although even some of them claimed they couldn't do so simply because no one could afford their commodity.

"Remember the caller I had today?" she asked, deciding to bring up the matter of his cousin before dinner was served. He had already taken an interest in her cleavage.

"Yes. In fact, I meant to ask about her. Who was she?"

Clarinda gave him a look of surprise. "So, you didn't recognize her?"

Daniel shook his head, a frown forming. "I did not see her," he replied, his attention torn from where it had been a moment before.

Sighing, Clarinda wondered how best to tell him of her conversation with Constance Fitzwilliam. "Do you have a cousin named Constance?" she asked, deciding to first be sure the woman wasn't an imposter.

Daniel straightened and turned his head fully to regard Clarinda, an eyebrow arching up in surprise. "Yes," he hedged. "She would be about ..." He considered when he last saw the chit and stiffened. "Five-and-twenty," he whispered. He didn't offer anything more about his cousin, but it was apparent to Clarinda he was recalling something from the past. Something not so pleasant.

"Her inheritance seems to be missing," Clarinda said, careful with how she made the statement. "Do you have any idea what might have happened to it?"

Daniel took a deep breath and held it a moment. "No doubt gambled away by my late uncle, Edward," he said, not trying to hide his disgust for the man.

Crestfallen, Clarinda settled back into the settee. "Oh," she murmured. After another moment, she asked, "Is there nothing to be done?" giving her husband her very best doe-eyed glance. "She's nearly out of funds despite how careful she's been with what little she has had since her father's death."

Daniel caught the look and straightened. "Well, I won't leave her destitute, if that's what you're concerned about. But last I knew, she had one of the most valuable stables in all of England. If she wanted to, she could sell her horses and be set for life."

Clarinda blinked. And blinked again as she regarded her husband. "What are you talking about?" she asked.

Daniel shrugged. "Uncle Edward gave her a horse—a filly—when she was young girl. He'd won it in a card game. Seems the mare was a product of a bay and some racehorse that had won the Ascot back in the day. Not knowing its true value, he forgot about it. But Connie, having grown up in the stables—she was a hoyden if ever there was one—she managed to find a suitable stud—I'm not sure who she found or if any money was exchanged for the stud service— and the next thing you know, she was the proud owner of a colt she named Mr.Tuttlebaum—"

Clarinda gasped. "*I've* heard of that horse!"

Daniel grinned. "Haven't we all?" he replied. "Made lots of money, which my uncle quickly lost. Some of it in David's gaming hell, come to think of it," he said with an arched eyebrow.

"Some? Or *all?*" Clarinda asked, one of her eyebrows arched up to match Daniel's. She knew of her first husband's gaming hell and exclusive brothel, of course, but she never considered who had lost their fortunes therein.

The earl shrugged. "Most of it, I imagine," he acknowledged. "Which is one of the reasons I will see to it Connie is provided with enough funds for a suitable dowry," he said before he finished off his scotch. He closed his eyes a moment, as if he had remembered something else.

Clarinda sighed. "I don't think a marriage is in her future, Daniel," she said softly. "She's already on the shelf. But I also think she will be happy to simply live the rest of her life in Sussex."

Daniel frowned. "She can use the funds to live on, I suppose. But I would like to know why there isn't some inheritance set aside for her. One that was protected from Uncle Edward." He paused a moment. "Did she say anything about the stables?" he asked then.

Clarinda shook her head. "Not that I recall."

"Hmm," he managed. The sound of the dinner bell sounded faintly through the closed door. "Ah, saved by the bell," he murmured, bussing his wife on her cheek when she gave him a quelling glance. "I'll do right by my cousin. I promise," he whispered. "In fact, I'll write her a cheque in the morning and send her a note that it's ready." Although he would prefer to simply have a footman deliver the cheque, he knew he should at least meet with her in person. And even though a good deal of time had passed since that night in the stables, he would carry the memory of it for the rest of his life.

Smiling, Clarinda gave him a kiss on the lips, a kiss that seemed to take the earl by surprise. "Thank you, my lord," she said as she made her way.

Daniel mumbled before saying, "Was Lady Pettigrew here today?" he asked then. "I could swear I heard her voice."

Clarinda sighed. "Yes, she was," she admitted. "I think she was feeling a bit sad."

"Oh?" Daniel replied as they made their way into the dining room. "Something happen?" *Besides Lord Pettigrew's mistress having left his employ to marry a baronet?* he nearly added.

The countess nodded. "She let her hairdresser go," she said with a roll of her eyes.

Daniel blinked. "I'm surprised she still has one. Doesn't she always wear a wig?" he countered.

Clarinda suppressed the urge to grin. "She does, but the girl could have stayed on to dress her wigs," he claimed. "When I suggested she hire her back for that reason, she said she tried to do so but discovered the girl had already taken a position in another household."

"Serves her right," Daniel said as he pushed in Clarinda's chair and then moved to take his own. "And good for the girl. I hope she ended up in suitable house?" he half-questioned, thinking it would be difficult to work for Lady Pettigrew.

"Well, that's the puzzling thing. When Lady Pettigrew went to the agency to get Foster back, she was told the girl had been hired by Lord Wakefield's majordomo for the earl's household."

Daniel frowned as he tried to remember if he had ever seen Charles Goodwin's majordomo. "Tall man, isn't he?" he said as a footman poured his wine.

"Yes," Clarinda agreed. "Why do you suppose Lord Wakefield would hire a hair dresser?"

The earl regarded her for a moment before considering the question. "I've absolutely no idea," he finally said. "But I rather imagine *The Tattler* will mention it in the next edition," he added before beginning his soup course.

Never having thought her husband to be a reader of the gossip rag, Clarinda regarded Daniel for a moment before allowing a giggle to escape.

She didn't notice Daniel's look of consternation.

CHAPTER 30
AN EARL RETURNS FOR DINNER

*S**even-thirty in the evening*

"I admit to being a bit surprised that you're still here," Charles said quietly as he gazed up at Eleanor. She was halfway down the main stairs and watching him from where she stood, one hand gripping the railing as if she needed it for support.

Perhaps she did.

"A few hours ago, I would not have been," she replied with a sigh. She took a step down and paused. At the same time, Charles took a step forward, his Hessian boots tapping on the marble floor of the main hall.

"And what, pray tell, kept you from leaving?" he asked. Nothing in his expression gave away whether or not he was pleased to see her, but Eleanor was quite sure she saw a hint of admiration in his eyes.

How could he not admire how she looked just then, though? Alice Foster had done wonders with her hair, and Miss Clos du Bois had brought the perfect dinner gown, it's deep sapphire coloring a perfect contrast against her pale skin and dark hair color. She had allowed the maid to use just a hint of lip color—the pot was in the top drawer of the dressing table along with dozens of pins and jars of powder and such, the cosmetics probably left behind by a former tenant of the townhouse.

Eleanor took another step down. "Well, first a lady's maid magically appeared at my bedchamber door," she said, her manner rather serious despite her words.

Charles allowed a grin. Chester had followed up, then, and he had seen to hiring a lady's maid. "Do you ... like her?" he asked carefully.

Taking another step down, Eleanor nodded. "I do," she answered. "Although I do have to wonder what happened to Lady Pettigrew's hair. Foster was dismissed because of it."

His brows arching, Charles gave a slight shake of his head. "I think it's common knowledge amongst the *ton* that Lady Pettigrew has no hair of her own, so she probably doesn't require the services of a hair dresser."

Eleanor had to suppress the grin she could feel lighting up her face. "Lucky me," she replied. When she saw his head angle to one side and one of his hands indicate she should continue, she sighed. "Then a modiste appeared with a trunk full of gowns and frippery and such—"

"Oh, thank the *gods*," Charles said dramatically. When he noticed Eleanor's arched eyebrow, he added, "There was some thought that Miss Clos du Bois was already engaged with another client and would not be able to see you until tomorrow. Which would have been entirely unacceptable, seeing as how you were left with so little in your valise."

Her eyes widening a fraction, Eleanor stifled the urge to inhale sharply. Had he looked into her valise when he took it from the brothel earlier that day? Or perhaps he was left with the impression it was nearly empty when she opened it the first time that day. Opened it and started bawling at finding some of her things missing.

"I do hope she *didn't* include a night rail in any of the clothing she left for you," Charles ventured, biting back the urge to curse when he realized he sounded like the very rake he was. "Forgive me, I did not really mean what I just said." He paused a moment, noting how Eleanor simply stared at him. "I did, actually," he countered himself. "Mean it, I mean. I cannot help myself, but I cannot abide the thought of you in yards and yards of fabric whilst you sleep."

Her brows furrowing, Eleanor seemed to think on that comment for a moment too long. "I can't really be sure if she did or she didn't include a night rail," she murmured, attempting to stop the blush of color she could feel creeping up her neck. Did the earl have any idea what he had just said? What he had just admitted? Besides his words confirming he was and probably always would be a rake, he had thoroughly embarrassed her by suggesting she sleep *naked* tonight.

She took another step down. "But I do hope you're prepared to pay a rather large sum of money, because there is an entire wardrobe of bride clothes up there," she said as she motioned up the stairs.

"Including a wedding gown?"

Eleanor blinked, surprised at how concerned he seemed about what the modiste might have accomplished in the few hours she was on the premises. "Yes, I do believe there is a suitable gown for just such an occasion," Eleanor said with a nod. "Do you suppose I'll be wearing it anytime soon?" She took another step down.

"God, I hope so," Charles replied as he took two steps forward. "Tomorrow, if my lady is so inclined?"

Taking another step down, Eleanor paused and held her breath. *He wants to get married tomorrow?* And he seemed rather pleased by the prospect! Pleased, and not the least bit worried, or bothered by the thought of being leg-shackled. "What will my lord wear?" she asked, angling her head to match his.

Charles seemed taken aback by the question. It wasn't exactly what he had expected her to say. "Whatever Chester puts me into, I suppose," he replied in an off-hand manner. He took the remaining two steps to the base of the stairs. Given Eleanor still had two to go, she was nearly eye-level with him as he took her hand and raised it to his lips.

"He's a good man," she said in a quiet voice.

Charles felt a bit of envy at hearing the words spoken of his majordomo. "Yes, he is," he agreed with a nod.

"As is your brother."

The bit of envy turned to full on jealousy as Charles took a step back. "He is?"

The question was full of caution, and Eleanor furrowed a brow before she took the last step down. "He paid me a visit a while ago," she said, her voice still quiet. "It seems ... my *affections* were poorly placed."

Eleanor wondered briefly if Lady Priscilla felt any affection for the men she would apparently be welcoming into her bed, or if she only proposed their arrangement out of curiosity. Once her curiosity was sated, though, what then? Would she be satisfied with a loveless union? Or would she be left with child? Or would they continue their occasional ... *what was it called?*

A *menage â trois.*

She shook her head, not wanting to give it any more thought.

Charles frowned. Did Eleanor feel affection for Arthur? Or no longer? "Where ...?" He stopped and blinked a few times as he considered how to ask his next question. "And on whom are your affections directed now?"

Eleanor took another step down so that she stood nearly eye-to-eye with the earl. "I must admit, I no longer feel affection for your brother," she said with a sigh. "Or rather, I do, but in an entirely different manner."

Charles closed his eyes and felt the sting of her words. She *did* feel affection for his brother, then. "And what is different now?" he asked, his question a mere whisper.

"He is your brother. If I marry you, he will be my brother as well," she replied simply.

Swallowing, Charles nodded. "True," he agreed.

Sighing, Eleanor regarded Charles for a moment. "He was quite ... *firm* in his opinion that I should know something of his character," she explained. "Seeing as how we will be related. By marriage. And given the gossip that is apparently more truth than not."

Charles held his breath, wondering what his brother had said.

What he had done. "And what was it about his character he wished you to know, my lady?" he asked carefully.

He hardly knew how to describe the rumors of his brother to a gently bred daughter of the *ton*. Would Eleanor even know what the term meant? Understand the ramifications? His brother would be in danger of arrest for the rest of his life should anyone pay witness to him with in the company of another man. "There were rumors he was a molly, but—"

"He is a molly," Eleanor whispered, glancing about as if she feared a servant might overhear her words. "I know what it means, my lord," she claimed when she noticed his look of shock. "I may live in the country, but I do read. Books. Newspapers. And I do read *The Tattler*," she said with an arched brow. "I admit, I felt … *crushed* when he told me. When he explained how it was he could marry his intended and see to her happiness as well as his lover's."

Charles frowned again. "Lady Priscilla?" he clarified.

Eleanor nodded. "Apparently, she …" Her faced pinked up as a blush bloomed over her face. "She has certain … *proclivities* that make their impending union a perfect match."

Charles frowned, startled by her words. His head dropping back on his neck so that he was staring at the overhead chandelier, Charles wondered what Eleanor might mean. "When you say 'proclivities'—"

"She is looking forward to a marriage bed with two men," she whispered. "Something I cannot myself claim to want anything to do with."

Arthur had obviously shared far more with Eleanor than he ever had with his brother! "I should think you would be scandalized," he remarked in alarm.

Eleanor regarded him a moment, realizing he was probably more scandalized than she was. "Well, I was a bit when he explained the part about … three people sharing a marriage bed," she said, *sotto voce*.

Blinking, Charles frowned. "A menage â trois?" he whispered, his brows furrowing. "And Lady Priscilla is agreeable to the arrangement?"

A small smile appeared on Eleanor's face. She leaned forward, her lips next to his ear. "She is the one who *suggested* the liaison." An eyebrow arched as she watched how Charles's face changed with this bit of information.

"I would never have guessed it of a bluestocking," he whispered, one of his hands going to Eleanor's waist. "Perhaps I have been pursuing the wrong women with whom to share my bed twice a ..." His hand intercepted her wrist before Eleanor could slap his face, the sudden anger causing her face to redden with her ire. "I am *teasing*," he said quietly, his face leaning towards hers. "But I admit to feeling a bit of relief that you are not suggesting a similar arrangement for *our* union," he added when he saw her anger hadn't abated with his words. "I cannot abide the thought of sharing you with another man, my lady," he said, his manner sobering. "The idea that you felt affection for my brother had me quite vexed, I'll have you know."

Eleanor's head tilted up. "And yet, I will be expected to abide another woman in *your* bed?" she countered, her anger still evident.

Charles straightened as if he felt the slap she had tried to land on the side of his face only the moment ago. "You will *not*, my lady, for there will *be* no other woman in my bed but you," he claimed in clipped words. "Nor shall I pay visits to a brothel." He waved toward the table near the vestibule, "I should never wish to give you a reason to throw a vase at me."

Eleanor glanced at the now-empty table, her head dipping. "I am sorry about the vase. I truly didn't intend for it to break," she murmured.

Charles regarded her a moment before angling his head, wondering if perhaps she thought he might catch it as opposed to ducking so he wouldn't be hit by it. "Apology accepted, of course. The thing was hideous."

Eleanor arched an eyebrow. "You say that as if you're glad I threw it you!" she accused.

Shrugging, Charles allowed a sigh. "I suppose I am. The look I saw on your face ... you displayed such passion, El." He paused a moment as he watched her eyes widen in surprise. "I have never had a woman bestow such a look upon me as you did at that moment. Such anger. Such hurt. As if I had betrayed you somehow. And all I wanted to do at that moment was to make it all right. To turn that look of passion into what I saw you display this morning when I brought you to ecstasy."

Eleanor inhaled sharply, realizing she had been holding her breath as he spoke. "I suppose an offer of marriage goes a long way toward making it all right," she whispered.

Charles allowed a wan smile. "I never want you to feel such anger or hurt because of me ever again," he said quietly. "I shall endeavor to make you happy always, in fact."

Allowing a smile of her own, Eleanor leaned forward and kissed his brow. Wrapping her arms around his shoulders, she lowered her lips to his. "I shall allow you to, of course," she whispered.

Nodding, Charles leaned his head forward so their foreheads touched. "Marry me, El. I promise, I will honor my vows."

Eleanor stared at Charles, rather stunned by his words. "Even when I am round with child and my body is fat and ugly?"

The change in Charles' face had Eleanor tempted to take a step back, for he suddenly looked positively predatory. "Oh, *especially* then, my lady," he replied, his eyes narrowing. "I have heard tales around the gaming tables of how ripe and ready a woman who is breeding can be," he whispered, trailing his nose along the side of her face until his lips took purchase on her cheek and kissed her. "About how affection for one another grows with time. With each subsequent child."

Eleanor's eyes widened as she regarded him with surprise. "Have you now?" she replied, her breathing labored.

"Aye," he whispered. "But I suppose there must be some affection with which to start," he murmured, the tip of his nose trailing along her temple and down to where her jaw met her neck.

"I do believe my affections can be put back into effect with a bit of encouragement," Eleanor managed, wondering how she was going to remain upright. Her knees seem to quiver with the effort to keep her standing.

Rather relieved and wondering what might constitute encouragement, Charles wrapped his arms around her waist and shoulders and pulled her hard against the front of his body. His lips were on hers in an instant, pressing and suckling until they were locked into place and possessed hers completely.

When she responded by moving her hands to the back of his neck, he closed his eyes. She returned the kiss then, her tongue barely touching his as her fingers speared the dark hair behind his ears, her fingernails scraping his scalp to send shivers beneath the skin. Charles stilled himself and closed his eyes, reveling in the sensations her touches elicited, his own kisses light as feathers against the pillows of her lips.

The slight moan from Eleanor's throat drove him on, his lips leaving hers to trail down her jaw line to her earlobe to her neck and finally to the hollow of her throat. When he pulled away to take a breath, his eyes widened.

"And now?" he asked expectantly.

It was Eleanor's turn to blink as well as regain a bit of balance. She stared at him once her eyes finally cleared. "Now ... *what?*" she countered, rather sorry he had ended his kissing.

"Your affections," he answered in a whisper.

Eleanor regarded him for a moment. "And what of yours?" she countered, her voice not as quiet.

The earl seemed to think on the topic a moment. "I asked you first," he whispered and then realized how stubborn he sounded with his comment. He straightened. "I woke up feeling affection for you," he stated before he returned his attention to the space below her earlobe. He murmured something into her cheek and then pulled away when the sound of a bell rang farther down the hall. "What was that?" he asked in alarm.

Sorry to have his attentions redirected, Eleanor regarded him with a shake of her head. "The dinner bell, of course. You act as if you've never heard it before," she accused, moving her arm up to rest on his.

"That would be because I have not," Charles said as a comical expression crossed his face.

Eleanor allowed a grin. "Escort me, won't you?" she hinted with an arched eyebrow. "So that I might tell you of my affections. And give you my answer."

Charles finally allowed a sigh of relief. "Of course, my lady," he replied before leading them down the hall to the dining room, his breathing finally returning to normal.

CHAPTER 31
A LATE NIGHT VISITATION

Nine o'clock at night

"I have news!" Charles Goodwin announced in a voice filled with cheer once Giles had led him to the study in Randall Roderick's townhouse, just off the vestibule. The Earl of Reading had been reading, although his attention wasn't entirely on his book but rather on how he was going to propose to Constance Fitzwilliam the next day.

Randall stood up and regarded his visitor with a wary eye. "And probably too much to drink?" he hinted, glancing out the front window to find there wasn't a conveyance parked in the street. Nor a horse. "How did you get here?" he asked then, realizing the earl wore neither coat nor hat.

Goodness! It was worse than he thought! The Earl of Wakefield was so deep in his cups, he had left his hat and coat at White's and walked the entire distance to Curzon Street!

"Just a few glasses of wine with dinner," Charles countered, his brows furrowed.

Randall blinked. *Wine?* "Then, how, pray tell, did you *get* here?" he asked, waving toward the window that looked out onto the street.

Charles glanced over Randall's shoulder and lifted a finger. "I just live across the street," he replied, continuing to point to the terrace in front of which the hackney had parked and dropped off the young woman only the night before.

"*There?*" Randall countered, pointing to the same terrace.

"Aye. Nice place, and roomy enough for now. But I'll have to find something larger, probably within the year," Charles replied lightly.

The marquess regarded Charles Goodwin for nearly ten seconds before he angled his head. "And why might that be?" he asked carefully, as if he thought he needed to enunciate his words so that an inebriated man could understand them.

Charles straightened and allowed a self-satisfied smile. "I am getting married."

Not exactly words the marquess had *ever* expected to hear coming from the Earl of Wakefield, at least during his lifetime, Randall blinked. And blinked again. "*Married?*" Randall repeated, his brows reaching for new heights on his forehead before they suddenly furrowed. "Where is the Earl of Wakefield, and what have you done with him?" he asked then.

Charles allowed a smile, recognizing his very words being used against him. *What had it been?* Twenty-four hours since he had said the same words to the Rake of Reading? "I am ... *betrothed*. I am to be married tomorrow, should the bishop agree to give me a special license."

Shaking his head, Randall sighed. "They don't just *give* them to you," he replied. "They cost money. One-and-twenty guineas, last I heard," he stated. "I'll be acquiring one on the morrow myself. That is, if I am permitted to do so," he added, remembering that he still needed to pay a call on the Earl of Norwick. Even if Constance was of age, he still felt it necessary to let Daniel Fitzwilliam know he intended to marry the man's cousin. "Perhaps we can go to Doctors Commons together," he suggested, thinking he could do with a bit of company.

"And positively shock the bishop?" Charles asked with an arched eyebrow. "If I'm to believe news of my brother, it seems we won't be the only two in pursuit of a marriage license," he added with a knowing grin. "I can just see the headlines in *The Tattler* now." He raised a hand and swept it through the air. "'Two rakes and a molly to get married. Hell frozen over'."

Randall gave the young earl a quelling glance. "More like, 'Pigs seen flying over London'," he countered, a chuckle burbling forth. Then he sobered. "Who is she?" he asked in a quiet voice.

Charles took a deep breath and held it, surprised the question didn't have him experiencing heart palpitations. At least, not the kind he would have imagined having upon learning he was to marry. "Lady Eleanor Merriweather," he finally said.

The marquess frowned as he considered the name. "Was she the chit who was deposited in front of your home last night? At midnight?" he asked, his manner rather stern.

Lady?

Good God!

The earl sobered. "The very same. She ... She had a rather trying day at Lucy Gibbons' brothel yesterday," he started to explain and then noticed how Randall's eyebrows seemed to have difficulty in deciding if they wanted to be high or low or arched or furrowed. "Lucy kidnapped the chit when she arrived in town yesterday. Sent her to me as a birthday gift." He had a moment when he felt a bit sick upon thinking of what might have happened if Eleanor had ended up being sent to someone else. He wouldn't find himself on the verge of matrimony, of course, but Eleanor would be thoroughly ruined, with no hope of an advantageous marriage, no hope of a life within the *ton*.

Perhaps Lucy had known and had Eleanor sent to him thinking he would do right by her.

Charles shook his head. *Doubtful*, given how the madame had reacted earlier that day.

Kismet, then, could be the only explanation. Eleanor was destined to end up with him just as he was destined to realize she was his future.

"I find I am rather enamored with the chit," Charles stated. He dared a glance across the street, hoping Eleanor wasn't trying to escape out her bedchamber window. "I may even feel affection for her," he added, his brows furrowing with his words. He paused a moment before lifting his eyes up to see Randall's rather startled expression. "And to whom will you be wed?" he asked, realizing if he didn't change the subject, the marquess might very well end up passing out at his feet.

Randall considered Charles' words, deciding the man wasn't as inebriated as he first thought. "Miss Constance Fitzwilliam," he replied finally.

Charles gave him a blank look at first, and then angled his head. "One of Norwick's clan?" he guessed.

Randall nodded. "Cousin. Edward's daughter," he replied simply.

Charles angled his head, as if he were trying to remember something. "When ... When did you meet *her?*" he asked, wondering if perhaps the marquess had been courting the woman in private for the entire summer.

"This morning. In Hyde Park."

His eyes widening in alarm, Charles took a step back. "Dammit man," he said as he blinked. "You weren't joking when you said you wanted to marry," he said. "Does *she* know she's to be the Marchioness of Reading?"

Randall let out the breath he had been holding in a huff. "Not as yet," he allowed, "But I'm about to leave for Ludgate Hill in search of a wedding ring, and I know where she lives."

Charles regarded the marquess for a moment. "Why? Why her?"

The question had Randall rather stunned. Had he taken a moment to even think about what he was about to do, he might have a more ready answer for the Earl of Wakefield. But truth be told, he couldn't exactly explain what it was that had him thinking about Constance Fitzwilliam nearly every moment of that day.

"I truly feel affection for her," he answered finally. "We share common interests. She is beautiful. She is resourceful. She has been running a household in Sussex on her own for several years—"

"She has a racehorse."

Randall blinked, stunned at Charles' simple statement. *How did he know Constance had a racehorse?* "She does," Randall agreed. "As well as a cold-blood mare and several other horses," he agreed, berating himself for having divulged that last bit of information.

The younger earl seemed to deflate before his eyes. "You're marrying to get a damned *horse*, aren't you?" he accused.

"I am not!" Randall countered, annoyed at how Charles had suddenly turned from an amicable about-to-be-a-groom to his conscious in a matter of moments. "She has an appreciation for horses I have never seen in a person of her sex," he said in a hoarse whisper. "So, yes, that *is* part of the attraction," Randall admitted. "But I do ... I do *care* for her. I have thought of nothing *but* her for the entire day! I find myself wondering if she is safe. If she has enough to eat. If she has decent clothes, a suitable maid, and a comfortable bed," he went on, oblivious to the changing expression on Charles' face.

"You're in love," the earl said. The quiet words didn't sound like an accusation. Nor were they made in disbelief. They were merely a statement of fact.

"Oh, good God, I'm doomed," Randall said with a roll of his eyes.

Charles grinned. "Well, that makes two of us," he replied brightly. He glanced out the window and turned his attention back to the marquess. "Come get me when you're about to head for Doctors' Commons," he said. "And I'll join you."

Randall gave the earl a nod. "I suppose you've already bedded your bride-to-be," he ventured, one eyebrow arching up.

The other earl nodded. "A good thing, too, for if I hadn't, I wouldn't have known she was to be my wife."

Randall frowned but somehow understood the younger man's comment.

With that, Charles took his leave of Randall's study and headed back to his terrace, leaving Randall wondering a bit more about what might have happened the night before. He shook himself from his reverie, though, when he noted the time on the clock on the mantel and realized he had little time to make his next destination.

Ludgate Hill.

For once he had paid his call on the Earl of Norwick in the morning, he had only one thing left to do before taking Constance Fitzwilliam as his wife.

Buy some jewelry.

CHAPTER 32
A MARQUESS IN LUDGATE HILL

ine-thirty at night

At precisely half past nine o'clock that night, Randall climbed into his town coach. Having instructed the driver to take him to Ludgate Hill, he now considered which jeweler would have what he needed. *Do I even know what I need?* he found himself wondering, for Constance Fitzwilliam didn't strike him as a woman who coveted any particular gemstone, nor did he think she was partial to one particular precious metal over the other. Which left Randall in a situation he had never been in before—on his way to a jewelry store with no idea of what to buy.

He would need a ring, of course, decorated with an odd number of gems. Symmetrical in their arrangement. Not too large a central stone, though.

He imagined Constance's hand, remembered how her fingers had looked without gloves covering them. They were long fingers, he recalled, with oval fingernails. Any hard gemstone would do, although she had made mention of loving the color purple. *Amethyst?* Too common, he thought, remembering when a jeweler mentioned how many were being imported from Brazil. *Tourmaline? Tanzanite? Spinel?* He knew they were all available in various shades of purple. But what would be most valuable? *A purple sapphire,* he decided, with a pair of diamonds on either side. He hoped Rundell might have such stone in his shop.

And what about the precious metal on which it should be mounted?

Gold.

Yes, that would be best, he considered. Now he just had to ensure she would accept it—he rather doubted she would accept his suit without an inducement. He chided himself, remembering it would be entirely inappropriate to gift her with a necklace or bracelet—she wasn't yet married to him, nor was she his mistress. But he couldn't help but hope such a gift might soften her toward the idea of marriage to him.

Damn the rules! he thought then. He was going to buy her a necklace.

Although he had no idea how much Daniel Fitzwilliam would settle on her for her inheritance, Randall knew it would be enough for her to choose to live the life of a spinster comfortably. She wouldn't need Randall to make her way in life. Wouldn't need him in any capacity, he realized.

A blanket of melancholy settled over him for a moment as he imagined Constance turning down not only his gift of a necklace, but also his offer of marriage.

What the hell is happening to me? he wondered as the coach made its way through the dark streets of London. He had only known the chit for ... Randall checked his chronometer by the light of a gas lamp and sighed. *Twelve hours.* Never in his life had a woman so consumed his thoughts. Never had a woman intrigued him to the point that he wanted her company every moment of the day.

He imagined her occupying the seat across from him and then considered how much better it would be to have her seated next to him, her thigh pressed against his, her hand held in his.

I'll propose first, he thought, deciding he could give her the necklace when she accepted his offer. *If* she accepted his offer. Or perhaps he would give it to her no matter her answer so that she might reconsider her decision. Or he would give her both at the same time and insist she not give him an answer until the following day.

His lack of patience had him reconsidering that last thought. *Can I wait that long for her answer?*

Do I have a choice?

Some chits didn't provide an answer until months after the proposal! At least Lady Lily had kept her promise to give him her answer when she did.

The thought of Lady Lily brought him up short. Other than the few moments he had spent in her company at the charity, he hadn't thought of her since meeting the two women in the park that morning. His thoughts had been entirely on Constance. He sighed, rather relieved that memories of the young woman's rejection no longer had him feeling sorry for himself.

Now Constance might have that privilege, he realized.

He closed his eyes, imagining the two of them in the library in the house in Cavendish Square, sitting in front of the fire. She would be doing needlework while he read a book. Or pretended to read as he considered how he might pleasure her later that evening. How he might carry her up the stairs to the master suite. How he would undo the buttons on the back of her gown and push the garment off of her shoulders. How he would undo the ties of her corset and slip his hands beneath it to gently push it away. How he would skim his palms over her torso, his skin and hers separated by only the thin silk of her chemise.

Still standing behind her, he imagined undoing the tie at the top of the chemise. Imagined how he would allow his fingertips to graze her collarbones as he moved his hands to lift it from her body, slowly, so that the silk would barely touch her skin as it came off over her head, the frilly hem abrading her hardened nipples in the process. His hands would cover her breasts then, cupping them as he pulled her naked body against the front of his and kissed the nape of her neck, the tops of her shoulders, the space between her shoulder blades.

He was about to imagine more—much more—when the town

coach came to a halt. A moment later, the driver had the door open and the stairs lowered.

"I may be a bit longer than usual," he said as he stepped onto the pavement in front of No. 32 Ludgate Hill, relieved his imaginings had been interrupted when they were. A moment more and his erection would have been evident behind the placket of his breeches.

Randall paused as he regarded the central arch of the storefront for Rundell, Bridge & Rundell. Four majestic columns outlined the entrance as well as the colorful window displays on either side of the front doors. Four additional stories rose above the main floor, three of them fronted with columned windows and ironwork.

He considered how much he had spent on the baubles he had purchased therein. Surely not as much as Prinny, of course, but probably more than Lord Torrington.

Randall vowed that from now on, he would only buy jewels for a wife. Should Constance Fitzwilliam deny his proposal, the jewelers would have to find another customer—or several—to replace what he usually spent.

A footman hurried to open one of the doors, bowing as the marquess made his way into the building. Despite the late hour, a half-dozen shoppers milled about, studying the precious metals and gemstones, the array of candelabras and cups, tiaras and trays, pocket watches and swords—enough brilliance to overwhelm even the most jaded aristocrat.

Spotting the irascible Philip Rundell as he placed a newly finished brooch into a display case, the marquess hurried over and lifted his hat. "Good evening, Mr. Rundell," he said quickly. "I hoped I might find you here."

The older gentleman gave him a nod. "Lord Reading," he replied carefully. He frowned. "What is it?" he asked. "Did she not like the bracelet?"

Randall blinked. And blinked again when he realized the jeweler was referring to the widow to whom he had given a bangle only the week before. "She adored it, actually. But now I am in need of a ring.

Gold. A purple stone. Sapphire, perhaps? With multiple diamonds. Can you help?"

Rundell continued frowning, as if he took offense at Randall's query. He lifted a finger and crooked it as he led the marquess to a display case. He pulled a ring from a bed of black satin and held it up. Tiny diamonds surrounded a blue sapphire almost too large for the gold ring on which it was mounted.

"A bit ostentatious, I should think," Randall commented. *And more like what Torrington would buy for his bride*, he thought with some amusement. "Something a bit more ... linear, perhaps?"

Although the jeweler didn't roll his eyes, Randall was sure he wanted to. Rundell pulled another ring from the display case and lifted it close to his face, a loupe held between his eye and the stone mounted in a gold setting. He held out the ring so Randall could see it up close. "Like this?"

Randall studied the proffered ring, his eyes lighting up when he noticed the purple highlights reflected in a multifaceted stone set in the middle of a line of diamonds, each diamond slightly smaller than the one next to it. "I'll take it!" he said as he plucked the ring from Rundell's fingers, his words obviously surprising the jeweler. "I'm in need of something else, as well. An inducement. A necklace. Something that can't be easily removed once it's in place. With maybe a cameo or a locket or a ..." His mind raced as he imagined what such a necklace might best display. "A *horse*," he breathed.

Rundell angled his head to one side. "Any particular horse?" he asked carefully. "I've a silver charm." He moved toward another case and pulled out a tray of gold and silver trinkets, each an intricate shape intended for a young lady's charm bracelet. The silver one of a horse was three-dimensional, its mane and tail flowing behind it, its legs clearly in mid-stride.

"Yes!" Randall nearly shouted, his raised voice causing the low murmur in the store to cease completely. Heads turned in his direction to discover who might have made the loud comment. Ignoring the stares, Randall kept his attention on the charm. "I'll take it, too, along with a silver chain. A strong one," he reminded the jeweler.

"How long?"

Randall considered where the horse should rest when it hung from the chain around Constance's neck. If the chain was too long, the horse might end up beneath the bodice of her gown. But if it were short ... "So the horse rests in the hollow of her throat," he said in a low voice, one eyebrow arching up.

Angling his head to one side, Rundell screwed up his face as if concentrating. "A choker, then," he suggested. "I'll be a moment," he said before giving the marquess a nod and moving to the back of the store. He disappeared behind a curtain, leaving Randall to wait while he attached the trinket to a silver choker.

Realizing he still held the ring, Randall moved to a chair near the front of the store and took a seat, studying the ring as he angled it under the lamp lights. He smiled as he imagined how it would look on Constance, imagined how she might react to seeing the work of art for the first time. Her face would light up, her gorgeous blue eyes widening as a smile formed. And then he would briefly be the subject of her joy and attention as she reached up with one hand to rest it on his cheek while she stood on tip-toes and kissed him on the cheek.

If only, he thought, a wan smile forming on his own face at the thought of her initiating such a chaste kiss.

Philip Rundell reappeared from behind the curtain and glanced about, his attention finally settling on the marquess. In one hand, he carried a pasteboard box. Opening the lid, he angled it down so he could show off his creation to the marquess. "Will this suit, my lord?" he asked, rather pleased that the charm worked with the woven silver band that made up the width of the choker.

Randall studied the jeweler's work of art. He swallowed. Hard. "It will," he said with a nod, rising from the chair and reaching for the hinged box. "I'll pay you now, of course," he said as he followed the jeweler to the nearest counter, clutching the ring in one hand as he held the box in the other.

"Much appreciated, my lord," Rundell replied. "I will put the ring in a box, of course," he added. "And hope the intended recipient enjoys it as much as you do."

Randall nodded. "As do I," he murmured.

Within minutes, the marquess and his wrapped treasures took their leave of No. 32 Ludgate Hill.

The night ahead would be one of the longest of Randall Roderick's life, for how did one sleep when a proposal had to be rehearsed? A proposal as well as a request for permission to marry the chit.

A visit to the Earl of Norwick would have to come before a walk in the park, he realized.

CHAPTER 33

FOLLOWED BY AN EARL AND
A KNIGHT

en-fifteen at night

Charles Goodwin watched Randall Roderick take his leave of Rundell, Bridge & Rundell from where he stood in one corner of the jewelry store, the brim of his top hat kept low in an attempt to keep his identity a secret from the marquess should the man look his way. Despite their discussion at Randall's townhouse only the hour before, he was still rather surprised to find Lord Reading in the market for a wedding ring. From what he had said, the marquess hadn't yet proposed marriage.

When he saw the box the Mr. Rundell had brought from the back, he realized it was far too large for a ring. And then the jeweler had given him another box, a much smaller box far more suitable for a ring.

Once he was sure the marquess had left the premises, Charles made his way to where Mr. Rundell was completing a bill of sale at the counter.

"Pardon me, but may I inquire as to which ring Lord Reading decided to purchase?" he asked, as he held out his calling card in one hand while waving his other hand toward the display case containing an array of rings and bracelets.

The jeweler regarded him through the pair of spectacles that rested near the end of his nose and frowned. "My rings are one-of-a-kind, my lord," Mr. Rundell replied as he read the calling card. He didn't reach for it but moved to the display case to pull out a tray of rings. "However, it was similar to this one." He plucked a ring from the black velvet and held it up to a candle lamp. A row of five white gemstones twinkled from the gold band. "It featured a single sapphire, and the stones ..," he angled the ring to better show off its array of diamonds, "Were in a line on either side. This, of course, is made entirely of diamonds."

Charles was tempted to ask about the price of the beautiful ring, but thought better of it when he realized the jeweler was still frowning at him. "May I hold it?" he asked as he lifted his thumb and forefinger to retrieve the bauble.

"There are matching earbobs, of course," Mr. Rundell stated in a bored tone, making Charles wonder if he would be expected to purchase them. He held the ring for a moment, finally sliding it onto his pinky so he might picture how it would look on Eleanor's finger.

The rose-cut diamonds were quite impressive and larger than the gold band on which they were perched, although there was a series of gold filigree swirls separating the stones. *They will look stunning on her*, he thought. Should she ever find the need to defend herself, he figured they might act much like a set of brass knuckles, doing a good deal of damage to some rake's face should she take umbrage with him.

There was a passing thought of Eleanor using them against *him*, but he quickly put the thought out of his mind. He rather doubted she would risk damage to the ring by punching him in the face.

"I'll take the ring now. I'll hold off on the earbobs until the next special occasion," he added, realizing he had no idea when her next birthday might be. Perhaps he would get them for her for Christmas.

He inhaled sharply just then, realizing he would be a married man in time for the beginning of Parliament. Eleanor might already be with child. "On second thought, may I take a look at the earbobs?" he asked.

Mr. Rundell angled his head and pulled another tray from the display case before putting away the first one. One finger hovered over the tray as his eyes swept over the rows of earbobs. "Ah, here we are," he said as he lifted the earbobs from the black velvet.

"Jesus, they're huge!" Charles said as he regarded the pair of diamond-encrusted earbobs. The array of diamonds were arranged just as they were on the gold ring, smaller diamonds at the top and bottom and slightly larger ones in between those. In the middle was a large, round diamond. Filigrees of gold swirls separated the foil-backed stones.

"Suitable for a wedding gift or ... the birth of an heir," Mr. Rundell stated as he lifted his chin.

His heart racing, he hoped from excitement and not because he was about to faint, Charles nodded to the jeweler. "I'll take them now," he whispered.

Mr. Rundell regarded the earl with an expression that suggested he was rather impressed. "Of course. I'll put them into boxes right away," he said with a nod. "And will you be paying for them this evening? Or do I need to send the bill to your man of business?"

Charles gave a shrug, reaching into his waistcoat pocket for a wad of pound notes. "That depends on how much they cost," he replied.

Seeing the money, Mr. Rundell's eyebrow arched. Since most of his better clients were extended lines of credit that sometimes took years to pay, the usually surly jeweler felt an unusual urge to grant the earl a discount. "I'm sure we can work out a suitable settlement," he said.

Letting out the breath he had been holding, Charles gave the man a nod and began unfolding his money.

Five minutes later, Charles took his leave of the store, realizing he was one of the last people there. Most of the other patrons had left when the ornate clocks on display struck ten o'clock.

From where he sat in one of the chairs near the front of the store, Sir Arthur Goodwin lifted his head and nodded in the direction of Mr. Rundell. "I shall be quick, Mr. Rundell," he promised as he stood and made his way to where the jeweler stood shaking his head.

"Let me guess," Mr. Rundell said. "You're in need of a wedding ring."

Sir Arthur grinned. "I am. Something similar to the one you just sold my brother, but in a white gold, I should think."

For the third time in an hour, the jeweler took the tray of rings out of the display case and placed it in front of the knight. His customer studied a few of the rings before finally pointing to a white gold ring with a series of diamonds separated by tiny flutterbies. The entire band was decorated with the flutterbies, a motif he remembered had decorated the hair combs he saw in Lady Priscilla's coiffure when she had suggested their arrangement. "This will do nicely for Lady Priscilla," he murmured, handing the ring to the jeweler. "We're to be married in less than a fortnight, so I should like to take it with me tonight," he said as he pulled his purse from his waistcoat.

Mr. Rundell regarded Arthur with an arched eyebrow, rather surprised to hear that the man he was quite sure was rumored to be a molly would be purchasing a wedding ring. He sighed and nodded. "Was there some kind of contest? A wager perhaps?"

The knight blinked. "Whatever do you mean?" he asked as he frowned.

The jeweler shook his head. "Three wedding rings sold to three men I would never expect to enter into marriage, and all in less than an hour's time?" Mr. Rundell countered, an expectant expression on his otherwise sour looking face.

A slow grin spread over Sir Arthur's face as he considered the man's words. After a moment, he allowed a chuckle. "I see your point. Hades must be getting chilly."

Mr. Rundell didn't say what next came to his mind as he watched the knight take his leave of the jewelry shop.

I dare not step outside for fear of being hit by flying pigs.

CHAPTER 34
A MARQUESS PAYS A CALL
ON AN EARL

Nine-thirty in the morning of September 16, 1817
Daniel Fitzwilliam, Earl of Norwick, looked up
from the massive mahogany and cherry desk in his study to find the
butler on the threshold, his manner suggesting he had been there for
some time.

Having handled the Norwick earldom books for as long as his
twin brother had been the earl—and for the six months he'd had the
title since David's death—Daniel took some satisfaction in the
familiar work. He employed the same servants, purchased from the
same vendors, paid the same recurring invoices month after month,
and knew every account and its balance.

What bothered him now was the one that wasn't there. The
account that should have been. The account that would have seen
his cousin Constance set up with a generous dowry—or at least
monies on which she could live for the rest of her life.

Uncle Edward's affairs had been turned over to him upon the
man's death, although for the life of him, he couldn't remember
having been briefed on Constance and her situation. He hadn't seen
so much as a single invoice for the house in which she lived or for any
of her expenses. He had to surmise she was paying for everything—
and everyone's salary at Fair Downs—by herself.

No wonder she was nearly destitute!

Hildebrand cleared his throat, reminding Daniel of his presence.

"What is it, Hildebrand?" he asked as he set aside his quill.

The butler straightened and gave him a nod. "Lord Reading has asked he if might have a word with you, my lord," he said in the sort of voice he tended to use for visitors of some importance.

Daniel blinked. And blinked again. *Why would Randall Roderick wish to see me?* He was about to ask if the marquess provided a reason, but then Randall Roderick, Marquess of Reading, appeared behind his butler.

"I don't mean to appear impatient, but I shouldn't take more than a moment of your time, Norwick," he claimed, his hat hanging from one gloved hand. "I promise."

Daniel stood up, waving the butler away with a quelling glance. "Come in, Lord Reading," he said, deciding he couldn't very well chide the butler. The poor man had probably been on the threshold waiting to get his attention for nearly five minutes!

"To what do I owe this honor?" Daniel asked as he indicated an upholstered chair near the fireplace. He moved to the one placed adjacent to it, rather glad Clarinda had insisted there be some furniture of comfort in the otherwise austere room. She had seen to it the walls were lined in a warm mahogany veneer and the two windows were dressed in velvet drapes and silk sheers, but the room boasted little in the way of additional decoration, apparently because David had rarely used it. He hadn't needed to since Daniel did most of the work of running the earldom from Norwick Park.

Now Daniel was doing it every day from the Norwick House study.

Reading gave him a nod and waited for the butler to take his leave and shut the door before moving to the chair. "Your cousin, Lady Constance," he answered as he took a seat. He looked up to find Daniel staring at him in surprise.

"Pardon me, but I was just ... I was just contemplating my cousin's situation," Daniel said as he resumed his way to the sideboard. He caught two tumblers in one hand and a decanter of brandy in the other.

"Indeed?" Randall said as he gave an approving nod to the brandy. It wasn't yet ten o'clock in the morning, but a drink was most welcome just then. He was about to do something he hadn't imagined ever doing in his entire life.

Daniel took a seat and poured a generous amount in each glass. "I am at a bit of a loss as to how she has managed to keep the Norwick property near Boxgrove operating," he replied as he gave a glass to Randall. "I've kept the Norwick books for nearly ten years. I used to pay the bills for Fair Downs, but after Uncle Edward died, I can find no evidence she's ever forwarded an invoice or requested that an expense be covered by the earldom. It's a wonder the property hasn't been claimed by the throne."

Secretly glad to have his assessment of Constance affirmed—the chit had managed to keep a home and stables operating with little in the way of funds—Randall angled his head and gave Daniel a winning smile. "Resourceful woman, isn't she?" he responded. "Cares what happens to her servants, knows how to run a household, knows horses, certainly isn't a spoiled brat, and is a rather pretty woman. She would make a suitable Marchioness of Reading, don't you agree?"

About to take a sip of brandy, Daniel paused and stared at the marquess.

Before Daniel could say what first came to his mind, Reading angled his head, as if in warning. "I haven't ruined her, if that's what you're thinking, Norwick," he warned with a shake of his head. "My days as a rake are behind me, I assure you."

Daniel stared at the marquess for a moment. *You may not have, but someone else already did,* he thought then, wondering if Constance had mentioned anything about that awful night of her come-out, a come-out he and David had hosted at Norwick Park.

"Are *you* her protector now?" Randall asked.

Daniel angled his head, not quite sure how to respond. "Truth be told, Reading, I had completely forgotten about Cousin Constance until my wife mentioned her last night before dinner," he explained. "Seems she paid a call here yesterday, asking if Clare might request that I look into her missing inheritance."

Randall angled his head to match Daniel's. "And have you?"

The earl gave a nod toward his desk before finally shrugging his shoulders. "I just yesterday received queries from not one, but two different solicitors, and I've just returned from spending nearly an hour with a banker at Barings first thing this morning," he replied in the manner of a man who was weary of the topic. "I am of the opinion it doesn't exist in a monetary format," he said carefully. "But rather in the stables at Fair Downs in Boxgrove."

Randall stared at Daniel for several seconds. "A *horse?*" he half-questioned.

"More than one, I should think," Daniel replied with a nod. "A mare, her colt, one you may even remember from Ascot several years ago, and any others that may have been born since." He didn't add that he was curious as to the sire of the horse, Mr. Tuttlebaum, who had won the Ascot three years before, and the colt he remembered having made its debut the same night as Constance's come-out ball at Norwick Park. *Mr. Wiggins.* He allowed another sigh. *Where the hell did she come up the names?* Daniel had never attended a race meeting nor followed the sport, so he didn't know whom to ask about such things. Before today, he didn't have a reason to do so.

Randall frowned so that his eyebrows nearly formed into a single slash on his forehead. *A stable of racehorses?*

"How much do I need to settle on her? For her dowry?"

Daniel asked then, noting how the marquess seemed to stare off into space. He nearly asked the man if there was something else about Constance that had him wanting her hand in marriage, but Daniel decided the marquess' list of reasons was enough. *Constance must have made quite an impression on him,* he thought with some satisfaction. It was becoming quite clear she would make an excellent marchioness.

Shaking his head, Randall continued to frown. "I'm not looking for a dowry, dammit," he said with a shake of his head. "But she deserves her inheritance, Norwick. To do with as she pleases. See to that, at least.

"And give me permission to ask for her hand."

His eyes widening at Randall's demand, Daniel regarded the marquess for a moment before nodding once. "Done," he said. He lifted the decanter. "Shall we have another brandy and make a toast to it?"

Randall regarded the crystal decanter for a moment before giving his head a quick shake. "Thank you, no. With your permission, I shall take my leave of you and seek out your cousin."

Daniel held up a hand. "Allow me some time to see to it she comes for her inheritance," he said. "I'll write the cheque right now and send a summons."

Not particularly pleased by the delay Daniel's request would force on him, Randall finally nodded. "I'll seek her out at one o'clock," he agreed.

Before Daniel could stand up from his own chair, Randall was up and out of his chair and on his way out of the study. A moment later, Daniel heard the front door close.

Feeling a mix of relief and happiness, Daniel returned to his desk, pulled a blank cheque from his account book, and wrote in an even script, 'Pay to the order of Miss Constance Fitzwilliam the sum of fifty-thousand pounds.'

Pausing a moment, he wondered if he was really doing his cousin a favor. She wouldn't require a marriage in order to carry on at Fair Downs, but if she chose to turn down the marquess' offer of marriage, she also wouldn't have the protection a husband like Reading could provide.

At least she had nothing to fear from most of the men in the village of Boxgrove, he considered, given the majority were Benedictine monks who lived at the monastery located there. But he wondered about whom else might be employed at Fair Downs. Who saw to the stables? Was there a head groom? Stable hands? He couldn't imagine Constance being capable of all the work required to run the stables as well as the household.

Sighing, Daniel signed his name on the cheque with a flourish, wrote a quick note to summon his cousin, which he gave to a footman to deliver, and went about his accounting work.

CHAPTER 35
A COUSIN IS SUMMONED

Ten-thirty in the morning

Glancing at the clock on the wall in the breakfast parlor, Constance was curious. Had Randall Roderick returned from wherever he had gone when he left his townhouse earlier that morning?

She hadn't meant to spy on the gentleman. Hadn't meant to keep looking out the front window in the second-story parlor to watch him in the event he actually left his townhouse, but curiosity had her wondering about the man who lived so close, who had walked with her and treated her to an ice and insisted they do it again.

The temptation was almost too much to bear!

When she did see him take his leave of his house, she watched as he made his way toward Park Lane. *He's going to the park*, she realized almost immediately. She was almost to her bedchamber to fetch a bonnet and pelisse when she chided herself. She couldn't be going to the park. Not today. At least, not without Simmons, and her maid was busy doing laundry and the ironing. *And I shouldn't be going with the intent of meeting Mr. Roderick!* Nothing good could come from further interaction with the man. Instead, she had made her way to the breakfast parlor for her morning meal and found she could barely eat a thing.

Her entire night had been spent thinking of Mr. Roderick. Remembering how easy it had been to converse with the man. How handsome he was. How he had made her feel—as if she were the only woman in his life.

Although he had given her a reasonable explanation as to why he wished to see her again, she couldn't imagine why a man of his good looks and good fortune would have her best interest in mind. Perhaps he meant to spend enough time with her until he could offer her *carte blanche*. The thought had her heart racing just a bit too fast, and she chided herself for finding the thought as intriguing and as welcome as she did.

Constance would never become someone's mistress, of course, but the thought of sharing a bed with Randall Roderick had the flutterbies tumbling about again.

Having just read last week's issue of *The Tattler*, she knew what might be said if she, an unmarried woman, was spotted in the company of the man. At least only a few in London knew who she was or to whom she was related. Once word was out she was Lord Norwick's cousin, though, she would be subjected to the same critical perusals as every other woman in the *ton*.

"Pardon me, Miss Fitzwilliam, but there's a letter for you," Simmons said from where she stood on the threshold of the breakfast parlor.

Pulled from her reverie, Constance regarded her maid for a moment. "A letter?" she repeated.

For a few seconds, she thought Mr. Roderick had sent the missive, but Simmons quickly erased that supposition with her next words. "A footman just delivered it. It's from Norwick House, my lady."

Constance reached for the snowy white envelope, studying the red wax seal before she slipped a fingernail beneath it. The seal popped open, revealing a short note written in a decidedly masculine script.

Dear Cousin Connie, I learned only yesterday of your presence in London when Clarinda spoke of you before dinner. I rather wish you had asked to see me, as well, for I would have welcomed you. I wish to do so today. Please come to Norwick House at your earliest convenience.

Yours truly,

Daniel

Post Scriptum. I have your inheritance.

Constance lowered the parchment to her lap and dared a glance out the window in the direction of Park Lane. *My inheritance!* she thought with more relief than she thought possible. But a trip to Norwick House was obviously required to secure it, she realized with a sigh. Although she wasn't looking forward to renewing her acquaintance with the earl, she knew she had no other choice.

"Is it bad news? Is the earl evicting us?" Simmons asked from where she still stood watching her mistress.

Blinking, Constance gave her head a quick shake. "Of course not. He has merely summoned me. He has my inheritance," she said with a wan smile, rather liking how the words sounded spoken aloud.

The maid covered her mouth with the hands. "Oh!" she cried out. Although Constance had mentioned Mr. Roderick's offer of a position should she need a job at month's end, Simmons didn't relish the thought of having to work in a new household, and especially for someone she didn't know but for the few minutes they had walked together in the park the day before.

Smiling broadly, Constance reread the note and slowly folded it. "It seems I should change my gown. I need to take a walk to Park Lane again," she said with an arched eyebrow.

"Of course, my lady," Simmons said as she hurried out of the breakfast parlor, presumably to lay out a walking gown and half boots.

Constance followed her maid, although far more slowly and only after she dared another glance out the upstairs parlor window.

The sight of Randall Roderick climbing his front steps had her breath catching and the flutterbies tumbling about in her already queasy stomach. Taking a deep breath, she watched him until he disappeared through the front door. When would she see him again?

CHAPTER 36
A REUNION OF COUSINS

*E*leven o'clock in the morning

As Constance dressed, she considered hiring a barouche and driver from the mews behind the townhouse, but quickly changed her mind when she remembered how short the walk was to Norwick House.

And I'll have an opportunity to walk by Mr. Roderick's house, she thought with a grin. Checking her reflection in the bedchamber's cheval mirror, she wondered if the scarlet walking gown and pelisse were really the best color for her complexion. She knew the ensemble was at least two seasons out of fashion, although the matching hat was current—she had purchased it at Fitzsimmons and Smith her second day in London in an effort to make the ensemble more fashionable.

"I doubt I'll be long," she said to Simmons as she took her leave of the Norwick townhouse and made her way toward Park Lane.

Despite her best efforts, she couldn't help but glance toward the townhouse in which Randall Roderick lived. *Is he watching me?* The tiny hairs at the back of her neck tickling her just then. She imagined him standing in the second-story window, probably in his bedchamber, gazing at her. Although she told herself not to, she glanced about and allowed her own gaze to take in the window across the street and above her. Given the way the sun hit the glass pane, she was unable to see anything beyond, though.

Increasing her pace, she hurried on to Park Lane and along the row of stylish Palladian mansions until she reached the one known as Norwick House.

The butler opened the door before she had a chance to reach the top step, moving aside to allow her entry.

"Thank you," she said with a nod. "Miss Constance Fitzwilliam to see the Earl of Norwick," she added. She noted how the servant seemed surprised by her statement, but she realized he probably expected her to ask for Lady Norwick.

"One moment," he said with a nod as he gave her a bow and left the vestibule.

Constance took a deep breath, realizing this would be the first time she would see her older cousin since the night of her come-out. The first time since they had sworn they would speak to no one of what had happened that night in the stables. She had sworn the same to Daniel's twin brother, David, but he was dead now. *He took his secret to the grave*, she realized.

And her own secret? Had Daniel kept his word?

"Follow me, please," the butler said, his voice startling Constance out of her reverie.

"Of course," she managed as the butler led them down the same wide hallway she had been in yesterday, her footsteps echoing on the marble floor despite the beautiful tapestries and silk-lined walls. They passed the parlor door and continued on past paintings of ancestors she realized she should know. And then she was over the threshold of a man's study and staring at her cousin, Daniel.

"Cousin Connie!" he said with a huge grin. His brown hair was longer and bushier than the current styles allowed, and his sideburns were well past his earlobes in length, but given his impeccable suit of clothes and snowy white cravat, Daniel looked every bit the earl he had become as a result of David's death. "Good God. I was afraid I wouldn't recognize you, but I would know you anywhere," Daniel added as he stepped from behind the desk and hurried to her.

"My lord," Constance replied as she gave him a curtsy.

"Oh, call me Daniel, please. We're family," he replied. "Come. Have a seat," he said as he gestured toward the chairs that faced an enormous fireplace.

"I don't mean to take you away from your business," Constance protested.

Daniel noted her skittish behavior. "Nonsense. I've not seen you for an age, and we've a bit of business to settle, it seems."

Her eyes widening in surprise, Constance moved to do his bidding. "I received your letter. It is true you found my inheritance?" she asked, hoping she didn't sound desperate.

Or spoiled.

Daniel sobered and reached for a paper from his desk. "Well, that is one of the bits of business," he said as he handed her the cheque.

Constance dared a glance at the bank draft. "Twenty-thousand pounds?" she breathed, astounded by the amount.

"I do hope it's enough," Daniel said as he motioned her to sit down. She did so, more because she found herself unable to continue standing just then.

"I wasn't expecting it to be *this* much. Where ... where was it?"

Not sure how to answer, Daniel allowed a shrug before he took a seat. In an effort to gather his thoughts, he motioned to the footman near the door. "Bring tea and coffee, please. And cake," he added, thinking he would share any that were leftover with his wife.

"Oh, that's not necessary," Constance interjected.

Daniel regarded her for a moment, wondering at her nervousness. "Well, it is for me, cousin," he countered with a grin. "I've been balancing books and dealing with my banker all morning, and I could use a cup of coffee. Now, about your inheritance," he started to say before he was interrupted again.

"Pardon me, my lord, but the countess is wondering if she and the young ladies might be allowed to join you?" Hildebrand asked from the doorway.

Daniel gave his cousin an arched eyebrow and said, "By all means." He turned his attention back to Constance. "It seems your father may have gambled away all but what you've been using to run the estate," he said. "Fair Downs is an entailed property of the Norwick earldom, and yet I've not received a single invoice for the place since Uncle Edward died."

Constance stared at her cousin for a moment, rather surprised by his words. "Did I do wrong by seeing to it the bills were paid?"

Daniel shook his head. "Not at all, but ... what I am wondering is *how* have you been able to do it?" he asked. "As far as me or the two solicitors who are familiar with the situation can tell, my uncle didn't leave a pence unspent. Which begs the question—how have you kept Fair Downs solvent?"

Inhaling slowly, Constance angled her head to one side. "My mother's pin money, I suppose," she said. "She hid it in cubbies and nooks and crannies all over the house so that father wouldn't find it. But ... despite searching from cellar to attic, I've not been able to find any more of it. I brought the last of it with me a couple of weeks ago —Mrs. Cunningham offered me a ride to London, you see—and I feared I would be destitute at the end of the month."

Furrowing his brows so that a wrinkle of skin developed between his eyebrows, Daniel shook his head. "It's a wonder you made it through last winter," he commented.

Constance's eyes widened. "We have Mr. Bennett-Jones to thank for that," she said. "He owns coal mines nearby and saw to it we had enough to get us through the coldest days."

Daniel continued to frown. *Mr. Bennett-Jones?* "Lord Bostwick, you mean?" he clarified.

Her face coloring, Constance nodded. "Yes. I forget he's a viscount now. He and his wife have been most kind, and not just because of his investment."

Blinking, Daniel stilled himself. "Investment?" he repeated.

Constance nodded. "In the stables. He was determined to have his Arabian sire another colt with my Amasia, since she was the mare who gave birth to Mr. Tuttlebaum and Mr. Wiggins, so he has been helping with the expense of a stablehand to see to the horses at Fair Downs."

"Jesus," Daniel murmured. He shook his head, realizing he had cursed. "I apologize. But I ... I had no idea you were forced to seek monetary help from him—"

"Oh, but I wasn't. George Bennett-Jones offered, you see. He's quite determined to have a horse he can race in a few years," she explained, "And I think Amasia has at least one more winner in her. She's due to foal in the spring."

Daniel stared at his cousin for a long time. "It's my belief your father intended for those stables to be your inheritance," he said quietly.

Constance blinked a few times, surprised at hearing the earl's words. "But he knows I would never *sell* any of the horses," Constance countered. "We need the work horses for haying, and I ride the Trotter, and I could never part with Amasia."

Angling his head to one side, Daniel considered her words. "I expect he thought you would collect stud fees for Mr. Tuttlebaum and *race* Mr. Wiggins," he said.

Constance shook her head. "But I could not. Mr. Wiggins would never have qualified when he was three years old. He wasn't nearly fast enough." After a pause, she eyed her cousin for a moment. "Now that he's nearly six, though, he's faster than Mr. Tuttelbaum was, so it might be possible for him to race in the Ascot at the end of the next Season."

Daniel regarded her for a moment. "I see," he said with a nod. Having never owned a Thoroughbred and never having attended any of the race meetings, the earl was a bit out of his element. Then he remembered the visit by Lord Reading earlier that morning. Perhaps the marquess could see to it Mr. Wiggins was entered in the Ascot.

A commotion outside the study door caught his attention. "We'll pick this up in a moment. You're about to meet some more cousins," he said with an arched brow. He rose to his feet as his wife, Clarinda, swept into the room, her dark hair piled atop her head in a mass of curls and her yellow muslin skirts swirling about her legs as she carried a blanket-wrapped bundle in her arms.

"Miss Fitzwilliam! It's so good to see you again," Clarinda

gushed as she hurried over to Daniel, bussing him on the cheek as she handed him the baby. The servant who had followed her into the room placed another in her arms. She hurried to where Daniel's cousin sat and took the one remaining chair. "I'd like to introduce you to your late cousin David's daughters," she said as she angled the baby she held in Constance's direction. "Lady Dahlia Davida …" She motioned to the one Daniel held up. "And Lady Diana Dorothea. They're just over three weeks old," she said proudly.

Both babies, wide awake and actively moving about inside their blankets, sported dark hair and chubby cheeks.

"Oh, they're beautiful," Constance murmured as Clarinda settled Diana into her arms. Startled at the weight of the baby, Constance felt the oddest sensation as the baby's eyes seem to focus on her. "Oh! Well, aren't you just the most precious thing?" she whispered. She used a finger to push away the edge of the blanket and was startled when the baby's fingers suddenly wrapped around it and her legs kicked up. "Oh!"

Clarinda beamed as she watched Constance hold the older twin daughter. "They're just now up from their morning nap. I wanted to be sure you met them, especially given your good news."

Constance turned her attention to the countess. "Whatever do you mean?" she asked, her attention back on the baby when she made a cooing sound.

"Why, your having impressed Lord Reading, of course!" Clarinda said brightly. "He is a catch, to be sure, even if he's better known as the Rake of Reading—"

"Clare!" Daniel interrupted. His countess turned her attention his way. "I don't believe the marquess has had the opportunity to …" He allowed the sentence to trail off, one eyebrow arching in the process.

"Oh, but surely Constance knows he's about to make an offer," she countered, not the least bit deterred by her husband's warning.

Constance gave a nervous laugh, her gaze on the baby finally broken. "I'm sure you must be mistaken, my lady. I've not been …

courted by anyone here in London, and I certainly don't know Lord ... *Reading*, did you say?"

Clarinda turned her attention from her husband to Constance and back again. "But, I thought you said he asked your permission this morning when he was here," she argued.

"He *did*," Daniel acknowledged, his words clipped as he gave his head a quick shake in her direction.

"*Who* is Lord Reading?" Constance asked then, her sudden confusion wiping away the grin she had been displaying for the baby. Diana frowned and appeared about to cry when Constance realized she needed to resume her playful faces or be holding an unhappy baby.

"Why, the Marquess of Reading, of course," Clarinda replied. "Randall Roderick. According to *The Tattler*, you were seen at Gunter's Tea Shop with him only yesterday."

Her head jerking up, Constance regarded the countess with an open mouth and an expression that suggested she might faint at any moment. "But, that cannot be. He ... he never once mentioned he was a *lord*," she managed to get out. *And he never once implied he intended to make any kind of proposal.*

Sensing the distress of the one who held her, Diana's face once again screwed up into a frown, and she let out a cry. Instinctively, Constance raised the babe to her shoulder and patted its back.

Clarinda exchanged a glance with Daniel and sighed. "He's quite rich," she offered with a shrug.

"Yes, I did get that impression when he spoke of his house in Cavendish Square and his property in ..." Reading.

Damnation! All the signs were there, and yet, because he hadn't introduced himself as a titled gentleman, she had assumed he was merely a well-to-do cit.

"And don't forget the stables," Daniel said, one of his fingers in the possession of the baby he held. "If Mr. Wiggins is race-ready, I'm certain Reading would have the contacts necessary to get him into the Ascot."

Constance gave him a nod. "No doubt," she murmured, a hint

of panic threatening her morning meal. "I really should be going," she said.

"But the tea will be here at any moment," Clarinda replied as she moved to take the baby from Constance, realizing the woman was about to leave even if the tea arrived right then.

The loss of the warm weight of the baby from her shoulder had Constance feeling even more stunned than she already did. She would never have one of her own to hold like that. Never have one to love like her cousin and wife did. "Thank you, but I really must take my leave," she managed to get out before she stuffed the cheque into her reticule and curtsied.

"You're welcome anytime," Daniel said as he quickly got to his feet, his bundle cooing with the sudden movement as he bowed.

Constance curtsied again to the countess and took her leave of Norwick House.

Clarinda and Daniel watched as his cousin hurried out of the study, their gazes turning on one another and then finally to the babes they held.

"I made a cake of that, didn't I?" Clarinda murmured to the daughter she now held.

Diana stared up at her mother and burped rather loudly.

CHAPTER 37
TRUTHS BE TOLD

*O*ne o'clock in the afternoon

"You're looking especially beautiful this afternoon, my lady" Randall said as he came abreast of the woman in scarlet and offered her his arm.

Constance Fitzwilliam paused on the crushed granite path, apparently surprised to find the very man she had been thinking about right next to her, as if she had conjured him into appearing with her thoughts.

She had been deep in thought—Lady Norwick's words had been rattling about in her brain—and she hadn't heard—or seen—his approach from the carriageway.

"How do, Lord Reading," she offered, giving a short curtsy to the man who had filled her dreams the night before.

Randall sighed, holding out his arm again. *Lord Reading?* Well, either she had asked as to his entire identity or someone had told her. *Norwick, probably.* "As I said yesterday, I would prefer you call me 'Randall'," he murmured.

Hesitating before placing her arm on his, Constance eyed the man with suspicion. "Calling you by your given name seems a bit ... informal, especially since you're a lord, and we only just met yesterday morning."

The marquess considered her words. "We may have only just met, my lady, but it feels to me as if I have known you my entire life," he countered. "I wonder why that is."

Gasping and once again pausing on the walkway, Constance shook her head. "I assure you, my lord, we had not met before yesterday," she repeated, wondering if Lord Reading had her confused with another woman. Having just learned of his reputation from Clarinda, she now suspected his only reason for pursuing her on this day was to offer her *carte blanche*. Why else would a marquess wish to be in her company other than to offer her the position of mistress?

Although the vocation would have alleviated her financial situation—she was quite sure he would have provided a townhouse and enough pin money for her to live on for at least a year—she certainly didn't need to accept such an offer now that she had Daniel's cheque in her reticule. *Fifty-thousand pounds!* She could return to Boxgrove and live on that sum very comfortably for the rest of her life.

"I certainly don't know why you would think you have met me before," she finally answered. Recalling their discussion about her identity only the day before, she angled her head. "After your query about my true identity yesterday, it's a wonder you made no mention of your *full* identity when you introduced yourself," she accused, remembering how confused she had been upon hearing Clarinda's comment. *Lord Reading.*

The Rake of Reading.

The marquess took a breath and held it a moment, realizing she did have a good point. "Touché, my lady," he said with a grin.

Although Constance thought she should feel some level of satisfaction at hearing the lord's admission, she found she did not. It was far better to think of Randall as simply a well-to-do cit, a man who might have been amendable to a marriage of convenience should she need his funds to keep Fair Downs solvent. Given his lofty title, though, she found herself uncomfortable in his presence. Much like how she felt in the company of Daniel Fitzwilliam until he had welcomed her so warmly. *Cousin Connie!* As if there had never been that horrific night in the stables. As if they both hadn't been aware of what David had done to her attacker that night.

"I am happy to have found you this afternoon," Randall said, hoping she wouldn't realize he had simply followed her to the same place in the park where they had met the day before when he watched as she left Norwick House, her expression troubled and her steps rather slow. "We have much to discuss. And I ... I have a proposal I would like you to consider. One that I believe will be amenable to the two of us."

Constance could feel her cheeks start to burn with embarrassment. She had guessed right then, she realized. Unsure of how to respond, Constance took a step back. "I beg your pardon, my lord, but I do not believe I should be considering *anything* you propose. I ... I must go," she said, giving a quick curtsy before turning back from whence they had come.

Caught off-guard by her cold response, Randall was about to ask what had her so upset and instead realized he felt rather offended by her comment. Reaching out with one hand, he hooked it into her elbow and pulled her back toward him. Spinning about and bit off-kilter, Constance let out a yelp when she collided with him.

"Pardon me, my lady, but just what did you think I meant when I said I wanted to discuss a proposal with you?" he asked, his expression one of hurt more than anger.

Regaining her footing and trying to do so without having to hang onto the marquess' arm, Constance shook her head. "I thought you were going to offer to help me and then ... and then *demand* ... something in return," she finally said, a tooth catching her lower lip. "But I don't *need* your help."

Randall watched the tooth as it deformed the pillow of her lower lip, still wondering what she thought until it seemed to suddenly hit him upside the head. "Oh, my *God!* You thought I was going to ask that you be my mistress!" he whispered hoarsely. He angled his head back so he was regarding the white, puffy clouds above. He shook it and sighed loudly.

Constance swallowed, her eyes widening at his apparent shock.

"Clearly not what you had in mind," she murmured, wondering why she felt bereft that he wasn't going to offer her *carte blanche*. She wouldn't have accepted, of course, but to know he wanted her in his bed would have been a boon to her ego just then.

"My lady, I am not looking for a *mistress*," Randall stated quite firmly. "I'm looking for a *wife!*"

Constance blinked. And blinked again as she considered his claim. *Well, this is unexpected.* She had to suppress the urge to laugh, both at herself and at him. "You cannot expect me to believe you're having difficulty finding a *wife*, Lord Reading," she said with humor she hadn't felt in weeks. She could feel her cheeks heat up with embarrassment, feel the pink color her cheeks. Despite the seriousness of their earlier conversation, she found she couldn't help but smile at his expense.

Taken aback by her response, Randall gave a huff. "It's not nearly as easy as it sounds," he countered, rather glad the topic had her smiling. She was beautiful when she smiled, her blue eyes bright and her cheeks glowing as they lifted on her face.

"You're a marquess!" Constance stated, chiding him with her comment.

Randall nodded. "I am," he agreed, his smile matching hers. It disappeared as quickly as it had appeared, though. "However, I also have a reputation as a rake, as you have apparently discovered." He sighed. "Norwick told you, I suppose?"

Her smile slowly fading, Constance shook her head. "His countess," she murmured, realizing Clarinda's reference to an *offer* meant a marriage proposal.

Randall hissed, feeling a bit annoyed with Clarinda Fitzwilliam. "A reputation that does me no favors when pursuing a wife," he remarked dryly.

Constance sobered even more. "Why would a man such as yourself even be interested in *me* of all people?" Constance asked, her brows furrowed.

Randall managed a shrug, realizing she had put forth a rather interesting query. Why, indeed, was he interested in her? *Am I so desperate to marry that I merely selected the next woman with whom I came in contact after Lady Lily's refusal?*

No. That wasn't it.

He was intrigued by Constance. Interested in her. Impressed with her. And she had horses, perhaps one who could race. "I cannot say exactly, my lady," he finally replied, not sure what else he could say to answer her simple question.

The young woman shook her head, obviously not believing his claim. "Cannot? Or won't say?" she asked, her manner displaying her growing impatience.

Randall swallowed, deciding he was going to have to tell her something. "I ... I found you ... intriguing, interesting, resourceful," he finally admitted. "And then, when I discovered your interest in horses and the unfortunate situation with your inheritance, I—"

"*What?*" Constance interrupted, her hands gripping the handle of her reticule. "How did you learn about my *inheritance?*"

Realizing he had been caught, Randall nearly rolled his eyes. If he told her how he had learned of her missing inheritance, he would have to tell her *everything*.

One hand went to his pocket, where the ring he had purchased the night before was wrapped in black velvet and nestled next to the slim box that contained the choker with the horse charm. He almost drew out the box, thinking he could deflect her question with the jewel. But then he figured if he didn't tell her the truth now, it would no doubt come out at some point in the future, perhaps in conversation. Better he tell her now and risk her ire than try to fix it later, he decided. "I learned of your situation from your solicitor," he said quietly.

Feeling as if she had been punched in the stomach, Constance took a step back and regarded Randall with a look of confusion. "Did he ... did he *hire* you to look for it?" she asked, thinking that could be the only explanation for how he would know about her.

Was he an investigator in addition to being the lord she had just learned him to be?

"No," Randall replied. "I paid him a visit after you left his office.

I ... I was concerned ..." He sighed. "Remember, I saw you go into his office. You seemed ... rather upset when you left."

Her eyes widened in alarm. "You *followed* me?" she asked in dismay, her breathing coming in short pants. "How dare you? Why ... *why* would you do that?"

Randall took a deep breath, realizing she was quite incensed. Would presenting her with the choker help the situation or only make it worse? He glanced around as if he were looking for an escape. "I cannot say exactly," he finally answered.

Constance blinked. She had to relax her fingers If she hadn't been wearing gloves, she was sure her nails would be leaving indentations in the palms of her hands. "You expect me to believe you cannot form a ... a reasonable explanation for your having followed me?"

The marquess allowed a sigh. "I saw you leave your home without the benefit of a chaperone. I couldn't allow you to simply walk the streets of London without an escort," he countered, his voice sounding ever so reasonable.

The words caught her off-guard before she realized that for him to have seen her leave her home meant he had been watching her house. "You were spying on me!" she half-accused.

"I was not," Randall answered right away. "I just happened to glance out the window when you took your leave of your townhouse. You didn't have a chaperone, and since I was about to head in the same direction, I merely thought to keep an eye on you. To be sure you arrived at your destination. The streets of London are not safe for a woman such as yourself—"

"You expect me to believe you had business at the same time as me? In the same direction?"

"But I did," he assured her. "I paid a visit to Lady E's 'Finding Work for the Wounded'. As it turns out, the charity's offices are located right next door to your solicitor's office."

Constance listened to Randall's words, her initial anger subsiding when she remembered him having said that he had seen her the day before. "I do recall you mentioning you had seen me when I was leaving Mr. Barton's office," she admitted finally.

Randall nodded. "I did. I was dropping off my donation and paying my respects to Lady Lily."

At the mention of Lady Lily, Constance felt a bit of jealousy. *Lady Lily?* Who was she? "Are you ... courting her?" she asked in a small voice.

Seeing the sudden change in Constance, Randall felt a glimmer of hope. "No. In fact, I was congratulating her on her recent marriage to Mr. Overby," he replied lightly. "And I admit, I was a bit concerned for her welfare since she was volunteering her services in an office that consists mostly of men whose clients are all men." When he noticed Constance's look of shock, he added, "As it turns out, her husband's uncle is one of the employees there. He is acting as her protector whilst she is there. And he's doing a fine job. Until he discovered I was there to make a donation, he seemed ready to wrestle me to the ground before allowing me a word with Lady Lily."

Constance allowed a nod. "She is a blessed woman to have not only a husband she loves but a relative to see to her safety," she commented, her indignation with him finally dissipating.

"My lady," Randall said quietly, his manner sobering. "With your permission, I would like to give you something."

Constance stared at him, wondering at the sudden change in him. "I'm sure that's probably not a good idea," she started to say, her head shaking as she watched him remove a slim box from his waistcoat. The pasteboard was covered in dark velvet. Although she had only been given one piece of jewelry the night of her come-out— a gift from her father—she knew what velvet boxes contained. "What ... what is that?" she asked, her voice barely a whisper.

Randall regarded the box a moment, positioning it so the hinge was facing him. "I had Mr. Rundell make this for you," he replied, opening the top lid to show her the silver choker. The horse charm, a bit askew, slipped into place when he gave the box a slight shake. "You see, I was impressed with your love of horses," he added. *And roses, and bubbles in your bath water, and in your champagne glass, and the color purple.*

Before Constance had a chance to protest, he removed the choker from the velvet lining and gave her the empty box. She grasped it by reflex. Had she not, it would have fallen to the ground as Randall used his other hand do undo the clasp. He was behind her and wrapping the silver around her neck as she gasped and held her breath, one of her hands going up to finger the horse charm as it settled into the hollow of her throat.

"Mr. Rundell?" she repeated. "The silversmith?" she breathed, stunned by the weight and feel of the tiny interlocked chains that made up the band on which the charm was attached.

"The very one," Randall said with a nod, moving around her so that he once again stood in front of her. He angled his head as he regarded the jewelry. The horse rested right in the hollow of her throat, just as Mr. Rundell assured him it would.

Randall noted her stunned expression before he allowed a grin. "It looks far better on you than it does in the box, my lady." He paused to take a breath. "I do hope you'll wear it in public. There's no reason anyone need know it was a gift from me."

Constance regarded him for several moments, quite certain he intended to offer her *carte blanche* if she didn't agree to be his wife. He still hadn't given her a reason as to why he considered her for the position.

How much did he spent on the necklace?

He had been speaking of a married woman, sounding as if he might have felt affection for the young lady. Had he intended to take her as his wife before she decided on another man to marry? If he couldn't have her as his wife, did he intend to employ her as his mistress?

Well, there was only one way to find out.

"Have you ... made an offer to anyone?" she asked, wondering at the odd sensation she felt upon thinking of him with another woman. *Is he going to ask me?* Her pulse raced with the thought.

"I did indeed," he said matter-of-factly, rather glad the comment no longer had him feeling a bit sick. "She was a maid, you see. A very lovely young woman," he added with a nod, as if he dared the earl's cousin to counter his claim.

Constance's eyes widened. "Why ever would she turn down a marriage proposal when she could have been a marchioness?" she asked, at once feeling relief and then even more nervous. The nervousness had her breathing a bit too quickly, every inhalation enhanced by the sensation of the warm metal around her neck.

"Why indeed?" Randall countered, a sly grin lifting one corner of his mouth. "And yet, she did." After a pause, he shrugged. "Truth be told, she turned me down in favor of a clerk."

"A clerk?" Constance moved one hand to rest on her middle, as if she had been struck by a physical blow rather than by the simple word. Relief once again settled on her and she allowed a wan smile.

Seeing her reaction, Randall felt an inkling of hope. "She loves him. Probably has since the boy saved her from ruination." Waiting a moment, he closed his eyes and said a silent prayer. "He loves her, of course," he said, wondering why he thought it important she know that last bit.

Constance considered the comment. "Then, will she marry her clerk?" she asked, still a bit stunned that a young woman—a woman who had been a maid—would forgo a life of wealth and privilege in exchange for one that might not be so comfortable.

"She already did. A few days ago, in fact." Noting her continued consternation, Randall added, "Do not despair on her behalf. She is the Lady Lily I saw at Lady E's charity yesterday. She is the sister of Lord Trenton. He would not have allowed the union had he thought Mr. Overby unworthy of her."

How she had missed knowing about the connection between Lord Trenton and his sister? She could swear the copy of DeBrett's at the Norwick estate in Sussex listed only the *one* living offspring of Graydon Trenton and Charity Fitzsimmons—Gabriel Wellingham, the current Earl of Trenton.

Then the reason dawned on her. "She was illegitimate," she said in a whisper.

"Indeed," Randall confirmed.

Constance's eyes widened again. "And yet, you made her an offer of marriage," she whispered hoarsely. Despite her quiet words, the comment came out as an accusation.

"I did," he agreed. "I was ... enamored. I thought her ..." His voice trailed off as he realized the sting of Lily's decision hadn't softened as much as he thought. "I thought her a brave young lady who would do me proud."

He didn't dare mention that he thought himself in love with Lady Lily, although he probably had only been for a brief time. She had been the first woman he considered for the role of his marchioness. The first woman with whom he hadn't done something scandalous when he had taken her into Lord Weatherstone's gardens.

When he noticed how Constance seemed to wait for him to say more, he added, "But I believe she was a bit intimidated by the fact that she is the same age as my oldest son." The words were out before Randall realized to what he admitted.

Inhaling sharply, Constance stared at Randall. "Your *oldest?*" she repeated, wondering how he could have sons and not had a marchioness. Unless he had married before inheriting, of course. And then been widowed. "Have you ... have you been a widower very long?" she hedged, finding her opinion of the marquess changing.

His eyebrows drawing together, Randall realized almost immediately why Constance would assume the best of him.

Bless her heart.

"In fact, I have never been married, my lady. My sons are all bastards," he stated, not bothering to suppress the wince he always seemed to display upon making the admission. He rather wished he could have put off telling the young woman about his boys, but he decided it was far better for her to know now than for her to find out from one of the London gossips who always reveled in putting voice to such details.

Constance looked as if she were about to faint. "M ... more than one?" she managed, her breaths once again coming a bit too fast. For a moment, she had thought the marquess was about to ask for her hand in marriage, and despite her original desire to simply live her life as a spinster, she had actually imagined a life as a married woman.

Imagined a life with Randall Roderick.

Randall let out the breath he had been holding. "Four, my lady," he finally admitted. "The mother of one of them was married to a man who could not give her a child, and she desperately wanted one, and he needed an heir, and so I ..."

As her vision grayed around the edges, Constance merely gave a nod in response. A moment later, she was falling through darkness.

CHAPTER 38
A COURTSHIP BEGINS WITH
A FAINTING SPELL

One-thirty in the afternoon of September 16

Having some experience with fainting women, Randall Roderick was quick to recognize the symptoms of a woman whose head was about to drop backwards as her body slumped, as if in slow motion, to the ground. The culprit could almost always be identified as a corset drawn too tight by an overeager lady's maid. However, on this day, he was quite sure *he* was the reason Constance Fitzwilliam's eyes clouded over and her head dropped back.

Or at least his news about his bastard sons.

He had an arm behind her shoulders and another behind her knees well before she fell to the crushed granite path.

Dammit all to hell, he thought as he glanced toward the east in an effort to determine how far it was to Lord Devonville's residence. The fellow marquess was no doubt in residence, and even if he weren't, his butler, Hatfield, would allow him entrance and a guest bedchamber in which to place Miss Fitzwilliam.

A glance to the west had him spying the park bench he had occupied only the day before. Although it wouldn't allow for the same comfort as a bed, it was much closer in proximity.

He opted for the park bench, and not just because of its proximity. He wanted to be present when Constance awakened. He *needed* to be present. He still had things to tell her. Things he needed to say. Explanations to provide.

He glanced down at her prone body as he made his way with quick, measured steps. She was beautiful, her mouth open just a bit, her lashes dark arcs lining her delicate eyelids. Her cheeks had been rosy while they walked. Now they were pale, as was her forehead. Given the way her head hung beyond the support of his arm, her hat's brim no longer shielded her face from the morning sun, and her skin appeared almost translucent. He had to bite back a smile when he spotted a series of freckles on her nose.

He imagined her sleeping in his bed, his own body pressed up next to hers so that he could hold one of her breasts while they slept. Perhaps he would tuck her body against the front of his own for shared warmth in the cold winter nights. Or perhaps she would prefer her head be tucked into the small of his shoulder while one of her bent legs lay between his, the top of her thigh cradling his manhood.

Randall had to shake his head. It was hard enough to walk while carrying Constance. An erection would make it nearly impossible.

Upon reaching the park bench, he simply lowered himself until he was safely seated, Constance still held in his arms. He dared a glance around, hoping no one could see them. He listened intently for the sound of voices, but heard only birdsong.

Sure they were alone, he relaxed against the back of the bench, readjusted the arm behind her shoulders to give her neck some support, and waited until her lids fluttered open.

Having experience with women who had fainted, and then being in their presence when they came to, Randall knew exactly what to say.

At least, he thought he did.

"Good afternoon, beautiful," he whispered.

Her eyes widening in alarm, Constance gave a shriek and kicked her legs, forcing Randall to give up his hold on them. He had to prevent her from falling off of him completely and onto the crushed granite below, though, so he simply moved his now-free hand to secure her other shoulder.

To any passing park patron, the two would have appeared as a randy couple on a bench, perhaps engaged in a bit of kissing. If they had looked a bit closer, however, they would have noticed how the young lady struggled to free herself of the man who held her.

"My lady, be *still* or you'll fall on your bum!" Randall said with enough force that Constance ceased her movements. She glared at him and then dared a glance around where they sat. "Where ..? What *happened?*" she asked in alarm.

"You fainted. I caught you. I carried you here."

Constance sighed and dropped her head onto his shoulder. Randall heard as much as felt her sudden sob. Concerned, he shook his head. "Please don't cry, my lady. I'm quite sure no one has seen us," he said quietly, wishing her hat had come loose from its pins. Its brim was preventing him from dropping a kiss onto her forehead, which is what he wanted to do at that moment. Anything to console her. Anything to make her want him.

"How many?" she whispered.

Randall was about to ask as to what she was referring when he realized she was wondering about his sons. "I have four sons," he replied, about to continue by telling her their names when she removed herself from his hold, and from the bench, and was suddenly standing up, a bit unsteady on her feet. Randall stood up as quickly as he could. "I have seen to it they are with good families. Two have my name. They are being educated ..."

But Constance wasn't listening to a word Randall Roderick spoke, for she had remembered the tales she had read in *The Tattler* about the exploits of the Rake of Reading. *How could I have been so foolish not to realize who he was?* Randall Roderick was the Marquess of Reading.

Clarinda had said so. She had even mentioned his nickname.

"The Rake of Reading," Constance said in a whisper.

Randall frowned, realized she had just then been reminded of who he was. "I am. I ... I *was*," he amended with a nod. "But no longer."

Constance regarded the marquess for a long time before she shook her head. "Thank you for your assistance today. Good day." With that, she took off on the path that led to the east, her quick steps making her appear as if she were running away from him.

Randall watched her as she took her leave him, half-tempted to go after her. She was alone, after all. Unprotected. But the path she followed was open, surrounded by parkland, and would take her to Park Lane. From there, he knew she could find her way to Curzon Street.

Sighing, he turned in the opposite direction, intent on taking the long way back to his townhouse. Before he had even made it to the pavement, though, he turned around and quickly retraced his steps, heading back on the path that he had used when he came into the park the day before.

He could see Constance up ahead. Despite her head start, she now walked slowly, occasionally appearing as if she were having difficulty walking. Perhaps she had turned an ankle. Or her half-boot heel had come loose. Randall quickened his pace until he came abreast of her, a bit out of breath with his exertion. "I will escort you to your home," he stated firmly, one arm jutting out in her direction.

Her eyes filled with tears, Constance regarded his arm for a moment and finally lifted her own so her gloved hand gripped his sleeve. "I shouldn't even be *seen* with you," she said before sniffling.

Randall was quick with his handkerchief. "Nonsense," he replied as he handed it to her. "How will anyone know we are courting if we're not seen together on an innocent walk in the park?"

Wiping her eyes with the handkerchief, Constance inhaled sharply. "But ... we are not *courting*," she replied, stunned at hearing him use the term so casually. Despite her earlier wish that he consider her for matrimony—back when she thought of him only as a cit— she now found the idea of being married to him impossible.

He was a marquess.

He was the *Rake of Reading!*

"*I* am," he responded, his attention on the path ahead. He held his head high, determined to keep his second chin from appearing while he rehearsed marriage proposals in his head. "I would like you to be my wife."

Constance felt as much as saw the gray attempt to cover her vision again, but she fought off the sensation and took a deep breath. "Thank you for the use of your handkerchief," she murmured as she handed the square of linen to him.

Randall regarded the fabric before taking it from her, stuffing it into this coat pocket. "You're welcome," he said with a sigh. "If you're opposed to the idea of being a mother to my boys, I understand completely. I am not in need of a mother for them. Nor do I expect you to ever make their acquaintance if you don't wish it. I am, however, in need of a mother for my *heir*. But more importantly, Miss Fitzwilliam, I seek a wife," he said as they reached Park Lane.

Constance inhaled sharply. "I hardly see the difference, my lord," she replied, her eyes darting about as she hoped they weren't seen by anyone. She could just imagine what *The Tattler* might print should one of their so-called reporters provide a story of their morning in the park. They had apparently already mentioned their visit to Gunter's Tea Shop the day before. The Countess of Norwick had mentioned it when she visited her cousin.

Randall considered how much to say. Did he dare tell her of his hopes for a life that didn't include men's clubs every evening? That didn't include a steady stream of widows in search of a bedmate for a few hours every night?

"I seek a woman to sit with me by the fire at night," he said as he slowed their steps to allow a curricle to pass by before they crossed Curzon Street.

Constance dared a glance at him then, struck by his simple words. "And later?" she prompted, wondering how much he would admit to her.

"A woman to share my bed. The same woman every night, of

course," he added, wanting to be sure she understood him completely.

"And after that?"

Randall blinked at the question. "To wake up next to me. To have breakfast with me. To share a walk in the park. To have dinner, to attend balls and soirées and ..." He paused a moment. "To share a kiss behind a potted palm."

Constance might have gasped except she found herself attempting to suppress a smile. "Not in the gardens?" she teased.

Randall gave her a quelling glance. "Careful. I've a mind to kiss you right here and now in the middle of the street."

Sobering quickly, Constance found she should have been shocked by his comment and instead found it rather exciting.

Climbing the steps to the Norwick townhouse, the two paused at the top as Constance pulled a key from her reticule and moved to open the door. "Thank you for the escort, my lord—"

"Randall," he corrected her. "You shall call me Randall. *Reading*, when we're in public, if you really must," he amended when he saw her look of surprise. "I have something else for you," he said as he fingered the ring in his waistcoat pocket. "Please, I beg you allow me to give it to you," he added as he watched her unlock the door, his one other thought on why a butler didn't see to opening the door.

Constance regarded him for a moment. "Good day, my lord." She stepped inside, gave him a curtsy, and shut the door.

Randall heard the *snick* of the lock before he turned around. Taking a deep breath, he was about to head for his own townhouse when he realized he would eventually turn around and make his way back to the Norwick townhouse. If others hadn't paid witness to their stroll from the park, they would certainly notice him pounding on the townhouse door. Perhaps hear him yelling her name. Shouting his proposal at the top of his lungs. Making a bloody fool of himself. So instead, he made his way to the end of the street, turned left and then made his way down the alley.

Constance Fitzwilliam might have locked the front door, but

Randall Roderick was fairly certain he could gain entrance via the servants' entrance. And while on his way there, he considered how he might talk the woman into being his wife.

CHAPTER 39
AN UNWELCOME PROPOSAL

wo-thirty in the afternoon

Constance hurried up to her bedchamber, fighting back the tears she knew would come no matter how hard she fought them.

Tossing her reticule to the bed, she caught her reflection in the cheval mirror and stilled herself. She swallowed and moved closer to the mirror, studying the woman who stared back at her. The silver choker was magnificent. The horse charm was a perfect rendering of a racing horse, its shiny silver metal reflecting the afternoon light from the bedchamber's only window.

She stepped even closer to the mirror and lifted the charm between gloved fingers, admiring the workmanship of the tightly woven silver strands that made up the choker, sighing at the intricate details of the horse. Swallowing, she watched as the horse seemed to move, his legs in mid-gallop. Fingering the horse as it rested in the hollow of her throat, she decided the piece was exquisite.

A more perfect necklace could not have existed for her, she realized, but she could hardly accept it.

She checked her own reflection in the mirror again, wincing at her reddened nose. She was about to reach around and unclasp the necklace from behind her neck when she realized she wasn't alone.

"Is the idea of being married to me really so ... *awful* for you?"

Constance whirled around, stunned to find the Marquess of Reading on the threshold of her bedchamber. "How dare you?" she whispered, one hand going to the choker at her throat to give it a tug. The clasp and chain held despite her attempt to break it. *Damn the jewelers in Ludgate Hill!* The choker would make the perfect weapon if only she could fling it at him!

Randall shook his head as he quickly moved towards her. "I dare because I ..." He stopped, unwilling to say the words that came to his lips. Words he had hoped to hear her say first. Now it was apparent she would probably never say them.

Why couldn't the woman believe him when he claimed he was no longer a rake? Why couldn't she see just how desperate he was to marry? To have a family? To spend his evenings in front of the fire instead of at a men's club or in the bed of a willing widow?

"Because why?" Constance countered, her hold on the charm lost when she noticed his pained expression. She stilled her movements.

Randall regarded her for a moment, his breaths labored. He had climbed the backstairs two at a time in an effort to reach her before she had a chance to lock the door just in case she realized he had made his entrance through the back door. If she had slammed shut the door and locked it, he was quite sure he would have broken it open with a swift kick of his Hessians, his valet be damned. Instead, he found the door to her bedchamber wide open. Found her admiring his gift as she stared into her cheval mirror.

"A question better suited for you," he finally answered in a near-whisper. He took two steps forward but paused when he saw how she backed away from him. Another step back and she would end up pressed against a large mahogany wardrobe. "Why are you so adamantly opposed to marrying me?" he asked then.

Constance backed up another step, apparently needing the wardrobe for support. "I am merely opposed to marriage in general," she hedged quietly, hoping he would simply accept her hastily made up reason and take his leave of her bedchamber—and her life. "Please, do not take it personally—"

"Of course I take it personally," Randall countered, covering the remaining distance between them in three steps. He stood before her as she pressed harder against the wardrobe, her eyes filling with tears. "Tell me why. Please, I beg you."

Shaking her head, Constance suppressed a sob as a tear broke free. "I like my freedom to do as I wish," she whispered.

Randall angled his head to one side, the response obviously a surprise. "Freedom to ... to travel?"

Constance blinked and nodded. "Yes," she answered, a bit relieved at his guess.

"To ... to pay calls and attend the theatre?"

She nodded more quickly. "Yes."

"To go shopping?"

Constance allowed a shrug. "I suppose, yes," she allowed.

"To bed any man you wish?" His head spinning, Randall had to close his eyes a moment to stave off the sensation of vertigo. The thought of Constance in bed with another man was simply too much to bear.

About to agree, Constance frowned and then gasped. "*No!*" she said with a good deal of disgust. "I've a mind to ... to slap you." And then, having given it some thought, she lifted her hand and swung it toward his face.

Despite his light-headedness, Randall easily intercepted her hand with one of his own, grasping it gently and leading it up to his face so it rested against his cheek instead of slapping it. He held it there as he continued to regard her, a sense of relief settling over him. "I ... I apologize, my lady," he murmured, his breathing still labored as his head lowered toward hers.

"However could you say such a thing?" she asked in a hoarse whisper, still offended by his comment and not the least bit happy he had prevented her assault so simply. Or that he still had a grip on her hand, although the way he held it was rather sweet. She noted how his eyes slowly lowered, the lids edged in a fringe of dark lashes finally closing off his deep blue eyes. Tiny lines splayed out from the corners of his lids, while the crease between his brows softened and then slowly disappeared. Then she realized how pale he appeared. Was he about to faint? "Are you ..? Are you unwell?" she whispered as his forehead came to rest atop her head.

Randall stilled himself, wishing the moment would never end. The scents of lemon and honeysuckle filled his nostrils, reminding him of summers at his estate in Reading. The sensation of the palm of her hand and her slim fingers against the slight stubble on his cheek reminded him of how his mother used to place her hand on his father's cheek before reaching up on tip-toes to kiss him. The warmth of her body, almost but not quite pressed against the front of his own, permeated his coats and seemed to surround him in a cocoon of comfort.

Oh, to be able to do this every day! To take just a moment and be one with Constance!

He lowered his lips so they came to rest on one of Constance's eyelids, eliciting a slight gasp of surprise from her. He barely kissed the delicate skin before moving his lips to her temple, to her earlobe, to the skin just below it before he finally pulled away and straightened. "I believe you have brought me back from the brink," he whispered. Slowly opening his eyes, he found her gazing at him with what could only be described as a look of confusion.

*C*onstance stared at the marquess for a moment, unsure of what to say or do. He was so close, she could feel his body heat through her walking gown. She could smell his cologne—sandalwood with a hint of spice—and the starch in his cravat. His kisses had been so light, they felt as feathers might when loosed from her pillow. Despite her determination to fight his effect on her, she realized too late she could barely breathe, as if her corset had been pulled too tight and her breasts had swelled. The heat between the tops of her thighs intensified, the pulse there apparent as it seemed to throb. She might have brought him back from the brink, but she felt as if she were falling over the edge.

"Marry me."

The simple words caught Constance by surprise, pulling her back to the present and away from whatever chasm she seemed about to fall into. She stared at the marquess before giving her head a shake to clear it.

"I promise you the freedom to do as you wish," Randall added, thinking she was about to deny him. "Except for the ... bedding other men, of course. I cannot abide the thought of you with another," he added.

Constance blinked before pulling her hand from his and allowing it to come to rest on his lapel.

There it was, then.

He might wish to marry her now, but when he discovered she wasn't a virgin, discovered she had already been with a man—willing or not—what then? His look of adoration would certainly change to one of disappointment. Perhaps of disgust. Anger, even. Better she deny his offer now. Thank him, of course, for she had given up on ever having a man look at her the way he was gazing at her at this moment. Beg his forgiveness and assure him that no one would learn of their private conversation. Or of his inappropriate kisses, innocent as they were given his reputation. "I am honored. I am. But I must ask for your forgiveness, for I cannot accept your offer," she whispered.

Tears streamed down her face as she watched his gaze change to one of confusion.

"Why ever not?" he breathed, his forehead once again coming down to press against hers.

Constance struggled to come up with a reason he would believe. "I am ... bad *ton*," she said quietly. "I would make a poor marchioness."

"Nonsense," Randall whispered. "You would have my protection. No one would dare ..."

"I am five-and-twenty," she stated, thinking her age might deter him.

"And I am five-and-thirty," he countered. He swallowed. "I probably shouldn't have admitted that," he added, his brows furrowing. "You think me too old for you, don't you?"

"Not at all," Constance argued. "It's just ... there are so many eligible young ladies. Daughters of earls and—"

"I don't want one of them," he countered. "I want *you*."

Before Constance could put voice to another word, his lips came down onto hers, effectively silencing any argument she might manage to invent.

In only a moment, her entire body was back to the way it had been when he had been holding her hand and kissing her temple. Although part of her argued she should push him away—push him away and run from the room—the other bade her stay and enjoy the sensation of a perfect kiss, for she had never been kissed like this. Never been kissed by a man so determined to *make* her his wife. So determined to change her mind. So determined to make her change her mind.

For a moment, Constance allowed the kiss as she reveled in just how pleasant a kiss could be. How simply wonderful it felt to be pressed against the front of a man, for although she was pressed quite firmly against the wardrobe, Randall's body had moved to pin her in place. Even if she had wanted to escape, she would have been unable to extricate herself.

But thoughts of escape were far from her mind, especially when one of Randall's hands had moved to hold her waist. Her one hand still gripped his lapel, but now her other moved up to his neck, the fingertips spearing the dark hair at the nape of his neck. She heard a moan and wondered if she had made the sound or if he had.

When his lips finally pulled away—she knew it was he whom did so for Constance didn't have the strength nor the desire to end the kiss—Randall allowed a heavy sigh. "I've a mind to make you mine right here and now, propriety be damned," he murmured hoarsely.

Her eyes widening in alarm, Constance gasped.

Frowning, Randall regarded her for a moment. "I wouldn't really, you must know," he said. "But I ... I cannot help but think I must *ruin* you just so you'll agree to be my wife." He paused and his frown deepened. "Damn, I sound like the worst possible libertine," he whispered with a slight shake of his head. His eyes captured hers again, aware of the effect his words had on her. She was pale, and her body seemed to shiver where his hands still rested against her. His brows furrowing, Randall watching as tears once again fell down her cheeks.

"You cannot ruin what ... already ... is," she whispered, a sob interrupting her final word. Her knees seemed to give out from beneath her. She would have fallen to the floor but for Randall's sudden grip on her waist keeping her up.

He replayed her words in his head, wondering if she said them with the intent of wounding him. Wounding him so he would take his leave of her and never return.

But the third time he heard them in his mind, the words had him realizing *why* she was so determined to see him leave.

He thought the worst, then, of course. She had taken a lover out of wedlock, perhaps thinking she would end up married to him. But the thought was soon replaced with other scenarios. Perhaps she was a widow—she was old enough—but why not simply tell him so? There was no shame in being a widow, unless perhaps her husband had committed suicide.

Randall shook his head.

What man would deign to commit suicide if he were married to such a gem as Constance Fitzwilliam? So that just left ...

"Were you ... willing?" he struggled to ask, his hold on her so powerful, her head ended up in the space below his chin.

"No," he heard as he felt her attempt to shake her head.

Damnation! "I'll kill him," he vowed, pulling his body away from hers so he could see her eyes.

Constance continued to shake her head, tears still leaving streaks down her cheeks. "That deed has already been done," she whispered. One of her hands searched for a pocket in her gown. She needed a handkerchief. *I must look a sight*, she thought, cringing when she noticed she had not only crumpled Randall's cravat, but left evidence of her tears on his waistcoat.

A linen was suddenly pressed against her cheek, Randall's hand holding it there as he gazed at her. "Did *you* ...?" he asked in a quiet voice, trying to imagine how she might have killed a man.

"No," she replied quickly, wiping her face and then moving to use the linen to dry his waistcoat. "I was quite ... unable, ... I assure you," she stammered, wishing the marquess hadn't extracted the truth from her. Time had dulled the pain. The nightmares no longer kept her awake at night. Now she would be reliving that night in the stables again and again.

Was reliving that night.

Randall kept his face as impassive as possible, not wanting to give away the sudden feeling of anger that bubbled up. "Under whose protection were you at the time?" he asked, his anger barely in check.

Constance resisted the urge to roll her eyes. She resisted the urge to simply smack the marquess in the nose. *A typical response for a man*, she thought. Blame the one whose protection she was under rather than the man who had committed the crime.

She worked hard to get her emotions under control and finally took a deep breath. "My cousin's, I suppose," she finally affirmed. "Which is why ..." She paused, wondering how much to admit. "Which is why he saw to it," she finally said, one eyebrow arching up as if she were daring the marquess to question how the situation was resolved.

Randall frowned, wondering what David—or perhaps it was Daniel—Fitzwilliam had done to the offending man. But giving it some more thought, Randall wondered if that very situation had been what forced Constance to choose the life of a spinster.

How else could a woman of her quiet confidence and pretty appearance avoid courtship? How else could she put off the attentions of marriage-minded men in Sussex? He was quite sure she'd had no intention of marrying—maybe not even to him—and had simply lived her life to avoid the situations that would have landed her at the altar.

Had she not been ruined, she might have been married off a long time ago.

"What did he do?" Randall demanded, his voice still quiet.

His sharp tone had Constance jerking her gaze up to meet his. "I cannot say," she said.

Randall furrowed his brows, the stern expression obviously useful in dealing with stubborn servants and members of Parliament, but Constance merely took a deep breath, a sob causing a hiccup as she did so.

"What did he *do?*"

Constance regarded the marquess for a moment, realizing she had to tell him something.

Perhaps it was time someone else knew the truth, although she had promised David she would never tell.

But David was dead now.

Daniel knew, though. Daniel had been there, probably even paid witness to it.

"I promised I wouldn't tell anyone," she whispered.

Randall took a deep breath and let it out slowly. "How many people know?"

Sighing, Constance angled her head to one side. "Just two of us now," she whispered. "But he was so angry when he discovered what had happened, he ... he hates me. He despises me. I will never be—"

"*Who knows!?*"

The words were so loud, Constance gave a start. "My cousin. Daniel," she whispered. She had thought lightning might strike when she said the earl's name, but a sense of relief settled over her just then.

"Norwick?" Randall countered, wanting to be sure he understood correctly. At her nod, he realized what she meant when she said there were just two of them now. "Was it David who killed your ... rapist?" he asked in a hoarse whisper.

Constance bit her lower lip before allowing a nod. "My horse ..."

She paused, the hand with the handkerchief lifting back to her face as another tear appeared.

"Your horse?" Randall prompted, wondering what she had been about to say. Had David killed the man before or after he inherited the Norwick earldom? Given his age and hers—David was at least fifteen years older—Randall knew it had to have happened after he inherited the title.

"Yes, Amasia, the mare. She was in the stables at Norwick Park because I took her there when I went to live with David and Daniel." At Randall's frown, she added, "My mother had died that winter and father ... father was in mourning."

Randall imagined Edward Fitzwilliam doing his mourning from the bottom of a bottle of brandy, but he kept his comment to himself. "And?" he prompted.

"She was foaling. I had checked on her before my come-out ball started, but ... And then, after the supper dance, I went back out to the stables. There was a man there. Someone I didn't recognize. The colt—Mr. Wiggins—had just been born, and I was ... I was about to go into Amasia's stall when ..." She let out a cry. "He was there to steal the horses."

Randall's arms were around her in an instant, pulling her hard against the front of his body. He was about to quiet her, tell her she needn't put voice to the rest of what had to be a horrible nightmare of a night, but he realized she probably wouldn't have heard his words. She seemed truly and completely in the past.

"David must have heard me scream. I know I screamed before he slapped me so hard, my head ..." Even now, she could remember how dazed she had felt, how stars had danced in front of her eyes so that she was nearly blinded by them. Perhaps she couldn't remember much more than the pain she had felt when she had been pushed onto the stable floor, or the sound of her skirts tearing and of the horses' neighs of alarm.

"He would not be found guilty," Randall said in a whisper, thinking she had feared for David's welfare. He was an earl at the time, after all, and almost immune from arrest and trial.

"He hit him with a shovel, and then he choked him to death," she whispered, tears streaming down her cheeks.

"And if he hadn't, I would hunt down the man and do it myself," Randall vowed, his voice quiet as he pulled her back into his arms.

Constance clung to him then, burying her head into the small of his shoulder. "Daniel would have," she choked. "Which is why I think he despises me," she said through a sob.

Randall frowned, wondering why she thought such a thing. "He does *not* despise you," he whispered.

Pulling her head away from his shoulder, Constance stared at the marquess through tear-filled eyes. "How would you know?"

Realizing he had to admit to having paid a visit to the Earl of Norwick, Randall inhaled. "I had to ask him for permission to marry you, of course," he said. "And make sure you received the inheritance you had coming to you."

Shaking her head in disbelief, Constance stared at the marquess. "When ...? *When* did you speak with *Daniel?*"

"This morning."

Constance angled her head, confusion apparent on her face. "Why? So my inheritance can become my *dowry?*"

Before she could finish the question, Randall shook his head. "It is yours to do with as you please, my lady," he assured her. "I don't need a dowry. I just want *you*. I made that very clear to Norwick," he said as he pulled her close.

"This morning?" she whispered.

Randall nodded his head. "Yes. I went this morning," he murmured, and then remembered Daniel's expression when he mentioned his desire to marry Constance. Relief, perhaps. Guilt, certainly. Arranging a match for his ruined cousin had to be in his best interest, even if it meant bestowing her with the inheritance she deserved.

And nothing had been said about the value of what was in the stables at Fair Downs.

•   •   •

"*W*hat about yesterday?" It made no sense. They had barely spoken to one another before their walk to Gunter's. "Why were you at Norwick House yesterday afternoon?" Constance asked, no longer resisting his hold on her.

The marquess sighed and kissed the top of her head. "Fate, my love," he whispered. "Destiny." *Curiosity, really*, but she didn't need to know that.

Destiny. Constance took a deep breath, inhaling the scents of sandalwood and starch as she considered the word. *A good name for a horse*, she found herself thinking. "And why didn't you introduce yourself as a marquess?" Of all the topics they had discussed while they walked and enjoyed ices at Gunter's, at no point had he mentioned his title.

Randall sighed. "If I had, you would have thought me a rake based on my reputation. Based on my nickname," he replied. "I wanted you to form your own opinion rather than that of *The Tattler's*," he added with a shrug.

"I thought you a rake even before I knew who you really were," Constance countered, her voice quite serious. But the gleam in her eye and her barely suppressed grin gave her away.

"And yet you allowed me to escort you to Gunter's," he accused.

Constance allowed a watery grin. "I did." She sighed. "But remember, I was hesitant."

Randall nodded. "I remember," he sighed. He kissed the top of her head again. "Now will you marry me?"

Angling her head so she could regard him a moment, she asked, "Will there be bubbles in my bath and in my champagne glass? Horses in the stables? A purple salon with roses?" she asked with a teasing grin.

Smiling, Randall nodded. "Yes to all," he replied. "At least, there will be when the decorator finishes your salon at the house in Cavendish Square."

Her eyes widening at his response, she asked, "When will he start, do you suppose?"

Randall shrugged. "He better have started yesterday," he answered, his manner suggesting there would be hell to pay if he hadn't.

Her eyes wide, Constance realized just how serious the marquess was about making her his marchioness. "And the choker?"

Randall nodded. "Last night. I have your ring, too," he added with a teasing grin.

Purring into his cravat, Constance nodded her head. "Then I suppose I will," she murmured.

"You will ... what?"

Constance grinned. "Marry you, you rake."

Randall allowed a sigh and kissed her quite thoroughly.

CHAPTER 40
A MARRIED LIFE BEGINS

ine o'clock at night, September 16, 1817
Eleanor Merriweather Wakefield regarded her reflection in the cheval mirror, rather stunned to find she looked rather beautiful just then. Her entire body, naked and still flushed from her wedding night couplings with her new husband, made her appear rather wanton, much like the naked whores she had seen in Lucy Gibbon's brothel her first day in London.

The day before yesterday.

The trunk of wedding clothes left behind by the modiste did include a night rail, but Charles had forbidden her to wear it. "Perhaps when it is a bit chillier," he suggested with a shrug.

Eleanor rather doubted there would ever be a chilly night in their bedchamber.

Her gaze took in the entire bedchamber, finally falling on a card table and two chairs. At Charles' behest, Chester had set up the furnishings during their hastily arranged wedding ceremony and left a box there for their return—a box containing a three-hundred-piece puzzle. A gift from Arthur, the puzzle's wooden pieces now lay strewn about the table, only a few of them put together.

There were more important things to do on a wedding day, after all.

She slowly turned so her left side was reflected in the mirror. One of her hands slid down the front of her body, coming to rest where she hoped a baby might have been conceived with that evening's lovemaking.

She dared a glance toward the bed, grinning at the sight of Charles passed out on her bed, the bed linens mussed and the counterpane in a heap on the floor. There was a thought she should get some sleep—she was quite sure Charles' insatiable appetite for her would require she succumb to his request for just one more opportunity to pleasure her before dawn lit the sky.

A frisson passed through her entire body just then, reminding her of just how he had kept his promise. Even when he wasn't atop her, he had her feeling sensations of pleasure she had never felt before.

Eleanor turned so her other side was displayed in the mirror, grimacing at the sight of a slight bruise, one she had sustained when attempting to leave the bedchamber by way of the window the day before.

What had she thought to do once she was out of the window? She might have been able to shimmy down the side of the house, gripping windowsills and finding toeholds in the clapboard siding, but she rather doubted her skills as a tree climber would have landed her on the ground in anything other than a heap of muslin and broken bones.

But Charles had come to rescue her. Come to pull her from the window. To admonish her, as if he truly cared for her. But mostly, she thought, because he didn't want the neighbors to see her and ruin her reputation.

Even if she was already ruined.

Smiling, Eleanor spun around in the front of the mirror and only stopped because she realized she was being watched. And because she was suddenly feeling a bit dizzy.

Embarrassed, she ducked her head and moved back toward the bed.

"You needn't have stopped on my behalf," Charles murmured as he sat up in the bed. His hair, tousled from his brief sleep and their lovemaking, stood out from his head. "If I had half your energy, I would be right there with you dancing about," he claimed, his voice sounding as drowsy as he looked. "But I fear you have worn me out." Indeed, he couldn't remember a time when his body had felt so replete, so satiated he didn't think he could muster enough energy to take Eleanor's body again.

At least, not before the morning.

Eleanor moved toward the bed and climbed onto the mattress. "Are you telling me you're too old for this?" she asked in mock despair.

Charles chuckled. "Perhaps." He reached over to wrap an arm around her waist so he could pull her next to his body. "But if you sleep next to me, I promise I shall resume our marital bliss in the morning."

Stretching out next to him, she reached over and kissed his lips. "I look forward to it," she replied in a whisper, feeling rather tired. Her eyes closed despite her desire to lay and simply watch him while he slept. Lie there and wonder why she had ever thought herself attracted to his brother, who was no doubt enjoying his own brand of marital bliss in the townhouse he shared with his new wife and lover somewhere in Piccadilly.

Lifting her left hand to regard her wedding ring by the light of the one candle lamp that was still lit, she studied the round diamonds with their filigrees of white gold in between. Surprised her husband hadn't simply given her a ring from the Wakefield collection—she figured the earldom probably possessed several beautiful and expensive pieces—she rather liked that she was the first countess to wear this ring.

Countess.

The word brought another grin to her lips as she snuggled closer against Charles' body and closed her eyes.

Having watched her admire the ring he had given her earlier that morning when they had said their vows, Charles closed his own eyes and decided he would have to give her the matching earbobs. *A wedding gift*, he thought as he allowed a grin.

He might even allow her to wear them tomorrow night. Them, and nothing else.

CHAPTER 41
FOLLOWED BY ANOTHER

Eight o'clock at night, September 17, 1817

Randall lowered that day's issue of *The Times* and dared a glance at his wife. Holding an embroidery hoop so the light from a candle lamp illuminated the fine white fabric, Constance poked a needle threaded with green silk into the floral design. "How are you this evening?" he asked as he leaned in her direction, curious as to what she was creating with her even stitches.

Constance grinned. "I am well, husband," she replied, her grin widening into a smile. "The same as I was the last time you asked ..." She paused a moment to check the time on the elaborate clock above the fireplace. "Fifteen minutes ago," she added with an arched eyebrow.

The newspaper forgotten, Randall followed his wife's gaze to the clock. "Has it been that long already?" he asked, an impish grin forming on his face.

Lowering her embroidery to her lap, Constance gave her husband her full attention. "You're missing your club, aren't you?" she said, a sense of disappointment settling over her. As much as Randall had assured her he wanted to be settled with a wife, the marquess had never struck her as a man who would be content spending his evenings at home by the fire, especially now that they had taken up residence in his Cavendish Square mansion. Too large for just the two of them, she had to feel grateful for the army of servants it took to run the place.

Randall frowned. "I am not," he countered, wondering how Constance could say such a thing. "I am merely ..."

Horny.

Now that he was finally married, and well before Christmastime, he found he rather liked waking up next to his wife. He knew he would, her warm body nestled next to his in the master suite bed. In fact, he hadn't wanted to get *out* of bed that morning, but the day's duties—a meeting with his solicitor and another with his secretary—forced him to leave her side and ring for his valet. Even before Castor could get to the master suite, Constance had climbed out of their marriage bed, donned her silk wrapper, given him a kiss on his cheek, and made her way into the mistress suite through their shared dressing room.

The quick glimpse of her bare bottom and the side of one of her breasts in the morning light had Randall wishing he could simply pull her hard against his body so that he might continue what they had been doing all night.

Did she have any idea how much he wanted her back in that bed?

Right now?

"I am merely wishing we could ... *continue* what we were doing at this time last night," he finally finished, his hardening cock forming a bulge behind his doeskin breeches.

Not wanting to wait a minute more than necessary—it had been their wedding night, after all—he had kissed her senseless and then carried her to the bed in the master suite. He couldn't remember another time he'd had to slow his ardor, practice patience, and delay his release as he had done last night. But, oh the *ecstasy!* Over and again, he had pleasured her until she begged for him. Over and again, she had used the pads of her fingers to explore his body, inciting ripples of pleasure in places he didn't know could feel that way.

He dared a glance at the inside of his elbow, an involuntary shudder passing through his body as he remembered how first her fingertip and then her tongue had him considering his arm in a whole new light. And then she had moved her attention to his other arm and done the same to him there. It could have had something to do with how her breasts were pressed against his chest at the time, or perhaps how the fingers of her other hand were busy stroking his other shoulder and upper arm, or perhaps it was the heady scents of jasmine and sex that had him so aroused, but whatever it was, he wanted more. Much more.

He shifted a bit in the upholstered chair, hoping she wouldn't notice his discomfort.

She noticed.

"Oh!" she said, setting aside the embroidery hoop and standing up. She shook out her skirts.

Caught off-guard by her sudden rise from her chair, Randall struggled to get up when Constance used a hand to push him back down into the chair. "Where do you think you're going?" she murmured, positioning herself so one of her thighs was propped on his chair's arm. She leaned down so her lips hovered near his. When he didn't make a move to kiss her, she pulled away a bit. "As I recall, this time last night, you were kissing me," she whispered, one of her fingers lightly trailing down the side of his face.

Randall grinned and pulled her around so that she ended up sitting across his lap. "I was, wasn't I?" he replied as he leaned sideways and caught her surprised mouth with his own. He quickly lightened the pressure on her, allowing his lips to slide over hers until her slight gasp had him pausing and then dotting her lips with light, quick touches.

When one of her hands moved up to rest against the side of his face, he captured her lips in a crushing kiss at the same time one of his hands cupped a breast and smoothed over it. Her chest rising with his touch, Randall felt as much as heard her purr of delight. When he slowly released her lips, it was as much to breathe as it was to whisper, "And I hope I might be allowed to kiss you every night at this time."

Constance regarded her husband for a moment before realizing she must have looked like a wanton given how she was spread across his lap and the arms of the chair, her ankles clearly on display for any servant to see should they pass by the library. "Of course," she replied, not about to deny him what she was discovering to be a rather enjoyable pursuit. Her entire body vibrated as he held her.

"I find I rather enjoy kissing," Randall whispered, his lips moving along her chin and jaw line.

"You say that as if you've never kissed before," Constance whispered in reply, her own lips forming a grin. Her breaths, short and shallow, sounded as light gasps with his every touch.

"I *haven't* kissed like this," he murmured, his lips moving down her throat, along a collarbone to the hollow of her throat.

Constance stilled herself, her hands moving to either side of his head so that she could force him to look up at her. "You expect me to believe that, you bounder?" she accused in a teasing voice.

Randall's eyes widened. "As a matter of fact, I do," he replied, giving a slight shrug. "I mean, I have *kissed* before, of course. Just not ... like this. Not with such intimacy, and certainly not in a room with an open door, where anyone might walk in on us."

Truth be told, he had arranged with Giles for the servants to go to the theatre. They wouldn't be home until well past midnight.

Constance blinked. And blinked again as she dared a glance toward the open door. *Did the marquess forget he had arranged for the servants to attend the theatre this evening? And given strict instructions they weren't to return until after midnight?* Perhaps he was merely teasing, but it had her thinking about the amorous behavior of couples when they wanted to steal a kiss. And about Randall's kisses as he held her on his lap.

No wonder couples took advantage of the discreet cover of potted palms and libraries and secret alcoves whilst at balls and soirées. No wonder they took walks in the dark gardens, pausing for liaisons behind tall hedgerows. No wonder they pulled shut the curtains in their town coaches as they bounced along the streets of London.

Kissing was a delightful pursuit!

Constance dared a glance at where his hand was still cupping one of her breasts. "Then perhaps we should kiss in a more private place," she suggested with an arched eyebrow. Leaning back, she used her other hand to turn down the candle lamp so its light was barely visible.

Randall dared a glance around the room and allowed a shrug. "Next time, I'll shut and lock the door," he murmured, leaning down to kiss the tip of her nose.

Constance speared her fingers through his silken hair, pulling his head down so that she could resume the kiss, moaning when his tongue found hers. A moment later, she was well aware of his arousal pressing against her hip. The space at the top of her thighs throbbed in anticipation. Although she had thought she felt a bit sore earlier, desire for him had her wishing he would suggest they retire to his bedchamber.

Now.

She considered her position, considered how she might attain some relief. Perhaps if she repositioned herself so that she straddled him, much like she would do when riding a horse, she could press herself against him. Perhaps he would understand her plight and use his hand to rub the spot as he had on one occasion last night.

She had barely finished the thought when she lowered her legs to the floor and lifted her hips from his lap. She pulled her lips away from his, struggling to catch her breath. "My lord, I beg your pardon, but I need ..." Bunching up her skirts around her thighs and then finally pulling her gown up and over her head and tossing it aside, she placed her knees on either side of his thighs and steadied herself with a hand on his shoulder.

Randall blinked. And he blinked again when he realized what she intended. His fingers fumbled for the fastenings that secured the placket of his breeches. Once he had them loosened, his breaths so short he was nearly panting, he struggled to push down the offending flap along with his smalls. His manhood, engorged and already wet at the tip, sprang free, seeking the warm, wet sheath poised above it. He scooted down in the chair, positioning himself so that he could impale her as his hands took possession of her hips beneath her chemise and pulled her onto him.

Their mutual moans sounded at the same time as two became one. "You needn't ever beg my pardon should you need ..." He paused. "Anything," he managed to say, reveling in the sight of her upturned face above him. Moving his hand beneath her chemise, his fingers seeking her bare flesh where her body met his, Randall felt a great deal of satisfaction when his thumb found its mark. Her entire body seemed to arc as he rubbed her womanhood, his other hand holding her hip so she couldn't lift herself off of him.

When he felt her clench on his manhood, when he saw how her breasts mounded over the top of her corset, when he heard her mewling turn to a cry, and when he felt her body quake, he let go his hold on her, and moved his hands to either side of her waist so he could lift and lower her onto his turgid manhood. He entered her over and over again until ecstasy gripped him, held him, took control and finally eased away. His loud groan probably filled the library; he hoped it drowned out Constance's cry of his name and didn't bring a neighbor rushing to discover what travesty might have occurred therein.

Breathing heavily, Randall straightened in the chair as he wrapped his arms around her waist and pulled her hard against the front of his body, his face pressed against the space above her breasts. "I didn't used to like being surprised," he murmured when he could finally breathe somewhat normally. "But, I do believe I have changed my mind."

Constance lowered her head to his, one cheek resting in his dark hair as her arms leaned on his shoulders. "I cannot tell you how relieved I am at hearing you say that," she replied in a whisper. Her entire body shivered again as his manhood moved inside her.

Randall gripped her tighter. "I do hope you're not uncomfortable my love," he said as he relaxed a bit. He still clung to her, as if he needed her for support. Or perhaps for warmth. The fire had subsided so that only a few embers remained lit in the fireplace.

Sighing, Constance allowed a grin and kissed his hair. "I am rather content, actually," she murmured, rather liking how he had finished his query. *My love.* Of course it was too soon to expect the marquess to have feelings beyond simple affection for her.

Or lust.

She knew very well of his lust. He had told her in no uncertain terms that he wanted her in his bed. "Every night," he had said. The memory had a frisson passing through her entire body, the resulting pleasure forcing another sigh of contentment from her lips.

Smiling, Randall lifted his head from where it rested and glanced up. "I shall endeavor to see you pleasured as often as you'll allow me," he said, his voice quiet in the darkening room.

"And I shall endeavor to allow you to," Constance replied with a teasing grin.

Randall allowed another sigh. "Does that mean I am allowed to speak of my love for you, too?" he asked, once again pulling away so that he might gaze up at her. He felt the jerk of surprise in her body, watched as her eyes regarded him in wonder.

"I would never prevent you from putting voice to your thoughts, my lord," Constance whispered.

Kissing the hollow of her throat, Randall wondered if Constance would ever feel for him what he had come to realize he felt for her. Perhaps it had begun as lust—lust coupled with the desire to have a woman share his evenings as well as his bed. Share their breakfasts in the morning and walks in the park in the afternoon. Dinners by candlelight.

But now he knew he wanted more. Needed more.

"Then let me ask you something," he replied finally. "And I beg you to tell me the truth."

Her eyes widening with the question, Constance nodded. "I will," she agreed, wondering at his sudden seriousness.

"Do you suppose you could ever wake up and discover you might ... feel *more* than affection for me?" he asked, his voice sounding almost loud in the quiet room.

Constance relaxed in his hold, the corners of her mouth turning up until she was smiling. "I already did. This morning, in fact," she said with a nod. After a pause, she arched an eyebrow. "Or perhaps it was before I went to sleep last night." When she sensed he was about to ask which time, her grin broadened. "One or two or all of the times," she added with a nod.

Randall sighed before allowing a chuckle. "I love you," he said, his nose pressing into the hollow of her throat.

"And I have probably loved you since the moment you said your vows yesterday," Constance replied happily.

His lips were on hers once again, soft and ever so light until he drifted off to sleep on a long sigh.

EPILOGUE

*D*estiny
June 1821

Constance Roderick, Marchioness of Reading, watched as Destiny made the first turn, her excitement at seeing Amasia's last colt ahead of all but one other horse rather evident as she bounced a bit on her toes. Her husband stood by her side, one gloved hand clasped over the one she had looped around his elbow. Despite his glove, she could feel his barely contained nervousness in how his fingers seemed to tap at each stride.

"Damn, he's fast," Randall breathed, and then quickly apologized. "I beg forgiveness for the curse, my lady."

Grinning, Constance gave him a wave with her other hand. "You can curse all you want, my love, as long as I can join you," she answered, her voice a bit louder so that she could be heard over the cheers and cries of the crowd surrounding the finish line.

Having never attended any of the race meetings run by Mr. Tuttlebaum, Constance found the frenetic atmosphere of Epsom Downs infectious. Everyone seemed excited, happy even, to be watching the Thoroughbreds as they made their way up the slight incline that started the race, around the turns that made up the U-shaped track and down the hill to the finish.

Even when Destiny had run the course the day before, a practice run meant to allow him to shake off the weary walking that brought him from Reading to Epsom Downs the week before, he had done so much faster than expected. Probably much faster than he should have run.

His jockey, Mr. Granger, claimed he couldn't slow down the Thoroughbred if he tried. "He's a runner," the man had said when he dismounted the day before. "And now that he's been to a few of these race meetings, he knows what to do."

The race season had been as invigorating as it was exhausting. At Lord Bostwick's insistence—the man claimed a need to remain close to his wife as she was due to go into confinement at any moment—Randall had seen to it Destiny made as many of the meetings as he could arrange given the travel involved between each town. At three, Destiny was the perfect age to beat all his opponents, winning money for his owners as well as those who placed their bets on him.

The only scare had been at Newmarket, when a vagrant had been stopped by Randall's security detail from attempting to lame the horse with a cut to his leg. The man claimed he had been paid to do it, and when he identified the miscreant who had hired him at the Jockey Club, the perpetrator denied any wrongdoing. Those present in the clubhouse, though, saw to it the man was barred from the building and from the racetrack. The incident was a reminder to all those participating that race meetings were rife with cheating and scandal.

"Will he win, do you suppose?" Constance asked, realizing she had been holding her breath.

"If he keeps up this pace and doesn't stumble, he just might," Randall replied, one eye on his Breguet as the first three Thoroughbreds made it out of the last turn and headed down the hill toward where most of the crowd stood waiting. Clods of dirt sailed into the air behind each horse, the roar increased ten-fold, and Constance gave up her hold on her husband to jump up and down and clap.

Randall turned his attention from the race to watch his exuberant wife, remembering how radiant she had looked wearing the red satin ball gown he insisted she wear for the ball the night before. "I knew it would be gorgeous on you," he had told her when she appeared at the top of the stairs. "From the first day I met you."

Constance had given him a look that suggested he wasn't in his right mind, but she had hurried down the stairs and kissed him quite thoroughly. "You were such a rake."

Smiling broadly, Randall realized he would miss the finish unless he redirected his gaze to where the top three finishers flew over the line, Destiny leading the way.

Constance whooped and hollered as loudly as any of those who had bet their money on the black horse, and now that he had won, Randall joined her with his own celebratory whoops. Taking her into his arms, he danced her in a circle before they rushed off to join Destiny and his rider.

Even before they made it to the winner's circle, some of the crowd dispersed while others continued to display their happiness at the outcome.

"Congratulations, Reading," several called out. Randall tipped his hat to them, acknowledging their words with a grin and a 'thank you'.

Mr. Granger regarded the Rodericks from his perch atop Destiny. "He was even faster today, my lord," he claimed. "I do hope you'll have me run him at the Ascot."

Constance and Randall exchanged knowing glances. "When he's older, perhaps," Randall said with a nod. "We have another horse in mind for this year's Ascot," he added when he saw the jockey's look of disappointment.

"Another horse?" Granger repeated, his brow furrowing. "Which one, if I may be so bold, my lord?"

Constance leaned her head against Randall's shoulder. "I suppose word will get out before too long," she whispered. "We may as well tell him."

Randall turned and kissed the top of Constance's hat. "Granger," he said with a good deal of authority. "You'll be riding Mr. Wiggins at Ascot."

The jockey stared at Randall, the horse's name not familiar to him. "All right," he finally responded. "And how old is this Mr. Wiggins?" he asked, briefly wondering if his master knew that the horses had to a bit older to run the Ascot.

Constance nearly bounced on her toes, as excited about the possibility of Mr. Wiggins racing as Destiny's win just moments ago. "He's eight years old!" she said happily. "Isn't that just wonderful?"

Granger's face fell upon hearing the marchioness' words. He looked to Randall for verification. "My lord?" he said in a hoarse whisper.

The marquess allowed a mischievous grin. "Fear not, Mr. Granger. Mr. Wiggins is *fast*," he claimed proudly.

"Why have I not heard of him?" the jockey asked as he dismounted. "With such an unusual name, I should think I would have heard of him ... years ago."

Randall watched as a young stablehand hurried up with a bucket of water and an apple, one of the security men in tow. Seeing the man nod in Randall's direction, Constance breathed a bit easier. It wouldn't do to have their winner poisoned by his post-race water.

"Mr. Wiggins' sire has been in question until recently," Randall explained as the jockey came alongside. The two led Destiny past a crowd of winners and well-wishers. "Now that Viscount Bostwick has admitted to owning the sire, Mr. Wiggins has finally been properly registered with the Jockey Club," he explained.

Granger seemed surprised. "And the sire?" he asked, wanting to hear which horse was responsible for producing a fast eight-year-old he had never heard of.

"Bostwick's Bounder," Constance said with a grin. "George Bennett-Jones' Arabian was Mr. Tuttlebaum's sire as well, and surely you've heard of him," she said with pride.

George had won Bounder in a fencing match long before he inherited the viscountcy, she remembered. Recalling the day she had first laid eyes on the chestnut-colored warmblood as it stood in an adjacent pasture to the one in which the Fair Downs' horses grazed, Constance smiled.

She barely knew George back then, but she certainly recognized a fast horse when she saw one. Thinking Bounder would make a good stud for Amasia, Constance had merely borrowed the stallion from his pasture when George was in London. She personally returned Bounder the following day, rather proud she had been able to calm the excited horse enough to toss a lead rope around the Arabian's neck. Murmuring to Bounder the entire time she lead him to the Bostwick Estate stables had kept the high-spirited horse minding her every command.

Murmuring and a few apples she had stuffed into her pockets.

When she handed over the lead rope to the stablehand, she simply explained she had found the beast in the Fair Downs pasture.

When her father realized Amasia's colt was a potential racer, Constance told him about Bounder, not realizing at the time that the lineage information was important. Mr. Tuttlebaum wouldn't have been allowed to race if his sire were listed as 'unknown' in the Jockey Club.

A slow smile appeared on the jockey's face. "Mr. Wiggins and Mr. Tuttlebaum share the same sire?" he repeated, his eye lighting up in delight.

"Oh, it's even better than that, Mr. Granger," Constance replied.

Randall allowed a moment to pass before he chimed in. "They share the same dam, my boy."

The jockey didn't bother to hide his astonishment, nor his appreciation. "True brothers. You must enjoy riding him then, my lady," he said in awe.

Constance regarded the jockey with a wry grin. "I did for many years. But now I have a better mount," she said with a nod, her face taking on a sudden blush.

Had anyone been looking at Randall just then, they would have witnessed his own reddening complexion before he said, "And I do believe it's time for your ride, my lady."

Thank you for taking the time to read The Love of a Rake. If you enjoyed it, please consider telling your friends or posting a short review. Word of mouth is an author's best friend.

Thank you, Linda Rae Sande

EXCERPT

Read on for an excerpt from Linda Rae Sande's
Book 2 in "The Sons of the Aristocracy" series
The Caress of a Commander

May 1818

Will Slater, Earl of Devonville, stood on the landing at the top of the stairs leading down to the Worthington ballroom, his heart racing. *Damnation*, it wasn't as if he had never attended a *ton* ball before, but for some reason, he felt entirely out of his element. Entirely foreign to the festivities that had apparently already begun below. Entirely ill at ease.

"Are you all right?" Stephen asked from where he stood a few feet away on the landing.

Will glanced over at his half-brother, startled to find him looking more confident and far more excited about that evening's ball than any bastard brother had any right to. "You look as if you're *happy* to be here," he accused, tugging on his topcoat for at least the tenth time that night. Everything felt smaller, tighter, more oppressive than his naval uniform. At least he was wearing a scarlet waistcoat, although now that he could see what the other men in attendance were wearing, he realized he should have chosen a more embellished option featuring more embroidery, or more metallic threads, or more ... *more.*

Or he could have simply worn his uniform. He was allowed, of course, although since he hadn't retired but merely resigned from the British Navy, he didn't think it appropriate to wear a uniform.

Now he wished he had.

He glanced over at Stephen's ensemble, frowning when he realized the man was wearing the very waistcoat he should have been wearing. One with a good deal of embroidery worked with metallic thread. One that fit him as if it were made by Weston. Even his dance shoes were more appropriate. Black, with silver buckles.

Will was about to suggest they trade waistcoats when the butler announced them from where he stood off to the side. "William Slater, Earl of Devonville and Mister Stephen Slater."

Too late, he realized. Will nodded to the room below, as did Stephen, and they began their descent. He was aware of a number of *lorgnettes* being lifted to noses, of the slight pause in conversation, of eyes rising to regard them as they made their way down the stairs.

"Trade with me."

The words were out of this mouth before Will could think of the repercussions.

"What did you say?" Stephen replied, his eyes occasionally darting to the steps below his feet. Goodness! *How many were there?*

"Be the Earl of Devonville," Will replied quickly, his face kept impassive as he continued his descent.

Stephen blinked and resisted the urge to halt his descent. "And who will *you* be?" Stephen countered, giving a quick glance at his brother.

"You," Will answered. They reached the ballroom floor in another three steps. Realizing Stephen was staring in his direction, Will responded to a comment made to him by David Carlington, Marquess of Morganfield before waving a hand in Stephen's direction. He made his first introduction to the Carlingtons. "Lady Morganfield. Lord Morganfield. So very good meet you. I am

Stephen Slater," Will said as he bowed before the Marquess and Marchioness of Morganfield.

Stephen stared at his brother in horror. *What the hell?* He turned to find a bevy of young ladies rushing up with their mothers to meet him, and suddenly, all he could think about was how easy it was to say he was 'Will Slater.'

Too easy.

He gave another quick glance in his brother's direction along with an arched eyebrow. "You owe me," he said in a hoarse whisper when Will was close enough to hear.

"By the end of the night, you may feel otherwise, my lord."

Stephen blinked and regarded his brother with a hesitant grin before moving to the next woman in line to meet him.

ABOUT THE AUTHOR

A self-described nerd and student of history, Linda Rae spent many years as a published technical writer specializing in 3D graphics workstations, software and 3D animation (her movie credits include SHREK and SHREK 2). Getting lost in the rabbit holes of research has resulted in historical romances set in the Regency-era as well as Ancient Greece.

A fan of action-adventure movies, she can frequently be found at the local cinema. Although she no longer has any tropical fish, she follows the San Jose Sharks and makes her home in Cody, Wyoming.

For more information:
www.lindaraesande.com
Sign up for Linda Rae's newsletter:
Regency Romance with a Twist
Follow Linda Rae's blog:
Regency Romance with a Twist